MW00466266

2021

NO
ESCAPE

THE LEXI CARMICHAEL MYSTERY SERIES

BOOK THIRTÈEN

JULIE MOFFETT

Praise for Julie Moffett's
Lexi Carmichael Mystery Series

"The Lexi Carmichael mystery series runs a riveting gamut from hilarious to deadly, and the perfectly paced action in between will have you hanging onto Lexi's every word and breathless for her next geeked-out adventure." ~ **USA Today**

"I absolutely, positively loved this book…I found the humor terrific. I couldn't find a single thing I didn't like about this book except it ended." ~ **Night Owl Reviews**

"Wow, wow, and wow! I don't know how Julie Moffett does it but every book is better than the last and all of them are awesome. I may have 6 authors in my top five now!" ~ **Goodreads Reader**

"Absolutely loved this book! I love the concept of a geek girl getting involved in all kinds of intrigue and, of course, all the men she gets to meet." ~ **Book Babe**

"This book can be described in one word. AMAZING! I was intrigued from the beginning to the end. There are so many twists and turns and unexpected agendas that you do not know who's on the good side or who's on the bad side." ~ **Once Upon a Twilight**

"This series has been one of my happiest finds since I started blogging...It's going to be such a long wait until the next book!" ~ **1 Girl 2 Many Books Blog**

"Lexi Carmichael has to be the most lovable character I have come across. She is 100 percent geek and has zero street smarts, but she tries to think outside the box while putting herself in dangerous places without knowing how she got there. The author keeps you guessing who might be a double agent and who might want to harm Lexi." ~ **Goodreads Reader**

"I've read each of the books as it came out and loved everyone one of them. You never know where a Lexi Carmichael book will take you. The romance is stunning, the mysteries complex, and the characters are so real you will want to hug them. Humor and personal moments balance the intense suspense.' ~ **Amazon Reader**

"*No One Lives Twice* is an entertaining and fun novel for anyone who enjoys seeing the underdog computer geek come out of her shell to save the day." ~ **Once Upon a Chapter**

"I love Lexi and the gang. OMG lots of excitement, mystery and love. Couldn't put it down." ~ **Amazon Reader**

Praise for Julie Moffett's
White Knights Mystery/Spy Series

"This book is Hogwarts for geeks. It is the perfect blend of YA, computer geeks, and spies!… I am so thrilled to be sharing this book with you…because I loved it! Like—stop a stranger on the street and don't stop talking about this book until they run away screaming, thinking you've escaped from the psych ward! Crazy good!"
~ Ginger Mom and the Kindle Quest Blog

"Love this new YA spinoff series from the Lexi Carmichael series by Julie Moffett. Same great pace, excitement, mysteries to solve, hacks to make, character growth, and an ending that makes me excited for the next book! Geek girls rock!" ~ **Amazon Reader**

"I loved the whole entire concept of the book. This book had me guessing what was happening the entire time while not leaving me completely in the dark which was something that I personally LOVE. This book was completely intriguing, and it was just so AHHHHH, it was amazing. The book I believe targets all people of all ages. It has so many things that people who read Young Adult to New Adult to Adult books." ~ **The Hufflepuff Nerdette**

"Holy crap, I couldn't put this book down. I love the White Knights and their team, and this book was nonstop action ... I cannot WAIT to see what the Knights will be up to next!" ~ **Goodreads Reader**

"Absolutely loved it—great first book in a new series. This Y. A. series has already made my keeper list. Can't wait for the second book!" ~ **Amazon Reader**

"To say that I enjoyed this book would be an understatement. It was positively awesome and an epic read. I am not one that will usually get in a fan club moment on a YA novel, but this one does something for readers. It is smart, witty and just plain fun. Anyone between the ages 14 and oh heck 99 can enjoy this book. Trust me it is made for geeky readers, like me." ~ **Amazon Reader**

"What a great book for all ages! It shows how people with different personalities can come and work together and become friends. I love this series. I have only one problem, when can I read the next book?" ~ **Amazon Reader**

"Just when I thought this series couldn't get any better, Julie Moffett outdoes herself! This book is considered YA fiction, but it is truly a book for any age. You can get so caught up in this book that you forget the main characters are kids ... Tension, humor & thoughtfulness are all present & accounted for." ~ **Amazon Reader**

"Wow! Great book! Each one gets better and the characters blend together perfectly with their friendship and crazy abilities to work together. I laughed so much at times and then I'd be nervous waiting for the end results of their adventure plus tears at the end. Loved it!!!" ~ **Amazon Reader**

Books by Julie Moffett

The Lexi Carmichael Mystery Series
No One Lives Twice (Book 1)
No One to Trust (Book 2)
No Money Down (Book 2.5-novella)
No Place Like Rome (Book 3)
No Biz Like Showbiz (Book 4)
No Test for the Wicked (Book 5)
No Woman Left Behind (Book 6)
No Room for Error (Book 7)
No Strings Attached (Book 8)
No Living Soul (Book 9)
No Regrets (Book 10)
No Stone Unturned (Book 11)
No Questions Asked (Book 12)
No Escape (Book 13)

No Comment
(*a free character interview with Lexi Carmichael*)

All Lexi Carmichael titles are available in print
(*except for No Money Down*), audiobook, MP3,
and several are on CDs.

White Knights Mystery/Spy Series (YA)
White Knights (Book 1)
Knight Moves (Book 2)
One-Knight Stand (Book 3)

The MacInness Legacy
(Historical/Paranormal Romance)
The Fireweaver
The Seer (by Sandy Moffett)
The Healer

Time Travel Romance
A Double-Edged Blade
Across a Moonswept Moor

Other Books (Historical Romance)
The Thorn & The Thistle
Her Kilt-Clad Rogue (novella)
A Touch of Fire
Fleeting Splendor

DEDICATION

To my extraordinary brother, Brad,
who is the true Gamemaster.
and
To my Dad. My true-life hero.
I love you both so much. xoxo

ACKNOWLEDGMENTS

I couldn't have written this book without my amazing brother, Brad, and his incredible mind. This one is for you, big brother! Thanks also to my mom, Donna, my niece, Katy-bug, my sister, Sandy, and my sister-in-law, Beth, who either read the manuscript, kept me on track, or put up with endless discussions on plot twists and scenarios. Lucas and Alexander, thank you, too, my sweet kiddos, for putting up with me and eating leftovers when deadlines were looming.

Huge thanks also go to Sandra Herndon Ross, who is a wonderful virtual assistant and keeps me in line and organized (thank goodness). Also, to all the amazing, caring, and awesome members of my Facebook Readers Club—you guys are the ABSOLUTE best!

Kudos to my excellent cover artist, Su at Earthly Charms; my terrific copy editor, Sara Brady; the fantastic formatter, Amy Atwell; and last, but in no way least, my wonderful editor Alissa Davis.

It truly does take a village. I couldn't have done it without any of you! oxo

NO
ESCAPE

ONE

Lexi

NONE OF THIS was my idea. I wasn't even sure how I got here, really. Not in London, not in a limo, and not meeting my in-laws for the very first time at a high-end, exclusive restaurant. Most certainly not bringing my parents along for our first encounter. Although I *had* wanted to meet my husband's parents before our official church wedding, I'd envisioned a peaceful, low-key meeting with just the four of us in a quiet house in a quaint London neighborhood. Yet somehow, our first meeting had morphed into a swanky dinner on the Thames with my parents in tow.

How had I let this happen?

Social gatherings are not my thing, and this was possibly the most nervous I'd ever been in my life, when a weapon wasn't involved, and that's saying a lot. I'm just an introverted geek girl who desperately wanted to make a good impression on my in-laws. This situation brought out every single one of my insecurities. I had my mother to thank for this.

Slash, my husband, sensed my nervousness and squeezed my hand. Although he was a geek like me, he never seemed bothered by social affairs and somehow managed to keep a calm, unflappable demeanor. I envied him that.

At least the drive from our hotel to the restaurant went quicker than expected. There was very little conversation as Slash and I sat in the back facing my parents. As we arrived, our limo had to wait in line behind several others queued in front of the bevy of valet parking attendants. The attendants were being very solicitous to the two limos in front of us, and there was a small crowd of people waiting for the passengers to emerge.

A woman in a red gown got out of the first limo just as several camera flashes went off and the crowd started to jostle each other, apparently trying to get the best angle for a photograph. This happened again as the occupants in the two limos ahead of us disembarked.

"What's going on?" my mom asked our driver, leaning forward to speak through the glass partition.

"This is an exclusive restaurant among celebrities," our driver responded. "It's a regular hangout for fans and the paparazzi hoping to catch a glimpse of the rich and famous."

I felt sick to my stomach, imagining Slash's mom and dad having to fight their way through the crowd to meet us.

Could this get any worse?

Our limo crawled forward until it was our turn to disembark. Many in the crowd continued to jockey for position to view the celebrities ahead of us. But those who lacked the best views were already turning their attention to our limo. The attendant leaned forward, peering into the tinted windows, before opening the door.

I sat closest to the door, and once it was open, I

caught sight of a lovely dark-haired woman edging up behind the valet. Holding her hand was a man in a dark suit. I recognized them immediately from the many pictures I'd seen. It was Slash's parents, Juliette and Oscar. Juliette was wearing a beautiful rose-colored cocktail dress, and she looked a bit anxious, perhaps because of the paparazzi crowding around the limo area snapping photographs. A tall, blonde woman in a glittery silver dress holding the leash of a huge, white dog with a diamond-studded pink collar appeared to be the most sought-after celebrity, as she'd been mobbed by the photographers and the cameras were clicking at an insane tempo.

"I wonder who the woman is," Mom said, peering out the window.

"Who cares?" I groused. "They just need to make room so we can get out."

"I wonder why she has a dog," my dad said, his brow drawing together. "It better not be allowed into the restaurant. That thing is huge."

"It's a Kuvasz," Slash said. "It probably weighs a hundred pounds. They're widely known as the guardian breed for Hungarian royalty."

"Lexi, get out of the car," my mother said impatiently, waving her hand at the open door.

I slid to the edge of the seat and stuck one foot out the door, my hand reaching for the valet's. The valet helped me to the curb and reached inside to assist my mother.

I'd just taken one step when the huge dog spotted me.

For no apparent reason, it went on full alert, immediately breaking away from the celebrity and loping toward me. The woman shouted, trying to follow the dog, but the photographers, sensing drama, began snapping like crazy, circling her so she couldn't get free.

"*Noooo!*" I breathed in horror, backing away from the limo and the dog, trying to melt into the crowd. Animals and I did not have a good rapport. What did it want from me? I hoped it would lose interest if it couldn't see me, but the dog latched onto my position like a heat-seeking missile.

It threaded its way through people before cornering me, woofing once, and leaping through the air, its huge paws landing directly on my chest. Given the combination of the dog's weight and my backpedaling, I screamed and fell backward into someone behind me.

The three of us hit the pavement as one giant lump.

I lay there, unable to move, trapped between a stranger and a giant dog whose apparent mission in life was to lick me like a Popsicle.

I wanted to scream again, but it was too dangerous to open my mouth. I finally felt the weight of the dog removed from my body and managed to roll to my side and sit up. Slash had the dog by the collar, and the woman in the glittering dress had finally made her way toward him, shouting. Slash did not release the dog to her...yet. The dog continued to lunge at me, grinning, with a giant lolling tongue and a goofy look. Its enormous tail whipped against Slash's thigh as if this was a game and I was the giant chew toy.

Cameras were flashing, completely blinding me. Photographers crowded around us, taking photos from every angle. Paparazzi doing what they did best.

I turned to apologize to the person I'd brought down with me and looked directly at Juliette, who'd also managed to sit up. She stared at me, eyes glassy, dress torn, hair askew.

OMG! I'd taken down my mother-in-law.

Having absolutely no context or idea of what to do in such a situation, I had to go solely off instinct. "Hi, I'm

Lexi," I said, pushing the wet, slobbery hair out of my face and thrusting out my hand. "Your new daughter-in-law."

She looked at me, shock and horror evident in her expression.

I heard Slash's soft voice in my ear, his hand on my arm. "Come on, *cara*. It's time to go."

What? He expected to go to dinner after this?

My eyes suddenly snapped open, my hands squeezing the soft leather of the living room recliner beneath me. My handsome Italian American husband sat perched on one side of the chair, our cute Christmas tree visible over his shoulder.

I let out an enormous sigh of relief and pressed a hand to my forehead. "Oh, thank God, I'm home. *Home.* The dog didn't get me."

"Dog?" Slash lifted an eyebrow.

"Yes." I closed my eyes, my heart still pounding. "There was a restaurant in London, and a woman with a big dog that jumped on me…and your mother. It was awful."

He smiled, cupping my cheek with his hand. "I assure you, there'll be no dog at Gio's wedding. You, and my mother, will be completely safe from an animal attack. But you do need to get ready. I just got a text—the limo will be here in five minutes."

TWO

Lexi

I HATE FLYING.

There, I said it. Hate, hate, hate. Regardless, I do a lot of it for a geek girl who detests getting into a vehicle that propels itself thousands of feet above the ground without a safety net. I used to think that experiencing so many flights would inure me to flying, but it hasn't. My recent plane crash should've been the perfect excuse for swearing off flying for the rest of my life, but no. Here I stood in my foyer, waiting for a limo to take me to the airport so I could pay money to have another near-fatal travel experience.

Ugh.

I hadn't slept well last night, which had caused the impromptu nap and subsequent dog/limo/mother-in-law nightmare. I should have known better than to read that article on flight in Scientific American before bed. Unfortunately, I'd discovered there was no mutual agreement among scientists on what generates the aerodynamic force known as lift. The aerodynamic theory of lift has been split into followers of a technical camp and a nontechnical camp, both of which have differing ideas on what keeps a plane in the air. I read both theories at length and came to my own conclusion that neither offers a complete or comprehensive explanation of all the physical forces that keep an airplane aloft.

So, yeah, reading that article about air travel made it *much* easier for me to fall asleep. Not.

Now, if I was talking about virtual travel, all would be cool. I'm all about virtual. That's my world, and it's where I'm the most comfortable. My name is Lexi Carmichael and I'm a twenty-six-year-old coder, hacker, and master of my own virtual domain. I double-majored in mathematics and computer science at Georgetown University and now work for a cyberintelligence company, X-Corp, in the suburbs of Washington, DC. Virtual flying, unfortunately, is not in my future. In three and a half hours, I'll be boarding a real airplane to Italy for my brother-in-law's wedding.

It seems weird to say "brother-in-law," because I'm only recently married myself. My husband, Slash, and I accidentally got married in quite an unexpected and nontraditional way just a few weeks ago. We're still having an official church wedding this spring with our families and friends, which I'd skip if I could, but I can't, since I'm half of the main attraction. But I couldn't stress out about my own wedding now because I was too busy freaking out about flying, as well as meeting my in-laws for the first time.

"Relax. It's going to be fine."

I stopped pacing the foyer and glanced at Slash, who leaned against the wall next to our suitcases. Dressed in dark jeans, a navy sweater, and a leather jacket, he looked dangerous and sexy all rolled into one. In some ways, he seemed out of place in suburban America, when he would have been perfectly suited to a fancy yacht on the Mediterranean Sea with no shirt, dark sunglasses, and hair blowing in the wind. But he'd laugh if I told him that, so I didn't. Besides, although he's nice to look at, I'm way more impressed with his stellar mind and hacker skills. He's the smartest person I know, and that's saying a lot, because I know a lot of really smart people.

He walked over and put his hands on my shoulders. "Still thinking about the nightmare?"

I sighed and tried not to look guilty. Social events always stress me out. Having to navigate a big wedding that included my husband's parents, whom I hadn't met yet, was daunting. "I'm thinking this is a really bad idea."

"Which part?" He looked directly into my eyes, knowing that more than anything, I appreciated forthright communication. He knew he'd have to reassure me at least a hundred times before we got to Italy for several different reasons. I guess he wondered which issue was bothering me the most.

"The *whole* part," I said. "Flying…again. Meeting my in-laws for the first time. Bringing my parents with us to meet your parents. Having to socialize with people I don't know. The list goes on, but those are the big ones. What were we thinking? Why didn't we just fly my parents to London to meet your parents without us having to go with them?"

He tucked a strand of my long brown hair behind my ear and spoke in the calm, reasonable voice he always uses when I'm on the verge of losing it. "We both agreed that having them meet in Italy, a neutral location, *before* our wedding made the most sense. Gio's wedding provided the perfect opportunity with lots of people around, taking the focus and pressure off us. I know you don't like to fly, but we'll be traveling together, which you assured me makes it a bit easier for you to manage. Right?"

I nodded reluctantly. "Right."

"And I do believe it was you who said it would be a wise move if our parents met at some place *other* than at our wedding for the first time."

I pressed my hands against my temples. "I *know* I said that. I'm just reserving the right to second-guess myself."

He chuckled, pulling me into his arms and resting his chin on top of my head. I was being irrational and cranky, but social pressure always did that to me.

"They're going to love you, *cara*. They already do."

"They love what you said about me. What if they don't love the real me? Or what if I say or do something stupid, like trip and fall on your mother when we first meet, or my parents tell them an embarrassing story about me growing up, and they end up intensely disliking us?"

"Then let's have a plan." His brown eyes softened as he tucked another strand of hair behind my ear. "If you trip or stumble when you meet my parents, I'll catch you before you fall. If your mom starts telling the story about the time you stuck a Darth Vader Lego figure up your nose, I'll give my mom permission to tell the story about when I was six, ate a dozen cannoli, and threw up all over Nonna's house. Then, if anything else goes sideways, we'll have a secret signal. How about you tap the right side of your nose if you need a rescue, and I'll do the same?"

"I like the idea of a plan," I said, mulling it over. "I just have to tap my nose? I can do that."

"You can."

A honk sounded out front. Slash released me, opened the door, and waved. "It's the limo with your parents. Time to go."

Before he reached for our suitcases, his arms

encircled me one more time, one of his hands resting at the small of my back. "Look, you've got this. *We've* got this. We're already family, and we're going to stay that way no matter what happens, okay?" He pressed a light kiss on my mouth, and I caught the scent of mint toothpaste and felt the slight scratch of the scruff on his cheeks.

I wanted to wrap my arms around his neck and stay like that forever. It was moments like this that reminded me how lucky I was to have him. Romantic love was exciting and captivating, and I enjoyed the benefits of that, but for someone as logical as me, finding a compatible partner wasn't just about physical attraction or pairing up with someone who matched my exact likes and dislikes, although that was helpful. It was about finding someone who could help me grow, bring me out of my shell, and help me to see what was holding me back in life. Slash had done that for me. He'd *always* done that for me. He'd given me the courage to make the life changes I desired and stood by me no matter what kind of anxiety attacks or second thoughts I had about it.

I took a deep breath. Freaking out wouldn't help anyone, especially me. "You're right, Slash. I'm over-thinking this. It's going to be fun. Besides, it's not our wedding—it's just a family get-together where everyone is going to like each other." I'm pretty sure he knew I was trying to convince myself rather than him. Still, the tenderness and kindness in his gaze caused my heart to turn over in my chest.

"That's my girl," he whispered against my cheek and then pressed his forehead against mine. "We've got this." We stood like that for a couple of heartbeats before he pulled away, disappearing out the front door with our suitcases, leaving me to lock up.

I took a moment alone in the foyer to collect myself.

I did feel a bit better, and I marveled how he could do that with just a few words. Still, as I set the alarm and locked the door, I couldn't help but worry the little black cloud of trouble that followed me around would want to come with us.

"Just stay here," I murmured to the cloud. "Please, I *really* need this to go flawlessly."

I had no idea if my request would work, but I figured begging was definitely worth a shot.

THREE

Lexi

"I HAVE A feeling I've forgotten something."

My mom searched in her purse, as if that would help her locate the elusive missing item. "You brought two gigantic suitcases for one week," I said. "I'm worried they're both going to exceed the weight limit. What could you have possibly forgotten, Mom?"

"I don't know, but I'm sure it's important."

I stretched my legs out, just like in my dream, and felt a nervous twinge. I had to remind myself we weren't in London, and we weren't headed toward a swanky restaurant, but the Baltimore airport. Slash and I faced my parents, with our backs to the limo driver, our legs splayed out next to each other. Fortunately, there was no large white dog in sight, though I barely restrained myself from searching the back of the limo just to make sure.

"Everyone has their passports, right?" Slash asked.

My dad pulled out two passports from his jacket pocket and waved them at Slash. "We're good on the passports. Clarissa, if you've forgotten anything, we can buy it in Italy. You said you wanted to do a little shopping anyway. It's been ten years since we've been there. Surely there are new things to purchase."

"That's true," my mom said, pulling out her compact and applying more lipstick. She already looked beautiful, so I don't know why she even had to use makeup. She effectively wielded her good looks as a board member on several charities, helping to raise millions of dollars for worthy causes. I'd inherited nothing of her looks except for her long legs and height, which unfortunately only served to make me look awkward instead of graceful.

"As long as I don't have to dodge bullets and bad guys." My dad pointed at Slash, which wasn't fair, because most of the trouble that happened around us was usually my fault. "I didn't bring or wear body armor, young man."

I was the only one in the limo who laughed, and I did it mostly to draw attention away from Slash. Dropping to the floor to avoid bullets had become second nature to my parents since they'd met Slash. There was a bit of contention between Dad and Slash over the heightened danger factor, even though I was a magnet for disaster before I met Slash. Somehow, he put the blame squarely on Slash, and Slash wouldn't disagree with him. They were working on getting past the danger thing but hadn't got there quite yet.

I didn't know what else I could do to ease that pressure, but I tried. "It's a wedding, Dad," I assured him. "The only potential shotgun that might have been in play would have belonged to the father of the bride. And seeing how Gio's bride, Vittoria, is already pregnant, and Gio is marrying her, the shotgun shouldn't be necessary at this point."

A smile touched Slash's lips, but my mom rolled her eyes. "For heaven's sake, Winston, forget about guns and life-threatening danger for five minutes. We're going to Italy. It's one of the most romantic spots in the world, perfect for lovers and shopping."

"And I feel compelled to mention we're going with our son-in-law, with whom danger has constantly been synonymous," he said. "How can we be sure we'll be safe?"

"Dad!" I threw up my hands in exasperation. "That's so uncalled-for. We're going to a wedding."

"After we spend time in a mysterious castle on a secluded island," Dad returned lightly. "It's a justifiable question."

I opened my mouth to respond, but Slash put a hand on my knee to quiet me. He didn't like me stepping between the two of them or defending him to my dad, even verbally.

Mom snapped her compact shut and slipped it into her purse. "Yes, about that, children. Why, again, are we going to a castle filled with puzzles and games before the wedding?"

I let out a frustrated breath and rested my head back against the limo seat. "I've already told you, Mom. It'll give us the opportunity to get to know each other a little better before our wedding while having fun."

"Why can't we do that sitting at a nice Italian restaurant?" Mom asked. "Why the castle thing?"

"Why not?" I responded. "It'll be an adventure, and you and Dad like puzzles. I thought we could all use a little fun."

"The castle visit is on me," Slash interjected smoothly. "Gio asked me to plan something for a few days before the wedding, where the wedding party could all come together and have some fun. I couldn't get to it because of work, so Lexi offered to help out."

"Work that had piled up while you two were in

Brazil?" my mom asked pointedly. "Where you two got married *without* family and friends."

"That was a matter of life and death," I said, hoping to cut off that line of discussion. I didn't want to go down that rabbit hole again. "We've already been over this a hundred times. Getting married in Brazil wasn't planned. Besides, we're not talking about *our* wedding—past or present—right now. You promised we could take a break from wedding planning and focus on this trip as a family. Remember?"

"Of course I remember. And I do appreciate Gio giving us an opportunity to meet Slash's parents and brothers at the wedding. I'm also sure the island you've chosen will be lovely, as will the activities you planned. You're right, I do love puzzles. It's just it seems a little odd as a family activity."

"Technically, I didn't plan a single activity," I said. "Slash and I were able to book the location and guest accommodations. The activities are included."

"Escape rooms in a castle."

"Yes, Mom, escape rooms in a castle."

"Well, it seems rather unusual. Explain the concept of escape rooms to me again, darling."

I adjusted my legs again, trying to stretch out to a more comfortable position. "As far as I understand it, the castle contains a series of escape rooms with puzzles and clues you have to figure out as a team. You must work together to figure things out, and in doing so, you get to know each other. Think of it as breaking the ice, but in a more heightened way."

"I should mention, this isn't just *any* escape room or castle," Slash added, looking out the window. He constantly scanned the environment, always on alert for any sign of danger, which sounds ridiculous if you don't know us. If you know us, it makes perfect sense.

"The castle, which was built in the fifth century, was named Castrum Augustus, after the Roman emperor Romulus Augustus," he explained. "The emperor used the castle as an occasional summer vacation spot. When the emperor was not in residence, it was used as a defensive outpost. It was taken over many times by different marauding forces over the centuries. The castle received a major renovation in the fifteenth century by Alfonso V of Aragon when he conquered the surrounding territory, including the island."

My dad's face lit up. He loved history and architecture. When I was younger, we took a lot of trips to the museums. Of course, I preferred the science museums, but I still enjoyed the history lessons and learning about new cultures and people.

"It sounds fascinating," Dad said. "I look forward to seeing it. What happened to it after that?"

"By the turn of the twentieth century, an Italian noble family, Migliaccio, had owned the castle for about two hundred years," Slash continued. "To be able to afford the upkeep, the castle was opened to the public in 1913. Unfortunately, Mussolini and his Fascist government took it over during World War II, and in the years following the war, the castle fell into serious disrepair. It was eventually purchased from the Migliaccio family in the late 1980s by Italian billionaire and tech giant Rocco Zachetti, who restored it to its full historical grandeur. A decade later, he turned the island over to his son, Dante, who had added significantly to the family fortune by being an early investor in video games. Today Dante Zachetti is the secret money behind several of the most successful game developers around the world. He's supposedly even more reclusive than his father. He's reputed to have a serious fascination, some might even call it an obsession, with games and puzzles."

"Sounds a bit like you, Lexi," my mom quipped with a smile. "Except your games are virtual."

"Virtual games *are* the best," I said. Still, I appreciated her acknowledgment of my gaming skills, and she seemed intrigued by the escape room concept, which I appreciated.

"It all sounds quite interesting," Dad said. "But how do you get an escape room in a castle from all that?"

"As I mentioned, Dante Zachetti is a bit of an eccentric," Slash replied. "He lived in the castle for many years, tended to by his groundskeeper, butler, valet, chef, and housekeeper. He has never married and never had children. About ten years ago, he moved to an estate in Naples and began secretive work on the castle. Suddenly, a few years ago, he began inviting select groups of friends and colleagues to the island to solve a series of puzzles and challenges he'd built at the castle. Word is, he'd visited several escape rooms and decided he could do better. He wanted to match minds with some of the smartest people on the planet."

"That's the perfect example of someone with too much money and nothing to do with it," Mom said.

"How strange," Dad said. "Why would someone do something like that to a historical site?"

"It *is* a bit odd," I agreed.

"Rumor is Zachetti was bored intellectually and desired a challenge," Slash said. "That's just speculation, however."

"What a peculiar man," Mom said. "So, how many of those bright minds have solved these escape rooms?"

"None," Slash replied. "At least to the best of my knowledge. Supposedly dozens of people have tried, including some of the most accomplished scientific and engineering minds in Europe invited personally by Zachetti. But no one really knows the results. Those who have done it aren't speaking, other than to indicate they failed. It's not surprising the participants at that level don't talk much about their failure, because they probably aren't used to it. Nevertheless, it's a mystery, which we will be able to experience firsthand."

Mom shook her head. "How in the world did *we* get invited?"

"It's kind of a strange situation," I said. "I read about the escape rooms being set up at Castrum Augustus when I searched the web for unique activities in that part of Italy. It came up in an article in *Scientific American* magazine from a few years ago. The magazine's puzzle editor mentioned a conversation he'd had with a leading mathematician who'd just returned from an interesting experience. The mathematician had been part of a group of puzzle solvers invited to tackle a series of escape room-type challenges constructed in a renovated castle off the coast of Italy. He said the castle was located in a fabulous and exotic Italian setting, and the puzzles were devilishly wicked. The editor said the mathematician wouldn't describe the puzzles or how the group did, but noted it was the experience of a lifetime. That sounded like something interesting to do with the wedding party. So, without knowing the full history or background of the castle, I called up and inquired about renting the place for a few days. They told me access to the castle was by personal invitation only from the owner, Mr. Zachetti himself, and not for rent. I realized what a dork I'd been by calling them up after I read more about the history of the castle and Zachetti, then learned what a huge, exclusive deal it is. Oops."

"If it's such a big deal, how did you get this Zachetti character to change his mind about us?" Dad asked.

"I didn't," I answered. "A couple of days later, I asked Father Armando if he knew what might be fun to do in the area, as I was out of ideas. He asked me what I'd already looked at, and I admitted that I'd tried to get us booked at Zachetti's castle. He didn't say anything about it but promised he'd help me find a suitable spot for us to gather. A few days later I received an email from Dante Zachetti inviting us to the castle for exactly the days we needed. I suspect Father Armando was instrumental in that, but he won't confirm it. It was a little odd, but since Gio was really stoked about it, that made the decision easy. I figure we're all game to give it a try, right?"

"Yes, of course, but it means we're going to be taking on the same challenges that even the brightest technical and scholarly minds in Europe purportedly couldn't solve," Mom said. "That seems quite daunting."

"True. But one way or the other, it will definitely make for a cool adventure."

"I think it sounds fascinating, Lexi." The astute lawyer brain in Dad seemed excited about the possibility. "I've never done an escape room, but you know me. I'm always up for a good puzzle, as is your mom. Right, Clarissa?"

"Of course." My mom patted his knee. "It just seems an unusual way to meet Slash's parents. But we're here, aren't we? So, bring on the puzzles."

That was one thing about my family. For as long as I could remember, we'd always had game night at our house. Puzzles, cards, board games, all of it. When my brothers and I were younger, we had game night several times a week after dinner. As we got older and more homework and after-school activities piled on, family game nights had become fewer. Then my older brothers, Rock and Beau, left for college, leaving me alone with my folks. We still had game nights, but they were rare until I'd left for college. In a strange moment of nostalgia, I realized how much I missed it.

"You're really good at puzzles, Dad," I said. "Which, not coincidentally, makes you an excellent lawyer."

"Why, thank you," he said, grinning at me. "But your mother is the real puzzle beast. Honestly, I think you and your brothers got your smarts from her side of the family."

I stared at him taken aback by his comment. Dad thought I got my smarts from Mom? Sure, she was intelligent and wicked good at puzzles, especially word games and crossword puzzles, but she'd always been so focused trying to push me into activities like ballet, dating, and girly things that I'd kind of forgotten she'd graduated from college with a bachelor's degree in psychology. She hadn't ever used her degree, as far as I knew, but the more I thought about it, she did have amazing success with people, fund-raising, and getting her way. Maybe leveraging her social skills and extraordinary good looks was just a strategy to get people to underestimate her.

Interesting I'd never considered that before.

"Regardless of what happens, our castle experience should be a once-in-a-lifetime opportunity for certain," Slash was saying.

I agreed 100 percent. I *loved* a good challenge. Plus, I hoped everyone would be so busy exploring the grounds and trying to solve the puzzles, no one would have much time to talk to me, ask me questions, or want to discuss my upcoming wedding plans.

Our driver pulled up to the airport departure area and helped us unload our suitcases from the trunk. Slash gave him a tip, and we schlepped our suitcases into the airport, decked out for the holidays. An enormous Christmas tree stood in one corner, decorated with hundreds of silver and gold balls and blinking white lights. Christmas music played over the loudspeakers. Everything was in the full festive spirit of the holiday.

As we headed toward the Alitalia airline counter to check our baggage, I pulled up behind a guy in a full Santa Claus suit, including boots, hat, and coat. Apparently, Santa was headed to Italy, too.

My dad, Mom, and Slash came up behind me. Slash pulled his suitcase and one of my mother's enormous ones. Dad had his suitcase and my mom's other one. Mom carried her large carry-on and purse. She happily peppered Slash with questions about Italy this time of year, and I smiled a bit, glad that she seemed to be having a good time already. Maybe things wouldn't be so bad after all. She came to stand beside me, reaching over to brush a strand of my brown hair off my shoulder.

"Italy at Christmas," she said. "It will be lovely, Lexi."

"I'm sure it will be." I reached into my purse for my passport, accidentally elbowing Santa in the side. My elbow hit something hard, and pain zinged from my funny bone down to my wrist.

"Ouch," I said, rubbing my elbow. "Dude, you've got some hard ribs there."

Santa glanced over his shoulder at me, his eyes narrowing. "Shut up."

Jeez. Ho, ho, ho, *not*. Guess Santa wasn't in a good mood, and…he was also sweating profusely. I couldn't believe he planned on traveling all the way to Italy in that suit. "Look, I'm sorry. I didn't mean to elbow you. It's just kind of crowded in here with all the Christmas travelers and—"

Santa suddenly whipped an automatic weapon out from beneath his red coat and fired several rounds toward the ceiling.

"I said shut up!" he roared at me.

Holy holiday!

This Santa wasn't packing presents.

FOUR

Lexi

I FROZE, SHOCKED by the incongruity of Santa Claus with an automatic weapon.

For a split second, the world narrowed to just the two of us. A loud roaring noise filled my ears, and although my brain screamed at me to run, my eyes were locked on his, my feet rooted to the floor.

"Drop!" someone shouted from behind me, but the voice seemed to take a long time to reach my ears, so when I finally heard it, it sounded more like drooooooo-ooooooop.

My mom, who was standing slightly diagonal to me and just behind Santa, immediately dropped to the floor, covering her head with her hands. But everything in my vision had changed to slow motion, so it seemed to take her forever to fall, as if I could see every moment of her movement occurring in a split-second time frame.

I felt a hand on my arm—maybe it was my dad's or maybe it was Slash's—pulling me backward. But my legs felt heavy, and I stumbled. Christmas music still played in what seemed like delayed time over the loudspeakers.

I'm dreeeeeeeaming of a whiiiiiite Christmaaaaaas…

Santa shouted something at me. I couldn't make it out, but it didn't seem friendly. His mouth moved in slow motion, his lips forming words I couldn't understand.

At some point I realized Santa no longer pointed the gun in the air but was bringing it down inch by inch. I waited for my life to pass before my eyes, but it didn't. Instead, two things happened simultaneously.

As the position of his gun lowered, Santa took a step backward and promptly tripped over the prone figure of my mom. The scene again unfolded in the delayed time of my vision. His legs flew up in the air, his body twisting as he struggled in a futile effort to stay upright. At the same time, a dark figure flew slowly through the air from behind my left side, his hands stretched out. That figure landed on top of Santa at exactly the moment he hit the floor flat on his back. I caught a glimpse of a black leather jacket.

Slash!

Shots were fired. Something hit me hard from behind, knocking me to the floor and forcing the breath from my lungs. As abruptly as it had started, the time warp I'd been locked in passed. My cheek was pressed to the cold airport floor. My senses were assaulted with real-time screams, a blaring alarm mixed with the Christmas music that was *still* playing, and the sounds of pounding feet and people shouting.

I squeezed my eyes shut and tried to get the heavy thing off me, but it wasn't budging. After what seemed like forever, the weight was lifted, and someone dragged me several feet away.

"Are you all right, ma'am?"

I sat up and blinked a couple of times. A policeman dressed in a flak jacket and earpiece, with his gun out, knelt next to me, looking at me with a concerned expression on his face. "I think so."

"Sorry. I brought you down for your protection. Are you injured?"

I patted my arms, legs, and head. All seemed in order. "I'm fine. But my mom, my dad, and…husband. My husband, he jumped Santa. Where is he?" I twisted and tried to stand on shaky legs to see the spot where we'd been standing in line, but there was such a crowd of people in the area, I couldn't see them.

We were joined by a man in a dark suit, wearing an earpiece. "I'm sorry, ma'am. You'll need to come with me." The policeman stepped back, deferring to the suited man, who flashed a badge.

"Are you the TSA?" I asked.

"Yes, ma'am, and you need to come with me right now."

"Am I in trouble?"

"No. Of course not. We just need to ask you a few questions."

"I'm sorry, but I need to check on my family first."

"Don't worry. We'll bring them to you. We must go now." He took my arm, pulling me away from the action. We passed a lot of policemen and people huddled into groups protected by security and police. I was honestly amazed at the level of security and how fast they had responded. He led me to a side door and into what looked like a security control room. Dozens of monitors were hanging from the walls, showing what looked like every angle of the airport. Phones were ringing, people were running around the room, and staff was barking orders. The TSA man steered me to a small room off the command center with a desk and a few chairs.

I thought it odd I'd been brought to this location for

questioning. I wondered why there were no police present since a crime had obviously been committed. But given we were in the airport, I figured it qualified as a federal offense, hence the TSA involvement.

He closed the door and asked me to sit. I sat gingerly on the edge of the chair. "Can you tell me what happened out there?" he asked.

"Who exactly are you?"

"Oh, sorry. I'm Frank Marks, a BDO." He pulled out a wallet and showed me an ID.

I studied it and then looked up at him. "What's a BDO?"

"BDO stands for a behavioral detection officer. We observe passengers in the airports, in person and on camera, looking for behaviors that might be suspicious. You know, like a cold, penetrating stare, or excessive sweating, or nervous behaviors of any kind. We already had eyes on Santa when you bumped into him in the baggage line. May I see your identification, please? Where are you headed?"

I'd been wearing my purse across my body, so it was still attached to me. I fished out my passport and handed it to him. "I'm traveling to Italy with my husband and parents. We live in Silver Spring, Maryland, and are headed to a family wedding."

"All right." He reviewed my passport and snapped a couple of quick photos of it with his phone. "So, what transpired between you and Santa?"

"Not much. My family and I got in line at the Alitalia counter to check our baggage. Santa was already standing there in front of us. It was crowded, so when I reached into my purse to get my passport, I elbowed him by accident. But instead of a bowl full of jelly, I hit something hard under his red coat."

"You didn't wonder what it might be?"

"There was no time. I said 'ouch,' because I hit my funny bone. Then, as I rubbed my elbow, I mentioned he had hard ribs."

"How did he respond to that?"

"He told me to watch it. It wasn't a friendly tone. I began to apologize, explaining it was crowded because of the holiday travelers. That's when he pulled out an automatic weapon from beneath his jolly red coat, screamed at me to shut up, and fired a few rounds in the air."

"Did he say anything to indicate a motive before he started shooting?"

"No. He wasn't much of a conversationalist."

Frank scribbled some more notes. "Did you know him?"

"I'd never seen him before in my life, and I have an eidetic memory, so I would have remembered."

Frank looked up, surprised. "Okay. Then what happened?"

"After that, everything seemed to happen in slow motion. Someone behind me shouted for everyone to drop to the floor. That was likely my husband. My mom, who was standing near me and slightly behind Santa, followed directions and dropped immediately, covering her head with her hands."

Frank looked impressed. "Just like that? She's done that before?"

"It's kind of a long story, but, yes, she's done it before. Anyway, unlike my mom, somehow, I couldn't move. Maybe I was worried he'd shoot my mom, dad, or husband. I can't remember exactly what was going through my head at that moment. Anyway, I'd locked eyes with Santa, and he seemed focused on me. Then he pulled his gun down from the air where he'd shot the first round, possibly preparing to shoot me. But he took a step backward and promptly tripped over my mom. My husband jumped on him as he fell. I heard the gun go off again. Can you please check if my husband is okay?"

"Is your husband the guy wearing a leather jacket?"

"Yes. Did you see him?"

"I saw him on the camera. Does he work in law enforcement or the military?"

"No. He works for the NSA...in computers."

Frank's eyebrow lifted. "Okay, I'll just go check on his status. Please stay here. I'll get right back to you."

As soon as he left, I began pacing the small office. Ten minutes later Frank returned. He opened the door, and Slash stepped inside.

"Thank goodness. You're okay." I ran to Slash, throwing my arms around him and hugging him tight.

He squeezed me tightly and then pulled back, cupping my face in his hands and pressing a kiss on each cheek. His expression was tight with concern. "You were worried about me, *cara*? You faced him down. What were *you* thinking? All those lessons we did in dropping and protecting your head. I told you to drop, but you just stood there."

"I know. I'm sorry, Slash. It just happened so fast, and I think a part of me wanted him focused on me so he didn't shoot at my parents or you."

He let out a sigh. "We're definitely going to have to address that urge of self-sacrifice. I was able to wrestle the gun away from him seconds before airport security arrived and took him into custody. Your mom is the real hero for tripping him, even if it was accidental."

"Where are they? My parents? Are they okay?"

"Right here, pumpkin," my dad said, stepping into the office. Dad had his arm around Mom, and they both looked shaken but unhurt. I ran over, hugging them both at once. They held on to me tight for a moment.

"Oh my God," I said, pulling away and swiping at

my eyes. "I'm so glad you're okay." I had a lump in my throat that wouldn't disappear even when I swallowed. "Mom, you totally saved the day."

My mom pressed a hand to her chest, looking surprised. "I did?"

"You did. You dropped exactly when Slash told you to. Santa tripped over you and lost his balance. Because of that, he didn't shoot me, and Slash was able to get control of the gun." I looked over at Frank, who stood by the door. "Did anyone get hurt?"

"No one got hurt thanks to the quick thinking of all of you."

I closed my eyes in relief. At least one thing had gone right. "Who is Santa?" I asked. "Is he a domestic terrorist? I'll be honest, he seemed pretty inept for a terrorist." Unfortunately, I'd had firsthand experience with a couple of terrorists in my lifetime, and Santa just didn't fit the profile.

"We've got a lot more work to do on that front before we can come to any conclusions," Frank said. "However, in connection with that, there are more people who need to talk to you."

"We can't miss our flight," I protested. "We're going to a wedding. We don't know anything else about Santa. It was a totally random encounter."

"I understand that, and I'm sorry," Frank replied. "Regardless, I'm afraid you're going to miss your flight. That being said, we'll try to make arrangements to get you on the next available flight out. We're also working on collecting your baggage."

I glanced at Slash, who shrugged in resignation. Looked like we didn't have much of a say in the matter. I just hoped we didn't have to tell the wedding party why we were going to be late, although I couldn't see how we could avoid it.

"Everyone, please follow me." Frank motioned for us to follow him out of his office.

I exhaled a deep breath, wishing I could shoot my little black cloud of trouble out of the sky or capture it in one of those *Ghostbusters* machines where it could be locked up forever. But, no, it seemed determined to follow me at every freaking turn. Maybe just once it could give me a break.

"I'm sorry," I said to my family as we walked through the airport.

"It's not your fault," Slash said, pulling me to his side and kissing my temple. "Thank God no one was injured."

"I'm in full agreement with that," my dad said. "By the way, about that body armor, Slash, I do believe you assured me I wouldn't need it."

I closed my eyes, thinking it was going to be a long week if my dad kept needling Slash like this and I had to be quiet about it. Slash murmured a soft curse in Italian under his breath and raked his fingers through his hair. "Maybe it would be wise, just to be on the safe side."

"Do I need some, too?" Mom asked.

"Put it on the list, Clarissa," my dad said. "We'll buy the best Italy can offer. No sense waiting until we get back. Like Slash said, just to be on the safe side."

FIVE

Lexi

IF YOU'RE GOING to fly to Europe and can afford it, first
class is definitely the way to do it. Actually, chartering a
private plane is *the* way to do it, but that, as well as first-
class seating, was a luxury I could never have afforded
before I met Slash.

In addition to his gig at the National Security
Agency, Slash founded a private company in New York
called Frisson that provided the government with special
simulation-based training, data integration, and fusion
analysis, among other things. It generated a good amount
of money, so it gave us the extra funds to charter a plane
to take us and my parents to Italy if we so desired. We
desired, but when Slash tried to charter a flight for the
dates we needed, there were no planes available. So, first
class on a commercial airline became our option of
choice, which was what my parents would have chosen
anyway.

When Frank had someone rebook our flight two
hours past the original one, I worried first-class seating
wouldn't be available for my parents. Luckily the flight
had two first-class seats available, which was great for

my parents, but Slash and I were relegated to economy. I didn't complain, because I was thrilled we were able to make the flight in the first place, and that's how I was used to flying anyway. Slash, being Slash, never complained and seemed content to sit next to me, even though his long legs were squished against the seat in front of him. I was just grateful we were in a row that had just two seats on the left-hand side of the plane, so we didn't have to be too near any other passengers.

I gripped his hand tightly as we took off. It wasn't until we'd reached cruising altitude that I relaxed a little. I leaned back against the seat but still held on to his hand.

"That whole Santa-shooting-up-the-airport thing was not the way I intended for this trip to start," I said. "Do you really think Santa was just after his ex-wife?"

"That's what he confessed," Slash said. "Investigators confirmed she was one of the customer service agents handling the check-in and baggage at the Alitalia counter at the time of the shooting. They divorced last year, and she got the kids. She already had a restraining order against him. You bumping into him probably saved her life."

"So, he was just going to shoot his ex-wife right there in the airport?"

"That's debatable. He told investigators he wasn't going to hurt her. He just wanted her to listen to him. I'm not sure I buy that."

I shook my head in disbelief. "What person in their right mind takes a gun to an airport?"

"A person who *isn't* in his right mind," Slash said. "Thank God no one got hurt, especially you." He reached beneath his shirt and slipped out a small cross that had once belonged to his father and kissed it. "Now that we know the black cloud is accompanying us to Italy, we have to stay on high alert."

As if I didn't already have enough stress as it was. I closed my eyes, took a few deep breaths, and tried not to think about it. "Were you able to reschedule the driver to pick us up at the airport?"

"I was. I also got a message to the boat captain. He'll wait for us, as well."

My eyes flew open. "Oh, I totally forgot about that. We have to take a boat to get the island, of course."

"Sorry, *cara*. I know boating is not your thing. At least I was able to charter a decent one with an experienced captain. It only takes about twenty minutes to get to the castle via boat. During the day, it's supposedly a beautiful view. Since we'll now be coming in at dusk, I'm not sure how much we'll be able to see from the water. Regardless, I feel fortunate we've been delayed by only a few hours, and I'm feeling extra lucky that they had enough seats on this flight to accommodate us, including first-class ones for your parents."

"Me, too." I squeezed his hand and he squeezed back. "We have a lot to be thankful for."

"I was also able to speak with Father Armando, and he said they're going to hold dinner for us. So we shouldn't miss much of the gathering. He'll tell the others what happened and is grateful all of us are okay."

A flight attendant walked down the aisle, stopping at our seats. "Excuse me," she said. "My supervisor called and asked me to take care of you. We heard what you did in the airport, and we're upgrading you, on the house. If you'd gather your things, we'll be moving you to first class."

"I didn't think there were any extra first-class seats," I said in surprise.

"We had two no-shows, so you're in luck."

We started gathering our stuff when an announcement came over the speaker. "This is your captain speaking. I believe many of you were in the airport and either heard or experienced the excitement with the gunman that went on earlier this afternoon. What you may not know is these two passengers were instrumental in stopping that man and ensuring no one got hurt."

Slash and I froze, clutching our belongings, as the flight attendant beamed and swept out her hand toward us. Everyone suddenly started wildly clapping and cheering.

I wished the airplane floor would open and drop me out. Not really, but still. This was excruciatingly embarrassing. Slash seemed as uncomfortable as I did.

An elderly woman sitting in the aisle seat across from us squinted at Slash. "Wait. I know you. Aren't you the guy that stopped a robbery and saved a kid at a gas station a few months ago? You're the Tampon Hero."

Now I was pretty sure Slash wished the plane door would open and jettison *him* out. That incident had happened while he'd been picking up a box of tampons for me; he'd stumbled into a robbery gone bad and had single-handedly brought down the bad guy. The cool thing was he was perfectly fine picking up tampons for me, but he wasn't so wild about his new nickname. I think he had to threaten some lives at work to get them to stop calling him that.

Could this get any more mortifying?

A murmur went through the cabin. "Yeah, that's him," someone said. "The Tampon Hero." The cheering got wilder and more frenzied, except now there was laughter.

Slash hadn't moved a muscle. I put a hand on his arm, hoping to defuse the situation.

"Please follow me," the flight attendant said cheerfully, having no idea how mortified we were by the attention. People held out their hands for high fives as

33

we walked up to first class. Slash clapped a few, but I touched no one. Thankfully, once we arrived, they drew a curtain behind us, giving us a bit more privacy.

"Oh, I'm so glad you're here," Mom said. "I saw these open seats and thought it wasn't fair you weren't here, because you'd already paid for them."

"It's okay, Mom," I said, stowing my carry-on in the overhead storage. "That was nice of them to move us up here."

"And the captain publicly recognized Slash's bravery," Dad said. "Another dangerous situation he was lucky to survive."

I glanced at Slash's face, which had a pained expression. "Can we not talk about that right now, Dad? We just want to relax a little."

"Of course. Relax away."

Slash and I sat down and buckled in. The best thing about these first-class seats was that they had a small privacy panel that could close out everyone else around us. For several minutes we sat there sipping the complimentary champagne and orange juice and nibbling on butter cookies until we relaxed.

"That was excruciating," I finally said.

"The worst. But we're on our way, and that's what's important. Everything else is superfluous. Our delay was minimal, and we'll soon be in Italy with my family."

I think that was supposed to make me feel better, but talking about meeting his family only served to heighten my anxiety. "About your family... I prepared something to help me." I released his hand and shifted in my seat so I could dig a piece of paper out of my jeans' back pocket. I took it out, pulled down the seatback table, and smoothed the paper on it.

"I printed this out so I could study it," I said. "I also have it on my phone, but I figured it was safer to have it in both places. The printed version is easier for us to look at together."

Slash leaned over to see what was printed on it. "What is it?"

"A list of the dos and don'ts of meeting the in-laws."

Slash raised an eyebrow. "You printed a spreadsheet of rules on meeting the in-laws?" Before I could answer, he lifted his hand. "Of course you did."

"Slash, this is serious stuff. I want to make a good impression on them."

He studied my face for a moment, like he was going to say something, but instead, he tapped the spreadsheet with his finger. "So, what's on this spreadsheet?"

"Rules. What's appropriate and what's not."

He leaned back in his seat, an amused look on his face. "Oh, this should be good. Run the rules past me."

I glanced at the spreadsheet. "First rule—do not curse or discuss controversial topics such as politics, religion, or sex."

"Sex is a controversial topic?"

"Well, I'm certainly *not* discussing that with your parents," I said. "Not the first time I meet them, and hopefully not ever."

He considered, then nodded. "Fair enough. Keep going."

"Rule number two—no personal displays of affection in front of the in-laws."

Slash frowned and held up a hand. "For the record, I object to rule two and require additional clarification."

"Slash, you *have* to back me up on this." I looked at him earnestly. "These rules were written after much research by sociologists and people who have actually gone through the experience. They know what they're talking about. If I can follow these rules, all will go well and they'll like me."

"If I want to kiss my wife in front of my parents, I'm going to do it." He took my hand, rubbing his thumb across my palm.

My hands started to sweat just thinking of kissing him in front of my in-laws. "A small kiss is fine. But nothing overly suggestive."

"Since when are we suggestive in public?"

"Never. But still, I want all the rules on the table. Moving on to rule number three—let the conversation flow naturally. I shouldn't feel like I must answer every question, but I should be prepared to respond naturally and organically. As a result, I've got a list of potential questions and appropriate answers already inputted into an app on my phone. I've memorized most of them, so I feel fairly confident on that front."

"A conversation app is neither natural nor organic. What if they ask you a question that's not on the list?"

"I've already thought of that," I said confidently. "I'll simply steer the conversation back to a topic I'm ready to address."

"I see."

The way he said that made me worried. "You don't think I can do it?"

"I think you can. I'm just not sure it will go as you expect." He moved his hand from my palm and started playing with my hair, winding the strands around his finger.

I glanced over at him. "Why are you doing that with my hair? Are you trying to distract me?"

"Maybe. When you talk spreadsheet, it makes me want you."

I sighed. "Slash, are you taking this seriously?"

He grinned and leaned over, his lips grazing my ear. "Absolutely. Please continue. Is there a rule four?"

"Rule four is do not pretend to be someone you're not."

"I'm not sure why that's a rule. It seems like it should be a given. What's rule five?"

"Rule five is don't drink excessive amounts of alcohol. This shouldn't be a problem for me. I'm aware of my limits."

"Good. Is that all? Five cardinal rules?"

"That's it for the rules. However, there are a few additional guidelines that suggest further appropriate behavior with the in-laws."

"Five cardinal rules aren't enough?"

I narrowed my eyes at him. "There are ten commandments in the Bible. A few more guidelines in behavior rules with in-laws feels completely within acceptable parameters."

"If you say so." Slash dropped his hand from my hair and shifted in his seat, leaning over the spreadsheet. "What are these additional guidelines?"

I smoothed the paper, tapping on a line. "The first guideline suggests I should accept an invitation to do something your parents ask, even if it's out of my comfort zone. This will demonstrate my eagerness to familiarize and integrate myself with your family. Another guideline says I should offer to help them do things, since it will show I'm hardworking and dedicated when assigned to a task. I should also offer compliments and comment favorably on their fashion, friendliness, and parenting skills. They raised you, after all, so those skills must be sharp. Finally, I should learn their hobbies and interests and ask lots of questions about them so I can glean more insight into their personality." I folded up the paper and returned it to my back pocket. "It all seems fairly doable when it's broken down into actions and rules on a spreadsheet. What do you think?"

"If you're asking my opinion, I like rule four the best. Be yourself."

"I *am* going to be myself, just better," I said with confidence. "I just don't want them to feel like their son made a mistake."

"I can assure you that they will never, *ever* feel that way, especially because they know how happy you make me." Slash leaned over and kissed me on the nose. "Just be yourself, and they will love you as much as I do."

It was nice of him to say that, but I wasn't reassured. I knew they would have a lot of questions, and I wanted to be prepared to answer them as thoroughly and honestly as I could. "They're going to want to know more about me, especially given our situation is unique."

"In what way?"

"Well, we got married without them. You say your parents are okay with that, but are they really?"

"They are, and they understand there were extenuating circumstances. Besides, we're getting married in the church in just a few months, so it's not a big deal. If the pope is okay with it, so are my parents." He paused for a moment, lowering his voice. "Besides, you don't get to have all the anxiety about parents. Let's be honest here. Your dad doesn't like me. Tolerates me, perhaps, but liking me is a reach."

"If this is about my dad and the danger and body armor thing, surely you know he's just overreacting."

"Perhaps. Still, your dad knows that black cloud of yours didn't start coming around until you met me."

"That's not true. From the day I knocked the entire ballet class off the stage while prancing around as a tree to the time I set our kitchen on fire while trying to create a volcano at age six, he's known that trouble is synonymous with me. The trouble has only morphed into more adult fare since I've grown up. Guns, home invasions, plane crashes, terrorists. No way he blames all of that on you."

"I'm not convinced of that." He leaned his head against mine. "We're a pair, I guess."

"We are. Look, I didn't tell you, but I asked the black cloud to stay home. Obviously, it didn't. But maybe we'll get lucky and it's one and done with the Santa episode."

Slash lifted his head to check my expression. "You don't actually believe that, do you?"

I wished I did, but I knew better. "Just stay close to me while we're at the castle, okay? We'll be on a secluded island with minimal chance for outside forces to be at play. What could possibly happen?"

"I really wish you wouldn't say that."

"Good point," I replied. "No need to tempt fate or the black cloud into any more action."

"No. No need at all."

SIX

Lexi

WE GOT A decent night's sleep on the plane. The chairs reclined enough to make it feel close to a bed, and holding Slash's hand, I slept harder and deeper than I thought I would. Knowing me and planes, I was surprised it worked. I must have been more exhausted than I realized. More importantly, there were no nightmares. I guess an automatic-packing Santa in real life was enough for my subconscious.

Unfortunately, it took hours to get through customs. Thankfully, our driver waited for us at the airport. After a three and half-hour trip to the coast, we finally arrived at the ferry station, where a boat was waiting to take us to the island. We were originally supposed to have arrived early in the afternoon, giving us several hours to rest and get ready for dinner. But after all our unanticipated delays, we'd arrived just as dusk was falling. Worse, I still had to endure a boat ride, which I would not enjoy, because I get seasick. I just hoped if I did hurl, it wouldn't be all over myself right before I met Slash's parents.

Slash knew what I was thinking. He took my hand as

we got out of the car and squeezed it. "It's going to be a quick trip over, and you'll be fine."

Easy for him to say, as travel didn't seem to adversely affect him. Still, I didn't reply, because I didn't want to worry him, especially knowing my little black cloud was hovering.

We gathered our suitcases from the car and rolled them toward the boat. The captain, I presumed, loaded them onto the boat for us and then instructed us to walk a small plank to board. I followed my mom and dad onboard, ignoring the lap of the water against the hull.

Slash stayed on land for a minute, checking the car and making sure we hadn't forgotten anything. While standing on the deck next to the captain, I decided to practice my Italian.

"Buona sera. Grazie per averci aspettato," I said. Good evening. Thank you for waiting for us. Or at least that's what I hoped I said.

"*Piacere mio,*" he responded.

I was pretty sure he'd told me that the pleasure was all his. He then asked me something else, which, I think, was why we'd come to Italy. I wasn't sure exactly how to answer, but I tried to do my best to tell him we were coming for a wedding.

He looked at me a bit strangely and then grinned. "*Divertiti.*"

I had no idea what that meant, and he walked away after that, so I'd have to ask Slash later for a translation.

Mom and Dad had gone below deck, but I was staying on the deck for the bracing breeze and in case I needed to lean over the side and empty my stomach. Slash stayed outside with me and didn't ask why I didn't go below. He already knew.

I watched in silence as we pushed off from the dock. The boat's motor thrummed louder as the boat picked up speed, and water crested against the hull. I felt the first turn of my stomach and a bit of nausea. I gripped the railing, willing it to pass. Slash came up behind me, putting a hand on each side of me, holding me steady. I relaxed back against him, thankful for his calm presence.

"Tell me something else about the castle," I said, wanting him to keep my mind off the water.

"That you don't already know? You researched the island as much as I did, except I'm not as worried about the snakes as you are."

"Hey! Did you check my browsing history?"

He laughed. "No. Just an educated guess. I figure you also researched local spiders and various insects, too. Come on, tell me I'm wrong."

He wasn't. He knew me better than I cared to admit. Even though I'd spent significant time in a jungle and a rain forest, I hadn't bonded with any of the reptiles or insects.

The boat had started to move at a decent clip now, and the wind whipped my hair into my eyes. Slash stayed as solid as a rock behind me.

"The island is small, just over seven kilometers, or four and a half miles, from point to point," he said. "It contains beautiful, ancient trees, foliage, and flowers, not to mention dangerous cliffs and drop-offs, from which, given your tendency toward tripping, I intend to keep you far away. As you've likely already uncovered in your research, there are two kinds of venomous snakes present on the island, *Vipera aspis* and *Vipera berus*. The statistical probability that you will come across one of them on the island is less than .000003 percent. But even if you did and were bit by one, their hemotoxic venom is much less dangerous than, say, the neurotoxic venom of a cobra. So you can stop worrying about that."

"Ha. Just because I know the stats doesn't make me feel any better."

He chuckled. "Anyway, the castle is the only significant building on the island and is powered by generators. In addition to the purportedly elaborate escape rooms, the castle supposedly has a ballroom, pool, library, game room, and a beautiful garden, as well as several guest rooms, bathrooms, and staff quarters, all of which have been renovated and made available to Zachetti's personal guests."

"Have you ever seen a photo of Dante Zachetti?" I asked. "I searched online but couldn't find a single photo of him or his father anywhere."

"No. As I mentioned before, the family is extremely reclusive," Slash replied. "In fact, I'm still surprised he agreed to host us."

"It had to be something Father Armando said," I mused. "I can't think of why else he'd agree, and why he'd refuse payment."

"It is odd," Slash mused. "I don't think Father Armando knows Zachetti, and I don't believe Zachetti is a practicing Catholic. If he is, he keeps it very low profile. Anyway, I don't see why he'd feel he'd have to agree to inviting us. But you never know. Perhaps we'll find out when we get there."

"Perhaps. Regardless, we must thank him, since Gio is beyond excited at the prospect, and he thinks you're responsible for it."

Slash didn't offer further comment. I couldn't see the dock anymore, so I tried to keep a fixed-point stare on the horizon, which is supposed to help with nausea. But other than the faint glow of the moon and the lights from the boat, it had become almost entirely dark on the water. I couldn't see anything to focus on. "Maybe there's a catch, Slash. Zachetti sponsoring the entire wedding party seems less like altruism and more like there's something in it for him. What if there are some weird conditions we don't know about?"

Slash's arms tightened around me. "If we're uncomfortable in any way, we leave. I guess we'll find out soon enough."

The wind whipped my hair in a frenzy around my face, and the spray of the water misted us, so several strands plastered to my cheeks. I was certain to arrive looking like something the cat dragged in.

"There's the castle," Slash said pointing.

In the distance, atop a large rise, I could see lights shining.

"That's Castrum Augustus," he said.

As the boat moved closer, I got a better look. The structure loomed above the jagged cliffs, lights dotting the windows. Below the castle the red and green twinkling of buoys in the water signaled the safe path to the shore, or at least I hoped it did. The boathouse and dock came into view as we rounded a small outcropping. The boathouse and dock were lighted by several overhead lights positioned so they wouldn't interfere with the pilot's night vision. It was too dark to see much else beyond the pools of light at the dock and the dim pearls of luminescence that likely marked the path up from the boathouse.

We sensed rather than saw the breakwater and low cliffs on either side of the boat as we headed for a small dock. Behind us, we could hear the crashing of the waves on the looming cliffs, where huge sprays of water smashed violently against the rocks. There was a lone figure waiting at the dock, and as we got closer, he grabbed a tethering rope that was tossed to him by the captain. As we were maneuvered closer to the dock, my parents came up from below. Once the boat was secured, the captain illuminated the deck with overhead boat lights and prepared to transfer our luggage ashore.

"Good heavens, Lexi," my mom said when she saw me in the harsh white boat light. "What happened to you? Was it raining out here?"

I tried without success to smooth down my hair. "No, Mom. The sea was a little rough and we got sprayed. I'm fine." Since I'd gone the entire ride without hurling over the side even once, I considered the trip a full success, despite the current state of my hair and clothing.

Slash helped the captain and the man waiting at the dock unload our luggage. After our suitcases stood side by side on the dock, the captain informed us he'd be returning to the mainland and would come back for us in three days. Slash spoke with him for a minute, then unfastened and tossed him the tether as the boat pulled away, turning off its overhead lights.

As we watched the boat disappear, Slash turned to me. "So, what did you say to the captain earlier?"

"Nothing much. I practiced my Italian on him. I greeted him and said it was a beautiful evening."

"Anything else?"

"Well, I think he asked me what brought me to Italy, and I told him I'd come for a wedding."

"How exactly did you say that?"

I thought back for a moment. "*Sono allupata.*"

Slash choked and then started laughing. "No wonder."

"No wonder what? What's so funny? Did I say it wrong?"

"You told him...you were horny."

"*What?*" I stared at him in horror. "No way I said that. Is that really what that means?"

"That's *really* what that means." Slash laughed again. "No wonder he told me to enjoy myself."

"Ugh! I'm never speaking Italian unless you're around."

"Don't be ridiculous. Your Italian has improved quite a bit. Mistakes are a part of learning a new language."

A voice spoke behind us. "*Benvenuto.*" The man who'd been waiting at the dock, holding a large lantern and wearing a gray trench coat, greeted us. He looked to be about sixty years old with a nicely trimmed mustache and shock of gray hair. "Welcome to Castrum Augustus. My name is Lorenzo Conte, and I'm Mr. Zachetti's butler. Shall we get your luggage into the van? The castle, as you can see from here, is just a short distance, but it's quite cool out here with the wind blowing."

We introduced ourselves before helping him pile our stuff into the van. I watched him stagger a bit with one of Mom's suitcases, but with a little help from Slash, he got it inside the van and somehow managed to close the back.

Mom and Dad had already seated themselves in the van, and Slash helped me in before climbing in behind me and closing the door.

"We're quite pleased you've arrived at last," Lorenzo said as we drove away from the dock. His English was tinged with a British accent. "You're the final guests. I was dismayed to hear about your travel delay but hope we have allowed sufficient time for you to change clothing and refresh yourselves before dinner is served promptly at seven o'clock in the dining room."

I glanced at my watch. I needed a lot more than forty minutes to repair my appearance, as well as mentally prepare myself for meeting my in-laws and the rest of the guests, but I wasn't going to get it. A panicked glance at Slash confirmed he knew what I was thinking.

He patted my knee in sympathy. "*Grazie,*" Slash told him. "We'll make it work."

SEVEN

Lexi

MY FIRST IMPRESSION of the castle was that it wasn't exactly a castle. Instead, it was more like a mansion built atop the ruins of an ancient castle.

As we pulled up onto a circular stone driveway, I stared in awe. The new part of the castle was made of cream-colored stones built directly onto the gray stone foundation that had once been the original castle structure. The architect appeared to have followed the original design, building a mansion that mimicked a real castle with impressive turrets, large windows ringed with stone arches, and impressive balconies guarded by delicate iron railings. The castle was unmistakably Italian, with red terra cotta tiles perched on the roof. Two enormous, arched wooden doors were decorated with Christmas wreaths woven with red and gold ribbons and dotted with silver balls.

"Wow," I murmured as I exited the car. If the castle looked this stunning in the dark, I couldn't imagine how it would look in the daylight.

"Impressive," Slash said. I hadn't realized he had come to stand beside me. He slipped his hand in mine, and for a moment we marveled at it.

"Lexi, this place is beautiful," Mom said from behind me. "What a lovely idea to come here."

"It'll undoubtedly be an adventure," Dad said, also admiring the view. "Good job."

We helped Lorenzo unpack the van and followed him through one of the gigantic wooden doors and into the foyer. The inside didn't disappoint. Two gorgeous rose-colored marble staircases with elaborately carved handrails led to the next level and flanked a large open space. A huge iron chandelier, possibly original to the castle, hung down from the second floor and held actual lit candles.

To the right of the entrance stood a gigantic Christmas tree, dripping in white lights, satin ribbons, and huge pear-shaped crystals. But the Nativity scene caught my interest. Someone had created an entire mini village with an inn, running water, working lights, intricate backdrops, and a plethora of people and animal figurines. The engineering and design were so sophisticated, the geek in me immediately activated.

I walked over to examine it, and Slash followed. "This is extraordinary," I breathed. "I've never seen anything quite like it."

"We Italians take our *presepi* quite seriously," he said with a smile. "It's your Nativity scenes, as you call it. *Presepe* means crib. The crib will remain empty until Christmas Eve, when the baby is placed in it to great fanfare. But I agree with you, this one's exquisite."

I wanted to stay and figure out how the architect had done everything, but Lorenzo ushered us toward the area between the two staircases, near a large rectangular table with a pink marble top. Atop the table was a rustic Christmas centerpiece made of pinecones, gourds, and fir boughs, mixed in with red, white, and gold candles, all of which flickered from the draft of the open door behind us.

"That's the butler's table," Slash said softly. "It holds things that a butler might need, I suppose."

Perhaps it was normal for a castle to have a butler, but I didn't even know what a butler did. "This castle is mind-blowing."

Even my mom was speechless, and that's saying something. My dad looked around the room, whistling at the view.

"I'm so pleased you approve of the seasonal decor," Lorenzo said. "Mr. Zachetti spares no expense. Now, behind the staircase to your right is a small elevator that will assist you with getting your luggage to the second floor."

As we started to shuffle that way with our luggage, my mom asked Lorenzo a question. "Mr. Conte, you speak English so well. Where did you learn it?"

He seemed pleased, as well a little embarrassed by her compliment. "That's kind of you to say, *signora*. I studied several languages in London. I also speak French, German, and Spanish. Mr. Zachetti often has guests from diverse locations and prefers to have a butler who can appropriately and efficiently respond to the needs of everyone."

"It's such a wonderful talent to have," Mom said. "My tongue gets tied up whenever I try to say something in a foreign language beyond a basic greeting."

"I'm sure, madame, with a little practice, your grasp of the language could be quite sufficient."

"Oh, that's kind of you to say."

We took turns in the elevator getting ourselves and the luggage to the top. Lorenzo then led us down a hallway lit by golden sconces on the wall. He stopped at a wooden door to his left and, using an old-fashioned golden key, opened the room. "*Signore* and *Signora* Carmichael, this is your room." He helped pull the suitcases inside and handed my father the key before walking to the next room.

"Your room, *signore* and *signora*, is here," Lorenzo said. "Hopefully you'll find it satisfactory."

"I'm sure we will," I said.

Lorenzo opened the door and motioned for me to enter first, so I did, pulling my suitcase behind me. "Wow," I said.

A beautiful four-poster bed with elaborately carved wooden columns and gauzy white curtains commanded the room. The space also had a marble fireplace, two antique armchairs, and a small table.

"Is that a working fireplace?" Slash asked.

"It most certainly is," Lorenzo replied. "Beneath the blanket to the right of the fireplace is the wood. It will be replenished every morning."

"Excellent," he said.

I went straight to the balcony, opening one of two large glass doors that led out onto it. "Come look at the view, Slash." Cold air rushed in, causing the curtains to billow. Our room faced the sea, and the moon shone brightly on the water. Waves crashed against the rocks of the cliffs, and for a moment, the sound reminded me of my favorite hotel room in Salerno, Italy, where Slash and I had worked through one of the most challenging issues of our relationship.

"It's beautiful," I whispered.

Slash joined me, putting his arms around me, pulling me close. I wondered if he was thinking the same thing.

"If that will be all, I shall withdraw and give you time to refresh yourself before supper," Lorenzo said.

Slash left me and walked Lorenzo to the door, speaking to him softly in Italian. I closed the balcony door and sat on the satin ottoman before starting to take off my damp tennis shoes. When Slash came back, I asked him what he'd said.

"I asked him where my parents are located," he replied.

I looked up from untying my shoe. "And? Where are they?"

"Next door."

My stomach did a little flip. "So, we're sandwiched between our parents?"

"Looks like it." He shrugged. "This ought to be fun."

"Said no one ever." I tossed my shoes aside, peeled off my socks, and lay back on the bed. "Jeez."

"It'll be fine, *cara*. It's just for a couple of days."

"If you say so. We can do this, right? Please tell me we can do this."

"Of course we can do this. We just have to be ready for anything."

I sighed. Wasn't that the motto of our freaking lives? "Well…aren't we always?"

EIGHT

Lexi

SLASH AND I took a shower together in the interest of saving time, but one thing led to another and before we knew it, we only had about ten minutes left to get dressed. Still, totally worth it, in my opinion.

I blow-dried my hair in the bathroom while Slash shaved at the sink. Luckily, no one got electrocuted. I quickly slipped on a sky-blue dress and a matching cardigan sweater, the same outfit I'd worn for my engagement party. I had matching shoes that were low to the ground and snug. Only my parents and Slash had seen my outfit before, and I didn't care if it was a faux pax to repurpose it. I felt comfortable in it, so that drove my fashion decisions. Tonight, comfort was especially important to me since I was already so anxious about everything else. The last thing I needed was to be worried about a dress.

I paced the room, nervously twisting my engagement ring around my finger. The band was an antique gold setting with two entwining hands that met at a circle of white diamonds. A gorgeous blue diamond nestled in the center of the circle, winking and sparkling whenever it caught the light. It had belonged to Slash's beloved nonna, and she'd gifted it to him to give to me. Nonna and I had an interesting history that involved odorous perfume, a haughty cat, and the best food I'd ever eaten in my life. Somehow, despite language and geographic boundaries, we'd become pretty good friends. Her ring was the perfect one for me—small and unpretentious, but still beautiful and unique. I rarely wore jewelry, but I loved that ring more than I could say.

After Slash left the bathroom to get dressed, I went in to put on makeup, just enough to find the sweet spot where my comfort equaled the minimum of socially acceptable expectations. I brushed my thick brown hair until it shone and left it long. I realized it hadn't been cut in a while, and it was longer than I'd had it in ages. Given all that had been going on in my life lately, there hadn't been an opportunity to get it cut. Plus, haircuts were not at the top of my list of favorite things to do. I didn't like being touched or handled by strangers, so I had to get myself mentally prepared every time. It was exhausting.

I came out of the bathroom just as Slash was putting on his suit jacket. He straightened his tie and turned toward me, holding out his arms. "What do you think?"

He looked handsome and smelled even better, so I walked up to him, winding my arms around his waist. "You're the most handsome man I've ever met, but don't let that go to your head." My words muffled against his chest.

He hugged me and chuckled, the sound rumbling in my ear. "And you're the most extraordinary woman I've ever known," he murmured, stroking my hair. "Despite your concerns, I'm looking forward to introducing you to my parents."

"I guess there's no backing out now…right?" I

looked up, half hoping he would have some magic excuse that would provide me with an escape. Unfortunately, he didn't.

He glanced at his smart watch, then kissed the top of my head. "It's showtime. Are you ready?"

"Emotionally, no. Intellectually, maybe. But it's one of those things I have to get through, right?"

"*Si.*" He put his fingers in my hair and lowered his mouth to mine, murmuring, "But you've got this." His lips were soft and sank into mine, touching, tasting as if it weren't enough. After a minute, he pulled back, resting his forehead against mine. He was breathing fast, and so was I, for that matter.

"I can't seem to get enough of you," he said. "It's magic."

"It's biology," I corrected him.

"Not all of it." His brown eyes lit with amusement as he kissed me one more time, his mouth lingering near mine. "We'd better go or we'll never leave this room."

I was totally okay with that scenario, but it had to be done. I left his embrace and picked up my purse, trying to steady my nerves. "Guess I'm prepared as I can be. I've got you, my spreadsheet, and the app on my phone to get me through this. Let's do it."

Slash smiled and held out his elbow. I slipped my arm through his with a deep breath. "I just hope everything goes right for once. Is that too much to ask?"

We knocked on both of our parents' doors before heading downstairs, just in case we caught them before they'd left for dinner. Neither couple answered.

"Are we late?" I asked, clutching my sweater tighter as we walked down the sconce-lighted hallway.

"We're not," Slash said calmly. "It's not quite seven.

It's likely that everyone went down a little early to enjoy a cocktail or two. I figured you needed the extra downtime and early cocktails was something you wouldn't want to do."

"You're right, as always."

We walked down the curving marble stairs instead of using the elevator. Lorenzo waited in the foyer. He'd changed out of his gray trench coat and looked quite dapper in a black suit and red bow tie. "Good evening," he said. "I hope your accommodations are adequate and you had sufficient time to rest and recharge."

"The room is beautiful," I said. "And we haven't even used the fireplace…yet."

"We're quite comfortable," Slash agreed. "*Mille grazie.*"

Lorenzo stretched out a hand to the right. "The dining room is that way. Cocktails and hors d'oeuvres are being served right now."

Slash patted my hand as we walked in the direction he had pointed. "Courage," he murmured.

As we got closer, the murmur of voices and laughter wafted down the hallway. Slash paused just outside the doorway so we could get a glimpse inside the glittering dining room before entering.

I had to blink twice because everything was so bright. A huge crystal chandelier hung over an enormous rectangular table set with gleaming dishes and silverware. Dozens of red and white candles formed a line down the middle of the table, causing the glassware and settings to sparkle wildly. Classical Christmas music played softly from artfully hidden speakers, and a roaring fire blazed in a huge white marble fireplace over which rested an exquisitely carved mantel. Above the mantel hung a gigantic portrait of a handsome man with long dark hair, a full beard, and dark, piercing eyes.

It was everything I'd imagined an Italian castle dining room would look like—not that I'd thought a lot about it.

"That's Zachetti in the portrait, I presume," Slash said.

Whoever he was, he looked kind of intense. "I wouldn't want to meet him in a dark alley."

Slash didn't have a chance to respond, because his younger brother, Giorgio, the groom of the upcoming wedding, spotted us.

"Romeo," he shouted before he bounded over to Slash, giving him a hug complete with heavy backslapping and cheek kissing. Slash had many names and aliases, but his family called him Romeo.

"Gio," Slash said with a smile on his face. He said something in Italian to his brother, and Gio laughed.

"What did you say?" I asked.

"I told him love looks good on him," Slash said. "And it does."

I'd met Gio briefly several months ago when he'd helped Slash save me from a Chinese hacker. I remember being shocked the first time I saw him, because he was so handsome. Even though they weren't biologically related, Gio looked like a slightly shorter version of Slash, with dark, wavy hair, brown eyes, and an extremely attractive smile. However, unlike Slash, who was quiet and reserved, Gio seemed to be constantly joking and had a great sense of humor. He was also incredibly charming and flirtatious.

Gio lifted my hand to his lips, keeping his eyes on me the entire time. "Lexi, *bella*, we meet again," he said in accented English. His voice was velvety and had that same hint of sexiness that I liked whenever Slash's English pronunciation slipped back into Italian. "What a joy it is to welcome you to our family."

"Congratulations on your forthcoming nuptials," I said, hoping that was an appropriate response to his declaration. I wasn't sure it was, because he laughed and pulled me toward him, kissing me noisily on each cheek.

"You're such a delight. Please, I wish to introduce you both to my beautiful fiancée, Vittoria."

Vittoria was, indeed, beautiful. Long, glossy black hair swept to one side in perfectly formed ringlets, heart-shaped lips, and stunning brown eyes with long eyelashes. She wore a glittering off-white dress with only one sleeve and an uneven hem, which was likely supposed to be a fashion statement, but my desire for symmetry made me wince. Slash had told me she was seven months along, but the baby bump was barely noticeable because of the flowing material.

Slash gently kissed Vittoria on each cheek and murmured something to her in Italian before she turned to me. I stood awkwardly, not knowing whether it was up to me to shake her hand or if I had to do the cheek-kissing thing that seemed the norm in Italy. Maybe I had to wait for her to make the first move. Why the heck hadn't I studied that part of the etiquette book before we'd left?

"Hello, Lexi," she said in a throaty voice, giving me a dazzling smile.

Thank goodness, she'd broken the ice first. "Hi, Vittoria. It's so nice to meet you." I thrust out my hand, and she shook it. I wasn't sure if that was proper etiquette, but it worked. We didn't have a chance to speak further, because we were mobbed by Stefan, Slash's older brother, and Tito Blickensderfer, a longtime friend of Slash's and, more recently, mine.

Tito, a former member of the Swiss Guard, had met Slash when they were working at the Vatican. I'd first met Tito when I was in Rome helping Slash's uncle with a hacking problem, and we'd become friends right away, which was unusual for me. I'd seen him only once since then, when he, Gio, and Slash had saved my life in Papua New Guinea. Tito was also good friends with Gio, and he was in the wedding party. Knowing Tito would be here made me feel better. At least I had someone other than Slash and my parents to talk to if things went downhill socially for me—something that was a real possibility.

"Hey, Tito," I said, wincing as he smashed me in a giant hug. He was a muscular guy, and even though he'd recently left the Swiss Guard, he still had his brown hair buzzed in a military haircut. "It's great to see you again."

He slung an easy arm around my shoulders. "Likewise. Thanks for the opportunity to play in a rich man's castle. I heard you had a little excitement at the airport."

"Yeah, Santa Claus gone bad. I'm sure Slash will fill you in on all the details."

He laughed. "You two have all the fun."

Before I could respond, Slash spotted Tito and they started grinning and slapping each other on the back, talking to each other in German. I suddenly faced Slash's older brother, Stefan, alone.

"Lexi, what a pleasure to finally meet you," Stefan said. Like Gio and Slash, Stefan had the same dark hair, chiseled jaw, and smoky brown eyes. Even if they weren't biologically related, they were a trio of seriously good-looking men.

Stefan lifted my hand to his mouth and kissed it. "I've been waiting to meet the woman who has completely captured my brother's heart. I hope we're able to find some time to talk this weekend. I've heard so much about you, and I'm looking forward to getting to know you better."

I grimaced inwardly. I had no idea what Slash had said about me, but I worried whatever it was, I wouldn't be able to live up to it.

After that, the faces, cheek kisses, and hugs became a blur. Stefan introduced me to his girlfriend, Alessa Thorne, a pretty, blonde woman in a black cocktail dress with a British accent. We chatted for a minute before Father Emilio Armando, a Vatican cardinal and the man Slash considered a second father, stepped forward to give me a kiss on each cheek. He was dressed in a black cassock with red trim and buttons, in what I presumed was casual wear for a cardinal. His eyes twinkled happily when he saw my shocked expression.

"Surprise!" he said.

It may not have been appropriate protocol when dealing with an important Catholic cardinal, but I threw my arms around him in a big hug. The gesture was unusual for me, but Father Armando was special.

"What are you doing here?" As soon as the words came out of my mouth, I blushed. When I'd made the reservations, we were told only twelve guests were permitted. After consulting with Gio, we'd whittled down the guest list to just the wedding party and my folks when Vittoria's parents weren't able to make it until the actual wedding. Although I was genuinely glad Emilio was here, it also meant we had thirteen guests. I hoped that was okay with Mr. Zachetti, because there wasn't much I could do about it at this point.

"I'll tell you later." He grinned but didn't offer any further explanation, and he moved on to talk with Stefan.

I'd come to the end of my rope in terms of social overload when I found myself face-to-face with a pretty woman in a dark-green gown. Her long, dark hair had been braided and hung down her back. Even without introduction, I knew at once she was Slash's adopted mother, Juliette. She looked much kinder in person than in my dream.

"Lexi, at last," she said softly. "How wonderful to meet you."

Slash somehow materialized at my side, slipping his arm around my waist, and leaning forward to kiss the woman on both of her cheeks. "Mama, I'd like you to meet my Lexi."

NINE

Lexi

I LOVED HOW he called me *his* Lexi. I couldn't recall him calling me that before. Just that little bit of extra love warmed my heart and went a long way to settling my nerves.

Juliette smiled at me, far prettier than photos showed, with high cheekbones, long eyelashes, and eyes that were more golden than brown. They softened with affection as she looked between Slash and me.

Was everyone in Slash's family drop-dead gorgeous?

I still hadn't said a word when Juliette took one of my hands in hers, pressing a soft kiss to each of my cheeks. "I'm so glad you could make it to Gio's wedding." Her English was perfect, with just a soft accent.

I finally found my voice. "I wouldn't have missed it for the world. It's great to finally meet you, Mrs. Thurlow-Davies. I've heard so much about you from Slash."

"Oh, please call me Juliette. And this was a wonderful idea to give us a few days before Gio's wedding to meet and get to know each other. I've already met your parents, and they are lovely people."

Gah! She'd already met my parents? I hoped my mom hadn't told her any stories about me yet. The embarrassing tales they could tell.

"You've met my parents?" I asked cautiously.

"I have. Your mom is beautiful and gracious, and your father is quite dashing."

I glanced over at my parents. My mom looked amazing dressed in a fitted red dress with sparkling diamonds at her ears and around her neck, her blond hair perfectly coiffed and her makeup flawless. My dad wore a suit with a red tie that coordinated with the color of her dress. It seemed unfair my parents, my husband, and now my in-laws were so good-looking with excellent people skills, whereas I sucked at all the above.

"They are so proud of you, Lexi, and rightfully so," she said.

I realized it was my turn to say something witty, but nothing leaped to mind, so I decided to lead with honesty. "Thank you for being so nice. I'm sorry, I can't think of anything interesting to say now. I'm nervous, a bit overwhelmed by all the people, and I'm not good at small talk."

Slash pressed a soft kiss against my temple, then slipped his hand into mine. His fingers, tapered and strong, squeezed mine gently, letting me know he'd always stand beside me in all my socially awkward glory.

"It's completely understandable," she said. "You've met a lot of people this evening." She noticed Nonna's ring on my finger and pulled it closer for a better look. "Oh, Lexi, the ring is perfect for you. We're so thrilled Romeo has met his match in you, and we couldn't be happier. I know we're going to get along wonderfully."

Her kind words made me feel better. Just then someone rang a bell to get our attention, and we stopped talking.

Lorenzo stepped in front of the group, commanding our attention. "Ladies and gentlemen, please have a seat at the table. You'll notice a white place card at each setting, and I ask you to sit at the spot you've been designated. We've arranged it so you'll be sitting next to someone you may not know well. We hope it'll encourage you to form new and lasting friendships and relationships."

I pressed tighter against Slash in protest. If they were separating us, I was in serious trouble. He was my guide, my buffer, and my savior when it came to social situations—and this was a *very* important situation to me.

What a freaking disaster.

"Let's talk more later, Lexi," Juliette said with a conspiratorial smile and headed toward the table.

"I told you she'd like you," Slash said, taking my hand. "Come on. We'll just be separated for a little while at dinner. You'll be fine."

I *wouldn't* be fine, but I didn't say so, because what would be the point? It didn't seem as if there was anything I could do about it, so I sucked it up and let him lead me toward the sparkling table.

We wandered up one side of the table until we found my name. I quickly glanced at the names on either side of me. To my right was Mia, Vittoria's teenage sister and maid of honor, and to my left was… Oh, crap. Slash's stepfather, Oscar Thurlow-Davies.

My breathing quickened. I would be squeezed between an Italian teenager and my British father-in-law with no help in sight.

What could possibly go wrong?

A voice in the back of my head reminded me that I *really* needed to stop asking that question.

TEN

Lexi

"DON'T WORRY," SLASH murmured, patting my arm. "Oscar's a good man." He looked around the room, presumably waiting to introduce me to Oscar before we sat. He didn't see him, and Lorenzo urged us to take our seats, so Slash kissed my hair and reluctantly left me gripping the back of my chair. I watched as he walked around to the other side of the table and sat between Stefan's girlfriend, Alessa, and the bride-to-be, Vittoria. All three sat down, and both women began chatting with him immediately.

He made it look so easy.

"May I?" a male voice with a distinctly British accent said, breaking into my thoughts.

"May you what?" I turned around to see a middle-aged man with thinning brown hair. He was dressed in a navy three-piece suit and a vest that seemed slightly too tight across his waist. His bow tie was red and askew, as if he'd been tugging on it. He seemed as uncomfortable in fancy clothes as I was.

He pointed at my chair. I looked at the chair and then back at him, hope springing in my chest. "You want to sit here?"

"No. May I pull the chair out for you? I'm Oscar Thurlow-Davies, Romeo's—or Slash's, as he prefers to be called these days—stepfather. You're Lexi, right? It's a pleasure to meet you at last." He stuck out his hand.

My cheeks heated as I took his hand and shook it. "Oh, hi, Mr. Thurlow-Davies. Yes, I'm Lexi. It's nice to meet you, too. I've been preparing myself to meet you. I mean, I've been looking forward to meeting you because you're Slash's stepfather." I snapped my mouth shut. Seriously? Could I sound any more like a dork?

"Please, just call me Oscar."

I stepped away from the chair. "Sure, Oscar, you can pull the chair out for me, if that's what you want to do. Not that you're going to want to do that every time we're at a table, but if we are, you can feel free to do so." I cringed at my babbling and wished someone would just shoot me.

Oscar gallantly pulled out my chair and motioned for me to sit in it. After I was safely tucked in at the table, he did the same for Mia, who showed up on the other side of me, before seating himself.

Slash glanced over at me, a smile playing at his lips. I think he liked it when I was pushed out of my comfort zone on occasion. I didn't mind a social challenge occasionally, but I was feeling overwhelmed in a room full of people, at least half of whom I didn't know, and had to strongly resist the urge to disappear to the bathroom and stay there for the rest of the evening. But having him in sight helped a lot, even if we were separated by a rather large table.

I suspected he knew that, too.

A young man and woman began moving in tandem up and down the table, filling our wineglasses and water goblets and offering an *aperitivo*, a small glass of liqueur people often drank before the meal in Italy. Tonight, it was prosecco. I didn't really care for it but downed it anyway because it was a small glass, and I was nervous and trying to fit in. Our glasses were quickly whisked away, and the next course, the *antipasto*, was served. Tonight, that was thick, crusty bread and an elegant selection of cheese and nuts on a small plate.

I glanced at Mia as she slipped her napkin on her lap. Following suit, I did the same with my napkin. I wasn't proud of it, but I was glad she was sitting next to me. Maybe dinner wouldn't be so difficult, as long as I had confidence the teenager had better table etiquette than me.

I tore into a piece of the bread and ate a small piece of cheese before Lorenzo rang the bell again to make another announcement. He stood to the right side of the table, near the door of what I assumed was the kitchen. Beside him stood several other people I hadn't noticed before but presumed were the castle staff. Lorenzo had said we'd be meeting them at dinner.

"Once again, welcome to Castrum Augustus." Lorenzo beamed as he looked around the table. "Our owner, Mr. Zachetti, is absolutely delighted you've decided to visit the castle and accept the exciting challenges locked within our walls." He swept out a hand toward the portrait above the fireplace, and my eyes were drawn to his dark gaze again. There were quiet murmurs at the table before he continued. "I wanted to take a moment to introduce you to our staff, who you'll likely see milling about the place during the day. If you require anything at all during your stay, please do not hesitate to reach out to any one of us."

Slash met my eyes across the table again and gave me an encouraging nod. I smiled, hoping I was radiating calmness and self-confidence even as I wiped my damp hands on the napkin on my lap. I'm sure he knew better.

"First of all, I'd like to introduce you to your resident chef, Carlo," Lorenzo continued. A handsome, dark-haired man dressed in an all-black outfit and apron stepped forward, lifting his hand in greeting. "Carlo has taken note of all potential allergies and food dislikes on the short online questionnaire you were asked to fill out before your arrival. But if anything has changed, please do not hesitate to let him know."

There was a polite smattering of applause at the table, but I didn't join in because Mia kept her hands firmly on her lap and Oscar didn't clap, either.

"Carlo is married to Eleanora, our housekeeper," Lorenzo said as a woman with a pretty smile and brown hair pulled back into a neat bun stepped forward. "If you require extra towels, sheets, toiletries, or anything else for your room, direct your needs to her. These two young and capable servers filling your wineglasses are their twins, Chiara and Ciro." The twins, whom I presumed to be in their early twenties, gave us a happy wave.

"Standing beside Eleanora is Matteo, the castle groundskeeper, who is also quite handy with tools," Lorenzo said. Matteo stood at least a half foot taller than Eleanora and was thin with a receding hairline. He looked supremely uncomfortable being highlighted and constantly wrung his gnarled hands together in front of him. I felt an immediate connection.

"You can thank Matteo for maintaining our beautiful gardens," Lorenzo said. "Now, last, although by no means least, is Brando Porizio, your gamemaster. Brando will lead you through each of the challenges and respond to any questions you may have."

Brando stood out from the others. He wore tinted glasses despite the fact it was night, and his shirt was forest green with an electric-blue tie. His stringy hair hung to his shoulders, and one piece was braided down the back. I immediately imagined him in a Volkswagen van wearing a tie-dye T-shirt and singing sixties music while strumming a guitar. Brando gave us a quick salute and flashed a smile. Was it my imagination or did his look in my direction linger before he stepped back in line?

"Well, he looks like a total nutter," Oscar muttered. "This should be interesting."

I agreed but didn't say anything. If things went south this weekend, it would be on my shoulders, and I didn't want to go down that rabbit hole when I was trying to stay focused on acting like a poised, socially competent, and normal daughter-in-law.

"Now, I'd like to play a welcome message from Mr. Zachetti himself," Lorenzo said.

Eleanora, the housekeeper, rolled in a large flat-screen TV on a cart. She positioned it near Lorenzo, who angled the screen to make sure everyone at the table could see it before turning on the TV with a remote.

"Here you go," he said, pushing another button. The screen leaped to life with classical music playing as a man with dark hair came into view. He sat at a giant mahogany desk with his back to the camera. On the wall behind him was an enormous image of the Roman Colosseum. Mr. Zachetti started to turn in his chair when the screen suddenly wavered and then froze.

"Oh, my," Lorenzo said. "It seems we are having technical difficulties." He pushed several additional buttons on the remote, but nothing worked.

I was just about to volunteer to help when Lorenzo turned off the television. "I'm terribly sorry it isn't working, but Mr. Zachetti wanted you to know how delighted he is that you're here and he hopes you will enjoy this one-of-a-kind experience over the next several days. Please, enjoy your dinner, and feel free to join us in the lounge afterward for a final nightcap."

The staff dispersed, with Lorenzo following Carlo into the kitchen. Chatter started at the table and after a minute, the young man, Ciro, placed a bowl of soup in front of me.

"What kind of soup is this?" I asked him. I was fond of most Italian food, especially if cooked by Nonna, Slash's grandmother, but I always felt better knowing what I was eating before I ate it.

"Minestrone, ma'am," he answered softly.

Thank goodness it was something I'd heard of before. He presented Mia with a bowl. She scooped up a spoonful and tasted it before saying something to him in Italian, and he grinned.

"He's as crazy as a cat in catnip," Mia whispered to me with a strange southern drawl when he returned to the kitchen to get more soup bowls. "It's not minestrone."

I paused, my spoon inches from my lips. "It's not?"

"It's not. It's a spicy version of *pasta e fagioli*, which is different from minestrone. He may be the son of the chef, but he obviously has no idea about food." She took another bite, a thoughtful look on her face. "It's excellent, by the way, if you like your soup spicy."

I didn't but wasn't going to admit that to a teenager. "So, you corrected him?"

"No." She ate another spoonful. "I told him you thought he was cute."

"What?" I looked at her in astonishment. "Why would you say that?"

She laughed at the expression on my face. "I'm just joking. Of course, I told him it wasn't minestrone soup. After that, I told him I liked his tie. I might have been flirting a little. Take a chill tablet."

It took me a moment to get there. "You mean a chill pill?"

"Oh, yes!" She clapped her hands. "That's it. I'm learning English slang at school. I'm an exchange student right now at Benjamin Franklin High School in New Orleans. That's in Louisiana, by the way, which is in the southern part of your America. America is *so* much fun. I love how they talk in the South. Everyone is friendly and loud, kind of like us Italians. But I especially love Louisiana, because the people there love their food just like we Italians do."

I had no idea if people from Louisiana liked their food more than people in any other state, but at the moment, I didn't have a way to confirm that. "I've actually never been to Louisiana."

"Never? Well, as my host mama likes to say, why, bless your heart," Mia said, pressing a hand to her chest. "You know, the way you Americans talk is almost as much fun as the food. Maybe you'll come visit me while I'm there."

The thought of traveling to a state I'd never been to in order to visit a teenager I barely knew was a huge statistical improbability for me. But even I knew enough social convention not to say so aloud. "How old are you, Mia?"

"I'm almost seventeen. My host mama says she's going to throw me a big shindig when it's my birthday. I just love the way my host mama talks. It is *so* different from the English I learned in Italy. I'm really excited you're here, Lexi. I hope you'll help me improve my English. Vittoria just thinks I'm crazy most of the time, making up weird phrases."

I was kind of leaning toward Vittoria's way of thinking, but I didn't say so. "Your English is good, Mia. Really good. Just take it easy on the slang."

"But I want to fit in," Mia said earnestly. "And be just like every other American teenager."

She grinned and resumed eating, so I returned to my soup. Mia was right, it was a bit spicy but good, and I was hungrier than I'd thought. I ate another piece of bread and finished off the soup. When I was almost finished eating, I looked up and realized Oscar was staring at me. Maybe he thought it was rude that I'd single-mindedly focused on eating without saying a word to him. I hoped I hadn't made any slurping noises.

I set down my spoon and quickly wiped my mouth with my napkin. "Is everything okay?"

Oscar's face was rather flushed, and sweat had started to gather at his temples. I didn't know if that meant he was hot, sick of me, nervous, or something else.

"The soup is a little spicy for me," he said, dabbing his napkin at his upper lip. "I didn't think to mention that on the food questionnaire."

Now that I thought about it, neither had I. I'd kind of assumed I would like all the food in Italy. At least, so far, that had been my experience. "I'm not a huge fan of spicy, either, but this doesn't seem too bad."

"Yes, well, spicy foods and I are not a good mix." There was an awkward pause, and then he cleared his throat. "By the way, I neglected to welcome you to the family, Lexi."

Wasn't that sweet? "Thanks, Oscar. I'm really glad to be a part of it."

While I was proud of myself for my smooth response, the conversation abruptly came to a halt because I couldn't think of what else to say and, apparently, neither could Oscar. I desperately searched for something to say when I remembered the guidelines for talking with the in-laws.

Get him to talk about himself.

ELEVEN

Lexi

"HEY, OSCAR, DO you have any hobbies?"

Oscar paused for a moment, his brows drawing together in surprise, or maybe confusion. Perhaps that had been too abrupt of a transition. I couldn't tell if I'd freaked him out or puzzled him or whether social discourse wasn't his strong suit, either. How would I know? I'd just met him, and Slash hadn't warned me that Oscar wasn't talkative or social. I *knew* we should have spent more time on the spreadsheet covering all the personality traits of his family. Because if Oscar also had trouble conversing, we were like the blind leading the blind, and who knew where that would lead?

My anxiety spiked, and I twisted my napkin in my lap. Now I wished I hadn't said anything and had just been glad he'd welcomed me.

"I enjoy apiculture," Oscar finally said.

I looked up in surprise. "Beekeeping?" Slash never mentioned Oscar's interest in bees before. "Really? Not soccer or afternoon tea?"

"Oh, I'm all for a good football match, and I do love my tea. But bees are my favorite hobby."

"Bees...that's unusual."

"You've heard of apiculture, then?"

I had, but I was deathly afraid of bees, wasps, hornets, and any sort of insect that flew, crawled, or stung. I'd been stung a few times and while I wasn't EpiPen allergic, I swelled up badly, which meant I always carried dissolvable antihistamine pills in my purse. I knew it wasn't logical or reasonable, but they scared the living crap out of me. Why someone would want to hang out with bees for the fun of it completely defied any logic I could imagine.

"Yes, but if you don't mind me asking, why?"

To my surprise, his eyes lit up. "Bees are so sweet and good for the environment and pollination. Besides, the byproducts are amazing. Honey, wax, and royal jelly. You've never realized what you've missed until you've tried the organic products. They're quite delicious."

I was perfectly okay with buying my organic products in the grocery store. But I had to say something positive and appear interested in his hobby—it was one of the spreadsheet rules.

"I find beehive mentality really fascinating." That was true, so long as I could examine the bees, their habitat, and behavior from a safe distance.

"You know, it really is," Oscar said, dabbing the spot above his lip and then gulping down more water. "Bees are quite sweet unless provoked. I'd love to show you my hives when you and Slash come to London. I've got two hives in the backyard."

Holy crap. In his backyard? "Your wife is okay with that?"

"Juliette? Yes, she loves the bees. I'm sure you will, too."

I managed to suppress a shudder. Seeing his beehives in person would never, *ever* happen in my lifetime.

Luckily, I didn't have to worry about that right now. That was a problem for another day. For the moment, I was simply grateful we were conversing on a topic that seemed to be going well and it wasn't about me.

"May I have your attention, please?"

Brando Porizio, our gamemaster, stood at the front of the table. The dinner chatter died down quickly. "Before we get too deep into the meal, I'd like to make a short announcement about the escape room challenges you'll face over the next two days," he said. "I must admit we're quite excited to watch you match minds with the creator of the escape rooms, Mr. Dante Zachetti. So far, no one has successfully solved them all, and in fact, it pains me to say no one has even come close. The challenges are quite complex and intricate, and you'll have to use all your mental acuity and creativity to solve them.

"There are also a few physical components to the challenges, as well, so please be prepared for that. Most importantly, however, you must work as a team. I suggest you determine your strengths quickly and work accordingly. I'm not taking questions tonight, but tomorrow morning, before you begin, I'll address any concerns you may have. What I did want to mention this evening is that in the event you're successful in solving *all* the challenges, there will be an impressive reward. Mr. Zachetti has informed me he'd be delighted to gift the bridal couple with an exceptional, all-expense-paid luxury honeymoon that includes the use of this island, the staff, and his fifty-foot yacht, as well as significant spending money to make sure the event is sufficiently memorable. Mr. Zachetti believes that performances are enhanced when there are appropriate rewards offered. We hope this offer provides sufficient motivation to you to succeed."

Gio jumped up from his chair in excitement, pumping his fist. "*Eccellente!* Oh, *si*, I'm absolutely motivated now. Let's do this!"

Claps, laughs, and excited chatter filled the dining room. Brando gave a flourishing bow and disappeared into the kitchen. Gio sat down and planted a big kiss on his fiancée's lips.

"Well, that's not dodgy at all," Oscar muttered to me. "Don't get me wrong, I'd love to see Gio and Vittoria win the honeymoon of their dreams, but I'm still not sure what an escape room is."

I took a sip of my Italian red wine, and as expected, it was excellent. "It's a room full of puzzles or challenges of some kind that you have to solve before you can get out." I set my glass down. "I've done a few of them before, and they aren't that hard. The rooms at this castle, I suspect, will be quite different."

"Well, Romeo, I mean, Slash, is good at puzzles, and apparently you are, too, so maybe we have a fighting chance."

Oh, we had a chance, but I didn't want to get his hopes up. I didn't want to discourage him, either. It was a fine line to walk. "There's always a chance."

Chiara stopped by to refill our wine and water. I noticed Oscar downed both glasses in quick succession.

"Are you okay?" I asked him. He was still sweating profusely and kept tugging on his tie.

He leaned a bit closer and lowered his voice. "Just between you and me, I hate wearing a tie. Feels like I'm being bloody choked."

"I don't blame you," I said. "I hate wearing a bra." I winced the second the words left my lips. "And... I think that wasn't appropriate to say to my father-in-law." My entire face heated.

He snorted, and I wasn't sure how to take that.

I didn't have time to stress about it, because Ciro set a plate of pasta in front of each of us at the same moment.

"It's *penne arrabbiata*," Ciro said before I could ask. "The sauce is made from fresh tomatoes, garlic, and dried red chili peppers sautéed in olive oil. It's one of Papa's specialties. You'll enjoy it, *si?*"

I looked down at it, considering. It looked good and smelled even better. "*Si, grazie.*"

Ciro returned to the kitchen for more plates, so Mia leaned over and examined my plate. "He's correct this time," she said, sniffing. "I love *penne arrabbiata*. But beware. As my host mama says, foods are best dressed up with a little Louisiana lightning."

"I don't know what that means," I said. "And English is my native language."

"It means the food has a strong...bite," she said.

"You mean a kick?"

"*Si.*" She tasted the food. "Yes, a kick. But it's good. *Deliziosa.*"

I cautiously sampled the penne. It was delicious, but certainly had a kick. I looked over at Oscar, who'd taken a bite and immediately drunk water.

Slash caught my eye across the table and smiled. I gave him a thumbs-up and took another bite of the penne. The more I ate it, the less spicy it seemed.

That didn't seem true for Oscar. After a minute, he set down his fork on his plate and dabbed his mouth again with his napkin. "This is a bit too hot for my palate." Oscar drank more water, then abruptly stood. His face was beet red. "Excuse me, would you?" He set his napkin on his chair and walked away.

I finished off my penne. I was full even though another plate of roasted vegetables had arrived. I sat back in my chair, speared a couple of the green beans, and sipped my wine. Since Oscar was gone and Mia was chatting with Tito, no one was bothering me.

Just the way I liked it.

After a few minutes, Mia turned to me. "Where did he go?" she asked, motioning toward Oscar's empty chair.

I shrugged. "The bathroom, maybe."

"The bathroom is that way," she said, pointing to the direction we'd come into the dining room. "I saw him go that way, which is where the outdoor balcony is located. Do you think he's okay?"

How would I know? I'd just met the man, even if he was now technically my family. I glanced down the table, where his wife and my mother-in-law, Juliette, was in deep conversation with my mother. I wondered what they were talking about and sincerely hoped it wasn't me. I wouldn't put it past Mom to tell Slash's mother about the temper tantrum I'd had when I was three because she wouldn't let me take my first notebook computer into the bathtub.

Jeez. The risk of interrupting and finding out they were talking about me was too great.

"I'll go check on Oscar." I stood, putting my napkin in the chair like Oscar had done.

No one paid any attention to me as I walked toward the balcony. A few of the large, elegant French doors had been thrown open, and I could feel the cool breeze and smell the ocean as I exited the dining room and strolled out onto the balcony.

I shivered, pulling my sweater a little tighter around my waist, looking for Oscar. I saw a dark shape leaning over the railing toward the end of the balcony a few feet away. I hurried toward it.

"Oscar?" I said as I got closer. "Are you okay?"

His reply was the most horrible sound I'd ever heard.

It was a cross between a hyena giving birth and the belching of an African hippo, and yes, I'd heard them both before. He projectile vomited over the side of the balcony, waving an arm at me in what I presumed was his way of telling me to stay back. He didn't have to worry. I quickly moved several steps away.

After a few seconds of that horrible sound, he rested his forehead against the balcony handrail. "I didn't know which way was the loo, but it's too late now. Dinner didn't agree with me. Obviously, I don't do well with spicy food."

Unfortunately, my stomach took that moment to churn uncomfortably. I pressed a hand against my midsection. I knew what was happening and didn't know how to stop it.

"Oh, no. I… I'm so sorry," I said weakly. "I have this problem."

He lifted his head and looked at me in disbelief. "*You* have a problem?"

I didn't have time to answer. Instead, I leaned over the balcony and threw up my entire dinner. I maintained sufficient presence of mind to calculate the wind strength, direction, and even anticipated ejection velocity to avoid any residue on my clothes. I was incapacitated for a least a minute and when I was done, I looked over in mortification at Oscar, who was staring at me with wide eyes.

Maybe I sounded like a hyena, too.

"I'm a sympathetic vomiter," I managed, using my fingertips to wipe my mouth. "I guess Slash didn't tell you that about me." I tried to laugh, but it came out as a dry heave instead. I leaned against the balcony on shaky legs.

"No, that didn't come up in conversation," Oscar said, still staring at me. "I'll have to have a talk with that boy."

Before I could say anything more, he barfed over the side again. I immediately followed suit until I could hardly breathe. We leaned against the rail, miserable and shaking, until we were startled by a voice.

"Excuse me. What's going on out here?"

TWELVE

Lexi

WE BOTH LOOKED over in alarm and saw Carlo, the chef, looking at us in concern. "Are you well?"

"Oh, Carlo, good evening," I said, trying to block his view of Oscar. "We're perfectly fine. We're just… getting some fresh air."

"Is everything okay with the dinner?" he asked.

"Oh, yes. It's fantastic. So…amazingly tasty." I could hear Oscar choking behind me and sensed my stomach squeeze in sympathy. "Thank you for checking on us. Oscar and I are just getting acquainted. We'll be right back in. We wouldn't want to miss dessert."

Carlo nodded a bit uncertainly but walked away. As soon as he was out of sight, Oscar threw up over the side again. I joined him. This was turning into a nightmare. I wasn't sure we'd ever get ourselves together enough to go back inside.

"Cara?"

Slash had somehow appeared beside me, moving so quietly I hadn't heard him. Of course, I'd been making a lot of noise, so he could have walked like an elephant and I might not have heard him. He looked over my shoulder in alarm. "Oscar, what's wrong?"

80

"Don't ask," Oscar said, leaning back against the balcony. "It's a long story."

Slash looked between his stepfather and me as if he were trying to figure things out. I decided to help him.

"You didn't tell Oscar I'm a sympathetic vomiter." I held my stomach and leaned my head against his shoulder. "So, now he knows."

"*Mio Dio,*" he murmured in shock, putting an arm around my shoulders, steadying me. "What happened with you two?"

"Dinner," Oscar said. "It was a bit spicy for me. Lexi came to check on me and unfortunately saw me in action. Apparently, she has a condition that compels her do the same if she sees someone vomit. So, here we are. Jolly good on us."

Slash closed his eyes, and I wished more than anything I'd stayed safely in my dinner seat.

"I think I'm finished, though," Oscar said, trying to be upbeat but not quite succeeding. "Which should be a good thing for you, Lexi. Right?"

"Right," I quickly agreed.

"Are you okay, *cara*?" Slash asked, tipping my chin up and studying my face in the moonlight.

"I think so," I said. "Luckily I didn't get anything on my dress… I hope. Can you check?"

Slash turned me toward the light and examined me. "You look fine. Oscar, are you steady?"

He sighed. "Actually, I'm a bloody wreck, but I'll manage."

Slash handed his stepfather a handkerchief from his pocket, a gesture I found both heartwarming and sweet.

Oscar took the handkerchief and wiped his face and hands. "Much obliged." He tucked the cloth in his pocket and straightened, fiddling with his tie. It was a losing battle, but to his credit, Slash didn't say anything or try to fix it. "I'd appreciate it if you didn't mention this to your mother."

"My lips are sealed," Slash assured him.

"Mine, too," I added. "As long as there's no more vomiting. Deal?"

"Deal," Oscar said as we headed back inside.

Slash and I hung back a little, and he pulled me in closer to his warmth. "This isn't my fault," I whispered before he could say anything. "I actually thought dinner was good. Maybe a *little* spicy, but not that bad. Oscar doesn't like spicy food. He left and was gone awhile. Since your mother was talking to my mother, and I didn't want to interrupt, I went to check on him. As soon as I saw him barfing over the balcony, well, it was all over at that point."

"How long have you two been out here?" he asked.

"Five minutes? Twenty? Hard to say. Feels like a lifetime."

"I thought you'd gone to the bathroom. I should have checked sooner." He muttered something to himself in Italian.

"It's okay. You know, I kind of like your stepfather. I have no idea what he thinks about me after the barf-fest, but at least we sort of bonded. Right?"

Slash kissed the top of my head, but it worried me he didn't answer my question. "We only have a little longer to get through dinner and then we'll call it a night. Think you can manage?"

"What else could go wrong?" I asked and then covered my mouth. "Nope. Pretend I didn't say that."

"I'll be watching you, so if you need to escape earlier, just tap your nose as we planned, and I'll make up an excuse, okay?"

I wanted to leave immediately, but I knew that would be impolite and draw attention to us, something I loathed more than sticking around. I figured if Oscar could suck it up, so could I. Plus, I would feel bad abandoning Oscar, in case something happened to him again. "Okay. Thanks."

We had just seated ourselves when the *dolce*, or dessert, was served along with coffee and a *digestivo*, an after-dinner liqueur that I recognized as limoncello. I avoided that, given the shaky condition of my stomach. Mia informed me the dessert was *zabaione*, a whipped light custard made with egg yolks, sugar, and a sweet wine and served in a dessert glass. It looked delicious, but I didn't feel like eating, so I poked and pushed it around, pretending to taste it. I noticed Oscar was doing the same when I glanced at him. He gave me a little smile, which made me feel that maybe we had made a connection of some kind, as strange as it was.

After another forty minutes or so, the table was cleared, and we were invited to retire to the lounge for a nightcap. I signaled to Slash that I was done, and he rose from the table to retrieve me. Everyone was milling about the room, laughing and chatting, so I thought it the perfect time for us to slip out. We headed for the exit but stopped when we ran into Father Armando.

"You promised me a minute to speak after dinner," Father Armando said to Slash.

"I did, but Lexi is tired. Perhaps we could do this tomorrow?"

"It's important to have a word with both of you tonight, but I promise to be as succinct as possible."

Slash looked at me uncertainly, but I nodded. "I'm okay, Slash. We can do it."

"Thank you," Father Armando said. "I know a place we can speak privately. Please follow me."

We trailed him out of the dining room, past the lounge, and into an unoccupied room that appeared to be a small interior office. A desk with a computer and a chair occupied one side of the room while a couple of bookshelves overflowing with books, boxes, and folders lined the other wall. Father Armando waved us toward a few chairs, and we sat down, looking at each other.

"Emilio, before you say anything, I have to thank you for whatever part you played in securing this venue for Gio and our family," Slash said. "I can't tell you how much this means to him, especially after all he's been through to get married in the church. He's thrilled to have this opportunity."

Father Armando placed his hands on his knees, smoothed his cassock. "Yes, about that. I must tell you, I had nothing to do with changing Mr. Zachetti's mind—well, at least not directly."

"How's that possible?" I asked. "A few days after I mentioned to you that we'd been turned down to visit the castle, his staff called to say Mr. Zachetti had changed his mind. No way that's a simple coincidence."

"You're correct. It's not a coincidence."

"Then what is it?" Slash asked.

Father Armando shifted uncomfortably in his chair and avoided eye contact with Slash. "Well, I may have mentioned it in casual conversation with…a certain someone."

"What certain someone?" I asked, looking between the two men.

Slash closed his eyes. "You didn't."

"I did, but I didn't *mean* to," Father Armando confessed. "I was just updating him on the plans for Gio's wedding and the topic *may* have come up. What happened afterward was entirely up to him."

"Wait, are we talking about the pope?" I asked. "You told the pope I tried to get us into Zachetti's castle?"

"As I said before, I *may* have mentioned it, and he *may* have taken it from there."

"I didn't think Zachetti was a practicing Catholic," Slash said. "Why would he entertain any request from the pope?"

"First of all, because he's *the* pope." Father Armando looked pointedly at Slash, and a slight flush crossed his face. "Secondly, it wasn't a request. Not exactly."

"What *exactly* was it, Emilio?" Slash asked.

Father Armando paused, as if choosing his words carefully. "As you know, the pope does not wager, gamble, or participate in any kind of betting."

"Of course not," Slash agreed.

"He may, however, have entered into a gentlemen's agreement."

"A gentlemen's agreement?" Slash raised an eyebrow. "Involving what kind of stipulations?"

"As you heard tonight at dinner from Brando Porizio, Zachetti's gamemaster, if you were to solve all the challenges in the castle, he has agreed to pay for Gio and Vittoria's honeymoon and throw in spending money as well."

"That's quite generous of him," I commented. "Not to mention motivating."

"Yes, but you see, Zachetti was not convinced the wedding party could stand a chance at solving even *one* of his challenges. After all, if the brightest minds in the scientific and gaming world had teamed against him and failed, what prospect would a family of unassuming Italians, Brits, and Americans, with no *known* credentials, have to solve them? So, the Holy Father told Mr. Zachetti he had every confidence that you could take on *all* of his challenges and come out victorious."

"*All* of the challenges," Slash repeated.

"Whoa. The pope *bet* on us?" I said incredulously.

"He made a gentleman's agreement," Father Armando gently corrected me.

I looked between Slash and Father Armando, who were staring at each other. I wasn't sure what was going on between them, but I had questions. "What happens if we don't solve all the challenges?"

The father broke eye contact with Slash and turned toward me. "If you fail to solve even one of the challenges, you lose, and the pope must make a donation to a charity of Zachetti's choosing."

"That's not so bad," I said. "I fail to see a downside, except Gio and Vittoria don't get their all-expense-paid honeymoon."

"It's not quite that simple," Father Armando replied.

I sighed and leaned back in the chair. "When is it ever?"

A smile touched Father Armando's lips. "The honeymoon story was told to the rest of the wedding party to keep *them* invested in solving the puzzles. And indeed, Dante Zachetti will grant Gio and Vittoria a spectacular honeymoon here on his island and yacht. But that's not the full agreement."

He paused, and I waited curious as to where this was going. "If you win and solve *all* the puzzles in the castle, Zachetti has agreed to make a significant donation to a charity of the pope's choosing."

I held up my hands. "Great. What kind of donation are we talking about?"

"Fifteen million euros."

"What?" I whistled in surprise. Was Zachetti that convinced, or so egotistical, that he believed no one could solve his puzzles? "That's a heck of a lot of money."

"It is."

"Which charity will be the recipient of the cash?" Slash asked, leaning forward and resting his hands on his thighs.

"The new state-of-the art orphanage the pope has been planning. It'll be able to house one thousand children from all over Italy. You both know how close building the orphanage is to his heart. Given an infusion of this amount of cash, it would become a reality much sooner than he ever anticipated."

Slash got a distant look in his eyes, and I could guess what he was thinking. He'd once been an orphan himself. That he could help bring the Holy Father's dream to reality would mean a lot to him. I had to give it to the pope. If nothing else, he certainly knew how to motivate Slash and, by extension, me.

"That's quite a challenge," I said. "Obviously there's a lot more at stake than a honeymoon. The orphanage, the pope's faith in us, *and* the pope's reputation are all riding on our capabilities. No freaking pressure."

"We're certain you, and your family, can handle it."

Slash stood, walking the length of the room and back, his thinking mode. "So, all twelve of us must participate in the challenges, correct?"

"Yes," Father Armando said. "Although I don't know the exact rules for the escape rooms yet. I've been told those will be laid out for you tomorrow before the first challenge, but on that one, Zachetti was clear. All twelve of you must participate."

That concerned me, because I wasn't sure how my mother, Oscar, Vittoria, who was seven months pregnant, and a teenage girl were going to handle or contribute to the challenges. Not to mention everyone else I didn't really know.

"Your presence here, Emilio, makes thirteen of us," Slash said. "How does Zachetti account for that?"

"Oh, I'm here as the pope's representative only, an observer to ensure the pope's interests are protected. Dante personally invited me. I am not expected to participate in the challenges. And, please, no one else must know of the gentlemen's agreement or it will become null and void. So, you will do your best?"

Slash exchanged a glance with me, and I shrugged, indicating I was in if he was, but leaving the decision in his hands.

A muscle in his jaw ticked before he gave a nod. "Your faith in us is not misplaced. We'll solve the escape rooms, Emilio."

"Of course you will," Father Armando said as he stood. "We have every confidence in you and your families."

While I appreciated that confidence, keeping everyone else engaged and committed to the challenges wouldn't be easy.

"Emilio, where's the orphanage going to be built?" Slash suddenly asked.

"Salerno, of course."

Of course. The pope had thought of everything. Salerno was a special place to Slash and me. We'd recently been given the proverbial keys to the city after helping avert a major disaster that could have killed dozens of people, including children. Plus, it was the place where Slash's biological father had been born and buried. It was a place we'd always hold close in our hearts.

"Salerno," I repeated.

Father Armando placed a hand on Slash's shoulder. "That's not all. The orphanage is to be named after your father. His Holiness knew that would mean a lot to you…in many ways."

Slash stilled, and after a moment, he slipped his father's silver cross out from beneath his shirt and kissed it. "*Si*, it does. I will do my best to make you both proud."

"You always do, my son." Father Armando smiled and his smile included me. "You *both* do."

THIRTEEN

Lexi

SLASH AND I passed out in each other's arms the minute we got back to our room and undressed. It had been a long day, and despite the sleep we'd gotten on the plane, we had to be in top form tomorrow. I had a million questions, but Slash wasn't going to know any of the answers, and neither of us had the mental acuity to entertain any of them before sleep. It just meant we'd have to face whatever was given to us in the morning and think on our feet. It was one of our strengths as individuals and a couple. If we had enough sleep, we could move mountains, or in this case, solve escape room puzzles.

At least I hoped so.

I was afraid I'd never get to sleep or that I might wake up in the middle of the night, but I slept like the dead until someone banged on our door. "Romeo?"

I shot straight up in bed before realizing it was Slash's mother.

Slash swung his feet over the side of the bed and shoved his legs into a pair of pants. He opened the door, still bare-chested. "Mama?"

They spoke rapidly in Italian before she gave him a quick peck on the cheek and left. He closed the door and faced me, running his fingers through his tousled hair. "Time to get up. Breakfast is being served, and Lorenzo announced that the gamemaster will be laying out the rules for the escape rooms in thirty minutes."

I sat up, bleary-eyed. Jet lag had taken more of a toll on me than I'd expected. My mouth felt like it was filled with stuffed cotton, and my stomach growled. "What time is it?"

Slash picked up his phone from the bedside table. "Half past eight." He held up his phone, moving it around. "And by the way, we have no cell reception or Wi-Fi here. I noticed last night."

"Me, too. I hope we don't have an emergency. I presume they have a landline phone just in case."

"One would hope." Slash shrugged. "Guess we'll find out."

We dressed quickly before I opened the curtains and windows to enjoy a breath of the crisp, cool air. Sunlight sparkled on the water, and I had to shade my eyes because it was so bright. "It's really beautiful here," I said.

Slash stepped up behind me, dressed in dark jeans and a black sweater. He gave my ponytail a little tug before circling his arms around my waist, resting his chin on the top of my head. "It is. Back at the ocean again. It seems to be our thing."

I really wasn't a fan of the ocean. Too much water, sun, sand, and salt. But it was growing on me. I put my hand on top of his. "So, what do you think? Are we ready for today? Can we successfully lead the group to solving the escape rooms?"

He considered my words for a moment. "Leadership isn't about being successful. It's about making everyone else better, which in this situation is going to be paramount. Having said that, if we're together, I believe we'll be able to solve any puzzle or mystery."

Spoken like a true leader. "Then, let's do this, Slash. By the way, have you spoken with Mia, Vittoria's little sister? She's trying to speak English like an American teenager."

He chuckled. "I noticed. She even insists on speaking with me in English, even though we're both native Italian speakers."

"She wants me to help her speak English better."

"Will you?"

"I don't know. Her English seems fine. It's the teenage slang thing that's throwing me off. I'm still trying to figure it out."

We walked downstairs, my sneakers squeaking a bit on the marble stairs. Everyone was gathered in the dining room again, helping themselves to a buffet of breakfast items. From my experience, breakfast in Italy consisted mostly of coffee or lattes and crusty bread or hard rolls with butter and jam. Then there was Slash's personal favorite when he was in Italy, an almond *biscottate* that he dipped in his coffee.

Slash stopped to chat with his brother Stefan when we came in, so I grabbed a latte, added more hot milk, and put a couple of thick slices of bread on my plate. Thankfully, there was no required seating for breakfast, so I sat at the table next to my mom and dad, who were talking with Mia and Tito while sipping their coffee. A bit farther down the table, Father Armando chatted with Oscar and Juliette. All of them waved when they saw me.

I waved back awkwardly.

"Good morning, darling," Mom said, leaning over and kissing both of my cheeks. She hadn't done that before, so it seemed she had effortlessly adapted to the Italian method of pecking people's cheeks as part of a greeting. "How'd you sleep?"

"Like the dead," I said, smearing some jam on my bread. "How about you guys?"

"Wonderfully, although your father and I got up around four thirty this morning. But we lit a fire in the fireplace and enjoyed a leisurely time of just lying around and talking. I can't remember when we did that last. This place is absolutely fabulous."

She looked beautiful and relaxed, dressed in white slacks and an emerald-colored sweater, green studs at her ears. Her complexion glowed pink, and her blond hair was pulled back at the nape of her neck. I'd gotten used to her beauty over the years, but I noticed the others in the room stealing glances at her. I wondered if she enjoyed the attention or whether it was just something she'd learned to live with. Maybe I'd ask her sometime.

My dad, on the other hand, looked more like me, with a hint of shadows under his eyes and his brown hair rumpled. But his hazel eyes sparkled when he looked at me, and I knew he looked forward to the challenges as much as I did.

"*Guten morgen*, Lexi," Tito said, lifting his coffee to me in a toast. "Ready for a fun day?"

"As ready as I can be. How about you?"

He lifted his hands. "*Gut.* I just hope I'm not the weakest link. I don't want to be the reason Gio and Vittoria don't get their honeymoon."

"I can't ever imagine you being a weak link, Tito." I took a bite of my bread. An explosion of tart blueberry jam exploded in my mouth. It tasted so delicious I closed my eyes. "Jeez, Italian food is so good."

"It's obscenely delicious," my mom agreed, nibbling on a croissant. "I could easily eat my way through Italy."

"That's totally my plan," Dad said, lifting his piece of bread to mine. I grinned and tapped it to his before we both took a bite.

"Good morning, ladies and gentlemen." I looked over to the entrance to the dining room and saw Brando Porizio, our gamemaster, standing there. "If I may have your attention, please."

I took a quick sip of my latte as the chattering in the room tapered off.

"We are quite excited to begin the games with you," he said. "As you may already know, all twelve of you must participate for the games to continue. What you may not know is that we'll have two separate escape challenges going on at the same time. You'll be split into two teams to work on the puzzles concurrently."

I shot a worried look at Slash across the room. Two concurrent escape challenges? If we were split up, how would that affect our accuracy at the puzzles? Or worse, if we were together, would the other group be able to handle the puzzle?

"Please talk a minute among yourselves to form your teams," Brando said. "Once you decide on the teams, I'll announce the challenges and you can decide which team will tackle which escape room."

We gathered in a huddle, and for a minute, no one said anything. Finally, Slash spoke, apparently the leader by default. "Does anyone have a preference on which team they'd like to be on?"

His question was met by silence and shrugs.

"Well, then the team division will be random." He looked around the group. "Lexi, you take your parents, Tito, Mia, and Oscar in one group. I'll take Stefan, Alessa, Gio, Vittoria, and Mama. Everyone okay with that?"

I noticed he'd done his best to keep most couples

together, which would have a certain comfort element. He'd split up his parents, but I knew Oscar better than Juliette at this point, so maybe he took that into consideration when pairing Oscar with me. Plus, since Slash had given me both of my parents, I couldn't help wondering if he was purposely avoiding my dad. That didn't seem like something he'd do, but it was a possibility.

"The teams have been formed," Slash told Brando.

"Excellent," the gamemaster replied. "Now, regarding the escape rooms. One challenge is outside in the garden, and the other is inside the castle. Please assign your teams to the preferred challenge."

"I'd prefer to be outside," Oscar said.

"I agree," Tito said. "Outside over inside any day for me."

"Me, too," Mia said.

Slash looked at me, and I shrugged. Didn't matter to me one way or the other. "Team A will take the outside challenge," he said.

"Perfect," Brando said. "I'd like to encourage Team A to return to your respective rooms for an extra sweater, a light coat, or hat, as today it's quite windy. While you are in your rooms, please empty the contents of your pockets, including any wallets and cell phones, and leave them in your room. You should have nothing in your pockets or on your person other than a watch or personal jewelry. Team B, since you are not returning to your rooms, please put personal items in the basket on the table. I assure you, your items will remain safe. Thank you for your cooperation."

I exchanged glances with my teammates—my parents, Tito, Mia, and Oscar. I wasn't sure what challenges we would face outside, but I hoped it didn't involve snakes, caves, or cliffs. I cast a glance at Slash, but he was in quiet conversation with his two brothers, their dark heads bent toward each other. I headed back to my room with my parents and the others on my team to gather our coats and hats.

When we finally reassembled in the dining room, Slash and Team B were gone, and we were alone.

The games were on.

FOURTEEN

Lexi

"WHAT DO WE do?" Mia asked, coming to stand next to me in front of the fireplace in the dining room. "Do we go outside or stay here twaddling our fingers waiting for the gamemaster?" She started wiggling her fingers.

"Um, Mia, I think the phrase you're looking for is 'twiddling your thumbs.'"

She looked at me confused. "You mean I can't twaddle my fingers? Then how exactly do I move my thumbs to twiddle them correctly?"

Lorenzo saved me from answering when he walked into the room, smiling at us. "Good morning, Team A." He quickly counted us. "Six. Excellent. Looks like everyone is here. Please follow me. The gamemaster will be with you as soon as he gets Team B set up with their challenge."

I wondered what Slash was thinking this very moment as I pulled on my windbreaker, zipping it up and stuffing my hat in the pocket. Would their challenge be hard? Would he be able to mobilize everyone to success?

And what did that mean for me? Would I be the

leader of the group? Should I? If I was the leader, did that mean success rested on my shoulders? If I failed, how disappointed would the pope and Slash be in me?

Ugh.

Somehow Dad must have sensed my anxiety because he placed a hand on my shoulder as we followed Lorenzo out of the dining room and down another corridor. "This should be fun," he said. "I know you're competitive, like me, but relax a bit. You look as if the weight of the world is resting on your shoulders."

It wasn't exactly the weight of the world riding on my shoulders, but the orphanage and the pope were counting on me. That was a heck of a lot in my opinion.

Eventually we arrived at a wide veranda with a few stairs that led down to a back patio.

"Please wait here until Mr. Porizio arrives to take you to your challenge," Lorenzo instructed us. "He should return momentarily."

Lorenzo disappeared into the house, so I walked to the patio railing and surveyed the backyard. The rest of the team followed me.

I had to give it to the gardener, Matteo, because the grounds were spectacular. Exquisitely manicured beds, stone walkways, pretty benches, and artfully arranged shrubbery led to a row of tall trees at the far end of the garden and what appeared to be a small hedge on the other side. Everything looked meticulous and beautiful. Combined with the sparkling ocean water and rugged cliffs, the view was magnificent.

"It's lovely, is it not?"

We turned around to see the gamemaster standing there. He still had that sixties vibe going on with a tie-dye T-shirt and blue jeans, but he also wore an unbuttoned dark blazer, a black knitted cap, and sunglasses. It was an eclectic look, but I guess that only meant his fashion sense was as good as mine.

I should have expected that, gamer to gamer.

"The grounds are breathtaking," my mom replied, pressing a hand to her heart. "If this is what the view looks like in the winter, it must be a stunning sight in the spring and summer when everything is in bloom."

"It is, even for someone who sees this on a daily basis," Brando said.

"Mr. Matteo has a green knuckle," Mia exclaimed. "That's what you say in America, right?"

"It's a green *thumb*," I corrected.

She looked at me, flabbergasted. "Thumb, again?" She glanced down at her thumbs. "Why are Americans obsessed with their thumbs?"

My mom smiled, clearly amused by Mia. "Thumbs aside, Mr. Porizio, Matteo's skills as a gardener are nothing short of magical. Please let him know I said that."

"Matteo will be delighted to hear that," Brando replied. "Now, Team A, if you're ready, please follow me."

Brando walked down the stairs and along the flagstone path to the left. We followed him, mostly single file. He headed for the grove of trees, and I noticed the ground rose gradually before sloping downward just before we reached the trees.

The elevation change masked a tall row of hedges that were invisible until we reached the tree line. From the veranda, I'd only seen the top of the hedge, and it looked like a single low hedge line. Close up, I could see the hedge stretched out quite far, and the height was roughly eight to ten feet, varying a bit, as if the top hadn't been trimmed recently. As we got closer, I realized the hedge wasn't straight, but curved and twisted into a huge, complex maze.

We stopped in front of the only entrance to the hedge I could see. Brando stood next to a metal sign on a post nearby that read Garden Maze. "We've arrived," he announced.

"A maze?" Tito asked in surprise. "That's our challenge?"

"That's not *exactly* your challenge," Brando said. "It'll be a bit more complex than that, I'm afraid."

I studied the maze entrance. Flanking each side of the path were twin marble pillars with carved alabaster vines.

"That's strange," my mom said. "Those columns look different from the ones I'm used to seeing. Why is the top round like that?"

My gaze rose to the top of the column. I didn't notice anything unusual, but I wasn't sure what I was looking for. I'd never spent much time looking at architectural columns.

Brando seemed delighted by my mom's observation. "You have a keen eye, Mrs. Carmichael, although if you've spent much time in Rome, you'd find column tops like this are not uncommon. These are the Roman version of the classical Greek column styles. We call them Tuscan columns, and they have the more rounded top, as you noted. Many of the Roman elite were quite enamored with Greek architecture, so you will still see a lot of the Greek style, even in Rome. I must say, however, your powers of observation for small details bodes well for how you might perform in the maze."

I looked at my mom in surprise. Since when did she know so much about Greek and Roman architecture?

My mom preened a bit with the compliment. She met my gaze and lifted an eyebrow at me. Maybe my dad was right and I *had* been underestimating my mother all these years.

"In order to complete this challenge, you must enter the maze, find a golden disc like this, and return it to me on the veranda within two hours," Brando instructed. He held up a round golden disc about three inches in diameter. "The disc will have a number engraved on one side."

We waited for him to continue, and when he didn't, my dad spoke up. "That's it? We go into the maze and retrieve a hidden golden disc within two hours?"

"That's it. One other condition is that everyone must be out of the maze before the two hours are up. Does everyone understand?"

I don't know what exactly I was expecting, but navigating an outdoor maze where I had to retrieve a golden disc without much explanation had not been in my repertoire of possibilities.

When no one said anything, Brando beamed. "Wonderful!" He glanced at his watch. "Two hours from now will be 11:47. Good luck with your task and may fortune smile on you."

Giving no further instructions, he turned and disappeared back toward the castle.

FIFTEEN

Lexi

WE STOOD THERE for a moment, staring dumbly at each other, until I realized everyone was looking at me.

"Ah…" I stammered. "Do you want me to take the lead on this puzzle?"

"Of course we do," my mom said. "So, now what?"

It wasn't exactly the rousing cry of confidence I might have hoped for, but no one was contradicting her, so I guess there was that. "We have to explore the maze and find the disc. Two hours seems like a long time for us to search a maze, especially with six people doing it, so there must be something tricky about how it's hidden. Unless anyone objects, let's divide up and explore every inch of the maze."

"Sounds good, Lexi, but how will we know which passages have been explored and which ones we still need to do?" Oscar asked.

"Good question," I said.

"The paths are made of rocks and gravel, so we won't be leaving any footprints," my dad said. "So, we'll have to think of another way to mark it as explored."

"How about at every place where the path divides,

102

we leave a small pile of gravel on the right side, just past the fork, to indicate the path has been searched?" Tito suggested. "That way we won't miss it or walk through it by accident."

"Sounds good to me," I said. "If we're systematic from the start, it should save us time later if we have problems figuring out what still needs to be searched. Does everyone understand what we're doing? We're going to split the maze into sections and comb it, all of us looking for a golden disc. If you find it, yell loudly."

Everyone nodded, and I blew out a breath, staring at the maze. "Okay, it looks like the maze divides into two directions. There are six of us, so let's split into two teams. Oscar and Mia, you're with me. Mom, Dad, and Tito, you go in the opposite direction. If any of you hit a dead end, backtrack until you find an unexplored path and follow that. Make sure to leave a pile of rocks to indicate the path has been explored. If anyone has any questions or finds something weird, just yell. We should be able to hear each other fairly well, and the gamemaster didn't say we couldn't shout or discuss things within the maze."

We plunged into the maze, the thick green foliage and branches making me feel slightly claustrophobic. I led the way with Mia in the middle and Oscar taking the rear. It didn't take long to realize it was going to be a lot more difficult than expected. There were no straight paths or ninety-degree corners. Everything was a curve, and I quickly lost track of where the entrance to the maze was located. But I couldn't worry about that now. We had to find the disc first and worry about getting out later.

As we came to the first fork, I sent Mia down it. "Make sure you build a little pile just a couple of steps down the path to show you've explored it. Keep going forward and shout if you find anything or if you need one of us. You okay with that?"

"Sure. I'm feeling as fat as a fiddle. By the way, what's a fiddle?"

"It's a musical instrument, kind of like a violin," I said. "And the saying is as *fit* as a fiddle. It means you're feeling good."

"Yes, exactly. That's what I meant," she said beaming. "I'm feeling good. But do violins actually feel fit in America?"

"We'll talk about that later, Mia, okay?"

"Okay," she agreed as she knelt and started to gather rocks.

Oscar and I exchanged a bemused glance and kept going, the gravel crunching under our feet. When we reached the next fork, I sent Oscar down it while I continued. When I came to the next split, I stood and thought for a moment. I knew it was statistically relevant that when people were faced with a fork in the road, most would pick the right-hand path. Just to be different, I took the left one. I knelt, built a pile of rocks, and moved on.

As I walked, I wondered what I should be looking to find. I didn't think the disc would just be lying in the middle of the path. The puzzles had to be worthy to challenge some of the finest minds in the world, and apparently, they were sufficiently difficult, because no one had yet been able to solve all of them. I needed to find the right balance between difficult and solvable. The best puzzles were doable if the secret was understood or if it was looked at from the right perspective. I just had to figure out that part.

The problem was the hedge walls were so dense, high, and thick I couldn't even get a glimpse of the next passage over. While the hedge tops were a bit ragged in places, the sides were well manicured and smooth, the sign of an excellent gardener. I tried forcing my way through the hedge wall without success. The branches were too closely packed, and the walls were too deep.

Suddenly, I realized I'd made a mistake. The gamemaster hadn't said we *had* to follow the maze, only that what we were looking for was in the maze. If I'd thought about it logically, I should have instructed someone to walk the outside of the maze looking for other entrances or some potential clue of significance. I debated going back to do that myself but decided I could still leave time to do it later.

I came to another fork and started to take the left path again until I saw a small pile of stones. Someone had already been here. I took the other path, leaving my own pile. This one continued for a short distance before forking again with both paths unmarked. Again, I went left and found a flat stepping-stone embedded in the center of the path with a Roman numeral III etched on it. I looked around, trying to discern the significance of the number. I saw exactly nothing except more of the smooth walls of the hedge. I lifted the stone up, but there was nothing underneath it. I even dug in the dirt beneath the stone but found nothing.

I replaced it and moved on. Although I couldn't tell for sure, my intuition told me I was running along the perimeter of the maze. There was no way to confirm it, as the hedges were too high and dense, and I'd become thoroughly disoriented. I considered using the sun as a navigation aid, however, the maze curved too much for the sun to help me.

Ahead and to the left of me, I heard Mia calling my name. "Mia? Did you find something?" I yelled.

"Two flat stones with Roman numerals on them."

My excitement leaped. "I found one, too. What were the numerals?"

"One and two," she shouted back. "What does it mean?"

"I don't know yet, but the stone I saw had the Roman numeral three on it. Keep looking."

I kept walking until I came to a dead end in the shape of a small teardrop-shaped alcove. A small sundial had been placed on a stone pedestal in the middle of the alcove. I quickly approached it, noting the time—10:15. That meant we'd been searching the maze for about thirty minutes. Although it told time, a sundial was not like a clock with twelve hours on the face. As the Earth spun, the shadow would change shape and position, thereby marking the passage of time.

This sundial was made of a greenish-gray metal embedded into a light-brown stone and firmly affixed to the pedestal. The face resembled a clock with Roman numerals with the hours spaced evenly around the dial except at the bottom. That was odd and made me look closer.

I wondered if there was a connection between the sundial and the round stone with the number III that I'd found, but if so, it wasn't obvious. This sundial's triangular blade that cast the shadow to tell time was tightly embedded in the sundial face. I recalled from a biography of Archimedes that the shadow-casting element on a sundial was called a gnomon. I tried to press and move the gnomon, to no avail.

I turned my attention to the pedestal. It was unremarkable, without markings or writings. I got down on my hands and knees and looked at every inch, pushing and pulling on everything, but got nothing.

I ran through the science of the sundial in my head, hoping something would jump out at me. Ancient civilizations, including the Greeks and Chinese, had used sundials to determine the change of seasons, calculate mathematics, create calendars, determine latitude, and study the stars. The sundial itself was clever in its simplicity. Unfortunately, nothing seemed to help me in terms of a search for a small golden disc.

Sighing, I backtracked my way out of the area onto a main path, when I stumbled upon my dad looking lost.

"Lexi, have you found anything yet?"

"Nothing except a sundial and stones with Roman numerals on them. How about you?"

"I saw a large rock with a Roman numeral five. Although, until you just said that, I thought it was just a large rock with the letter V on it. I wondered if something was being spelled out, but Roman numerals makes sense, too. What numbers did you see?"

"Three, but Mia saw one and two."

"Well, I also found an exit out of the maze. That reminds me, I did see another number stone, this one with an X on it, right near the exit. When I got outside, there wasn't anything to see. Just some more great views of the water, the cliffs rising above the beach, and the maze outside walls stretching out in both directions. No disc in sight."

A woman's scream caused us both to jump.

"That's your mother," Dad exclaimed. Before I could say a word, he tore off down the path.

SIXTEEN

Lexi

I RAN AFTER Dad. We scrambled through the maze, making sure at each fork we were going the right way. After about a minute, the screaming stopped, but we could hear people close by talking. We sped around a corner and found Oscar talking with my mom. For some reason, Oscar's face was beet red.

"Are you all right, Clarissa?" My dad pulled her into his arms and examined her worriedly.

"I'm fine, Winston. Sorry to frighten you."

Thankfully, Mom looked unhurt, if not a bit disheveled. Her hair had lost its perfect coiffure and wait...was her sweater on inside out?

"I tried to go through a spot in the hedge by the path over there." Mom waved her arm at the hedge behind me. "I thought it looked a little thin and there might be an opening. That's when I felt something crawling on my leg. It was an enormous lizard. I swatted at it to get it off me, and that's when it happened."

"What happened?" I asked as Tito came running around the corner.

"*Mein Gott.*" His hands were curled into fists, and he looked ready to fight. "Is everyone okay?"

"All good," I assured him. "A lizard crawled on my mom's leg." I turned to Mom. "Did it bite you?"

"No. I tried to brush it off, but it ran beneath my sweater. I screamed, pulled off my sweater, and that's when Oscar arrived."

We all turned toward Oscar, whose face had deepened from red to burgundy. "I sincerely apologize, Mrs. Carmichael. I was completely unaware of, ah, your state of undress."

Tito coughed, probably to cover a snicker, but Mom waved a hand. "Oh, please, Oscar. We're family now. So, you've seen my bra. All essentials were covered. No worries."

My dad seemed more amused than upset. I winced as Oscar's face turned a new shade of purple. Clearly, he was mortified. Poor guy. First his daughter-in-law vomits off a castle balcony with him, then said daughter-in-law's mother flashes him. Ugh. I'm not an expert on family dynamics, but even I knew things were not trending in my favor. Still, I wasn't sure who'd had it worse so far—me or Oscar.

I blew out a breath, pushing that aside for later. I had no time to worry about family drama right now. Time was slipping away faster than I liked, and I still had no idea how to find that golden disc. If we were going to solve this puzzle, we need to regroup and discover what, if anything, everyone had found.

Since everyone was here but Mia, we started calling her name to get her to join us. Within a couple of minutes, she appeared, looking confused.

"What's going on?" she asked. "Are we having a meeting?"

"We are," I said. "I need to know what everyone has found so far."

Everyone took turns repeating what they had found, mostly nothing. We all agreed the maze was disorienting, with lots of intersections, meandering paths, and dead ends. Mia and my dad had each seen a marble statue but found nothing of apparent significance about the statue or its location in the maze. Most of us had seen the large stones with the Roman numerals.

"I think the Roman numeral stones are important," I said. "From what you've reported, we've found Roman numeral stones from one to ten, and we're missing only the stones with the numerals seven and eight. Let's see if we can find them. But hurry. We've been in the maze almost fifty minutes now."

I turned to Dad. "Could you find your way outside the maze again and this time circle it in its entirety to see if there's a hidden entrance that cannot be accessed from inside the maze?"

"You think there's another entrance to the maze from outside of it?" Dad asked.

"It's worth checking out. In fifteen minutes, I'm going to shout again. Everyone, follow the sound of my voice, and we'll meet up and compare notes. If anyone finds something significant before that, call out and we'll know to come right away. Also, don't just *look* for a clue. It could be a special scent, sound, or an odd look to the foliage that may cover up a hidden door. Go!"

Everyone shot into the maze in different directions. I headed in a direction I didn't think I'd been before. I went down several paths that had already been searched by someone else and found exactly zero. Desperation set in.

"Lexi?" my dad yelled somewhere over my right shoulder.

"What?"

"Just wanted you to know I got out of the maze and am circling it. Haven't found an entrance from out here yet."

"Keep looking."

I started jogging through multiple intersections where all the possible paths had been explored already. When I came upon an intersection where three paths converged, I spotted another large stone with the Roman numeral VII on it. I stood beside it and started yelling. "I found stone seven. Come toward the sound of my voice as quickly as you can. Dad, if you can hear me, finish circling the maze and then join us as quickly as possible."

I kept shouting until everyone had found me. When we were assembled, I pointed to the stone under my foot. "I've found the stone with the seven on it. That means the stone with the eight is the only one we're missing. Did anyone notice a relationship between the numbers and where they were found in the maze?"

"Keeping that type of perspective was quite difficult due to the curving, convoluted nature of the maze," Dad said. "But it seems to me the earlier numbers were closer to the entrance we came in at, and the later numbers were closer to the exit where I found the stone marker with the X. By the way, I found no exits other than the one marked with the X."

"That may be an indicator there's some part of the maze we've missed," I said. "Dad, go back to the exit where the X marker is and shout when you arrive. Tito, go back to where the nine stone is and call out. My guess is that the stone with eight should be triangulated between those. I'll stay here at the seven stone marker. Everyone else, fan out and look for anything else out of the ordinary."

A few minutes later, Tito called. "Lexi, I'm at the

nine stone." Another minute later, my dad shouted he'd made it to the X stone marker. If I triangulated their voices with my location, the stone with VIII should be somewhere in the middle and straight ahead of me. I headed quickly down the path, tracing an arc along one of the seemingly infinite number of similar curves.

I found nothing. The VIII stone remained elusive.

I stopped in the middle of the path, unsure what to do next, when I heard a slight whispering sound. The breeze picked up slightly, and I lost it. I circled the area once more, standing downwind and straining my ears. At last, I heard it again, slightly louder as the wafting breeze carried the sound to me more clearly.

It sounded like a trickle of running water.

"Has anyone seen a fountain or heard water running?" I shouted.

"Not me," Mom shouted back. "Did you find something?"

"Maybe," I yelled. I tried to push forward on the hedge where I could hear the sound, but it was too thick and dense.

I needed some help, and fast. "Everyone, come toward my voice again. Now."

SEVENTEEN

Lexi

WHEN EVERYONE WAS assembled again, I spoke. "Listen carefully and see if you can hear anything."

Everyone fell silent, listening.

"I hear it!" Mia shouted first. "It sounds like water dripping, and it's coming from that hedge, right there."

"You mean the one without an entrance," I said wryly. "We need to find a way through. Everyone, take a section of this hedge and go piece by piece to see if there's a door or an opening we're missing."

We lined up about six feet apart and began going down the hedge, painstakingly searching and poking at it. A couple of minutes later, Tito called out, "I found it!"

We all raced toward him, but he'd vanished.

"Tito?" I called out. "Where are you?"

We studied the hedge, but it appeared impenetrable. With a laugh, Tito's head poked out of the hedge a few feet away from me. "Here," he said before disappearing again.

I reached the spot where Tito's head had been but saw no opening. I stuck my hands straight into the hedge and discovered it had no interlocking branches. I pushed forward through the covering growth and found myself in a tunnel of hedge before it opened into a mown area about as wide as a small tennis court. Tito stood smiling at me, a large stone with the number VIII set in the grass at his feet.

"We found it!" I shouted at the others. "Push through the hedge. The branches aren't interlocked."

Mia came through next, followed by Oscar, Mom, and finally Dad.

"Brilliant," Oscar said, looking around in surprise. "A secret garden within the maze."

There were only two other objects besides the stone VIII marker inside the hidden garden. Near the center, a large Roman sundial sat on the ground enclosed within a circle of marble. At the far end of the garden, near the hedge, stood a large fountain with a marble statue of a woman in a long, flowing robe and two children. The woman held an urn above the children, the water trickling out of it. The trickle of water was what I'd heard when passing the hedge.

I skipped the sundial for now and headed for the statue. When I got closer, I saw the water spilled out of the woman's urn through a spout that split the flow of water into two streams. Each of the streams fell into separate cups being held aloft by two young boys, who were identically aged and dressed. The water overflowed their cups and ran down their arms and bodies back into the pool that surrounded the statue.

"It's beautiful," my mother said, coming to stand beside me. Mia followed her. "Is there a significance to it?"

"Probably," I said, although I wasn't sure how.

I walked around the statue a few times, then headed back to the sundial, where Oscar, my dad, and Tito were studying it. The metal sundial was set in a wide, flat circle of marble. Just outside the marble base, in the grass, a ring of round stones the size of a man's hand were equally spaced around the base.

"Do you see anything unusual?" I asked them.

"Not really. It looks like an ordinary sundial," my dad confessed. "What do you think?"

I examined the sundial, comparing the time with my watch. "It's much larger than the one I saw in the alcove, which reminds me we now have less than twenty minutes to solve the puzzle and get back to the veranda."

We started to wander around, but I decided to focus on the sundial. Its gnomon was an angled bar of metal similar to the smaller sundial I'd already come across. The sundial was marked around the edges in Roman numerals like the other sundial had been.

What did it mean? What was I missing?

I caught movement out of the corner of my eye and saw Oscar moving around the sundial, apparently counting the small stones that circled it. Before I could ask him what he was doing, my dad shouted at me from the fountain.

"Lexi, come quick! We've found another clue."

EIGHTEEN

Lexi

I DASHED OVER to the fountain with Oscar, Tito, and Mia hot on my heels. "What is it?"

"This," he said, pointing to the back side of the woman's feet. There were tiny numbers etched there.

I squinted and saw the number 1150. The number was in the shadow of the statue and was hard to see unless you had a sharp eye. "Good catch, Dad."

"It wasn't me," he said. "You can thank your mother."

Well, well. Mom had certainly stepped up her game on this challenge. "Thanks, Mom." She beamed, and I realized with a jolt of surprise she was really enjoying herself.

"You're welcome, but I have no idea as to the significance of the number. That's your job, sweetheart."

"Did you say 1150?" Oscar mused. "That number seems odd to me."

"It's even," Mia pointed out.

"That isn't what I meant."

They bickered good-naturedly, but my brain was racing furiously. "Why is 1150 in Arabic numerals?" I asked. "Every other number in this garden has been in Roman numerals."

"Roman or Arabic, the clock ticks on," Oscar said. "We have eleven minutes left."

Panic bubbled up, but I forced it down to concentrate. The answer had to be right here in front of me. "That number must relate to the sundial, but how?" I left the fountain and returned to the sundial to study it.

Tito, Oscar, and my dad came up behind me, staring at the sundial, all of us hoping the solution would somehow present itself.

"I don't know if it helps, Lexi, but I counted 216 stones surrounding the sundial," Oscar said. "That means nothing to me, but Romeo tells me you're quite good at math, so I thought I'd throw it out there."

Numbers. He was right. That was my strength. I quickly did the math and determined that if there were 216 stones surrounding the sundial, that would equal about six stones per hour for each of the hours of daylight on the sundial.

"Six stones per hour, or one every ten minutes," I mused aloud.

"That's it!" my dad suddenly yelled almost giving me a heart attack. "It's time, Lexi. The 1150 refers to a time—11:50."

My mouth dropped open as I suddenly understood. I raced to the rocks positioned on the arc between the XI and XII. I eyeballed which one most likely represented 11:50 and bent down to pull it up. It didn't budge.

"This has to be it!" I exclaimed in frustration. I desperately tried to pull up the stones on either side just in case my math was off, which I knew it wasn't. Still, no luck. Nothing budged.

"What are you doing, Lexi?" Tito asked, clearly confused. I glanced up and saw everyone was looking at me as if I'd completely lost it.

"The one-one-five-oh is time, and it's telling us

which of the stones to look under," I explained. "It should be where the disc is hidden." I pointed to the stone I had originally tried to lift. "That's the spot for 11:50, but the stone won't budge."

"Let me give it a try," Tito said, bending over. He tugged at it for a minute and abruptly stopped and started laughing.

"What's so funny?" I asked.

"It's funny because we're trying too hard." To my astonishment, he pushed down on the stone and, with a flick of his wrist, popped it open. Reaching into a hollow cavity, he lifted out a golden disc with the number 509 engraved on the top.

"The stone was hollow?" I said in shock.

"The stone wasn't a stone." He grinned and handed the disc over to me. "Just a fake rock with a hollow center big enough to hide this golden baby."

After a moment, I leaped to my feet and hugged Tito. Everyone started cheering and congratulating each other.

"We haven't won yet," I reminded them. "We have to return the disc to the veranda and get out of the maze." I checked my watch. "And we have six minutes to do that, so let's get going."

Once we got out of the hedge, I worried we'd never figure out a route back through the maze in time. I paused, trying to figure out how to proceed. My dad must have realized my dilemma because he put a hand on my arm.

"We can take the side exit near the stone marker with the X on it and get out more quickly," he suggested.

"Great idea, Dad," I agreed. "Brando didn't say we had to go out of the maze the way we went in, so let's do it. Can you lead us out?"

"Of course."

We ran now, following him as quickly as we could. I was acutely aware of the time ticking past until my dad suddenly stopped at a stone marker with an X on it. "The exit," he said, bowing and sweeping his hand out.

"You did it, Dad," I cried. "Come on, everyone, let's run back to the castle."

Collectively we raced as fast as we could around the outside of the maze toward the castle. I tried to calculate how much time it would take us to get there and had a sinking feeling we wouldn't make it in time. No way I could push my parents or Oscar to run any faster.

My mom stopped and waved me forward. "Go on without us, Lexi. Run as fast as you can and give the gamemaster the disc. Hurry."

I didn't waste time arguing or answering. I just started running as hard as I could, pumping my legs. For the twelfth time in the last three months, I reminded myself that I needed to develop a consistent exercise routine, especially since my life with Slash always seemed to involve running away from, or toward, something dangerous. If I intended to survive that lifestyle, I was *really* going to have to up my exercise game.

About halfway back to the castle, I realized I should have handed off the disc to Tito, who was in much better shape than I, but it was too late now. I wasn't going to stop now.

I made it to the veranda, raced up the steps, and skidded to a halt right in front of the table where the gamemaster sat having a cup of tea. A quick check of my watch indicated I had less than a minute to spare. Pausing to breathe, I placed the golden disc on the table next to his teacup.

"The number is 509, and we've solved the challenge," I said, gasping for breath. "We did it."

He glanced over my shoulder. "Where's everyone else?"

"On their way."

Brando clucked his tongue. "Ah, but one of the puzzle requirements was that you all had to be here. If not, then even though you've solved the puzzle, you can't win."

I considered for a moment, then shook my head. "Actually, that's *not* what you said. I happen to have an eidetic memory. You didn't specify that everyone had to be on the veranda, only that we had to be out of the maze, and that you had the disc. We are all out of the maze, and you have the disc."

Turning, I pointed into the distance, where these rest of the team appeared along the side of the maze. "As you can see, we are all accounted for and out of the maze, as instructed."

Brando stared at me for a moment thoughtfully and then smiled. "Well played, Miss Carmichael. You and your team have successfully met this challenge." He slid the disc back toward me. "Keep it. You may need it later."

He stood and disappeared into the house. Releasing a tight breath, I headed back toward the group to fill them in. When they saw me walking toward them, Mia and Tito broke away from the others, running ahead to greet me.

Tito reached me first, followed by Mia a couple of seconds later. "Did we win?" Mia asked, skidding to a stop next to me, panting. "Please, tell me we won."

"We won," I said, grinning. "One challenge down, and who knows how many more to go?"

"Hurrah!" Tito pumped his fist in the air and then lifted me off my feet, spinning me around until I was dizzy. "We're going to slay this escape room thing."

"One puzzle at a time," I cautioned, wobbly on my feet. Still, I couldn't help but smile as I was mobbed by the rest of our team.

We were one step closer to funding the orphanage in Salerno. Now it was up to Slash to get his team through.

NINETEEN

Slash

I THOUGHT ABOUT Lexi and how their team would do as the gamemaster led us up the right-side staircase and down the end of the hall past our bedrooms. I reminded myself that being separated on to different teams was the right decision. She was the smartest woman I'd ever met. I had full confidence that if anyone could lead the team to success, it was Lexi.

On the other hand, my amazing wife also had a little black cloud of trouble that followed her around like a favorite pet. That worried me. But I put that aside for now to focus on the task at hand.

The gamemaster stopped in front of a large, wood-paneled door with a keypad mounted on the wall. He turned to type a code on the panel. I slightly shifted my position to try to catch a glimpse of the code, but he effectively blocked the view, and the door swung open. He invited us to enter, so one by one, everyone filed in.

I waited until last to go in. Brando's eyes met mine as I walked past, but that didn't stop me from glancing at the keypad. One brief look told me everything I needed to know. Standard security cipher lock. Not top-of-the-line. Given some time, I could bypass it. Clearly, the purpose of this keypad was merely to serve as an effective lock to keep guests from peeking into a room ahead of a challenge.

Brando followed me in and left the door open behind us. I did a quick sweep of the room. Medium-size, with a high ceiling and no windows. Only one obvious exit, the one we'd just entered.

What was in the room, however, was most curious. Sitting directly in the center was an enormous bronze statue of a bull, dwarfing everyone. Brando guided us so that we were facing the right side of the bull. The statue had been placed on a raised dais with two steps leading up to the platform. Everyone stood in awe, looking at the bull. I remained near the door, leaning back against the wall and watching the gamemaster carefully. He seemed very confident and in control. However, in my experience, such individuals were occasionally betrayed by their confidence and unintentionally gave away more than they intended.

"This challenge is quite straightforward," Brando said. "All you must do is remove the gold ring from the bull's nose and use it to exit the room."

Several of the team began chattering excitedly and wandered toward the head, pointing at a large golden ring that had been placed through the nose of the bull statue and pulled tight with several interlocking ropes. I adjusted my position so that I could better see the bull's head. After a quick glance at the ring, I kept my eyes on Brando.

"You will have two hours to complete the challenge and exit," he continued. "When I leave, closing the door, the clock over the exit door will illuminate with a two-hour countdown. This will help you keep track of the time and coordinate your actions in an effective manner.

If you have not exited by the allotted two hours, I will return and will retrieve you. Good luck, or *in bocca al lupo*, as we say in Italian."

He gave a short bow and then headed for the door, his gaze meeting mine one more time, acknowledging my scrutiny without betraying any secrets, before the door shut behind him. As soon as he was gone, the clock started counting down.

Everyone started throwing out ideas. Gio and Stefan immediately mounted the platform to take a closer look at the ring. I stayed where I was, taking in the big picture, compartmentalizing what we were up against with this challenge.

Since I currently viewed the bull from the side, I could see its dominant feature was a heavy leather harness that wrapped around its chest and was secured by a rope that ran along the side of its head, attaching to the harness with a massive, complex knot.

I walked around to the front of the bull. The large gold ring sat directly in its snout, set into the statue amid flaring nostrils. The ring's diameter appeared to be the span of a man's large hand, and it was as thick as a finger. Looped through and around the gold ring were three ropes of different thicknesses. The thinnest rope ran from where it attached to the harness on both sides and was looped twice through the ring. The huge knot sat directly at the point where the rope attached to the harness on either side. My gaze flicked back to the ring. The two loops on the ring for the harness's rope were at the three and nine o'clock positions.

Interesting.

The fattest rope appeared to be about one inch in diameter and dropped from the ceiling, running through the top of the ring, directly next to the bull's nose. It did not make an additional loop before returning to the ceiling. The ends of that rope were secured in the ceiling at least ten feet above the head of the bull by separate heavy metal collars that were bolted into the ceiling. Through the bottom of the ring, there was a medium-size rope about three-quarters of an inch across. This rope looped through the ring, and both ends ran through a hole in a four-foot-high wooden hitching post. The two ends were knotted on the far side with a complicated set of knots and rings.

Stefan, who had been examining the hitching post, threw me a glance over his shoulder. "Looks like we have to remove all those ropes in order to free the gold ring."

"We'll have to do more than that," Stefan's girlfriend, Alessa, corrected him. "Because as far as I can see, in addition to the ropes holding the ring tightly in place, it's also still inside the bull's nose. How are we going to free the ring from his nose even if we unravel the knots and remove the rope?"

It was a good question. "I presume there's a latch or some mechanism on the ring that'll permit us to separate it and remove it from the bull's nose once we loosen the ropes," I said. "But first things first."

"How are we going to loosen all the ropes? Vittoria asked. "One of those ropes is attached to the ceiling. We don't have anything to cut it and, unless I'm missing something, I don't see any ladders in here." She looked around the room as if to confirm that statement. "In fact, there isn't *anything* else in this room but this *enorme* bull."

That was my cue to get things going.

I pushed off the wall. "There's a way to solve this puzzle, we just have to find it. In fact, the best puzzles usually seem impossible until you know the secret. Our job is to find that secret. So, let's start by going over this room and the bull very carefully. The time spent evaluating this puzzle will be well spent. Gio and Stefan, let's get a closer look at that bull and the ring. The rest of you, check the platform, the walls, the doors, and the floor. Every inch of this space needs to be examined."

I climbed the platform and stood next to my two brothers and my mother, who had also decided to join us on the platform. Everyone else stayed below, looking around.

"This is not bronze," my mother said to me in Italian. "It's wood. But it's solid wood and seems quite thick."

I touched the side, realizing she was right. I mobilized my brothers, and we tried to lift or move the bull. It didn't budge, clearly well anchored.

I turned my attention to the leather harness that encased the bull's shoulder and wrapped around its belly. The straps were thick and attached to each other with rivets. I tried to pry off a rivet without success. There were no obvious buckles or way to remove the harness short of cutting it off. Gio started methodically checking the rivets, looking for one that might be loose, and I left him to it.

Vittoria had started examining the knot on the back of a hitching post at the front of the bull. "This is odd," she said. "After passing through the hole in the hitching post, one end of this rope stops within a ring that's approximately the same size as the hole in the hitching post. The other end is embedded in this long, thin piece of wood. There's no way the ring can fit through that hole, so it must be the piece of wood that has to be freed to pass through the hole."

"Agreed. Keep working that angle," I said. Mama joined Vittoria. I liked seeing her and Vittoria working together. I hoped to see the same level of comfort with her and Lexi.

Turning my attention back to the task at hand, I decided to take the bull by the ring—literally. I reached up and grabbed it, pulling hard, but it would neither rotate nor move. It was pulled so tightly against the upper part of the nose by the ropes, I was unable to budge it at all. I knew it couldn't have been that easy, but it had to be eliminated as a possibility. Just the same, I checked every inch of the wood around the bull's nose and the ring itself in case there was a way to snap the ring or pull it from the nose, but I found nothing. That meant any unlocking mechanism on the ring would be hidden beneath that tight band of ropes holding it against the top of the bull's nose.

I glanced around and saw Alessa carefully examining the walls of the room, looking for any hidden opening that might provide a ladder or a hidden compartment that might contain a cutting tool.

She reached the exit door and took a step back. "There's no doorknob here," she called out in her clipped British accent. "How did our gamemaster get out of here?"

"The door was left open when we entered," I said. "He didn't use a doorknob to get out."

Nonetheless, I joined Alessa at the door. As she'd stated, there was no doorknob. I bent down to get a closer look. Instead of a doorknob, the door had a round indentation in the center that appeared to be the exact size of the large gold ring currently sitting in the bull's nose.

Her head bumped mine as she tried to get a better look at the indentation. "There appears to be a smaller indentation here right in the center of the circle," she said, tracing her finger over the tiny circle.

It was so faint I hadn't noticed it until she pointed it out. That circular area was about the size of a large fingertip or a thumb. I straightened, noticing a keypad like the one on the outside the door to the left of the indentation on the wall.

"How do we get out of here?" Alessa asked.

I looked between the keypad, the door, and the brass ring still firmly attached to the bull's nose. "I think to open the door we'll have to place the gold ring in the large indentation and either press the smaller circle and/or enter a code into the keypad. Perhaps in a particular order."

"If we can ever get the ring out of the bull's nose," Stefan called out. "It's not looking promising."

I studied the keypad more closely. "Did anyone happen to see the code our gamemaster used to get into the room?"

No one responded, not that I'd expected them to. But I'd noticed Brando had taken extra care to conceal the code from me, so it must mean something.

"I don't remember the code, but I seem to recall that he hit the keypad only three or four times," my mom said. "I'm sorry I didn't see more."

"It's okay," I assured her. "I presume we can't get out until we complete the challenge anyway." Just for the heck of it, I tried several combinations, to no avail.

"Hey, I could use some help here," Gio said, wrestling with the knots on the harness.

"I'll be right there," I said.

I instructed Alessa to keep examining the walls and floor and to go ahead and begin trying random codes on the keypad. On my way back to help Gio, I stopped to check on my mother's and Vittoria's progress at the hitching post. Vittoria was sitting on the floor with ropes in her lap, trying to untangle them, while my mother pulled at them gently.

"How's it going?" I asked.

My mom sighed, tucking a strand of her dark hair behind her ear. "Unfortunately, we're worse off than when we started. It is a complete mess now. We're attempting to backtrack to the original position and try something else."

I patted her on the shoulder. "Keep at it."

I did a quick time check, noticing that twenty minutes had already passed. I heard a grunt and looked up just in time to see Stefan hoist Gio onto the back of the bull. Gio began checking the harness and all the connections from his new angle. Stefan began a closer exploration of the underneath side of the bull.

"See anything, Gio?" I called up to him.

"Nothing," Gio said. "The harness from up here looks the same as below, and there's no apparent way to remove it. There's nothing else up here except the rope that runs up to the ceiling."

"Can you reach the ceiling?" Stefan asked, poking his head out from beneath the bull.

"Hell, no. Even if I stood on the bull's head, the ceiling is well over a meter above my head. But I'll see if I can pull the rope free from here."

Gio grabbed the rope and yanked on it. He gave it several hard tugs, but nothing happened. It appeared to be firmly attached to the ceiling.

"Perhaps you could shimmy up the rope and see if there is a way to disconnect it?" I suggested. "I presume you've done that once or twice during training in the special forces."

"That's a terrible idea," my mother scolded me, but before she'd even finished her sentence, Gio had shimmied up the rope until he'd reached the ceiling. Holding on with his legs and one hand, he inspected the rope attachment points carefully.

"The ropes are very well anchored," he called out. He

tried to push, pull, twist, and slide the end of the rope in its bracket with his free hand, without success.

"Check the bolts," I said.

"I already did, but there are no weaknesses, and they're too tight to twist off without a wrench." He tugged on the second rope but still no luck. "This thing is anchored tightly."

Defeated, he slid down the rope to the bull's head, careful to avoid the horns. He made his way to the back and then slid off, making the small jump to the platform. "I just don't see how we can release either end of that rope, short of cutting it down."

Gio and I walked around to the front of the bull to look at the head and golden ring again. The ring was set in the wood of the bull's nose about halfway up its nostrils. Much of the snout was hidden by the ring and the ropes.

"I already pulled on the ring," I said. "The ropes hold it tightly in place. I suspect it won't budge or rotate until we loosen those ropes."

"Maybe the eyes have a secret compartment with a collapsible knife?" Gio suggested, half joking.

It was a stretch, but I was open to all possibilities at this point. "Can you reach them?"

"If you give me a bit of a boost. Be careful not to skewer me on the horns."

I cupped my hands, and he put one foot in them as I lifted him up. He reached carefully between the horns and pushed on the glass eyes, but nothing happened.

"That's not good," Gio said as I lowered him down. "This seems like an impossible task."

"It's not impossible," I said. "We just have to consider our options."

"What options?"

"We have to solve at least one of the knots on the

harness to loosen the rope around the ring. Maybe that will give us enough ability to slide the ring around and find a hidden mechanism that will allow the ring to separate. I don't see any other options. Let's do that first and then worry about how to remove the ceiling rope and the ring later."

A quick glance indicated that Stefan had begun attacking the knot on the right side of the bull's harness. Gio and I went to help him. I compared the knots on both sides of the harness and quickly recognized they were different, but similar in complexity. I left Gio and Stefan to work on the left side while I went to work on the knot on the other side.

Each rope passed through a small but solid iron ring on the harness and formed an enormous knot the size and shape of a volleyball. It was tied in such a way that the end of the rope wasn't showing. I studied it for a moment. The rope wrapped around itself again and again until the surface was pebbled with extremely tight rope loops. There was a definite pattern to each knot, but it didn't offer any immediate insight as how to untie it.

No way to know unless I tried to unravel it.

I attacked the knot, listening with amusement as Stefan and Gio alternately cursed and praised the knot's genius.

"How's it going?" I called out after a few minutes.

"*Pazzo*. It's insane. How did they do this?"

"They designed it by computer," I replied, certain I was right. I'd read enough scientific articles by physicists and mathematicians who specialized in creating and untying incredibly complex theoretical knots. But how did Brando expect us to unravel such a complex knot in two hours without a computer?

"Great, a computer-generated Gordian knot," Stefan added in frustration.

"What's a Gordian knot?" Gio asked.

"It's one of the few things I remember from my Greek mythology course in college. It comes from an ancient Greek tale of a knot created by the peasant Gordius, who wanted to thank Zeus for making him a king. I don't remember how or why Zeus made him a king, but he did. In gratitude, Gordius dedicated his most prized possessions, an ox and cart, to Zeus. In the center of the town he now ruled, Gordius tied his ox to a post with a highly intricate knot, eventually dubbed the Gordian knot. An oracle then foretold that whoever untied the knot would rule Asia. For years, no one was able to untie the knot. Then Alexander the Great conquered the area, heard of the oracle, and decided to attempt it."

"Did he untie the knot?" my mother asked, still working on the knots at the hitching post with Vittoria.

"No," Stefan said. "He tried, but to his great frustration, he never could. So, instead, he sliced the knot with his sword, freeing the bull, which somehow was still alive, I guess. He then went on to conquer much of Asia."

Vittoria stood up, rubbing her back. "Perhaps that's a message that we should be looking for a way to cut the knot instead of trying to untie it."

"Hand me a sword, darling, and I'm all about the slicing," Gio said to her, holding up a hand as if he were wielding a sword. "I'm more of an action guy than a thinking guy anyway. I leave all that deep thinking to Romeo."

I rolled my eyes, but Alessa came up behind me to study my knot. "Perhaps Vittoria is right, and the legend is a clue that we should look for another solution."

"If you have one, I'm all ears," I said.

"I don't. But I'll keep thinking."

I studied the knot again. However it was created, the rope had to have an end. Another fact was that end must be near the surface, just cleverly tucked away and hidden. We just had to find it to unravel it.

"Look for the end of the rope," I instructed everyone. "It has to be near the surface."

"Easier said than done," Stefan said with a grunt. "These knots are so tightly wound and compressed, there isn't much surface to pull. Even when we do get purchase, it doesn't budge."

He was right. We needed something sharp and strong to pry the strands apart. But what? I stepped away from the bull and surveyed the room again.

My mother and Vittoria had made decent progress with the ropes at the hitching post. The end with the piece of wood was now at the end of a foot-long piece of rope as they were gradually figuring out the multitude of steps that need to be taken. I glanced at the bull again, and my eyes locked onto the horns. Those would be sharp and strong. Perhaps we could break one off. I wasn't sure if that was allowed, but I didn't see any other options.

I climbed back onto the platform. "Gio, Stefan. Give me a boost onto the bull. I have an idea."

My brothers boosted me up, and I moved carefully to the head. I examined the horns, determining the amount of force I'd need to break one off. I pulled on one of them, and to my surprise, it twisted easily. It took me two seconds to determine the horns were only screwed on. I gritted my teeth, annoyed at myself for not thinking of this before.

"The horns were only screwed on," I said. "Here, catch them."

I dropped both horns down to Gio and Stefan. Everyone started chattering excitedly, the anticipation of a breakthrough palpable. "Use the tip to pry at different spots at the knots, looking for the weak spot," I instructed my brothers.

I used the harness to hop down, and Gio tossed me one of the horns. I immediately used it to start attacking the knot on the other side of the bull's harness.

"It's working!" Stefan cried out.

I came over to investigate as he pried with the horn, separating the coils of the rope. Stefan and I helped him pull, and while the knot gave a little, it did not unravel and eventually refused to budge further.

"Damn," Stefan said, using the horn to poke at a different spot. I joined him with the other horn, stabbing the horn into the knot in a different location to release more of the tension. After a couple of minutes, we were able to push parts of the knot farther apart. At last, we were able to unthread the end, giving us about six inches of rope free from the knot.

"Progress," Gio shouted, pumping his fist in the air.

I wasn't quite as enthusiastic. I'd already calculated the time we'd need to unravel this entire thing, and it wasn't enough. We continued the process, but after another ten minutes we'd only unraveled about eighteen inches. The knot was stubbornly refusing to give up its secrets easily, and we were running out of time. I glanced at the clock, noting forty-five minutes remained. We had to solve the mystery of the knots quickly or there wouldn't be time to solve the rest of the puzzle.

"We're almost done here," my mother said. "Romeo, come take a look."

I handed off my horn to Gio and went to see what they'd done. To my astonishment, they'd nearly solved their knot.

"How did you do it?" I asked.

"Alessa and Vittoria are quite adept with their hands,

and we were fortunately able to solve the pattern of this knot." She stretched her arms over her head, rolling her neck. "I estimate we should be finished in a few minutes. How are things going with your knots?"

"Not so well, Mama. At this pace, I'm not sure we'll finish in time."

She patted my shoulder like she always did when I was frustrated. "Always look to the solution, *tesorino*, not the problem."

Alessa, who was sitting on her knees, her arms wrapped in ropes, untangled her legs and stood. "Seriously, this doesn't make sense. They can't expect us to solve all these problems in the allotted time. No wonder no one has ever completed these challenges. There must be some other, easier solution we're overlooking. What could it be?"

I'd long ago come to that conclusion, but my mother's words had struck a chord. Maybe the challenges and knots were a distraction, and the answer was far more obvious.

Start at the solution.

Getting out of the room with the brass ring.

"*Finito!*" Vittoria suddenly shouted, startling me from my thoughts. She'd somehow pulled the rope free. "We did it!"

Everyone gathered around to look. The women had successfully pulled one end of the rope through the hole in the hitching post. I quickly took the loose end and threaded it through the ring. There was just enough room for the piece of wood to pass through once, and then again to remove the second loop and free the rope from the ring.

"Yes!" Stefan said, planting a kiss on Alessa's lips. "You ladies are amazing."

I agreed, as this was real progress.

"Gio and Stefan, I need you to keep working on the big rope," I said. "We don't have much time. Mama, stay and help me here. Vittoria and Alessa, start searching the room again and see what we might have missed. There *must* be something. Look everywhere."

Now that at least one rope had been loosened, I returned to the nose ring. Without the lower rope anchoring it in place, I was able to wiggle it a bit. In fact, I could now lift the bottom of the ring up toward the ceiling a few centimeters. When I did it, I felt a slight catch. I lowered and raised the ring again, but this time I didn't feel the catch. I tried several more times without success.

"Can you rotate the ring now?" my mother asked.

"I'm trying," I said.

I studied the ring for a moment and tried pulling it while the ring was positioned downward. Nothing. I lifted it up again, this time agonizingly slowly until I felt that slight catch again and froze. After a moment, I tried to rotate it while it was in that position, and it finally moved.

I let out a small breath, the muscles in my arms and shoulders screaming. I carefully rotated the ring, rewarded with the appearance of a small gap that had previously been hidden beneath the wood of the nose. I felt the gap, looking for a release mechanism or way to unscrew the ring from the nose, but other than the slight gap, there was no way to release, break, or remove the ring.

I released the ring and shook out my arms. "I've got bad news. There is no release mechanism on the ring. It's solid."

My mother looked at me in surprise. "Then how do we get it off the bull's nose? Even removing all the ropes won't free it from the nose. That doesn't make sense."

I didn't have an answer, but no other solution presented itself. I reached up and felt all along the brass ring again, stopping on the slight gap. I rotated the ring until the gap was where the rope from the ceiling passed through the loop. I tried to push it through, but the rope was too fat to fit through the gap. I tried to force it, but it was clear after a minute that it wouldn't fit no matter how hard I pushed.

I looked up and down the rope to see if there were any places where the rope was thinner, but it all looked the same thickness. Still, I continued to rotate the ring until it was adjacent to where the rope that was attached to the Gordian knot on the right side. As I'd hoped, that rope *was* thin enough to pass through the gap. But it wouldn't go easily, because the second loop through the ring was on the other side.

The rope was pulled so tight, there wasn't quite enough slack to fit through the crack. I retrieved one of the horns and began prying apart the strands of the rope until I was able to fit some of the strands individually through the gap. Eventually, I was able to remove the rest of the rope from that side. With one side free, I had plenty of slack to rotate the ring to the other side, repeat the process, and drop the rope from the ring.

Like Alexander the Great, we'd succeeded in freeing the rope without having to solve the Gordian knot. Yet.

"You did it!" Alessa shouted, and everyone came around to congratulate me.

"It only means we have two out of three ropes off the ring," I said. "But at least we can stop trying to unravel the Gordian knots. The ceiling rope remains and, of course, the wood of the bull's nose holding it in place. I felt the wood between the ring and the nose, and it's incredibly strong. Even using the horn to hack at it, I don't think we'd be able to break through."

"So, what do we do?" Gio asked. He had his arm around Vittoria, and she rested her dark head on his shoulder.

I thought for a moment. "Let's review the remaining problems and visualize a solution. Mama, tell me what you see as the problems."

She looked at me and then the ring still encased in the bull's nose. "Step one. We must remove the rope from the ceiling in order to free the ring completely of all ropes. Step two. Figure out how to remove the ring from the bull's nose. Step three. Once we free the ring, we place it in large indentation in the door and either press the small circle or enter a code on the keypad that we don't know yet. And we must do all of that in eighteen minutes. Did I miss anything?"

As far as I could tell, she hadn't. But something had started to bother me, which meant that during her recap, something had stirred inside my head. A potential answer or solution, I hoped.

But how long would it take before it surfaced into my brain as an action?

There wasn't a minute to waste. "Gio, get up on the bull again and take another look at the ceiling bolts. Stefan, you help him. Mama, you and Vittoria check to see if there is anything we can do with the hitching post now that it's free of the rope. Perhaps that is why we needed to free the rope instead and freeing the ring was a distraction. Then go over the platform and the walls looking for any anomaly that we might have missed. Alessa, take another look at the door. Everyone, be quick, because we don't have much time."

"What are you going to do?" Stefan asked.

"Play to my strengths," I said, heading toward the keypad. A gut feeling suddenly told me the answer was at the door, and I never ignored my gut feelings.

I studied the keypad for a several minutes. It was a simple black keypad with blue backlight. The keypad display was digital, which meant no worn-out keypads where you could determine the password by simply looking at which keys had been pushed the most. A blue backlight was more convenient in the dark and harder for interlopers to look over your shoulder, through binoculars, or via other electronic means to see you punch in a code. But how did that figure into this challenge?

The keypad was important, but how? It meant we'd need a code to get out, and I hadn't seen a series of numbers or letters on anything.

Out of the corner of my eye, I noted Alessa peering intently at the indentation where the brass ring would go if we ever figured out how to remove it from the bull's nose. "Find something?" I asked her.

"Not yet, but I'm convinced that, as with the knot, the solution may not be the obvious one. Subtlety seems key to this challenge. Perhaps all we need is a combination to unlock the door. Maybe the combination is inscribed on the gold ring, and we don't have to remove the ring, just like you didn't have to untie the Gordian knots completely."

It was an interesting theory, even though I wasn't sure how you could misinterpret Brando's clear instructions—*remove the gold ring from the bull's nose.* Additionally, I'd already looked at and felt every inch of that ring with my fingers, and other than the small gap, I hadn't seen or felt an engraving of any kind.

But it didn't hurt to have confirmation of that.

Fired up by her train of thought, Alessa raced over to the bull and asked Gio for a boost. He gave her one so she could examine the golden ring up close. Like I had, she studied the ring carefully, looking on the outside and inside of the ring and rotating it so she could see all parts of the ring…and found nothing. No way to break it, no way to remove it from the bull's nose, and no secret code.

Nothing.

Disappointment showed on her face as Gio lowered her down. I realized I was not the only one who would take this failure personally.

"I thought I was on to something," she said dejectedly. "It just felt right."

I agreed with her. It *had* felt right.

I turned and studied the door again. The answer had to be right in front of me. What was it?

"This small circular indentation bothers me," I murmured. "I can't figure out its true purpose. Every piece in a puzzle has a purpose, so what could this be?"

Alessa bent down closely, peering at the indentation. "I thought maybe we would push it once we put the big ring here." Her finger ran around the large indentation. "But it doesn't look like you can push it. Other than being a smaller version of the large ring, I don't know what it's here for."

My brain exploded with the answer. "Alessa, that's it!"

"What's it?"

I strode over to the bull. Leaning up, I reached my hand over the large gold ring and shoved it all the way to the back left nostril of the bull. I wiggled my hand and fingers around, looking for a crevice or anything, but felt nothing.

"Hey, Romeo, what's going on?" Gio asked. I ignored him for the moment, but the entire team instantly surrounded me, convinced I was on to something.

I shoved my hand into the bull's right nostril. Approximately three inches back, in a slight hollow that wouldn't be visible to anyone looking into the nose, I felt a small, round metal object. I flipped it out of the hollow and dragged it out of the bull's nose. With a smile, I turned and presented it to Alessa.

"Your ring, madame," I said. "Thanks to your train of thought, we found it."

"There was *another* ring in the bull's nose?" Stefan asked, his expression incredulous.

"There is." I knew how competitive my brother could be, so I decided to jab at him a bit. "Thanks to Alessa, we figured it out. You'd better up your game, Stefan."

Alessa grinned at me and then raised an eyebrow at Stefan. "Guess I won this one, babe. Don't worry, there'll be more puzzles for you to prove yourself."

Stefan shook his head, but he smiled, and I could tell she'd impressed him.

"Just a minute." Vittoria threw up her hands. "I don't understand. There were two rings this entire time?"

"There were two rings," I confirmed, suddenly acutely aware of the time. "The roped ring was just a distraction. Alessa, is there anything engraved on the ring? A code or some numbers, perhaps?"

She turned the ring over in her hand and peered closely at the inside of the ring. "Yes. The number 395. Let's try it, but we have to hurry."

We all headed to the door. Alessa inserted the ring into the small indentation, where it fit perfectly. A distinct click sounded, and the keypad lit up.

"It worked!" Alessa gasped.

I quickly typed in 395. The keypad flashed once, and the door silently swung open. There was a moment of disbelief before everyone started shouting and cheering. Alessa was mobbed as everyone filed out, jostling and slapping each other on the back. Carefully, I reached down and took the small ring from the door, the last to leave the room.

As I stepped into the hallway, I looked back over my shoulder thoughtfully. There were lessons I needed to learn from this experience if we were going to be successful for the rest of them. Besides trusting my instincts, I needed to fully trust my team, because, as they'd just shown, they were more than capable.

My mother gave me a proud pat on the shoulder as I walked past and fell into step next to Alessa. I handed her the ring. "You present it to the gamemaster. You earned it."

As I said those words, Brando appeared in the hallway. "How very delightful. You're all here. If you'll provide me with the ring, I'll trade you for this golden disc to certify that you've completed the challenge."

Alessa beamed as she handed Brando the ring. He inspected it and presented her with the gold disc. "Congratulations! You've successfully solved your first challenge. Please accept our invitation to lunch, followed by another challenge this afternoon."

"Please tell me the next one will be easier," Vittoria pleaded, and everyone laughed.

Brando gave her a smile. "Oh, I assure you, they're all easy...if you know the secret. Now, please follow me."

TWENTY

Lexi

MIA FELL INTO step next to me as we headed back to our rooms to clean up before lunch. I looked forward to seeing Slash and hearing about their challenge. We hadn't been told whether the other team had succeeded or not, so I was anxious to find out.

"Lexi, I'd like to ask you something," Mia said as we were climbing the stairs. "Do you have a minute?"

I had no desire to chat, but Mia was, by extension, becoming part of my family, so I couldn't just brush her off. I expected she wanted to try another couple of slang expressions on me, so I stopped when we got to the top of the staircase. "Sure, what's up?"

"Vittoria didn't have a bachelorette party, so I'm fixin' to give her a big surprise."

Fixin'? Family or not, I sincerely hoped she didn't think I was going to help plan a bachelorette party, because that wasn't going to happen. Been there, done that, and didn't want to ride that crazy train again...ever.

"What did you have in mind, Mia?" I asked carefully.

"I want to play a prank on her."

"A prank?" Okay, that was a bit surprising. I hadn't expected that.

"Yes. I've already talked to Alessa, and she's in, too."

I stared at Mia for a moment, thinking. I wasn't sure where this fell on my spreadsheet of dealing with in-laws. The risk that the prank might backfire or embarrass me, or other family members, was awfully high. My record with these types of situations was consistently and statistically bad.

I needed time to figure out how to say no gracefully, so I stalled. "Thanks for including me, Mia, but I've got a lot going on right now and wouldn't have the time to plan anything. Can I get back to you on this?"

"Oh, you wouldn't have to plan anything. It's already planned. It would be a walk in the forest for you."

"Do you mean 'a walk in the park'?"

"Park! Yes, that's it!" She looked delighted. "You're the best, Lexi. Anyway, Alessa and I have a plan. We want you to be included because we're family now."

I felt trapped. I did not want to be considered anti-fun, but it was hard to stand firm when she played the family card, because that was my vulnerability. Still, I was smart enough not to commit to anything...yet.

"I really appreciate that you guys want to include me. I'll think about it, okay?"

Mia perked up. "Great. Let either Alessa or me know by tonight if you're in, and *don't tell anyone*. Not even your husband. We want it to be a complete surprise."

"Okay. I won't tell anyone."

When I got to our room, I found Slash at the bathroom sink, washing his hands.

"Hey, you," I said, giving him a quick peck on the cheek and handing him a hand towel. "How did the challenge go?"

"We solved it," he said, wiping his hands dry. "We managed to finish within the allotted time, but with less than a minute. Not a comfortable win, but a win, nonetheless. How about you guys?"

"We barely made it, too, and that was with me having to run as fast as I could with the disc to give it to the gamemaster. It reminded me I need to up my workout game." I turned on the faucet and washed my hands, too, splashing water on my face. "The maze escape room was seriously complicated, and they gave us only two hours. I'm worried about what comes next."

"Me, too. But good work, *cara*."

I wiped my hands and face with the towel and pulled my ponytail tighter at the back of my head. "At least we're two for two. What was your challenge?"

Slash provided a concise accounting of the events that involved removing a brass ring from a large wooden bull's nose.

"So, there were two rings," I said, musing it over. "That was the catch?"

"That was the catch. I should have thought of it earlier, but the knots and the complexity of the puzzle distracted me. That won't happen next time."

He reached behind me, releasing my hair from its ponytail. My hair fell loose around my shoulders. He tugged gently on a strand, pulling out a small twig and holding it between his fingers. "What did you guys have to do?"

I told him about the garden maze, the fountains, the stones with the Roman numerals, and how we solved the puzzle of the sundial. All the while, he combed my hair with his fingers, removing an inordinate amount of brush and sap while giving my scalp a light massage. It felt heavenly.

Finally, I finished up by telling him how my mother

accidentally flashed Oscar in the maze before screaming and scaring us all to death.

"Your mother took her sweater off in the maze?" Slash repeated, his hands stilling against my scalp. "In front of Oscar?"

"Yes, to get rid of the lizard. That's when Oscar came around the corner of the hedge and scared the crap out of her. Probably scared the crap out of the lizard, too, because it hightailed it out of there. He looked pretty mortified."

"The lizard or Oscar?"

"I presume both, but I'm talking about Oscar. You should have seen his face. It was a color of scarlet I'd never seen. Kind of alarming, actually. But don't worry, Mom assured him since her boobs were covered by her bra, it was no biggie."

Slash turned around and went to sit on the bed. I joined him so we were perched side by side, our thighs touching. "I'm worried by your lack of a humorous response. You don't think my mom talking about her boobs in front of your stepfather is going to be a problem for our family dynamics, do you?"

"Of course, not," he said. "Oscar is a grown man. Your mother is a grown woman. It was an innocent mishap." He paused and then looked at me. "What did your dad do?"

"Dad? He didn't do anything."

"That's good, at least."

"Why would you say that?" It took me a minute to get there. "Wait. Don't be ridiculous. My dad is *not* going to blame you for the lizard."

He gave me a pointed look that indicated I hadn't convinced him. "Okay, now I'm feeling like I need to start a family disaster spreadsheet. We already have a pretty good start on it if you include the shooting the first time you had dinner with my parents, the scare at our engagement party, crazy Santa at the airport, throwing up with Oscar, and now my mom flashing your stepdad. I'm sure I'm forgetting several others."

"You are." He put his hand over mine. "But no spreadsheet. Everything's fine with our families."

He sounded confident, but it didn't quite extinguish that small, niggling doubt that things on the family front weren't going as smoothly as I'd hoped. "Well, I guess I should look on the bright side. We have two escape puzzles completed. I wish I knew how many more we have to go. I just hope we're as successful as before."

Slash rested his forearms on his thighs as he leaned forward. "I suspect the puzzles will get increasingly difficult. We have to be sure to carefully review the instructions to each room or location, because they may offer the most valuable clues."

"I agree. Also, one thing I also observed is a focus on mathematics—numbers and patterns. That seems to hold for both challenges and will likely play a continued role in the puzzles."

"Undoubtedly. What did you think of the capability of your team?"

"I was pleasantly surprised," I said. "Everyone is quite clever and adept, including my mother. She was amazing. In fact, she was the one who found the hidden code on the statue that led to us solving the puzzle."

"I've also been pleasantly surprised. Stefan's girlfriend, Alessa, is quite intelligent and resourceful. We're lucky to have such talented families, aren't we?"

"We are." I put my head on his shoulder, slipping my hand through his. I'd had more than my fill of people this morning, and I wished we could stay here and skip lunch. But I could hear Slash's stomach growling, so I sucked it up and stood.

"Time to eat," I said as cheerfully as I could.

He gave me a look like he knew what I was thinking, but hunger won out and he didn't argue. We exited the room hand in hand, heading down the marble staircase until we reached the dining room. I was relieved to discover we could sit where we wanted for lunch, so I followed Slash, who headed toward an empty seat next to Father Armando.

"Congratulations on solving the first two challenges," the priest said as we sat down. "I knew you'd do it."

"Two down and several more to go," I cautioned him.

"Of course. But I have no doubt you'll succeed. Keep up the good work."

Juliette sat next me, and Oscar joined her. The table quickly filled up, and conversation inevitably turned toward the challenges of the morning and who had done what to figure out the puzzles. The conversation seemed animated and easy. If the point of the escape rooms was to get to know everyone better, it was certainly working.

I was a nervous wreck sitting next to Juliette without my teenage table-etiquette model nearby, so my anxiety heightened as the food arrived. I remembered to put my napkin on my lap, but my hands shook when Slash asked me to pass a plate of meats and cheese. I accidentally dumped a third of the plate on the tablecloth while handing it off to him. Slash calmly ate it from the table without missing a beat while chatting with his mother. I loved him so much for that and appreciated that Juliette hadn't pointed it out, either.

After eating sliced pears drizzled with caramel for dessert, I sat back in my chair, full and needing a serious nap. I thought it a clever strategy for the staff to feed us like this—to keep us lethargic and off our mental game.

Lorenzo arrived and told us we'd have one hour to

rest after lunch before reporting back to the dining room to receive our next challenge.

People began chatting, with some filing out of the dining room for downtime before the next challenge. Juliette excused herself from the table and went over to speak with Alessa, while Gio waved Slash over to tell him something. That left Oscar and me alone at our little corner of the table.

"So, Lexi," Oscar said, leaning forward. "I meant to tell you, I noticed something interesting in the garden today."

"You mean other than that crazy maze?"

"Exactly. In fact, I was quite surprised to see the island has its own little apiary."

I looked at him in astonishment. "Beehives? Here?"

"Yes, it's quite extraordinary. The staff must produce their own honey."

"That's…unexpected," I said cautiously.

"Well, anyway, I thought maybe you'd enjoy getting a closer look at the apiary with me. I'd be delighted to tell you all about the beehives."

I must have made a horrified expression, because he hastily added, "Of course, only if you're interested."

My mind immediately flashed to the rules for the in-law's spreadsheet that was folded flat in my back jeans pocket. Guideline number one stated I should accept an invitation to do something my parents-in-law extend to me *even* if it was out of my comfort zone. It would demonstrate my eagerness to familiarize with and integrate into the family.

Unfortunately, bees were so far out of my comfort zone they were in the stratosphere. But Oscar was right. We'd kind of gotten off on the wrong foot, so here was my chance to be the interested and invested daughter-in-law, ready for a seamless integration. I was sure there was a way I could stay a safe distance away while still showing appropriate interest.

What could go wrong?

"Sure, Oscar. I could do that. When did you have in mind?"

"How about right now?" He stood up. "I could use a walk and some fresh air to clear my head after that expansive lunch. We have a bit of time before the next challenge, so why not?"

I searched for some, *any* plausible explanation why I couldn't go at this exact moment, but nothing presented itself. My stomach dropping, I managed to respond. "Okay, I guess we could go now."

My heart started to race at the prospect as I wiped my damp palms on my jeans beneath the table. Oscar gallantly pulled out my chair, and I stood, hoping to catch Slash's eye, but his back was to me.

Oh, jeez.

"I don't think we'll need a jacket," Oscar said. "It's warmed up since this morning, and it's lovely outside. We should have the perfect opportunity to see the hives."

Lucky for me. Not.

I followed Oscar out of the dining room the same way Brando had led us this morning when taking us to the maze. We walked out on to the veranda and down the stairs to the garden. Oscar was right, it had warmed up enough that I felt comfortable in my long-sleeved T-shirt and jeans.

"Which way?" I asked, shading my eyes, wishing I'd brought my sunglasses.

"Follow me."

He led me to the right side of the maze and toward a wooded area. He stopped near an opening in the trees and pointed in the distance. "See those white structures?

Those are the apiaries. I noticed them in the distance when we came out of the maze."

I squinted into the trees and saw the structures he was talking about several hundred feet away. Hope rose in my chest. Maybe we could look at the beehives from here.

"How can you tell those are apiaries?" I asked.

He smiled broadly at me. "I just can. Come on. Follow me, and don't worry. Bees are harmless."

Easy for him to say. He apparently didn't mind swarms of insects flying around his head and landing on his body. I shuddered just imagining them crawling on me. Intellectually, I liked bees. I knew they were good for the environment and the planet and an integral part of our ecosystem. I just wanted to appreciate them from a healthy distance, which apparently wasn't going to happen today.

As we got closer to the hives, it became easy to spot the bees flying between the structures and the trees. Several white boxes were stacked on top of each other vertically. Some of the boxes had viewing windows, so the beekeeper could see what was going on in the hive. There was no way I was getting close to the viewing window with all the bees flying around. Still, I had to give it to Oscar—there was something mesmerizing about watching the bees buzz about.

"A good apiary is one that is secluded, has access to plenty of flora, and has direct sunlight," he said. "It must be close to water and have good air circulation, as honeybees need to keep dry. Natural ventilation and airflow are key to harvesting a lot of excellent honey."

I had to admit the science of it interested me, and the fact that Oscar cared about bees and the environment made me like him more. If only it were that easy to rationalize my fear of bees away. No matter how hard I tried to convince myself bees were harmless, my legs trembled, and my hands started to shake. Thankfully, Oscar was so focused on the hives he didn't notice.

We continued to approach the hive, getting much closer than I was comfortable with, stopping thirty or so feet away. My eyes were like advanced military radars trying to simultaneously track each buzzing object. Oscar must have noticed my increased breathing and tried to be reassuring.

"Don't be afraid, although I know that just saying it doesn't make it easier. These European honeybees do not sting unless they are threatened. They're just like the ones that I maintain back in England. Here, let me show you." He walked up to one of the hives where there was a small ball of bees on the outside and gently scooped them up into one of his hands. He turned toward me and offered them to me. I froze in place, completely terrified, unable to move.

I watched in a mixture of horror and amazement as the bees swarmed his hand, crawling all over it. Clearly, they didn't perceive him as a threat, and he was not being stung. It truly shocked me. He brought the bees up close to his face so that he could watch their movement even more closely. His expression was so calm and enraptured I forgot my fears momentarily. How could he be so at peace with such small yet dangerous creatures?

He turned to me and smiled. "I'm going to show you something bloody fascinating, Lexi. Do you trust me?"

Um, how was I supposed to answer that? There wasn't explicit guidance in the in-law's guidance on this particular circumstance, but I felt confident the advice would indicate that the proper response was for me to say that I trusted him. He was family, after all.

"Um…yes?" I hated that it was more of a question

than a statement, but we are who we are. "You aren't going to put one on me, right?"

"Of course not. Not without your permission. Now, close your eyes for at least a minute, and I'll tell you when to open them. When you do, you'll see how friendly these gentle creatures are."

I closed my eyes, my heart thumping so hard I feared I might have a heart attack. Subconsciously, I started counting the beats, trying to estimate my heart rate to determine if I was at risk of tachycardia. I'd conducted some serious online research about the risks of an excessive heart rate after my encounter with Guido, the giant dog who had followed me into a bathroom several months ago. I remembered vividly that a sustained heart rate of over 210 for a person my age could be very dangerous.

It always took me about thirty seconds to calculate the square root of eleven to seven decimal places, and I'd used that occasionally to measure time accurately in my head. I began simultaneously counting my pulse throbbing in my temples as I began solving the square root. I was sure that I was going to find my pulse was over 250. I was stunned to find that it was *only* 175, a level commonly reached by fit people involved in heavy exercise.

I heard some grunting sounds from the direction of the hives. I was tempted to open my eyes, but I had promised to trust Oscar to keep them closed for a minute, so I waited until my internal clock assured me that at least a minute had gone by.

When I opened my eyes, Oscar staggered toward me, grunting, and waving his arms in front of him. Only the outline of his face and head were visible, as everything above his shoulders was buried under a thick coating of bees.

For a moment, I could only stare at him in complete horror. Then, although I admit it wasn't one of my better responses to a crisis, I screamed at the top of my lungs.

TWENTY-ONE

Lexi

"OSCAR!" I SHRIEKED, stumbling backward. "They've swarmed you."

Although his head was covered with bees, he must have been able to hear, because he began waving his arms even more urgently. I presumed that whatever he had planned, Oscar must have spooked the bees so that they began attacking him, swarming his head and shoulders. He couldn't speak and the best he could do was grunt at me, clearly in desperate need of help.

There wasn't time to run back to the castle. He might be dead by the time I returned with help. It was up to me to save my father-in-law.

"Hold on," I said as bravely as I could. "I'll save you." Although my hands were shaking violently, I looked around for a tool or something to get the bees off him. Several steps to my right, I found a dead branch about five feet long. The branch was about an inch thick, and at the end it had several smaller branches growing out of it with a few small, dry brown leaves attached. It would be perfect to shoo the bees off his head and keep me at a mostly safe distance. I had to get a grip on the fact that I'd probably get stung. But I couldn't leave him at the mercy of the hive.

I grabbed the branch and turned back toward Oscar. When I saw him on his hands and knees, most likely succumbing to bee venom, I almost passed out.

"Hang on." Brandishing the branch in front of me and giving myself an internal pep talk, I approached him and the bees.

To his credit, he must have sincerely cared about me, because he leaned back on his knees and tried to wave me away. It was unbelievable. He was dying from a bee attack and yet his instinct was to protect me.

Determined, I stepped closer, raising my branch carefully over Oscar's head, intending to brush the branch near his face to scare away the bees, so he could breathe again. But as I started to lower the branch, I felt a tickle on my right forearm. Looked down, I saw a bee had just landed on it.

Swallowing a shriek, I jerked my arm back, dropping the branch directly onto Oscar's head with a thud, knocking him to the ground.

A cloud of bees scattered from his body, so I did what any self-respecting bee warrior would do—I shrieked and ran, certain they were coming for me next. I was rounding the edge of the maze when I heard a call from behind me.

"Wait, Lexi, don't run away. I'm fine!"

I turned, and to my astonishment, I saw Oscar walking a little unsteadily up the path from the hives. He was alive. Thank goodness, my blow must have knocked the bees off in time to save him. As he approached, I could see some blood dripping near his ear.

"Holy beehive. Oscar, are you okay?"

"Yes, I'm okay. Something heavy must have dropped from a tree and hit me in the head, scaring the bees away. I had limited vision with the bees around my face, so I couldn't see what it was."

I stared at him, not sure what to say first. "You couldn't see?"

"Not well. What did you think of the bees?"

"I think you're crazy lucky to be alive. They swarmed you, Oscar. I couldn't even see your head."

"The bees weren't hurting me, Lexi. I put them on my head on purpose."

"You did *what*?" My heart was beating at a crazy tempo, and my knees visibly shook.

"I wanted to show you how gentle they are. I opened one of the hives and took out a small mass of them and put them on my head. I expected them to form a sort of beehive hairdo where you could see that they are harmless if you treat them with care and understanding. Unfortunately, I must have grabbed a queen, because as soon as I put the mass on my hair, many of the rest of the bees in the hive swarmed to protect her. They weren't stinging me, but there were so many, they quickly covered my face and mouth. I didn't want to open my mouth to try and tell you not to worry, for obvious reasons. The best I could do was grunt to let you know I was okay and to stand back while I gently removed them."

"You put them on your head?" I repeated, still not comprehending. "On purpose?"

"Yes. I realized I must have frightened you when you screamed. Unfortunately, I tripped over a rock and landed on my knees. Then the next thing I remember, something hit me on the head. I was lying facedown on the ground, and the bees were gone. I got up and saw you running for help and realized you must have misunderstood what I was trying to show you."

"Misunderstood," I said weakly. "Yes, that's what is was. A misunderstanding."

"When I fell to the ground, a few of the bees must have been upset with being smashed, so they let me know they felt threatened. I have a couple of stings on my neck and hands, but it's no big deal. I've been stung hundreds if not thousands of times. Fortunately, I only swell up for a short period of time, and my body is quite used to it."

I sincerely needed a drink, or thirty-seven, to bring my anxiety down from the stratosphere. But we had less than thirty minutes until the next challenge, so I'd just have to figure out some way to suck it up and deal. "Well, I'm glad you're okay" was the best I could come up with for the moment.

We were silent the rest of the way back to the castle. All the while, I argued internally with myself about whether I should tell him the truth about the branch. The in-law guidance offered no advice for this situation. It was clear that I should be honest, but it really didn't say anything about volunteering information that might make me look like a complete lunatic.

"Lexi, stop for a second."

Oh, crap. Could he see the guilt on my face? Or had he finally realized that I was terrified of bees and that I'd been less than forthcoming about my interest and fears? I stopped to face him, a hundred ways to apologize running through my head.

He stepped up and brushed something off my shoulder. "I think our private conversation was bugged," he said, smiling. "Hope Mr. Bee won't share it with the rest of the hive."

I tried to laugh, but it came out more as a choking sound.

We made it back to the castle, and I waited until he disappeared into his room before going into mine. As I fished in my pocket for the key, I felt something move under my shirt and crawl around on my back. I froze in fear, every nerve in my body on full alert.

Holy crap. It was a bee. Maybe two. Maybe half the freaking hive.

As carefully as I could manage, I slid the key into the keyhole, my hands shaking, my breath coming so fast, I wasn't getting any oxygen to my brain. The crawling intensified.

OMG! It was more than one bee. They were walking all over me, moving slowly up my back toward my neck and face.

The key wouldn't turn, and I'd begun whimpering as I twisted it back and forth. Finally, the key turned, and I threw the door open with a bang.

Slash stood in the middle of the room, dressed only in his underwear and in the process of taking off his socks. A small part of my brain registered that he was changing his clothes, perhaps to something cooler than what he wore in the morning. But the rest of my brain was consumed with survival thoughts. He took one look at my face, and alarm flashed in his eyes.

"Cara?"

I was so panicked, I couldn't speak. I kicked off my shoes and ripped my shirt, jeans, and bra off. I threw them wildly around the room.

"Bees," I manage to hiss out between my clenched teeth as I tore off a sock while hopping around on one foot. "They're on me, Slash. Get them off! Get them off!"

"Bees?" Slash looked at me in puzzlement before realizing the door to our room was wide-open and we were both in a serious state of undress. He strode toward the door to close it. I heard an angry buzzing sound near my ear, and as I froze in horror, a bee buzzed around my head and landed on my shoulder. For a moment, the bee and I stared at each other before I shrieked.

"AAAAGH!" I ran toward Slash with the speed, accuracy, and determination of an NFL linebacker. "It's on me!" I shrieked.

TWENTY-TWO

Lexi

I COLLIDED HARD with Slash, who had one hand on the doorknob, presumably to pull the door closed. The momentum of my body accelerating into his propelled us both into the hallway with surprising force. Slash, who'd clearly been unprepared for my full-on tackle, stumbled a few steps before wrapping his arms around me and going down on his butt, me landing on top of him, writhing and hyperventilating.

Slash wrapped his arms around me, trying to calm me. "You're safe. Calm down."

"It's on me. My shoulder. Can you see it? Is it still on me?" I shoved my shoulder into his face.

"No. There's nothing on your shoulder. In fact, I don't see anything…" He paused for a long moment. "…except for our parents."

I immediately stilled and then looked up. Sure enough, both my parents and my parents-in-law stood in the hallway in front of their respective rooms, looking at us with wide eyes. Slash immediately rolled us over, trying to shield me with his body.

Thank God he still had his boxers on.

My mom looked shocked beyond words, and my dad seemed posed to fight Slash if it came to it. I couldn't even glance at my in-laws. My face burned hot with embarrassment.

"Well, this is totally awkward," I finally said.

"What happened?" Oscar asked. "Why are you both lying starkers in the hallway?"

"Oscar!" Juliette scolded him. "Mind your own business."

"He asked a legitimate question," my dad said, crossing his arms against his chest. "Why *are* you lying in the hall in a serious state of undress? And why did you scream? Is he hurting you?" He glared at Slash.

"Hey," Oscar said, stepping forward to defend his stepson's honor. "Romeo would never hit a woman."

"What? I exclaimed in horror, peering over Slash's shoulder. "No, Dad, no. Slash isn't hurting me at all. You've got it all wrong."

Thankfully, at that moment, my mom, social hostess of the year, broke the tension. "Gentlemen, take the testosterone down a notch. Can't you see Slash is trying to protect her honor?" She knelt beside me and Slash. "What happened, honey? A spider? You're white as a sheet. Let me take a look."

She unwrapped a silk scarf from her neck and draped it over Slash's shoulder. Then, before I could say anything, she reached between Slash and me, groping around for a nonexistent spider bite on my body.

OMG.

I wanted to die of sheer mortification. I was lying mostly naked beneath Slash in front of my in-laws, whom I'd just met. And poor Slash. I'm certain he never wanted to be this close to his mother-in-law with her hand blindly fumbling God knew where between our bodies.

"Mom," I managed to get out. "No spiders. I'm okay."

Slash tried to keep stoic and silent even as my mom pulled her hand out from between us, retrieving her scarf and straightening. "If you're sure you're okay, honey, we'll leave you two alone to do...whatever it is you're doing. Come on, Winston. Stop glaring at Slash, because clearly this isn't his fault."

They went back into their room, my mom pulling Dad with her. He looked reluctant to leave. I couldn't imagine what their conversation would be after seeing us like this.

Unfortunately, instead of leaving like my parents had, Oscar peered down at us. "I didn't scare you that badly, did I, Lexi? Are you sure you're okay?"

OMG. How was that even a question? Obviously, I was *not* okay. Not now, not in any universe, not *ever*. I might even have to consider moving to the moon on the next commercial flight. I honestly didn't think there was *anything* I could say in such a situation even if I googled it for the next six years.

Still, I hoped I hadn't given Oscar the impression I hadn't enjoyed his company, because I had. Just not the part where he'd decided to become Bee Man. However, to admit now that I was scared to death of bees after braving a viewing of a hive, and pretending I wasn't, would expose me as fake.

What in the world had I been thinking? I should have been honest from the start about my fear of bees. I was a complete idiot. How much worse could I screw this situation up?

I drew in a deep breath. "Oscar, I... I thought I saw a—"

"Scorpion," Slash smoothly interjected. "She thought there was a scorpion in our bed and ran out of the room.

I tried to catch her, but my feet got tangled and we ended up here."

I just stared at him. It was one of the nicest things he'd ever done for me, even though I couldn't ever imagine Slash getting his feet tangled up. Still, I almost dropped my hands from my boobs to kiss him.

"Come on, Oscar," Juliette said gently, tugging on her husband's arm, clearly embarrassed for us. "Leave the children alone. They're fine."

Oscar didn't respond, but he did give me one last worried glance over his shoulder.

As soon as their door closed, Slash got to his feet, hauling me up and into our room. He shut the door firmly and leaned back against it.

"Where exactly did you and Oscar go after lunch?" he asked.

I sighed and snatched a folded blanket from the foot of the bed, wrapping myself in it. I wasn't going to have this conversation while dressed only in my undies. "Last night at dinner, Oscar told me about his hobby tending beehives. Since I was following guideline number three on my spreadsheet—learning the hobbies and interests of your in-laws—I asked him several questions. As a result of that, Oscar *may* have perceived that I'm genuinely interested in bees, which, in fact, is true, but only in a theoretical sense."

Slash crossed his arms against his chest. "Go on."

"Well, today at lunch, Oscar said he'd noticed an apiary on the castle grounds after we'd completed the maze challenge. He invited me to check it out, and since I couldn't think of a good reason to decline, I said…yes."

"Although you're terrified of bees."

"Yes, Slash, although I'm terrified of bees." I glared at him. Had he heard nothing I'd told him about the spreadsheet and the important guidelines? "I was trying to follow guideline number one: Accept an invitation to do something with your in-laws even if it's out of your comfort zone. Obviously, that was *way* out of my comfort zone. But I really like Oscar, and I wanted to show my eagerness to integrate into your family."

"And by doing so, you violated rule number four: Be yourself."

I sat down on the bed, dejected. "I know. But I didn't expect him to cover himself in bees. I thought the bees were killing him, so that's why I brained him with a branch."

"You...*hit* Oscar?"

"That wasn't exactly the plan, but I wanted to get the bees off. I dropped the branch by accident, whacking him in the head. At least it worked, because the cloud of bees rose off him as soon as I hit him. But then he was on the ground and bleeding, and I thought they were coming after me, so I ran."

"You hit Oscar and ran?"

"Ran *screaming*, to be exact," I amended. "I thought I should go get help." I stopped and stared at him for a moment. "Are you going to repeat everything I say and make it into a question?"

"Maybe?" He stared at me as if afraid to know where the story might go next. I figured it was better to just tell him everything at once.

"The funny thing is, Oscar may or may not know it was me who clocked him with the branch. I'm leaning toward may not, and I'm fine keeping it that way for now. Anyway, as I was running away, he shouted and told me to stop, and that he was fine. I cautiously returned, and other than some apparent stings on his neck and hands, he was alive...although bleeding behind the ear. It's a miracle he only got stung a few times. He was completely swarmed with bees. They were on his face, head, arms. Everywhere." I shuddered just remembering it. "I thought he was going to die right in front of me."

"He's an experienced apiarist." Slash sighed and ran his fingers through his hair. "You should have told him the truth—that you're terrified of bees, spiders, and a wide variety of insects."

I felt worse than ever. "I know. This whole in-law thing is way more complicated than I expected, even though I studied really hard and prepared a spreadsheet. Now I've ruined everything."

He walked over to the bed and sat down, putting an arm around me. "You haven't ruined anything. This is my fault, too. I should have mentioned Oscar tended a small apiary. It completely slipped my mind. But you're overthinking this. My family loves you because I love you. You make me happy, and in turn, that makes *them* happy. You don't have to say or do anything to be part of our family, *cara*. You already belong just by being you."

He took my hand, running his thumb over the scar on my wrist, identical to the one he had on his. "We're in this together for the rest of our lives, remember? Just be yourself, have fun, and relax a bit around my family, okay? Trust me, they will love you for who you are, not for who you think they want you to be."

I sighed again, leaning against him. "You make it sound so easy."

"It's not. Exhibit A—your dad's and my relationship. But it doesn't mean we stop working on it." He reached up to touch my hair, then stood, heading for the balcony. He opened one of the balcony doors, letting the cool air in and causing the curtains to billow.

I pulled the blanket tighter around my shoulders.

"Why did you open the door? It's windy out there and I'm mostly naked, remember?"

"Oh, I assure you, I remember you're mostly naked."

"Then what are you doing? We have to get ready for the next challenge."

"I know, but I had to set the bee free first."

"Bee?" I leaped to my feet in alarm. "What bee?"

"The one that was tangled in your hair." Slash closed the balcony door and turned to grin at me. "But no worries, he's safe and you're all clear now. No more bees. But I *was* hoping you'd join me for a little search among the sheets for that missing scorpion. After all, we do have a bit of time before the next challenge, and we need to release some tension. Plus, we wouldn't want that poor scorpion waiting all that time for us."

I tilted my head at him, narrowing my eyes. "You just made that up about the scorpion, right?"

He gave me an innocent look. Sitting on the bed, he patted the spot beside him. "Why don't we take a closer look beneath the sheets and find out?"

I studied him. "You have a serious bad boy vibe going on right now."

"I'm *astonished* you know what a bad boy vibe is."

"Says the man who dressed in black and bypassed my apartment alarm to sneak in and watch me sleep the first time we met. Oh, I *know* what a bad boy vibe is."

His mouth curved into a grin. "So, this bad boy vibe…are you insinuating I'd disable my firewall for you?"

"Would you?"

"For you, I would. Now, come over here and kiss the bad boy who's willing to lower his firewall for favors from his wife."

I dropped the blanket and crawled toward him on the bed. My hair brushed against his chest, the muscles tensing under my fingertips as I splayed them against his skin. "Okay, but if a scorpion stings my butt, you'll owe me the newest, most expensive insular gaming headset on the market."

"Fair enough," he said, knotting a hand in my hair and pulling my mouth toward his. "But in the spirit of full disclosure, I'm absolutely getting the better deal."

TWENTY-THREE

Slash

LEXI AND I were the last to arrive in the dining room for the challenge. One glance at Mama's face confirmed she knew exactly why we were late. But her eyes danced with delight when she looked my way, making me smile. More than anyone, she knew my heart and how happy I'd become since I'd met Lexi.

Brando stood chatting with Lorenzo near the fireplace. Once he spotted us, he clapped his hands to get everyone's attention. "Welcome back. We're fortunate to have you continue with the games. Both teams had an excellent showing for the first round, so congratulations. Are you ready for the next set of challenges?"

"Challenges, as in plural?" Dad asked. "Will we be splitting into teams again?"

"Yes, there will be two concurrent challenges," Brando confirmed. "This time we'll let you choose your teams, but the challenge will be assigned randomly. Please discuss the composition of your teams. You have five minutes."

Two more challenges, two separate teams...again. I mentally sorted through the best plans of actions to move forward.

We gathered into one large group, and Alessa spoke up immediately. "Should we keep the same teams, Slash? It seemed to work well last time."

I'd already considered it, so I shook my head. "In my opinion, no. I suggest mixing it up this time and have three men and three women on each team. We could divide by physical strength and puzzle expertise, unless anyone has a different suggestion."

No one volunteered a different recommendation, including Lexi, who was watching me. She already knew I intended to separate us once again to help even out the teams' mental capability. If she didn't like that scenario, she didn't show it. Instead, she simply nodded at me.

"What does that mean in terms of who's on what team?" Clarissa asked.

I looked around the group, making an executive decision. "Team A will be me, Gio, Winston, Alessa, Mia, and Clarissa. Team B will be Lexi, Stefan, Tito, Oscar, Vittoria, and you, Mama." I'd taken a risk putting Winston on my team, but we had to work on our relationship one way or the other, and there was no better time than the present. Or at least I'd convinced myself of that.

There were no objections, so we split into our assigned groups and waited for further instructions from Brando.

"Your teams are chosen and set," the gamemaster said. "Regarding the two challenges—one involves games and the other water."

I glanced quickly at Lexi and saw her face go pale. Water was not her thing and would make any puzzle exponentially harder for her and, by extension, her team. Unfortunately, this time we couldn't assign the challenge to the team. I had to rely on chance, and I didn't like doing that.

The gamemaster held out his hands, which were folded into fists. "I'm holding a blue rock in one fist and a black rock in the other. The blue rock represents the water challenge, and the black rock represents the game room. I need one person from any team to come forward and choose a hand. Whatever rock they choose will be their team's challenge."

Before I could say anything, Mia darted forward. "Ooh, ooh! I want to choose. Can I?"

No one protested, so Mia studied the gamemaster's hands and then tapped his left one. "This one. Our team wants this one."

Brando opened his fist to reveal the black stone.

"Games!" Mia shouted, jumping up and pumping a fist in the air. "We got the games. I love games."

Someone groaned while others laughed at her declaration. Brando opened his other fist to reveal the blue stone. Lexi quietly met my eyes across the room. But instead of dread, I saw determination. Water or not, she wasn't going to let her team down.

"Team B, please return to your rooms and get dressed in your swimwear and meet me back here in ten minutes," Brando instructed. "Now, I'm not saying that you *will* get wet, but as water is involved, it's a possibility, and we want you to be prepared. Team A, if you have anything in your pockets, please empty them into the basket on the table and follow me now."

Having already anticipated that, my pockets were empty. I waited until everyone else on my team had left the room. I took one final look at Lexi, who gave me a thumbs-up before following my team to our next challenge. Brando made a right turn and went down another hall that ran behind the marble staircases that led to the bedrooms.

As we were walking, Lexi's dad fell into step next to me. "So, Oscar told me you had a little scorpion trouble in your room. You get that sorted out?"

I tried not to wince. "Yes, sir. All sorted."

"Good. I'm counting on you to keep her safe."

"With my life."

Gio overheard our conversation and stepped up beside us. "Trouble does seem to follow you, brother. Good thing you have Lexi around to keep you safe."

He and Winston laughed at my expense, and my father-in-law gave Gio a friendly slap on the back. I supposed I should be happy that Lexi's father at least liked *one* of the men in my family.

Brando abruptly stopped before a door with a sign.

"The Game Room," Mia read aloud.

"Isn't this entire castle a game room?" Clarissa pointed out.

"Indeed, it is," Brando replied, smiling. "Now, to complete this particular challenge, you must retrieve a golden disc like you found in the first challenge and exit the game room before the time is up."

"When does our time start?" Gio asked.

"The challenge will begin when the last person reaches the room."

"Reaches the room?" Alessa said. "What does that mean?"

Without answering, Brando opened the door. The room was dark until he reached inside the door and flicked on a switch. A light appeared as if at the end of a tunnel. "This way," he instructed mysteriously.

I took the rear position, so I was the last to arrive at the spot where everyone had stopped.

"Are you kidding me," Clarissa exclaimed. "Is that a slide?"

TWENTY-FOUR

Slash

I PEERED OVER Clarissa's shoulder and saw an open door revealing a chute leading to a basement or a lower level.

"A slide? Well, this is right down my aisle," Mia said, clapping her hands.

"Do you mean 'right up my alley'?" Clarissa asked.

I sighed. I was going to have to have a conversation with Lexi about what she was, or wasn't, teaching Mia, because it obviously wasn't working.

"What's the difference between an aisle and an alley? And why do I go up instead of down it?"

"I'll explain later, dear," Clarissa said, patting Mia on the shoulder.

"So, the game room is in the basement?" I asked Brando.

"Seems more like that's where the dungeon would be," Winston muttered.

"Au contraire, Mr. Carmichael," Brando said. "Castrum Augustus was a military fortification and did not possess a dungeon. However, it is an excellent suggestion. It might be a nice touch to add in the future.

Perhaps a place where we can intern participants who fail in their challenges. Sort of like the nonlethal equivalent of losing one's life in our games."

Everyone laughed, except me. I wondered as to the true purpose of the slide.

It was as if Brando read my mind. "I'm sure you're all wondering why Mr. Zachetti would build a slide into a castle. I assure you, it's only to make sure his guests have some fun."

"How steep is the slide and how do we know if it's safe?" Winston asked.

"I assure you, it's completely safe," Brando answered. "But I'll say nothing more, as I don't want to spoil any of the surprises."

"So, you're saying my pregnant fiancée would have had to go down this slide had her team chosen the game room?" Gio asked.

"We would not have insisted your expectant bride-to-be go down the slide," Brando said. "But, thankfully, we don't have to worry about that, do we? Now, when the last person slides down, I'll start the clock. You may not come back up the slide, so please, don't try."

"Do we *really* have to go down the slide?" Clarissa asked, her hands on her hips. "I have white slacks on. Can't we take the elevator?"

"I'm sorry, but you must use the slide. However, if you wish to forfeit the challenge, you may leave the way you came. Just keep in mind that all of you must go down the slide and participate to win the challenge."

Gio shrugged. "Fine. I'll go first and confirm it's safe. You're playing for my honeymoon, after all, so I might as well be the first to take the challenge. See you on the other side." Without another word, he stepped forward on the slide and practically leaped down. There was no sound for a bit, followed by a short scream and abrupt silence.

Everyone looked at Brando with wide eyes before Winston turned toward me, his expression sending a clear message.

Everything is dangerous when you are around.

I sensed a revolt brewing, starting with my in-laws, and no ready plan to mitigate it. I started to say something when Gio called out from below.

"Hey, that wasn't too bad. A little twisty but nothing special. It was fun. Come on!"

"Why did you scream?" Alessa shouted down to him.

"I was just kidding," Gio said, laughing. "Relax. It's perfectly safe, and the room looks interesting. Come down one at a time and I'll catch you."

"Well, that's good enough for me." Mia sat on the slide. "In a while, juvenile," she called out as she disappeared.

Winston and Clarissa rolled their eyes at each other, and I made a note to have my Mia conversation with Lexi as soon as possible. Meanwhile, Alessa stepped up to the slide. "My turn, I guess."

She slid down, leaving me, my in-laws, and the gamemaster in the room.

"Ladies first," Winston said to his wife, sweeping out his arm toward the slide. "Come on, Clarissa, you can do this. We're not going to fail because of a pair of white pants."

"Fine, but *you* go first," Clarissa said. "I want you down there to cushion my fall if it becomes necessary."

"Have it your way." Winston sat down and pushed off. When he called back up to her, Clarissa followed until it was just me and the gamemaster alone in the room, sizing each other up.

"I'll start the clock in fifteen seconds," Brando said

as I stepped onto the slide. "Good luck. I believe you'll find this puzzle quite challenging."

I pushed off, going down the slide at a good clip. Before I hit the bottom, I heard the door above me close. I braced myself so I landed smoothly when my feet hit the floor, then automatically swept the room with my eyes.

The exit door was on the far side of the room with a large digital clock showing a time of 1:59:56 and counting down. The walls were made of stone and were likely a part of the original castle. There were no windows or other obvious means of exit. Strange carnival-style music played through hidden speakers.

The ceiling was high and, oddly, covered with balloons, which were divided by colors and marked into sections by lines of white balloons. I counted quickly, noting there were eight different areas and nine colors of balloons including the white ones. Each balloon area was numbered by a small sign hanging from the ceiling in the middle. Along the left half of the room the balloons were numbered one to four, starting with the one at the far end. For the right half of the room, the balloon numbers ran from five, which was closest to the slide, to the number eight at the far end of the room.

The lighting was dim, but I made out two square game tables set up along the right stone wall. The one closest to me had a chessboard with what looked like a game in progress, a chess timer, a small pad of paper, and two chairs. Farther down the wall, another game table with four chairs had been set up, but I couldn't yet see what game it held.

Across the room from those tables stood an unusual, rectangular table. Two sculpted figures posed like Atlas supported the thick marble top on their backs. From my angle, it looked like large jigsaw puzzle pieces were scattered atop it. Farther along the wall stood a large scale with a circular dial that you might see at a carnival, the kind that would presumably show your weight if you stood on it. Behind that, there appeared to be an ATM.

What the hell?

"What do we do?" Alessa asked me.

The sheer chaos of the layout had to be part of the puzzle, so I considered the best strategy to start. "Let's explore the room for a few minutes. Note any items that strike you as potentially important. Avoid moving anything until we know what and where everything is. Let's take inventory before we decide on a strategy."

The team started to wander around. I headed toward the center of the room, where a pedestal with a rectangular top had been positioned. A dark wooden box, the size of a small microwave and ornately engraved with Roman-style vines and leaves, had been placed atop the pedestal. The box had a hunting bow with a notched arrow carved into the top. A combination lock, the kind you might find on a briefcase or a bike, was embedded into the side of the box. The lock had an eight-digit code.

I left the pedestal without touching the box and strode over to the table with the game I hadn't been able to see upon my arrival. The table was hexagonal in shape and covered with a board game, small tiles, and a tile holder that looked like the one from a Scrabble game. I'd only played the game a few times, but I knew Lexi's parents were enthusiasts.

The game seemed to be nearly finished, as it was covered with tiles and words already in play on the board. In fact, there appeared to be only one player left with any tiles to play. A pen and a small piece of paper with the handwritten words *48 points* sat at the lower right of the board.

I moved on, continuing to take inventory. A wall-size, garish carnival panel hung at the far end of the room, opposite the slide and adjacent to the exit door. Decorated with clowns, the panel had eight doll-size doors arranged in two rows of four. Six black gaming chairs were fixed to the floor and arranged in an arc in front of the panel. Plastic guns were attached by a cable and rested in a holster to the side of each chair. The carnival music came from camouflaged speakers I was now able to detect near the panel.

I startled when Gio's hand landed on my shoulder. "What is this—a circus?" he asked me in Italian.

"It's definitely starting to feel that way with the clowns, a scale, an ATM, and balloons," I replied.

"So, where do we start?"

I turned around to survey the room in its entirety. I honestly had no idea, but we needed to get going. "Okay, team, we've seen what's here. A wide variety of games, some traditional, some not. There's almost a circus feel to things. But it's time to get started. I suggest taking a quick look at the box in the middle of the room on that pedestal together, and then we'll decide how to proceed from there."

Everyone nodded in agreement, so we headed to the pedestal and examined the large carved wooden box in unison.

"It's got an arrow carved into it," Clarissa noted. "And a bow. Perhaps that's significant, although I don't see any archery targets in here. Yet."

I carefully examined the box mechanism. It had a hinged lid held shut by a latch and, of course, the combination lock.

Alessa peered over my shoulder. "The lock has

numbers, letters, and symbols, depending on which digit you spin. The first two-digit columns have letters, the third one has numbers, the fourth one has symbols, and the last four have all letters. Weird."

I gently turned the first digit of the lock with letters on it. The letters were not sequential and contained only five letters: B, K, N, Q, and R. The second column had the letters A through H in sequential order. The third digit had numbers sequentially listed one through eight, and the fourth had: +, #, !, ?, and 0-0. A quick examination of the final four-digit columns indicated they were duplicates of the first four.

I pushed and pulled on the carvings and corners, hoping to find another way to open the lid. I half hoped I'd get lucky and find a hidden panel or drawer but found nothing. I also tried to lift the lid from the hinge side without success. I tried a few random combinations, but nothing happened.

"Slash, check this out," Clarissa called. She stood on the scale and held a piece of paper between her fingers. "You'd think that if they'd spent money to put a scale like this on an island, it would at least work."

"It didn't weigh you?" Winston asked.

She waggled the piece of paper between her fingers and shook her head. "Oh, it weighed me, all right, but instead of confirming my weight on this paper, which I would have had to burn, it just says 'three.'" She stepped off the scale and brought the paper to me.

I examined it. Sure enough, it had one number— three—and nothing else on either side.

Meanwhile, Mia hopped up on the scale. "Hey, it weighed me correctly, too, but I got a piece of paper that says 'two.' What does that mean?"

I thought for a moment. "Clarissa, can you get back on the scale again?"

She obliged, but nothing happened. "It weighed me correctly, but it isn't giving me another piece of paper. How odd."

I approached the scale and stood on it. The needle moved until it accurately displayed my weight. A small piece of paper popped out with the number six on it. Clearly, we were each being assigned a number, possibly by our weight. But why?

"Everyone, examine the puzzle tables more thoroughly," I said. "Gio, come with me." I walked over to the carnival panel and looked between it and the chairs.

"It's a shooting gallery," I said. "You sit in a chair and fire at targets that presumably appear from behind the doors. But there doesn't appear to be any way to start the game."

Gio removed one of the guns and gave the holster a closer look. "There's a small slit next to the holster, but it is too thin for a coin, even if we had any, which we don't." He plopped into one of the chairs, holding the plastic gun in his hands. "You know, this kind of feels like one of those blasters you might find in a laser tag game." He pointed it at the wall and pulled the trigger, but nothing happened.

"We need to figure out how to start the game," I said.

I surveyed the room again. Mia and Clarissa stood near the Scrabble board table, Winston had migrated to the chessboard, and Alessa examined the jigsaw puzzle.

"This is strange," Winston said. "This chess game is already well underway. In fact, it's nearly finished. Can you check this out, Slash?"

As I walked toward Winston, Mia reached out to touch one of the tiles on the Scrabble-like puzzle. Clarissa quickly rebuked her. "Don't touch anything yet, Mia. As Slash cautioned us, we shouldn't move things until we understand what we're doing. Otherwise, we might lose a clue."

Clarissa glanced at me for affirmation, and I nodded my head, tipping an imaginary hat to her. That garnered me a dazzling smile as I joined her husband, my father-in-law, at the chessboard.

"Look at this," Winston said, pointing at the board. "The game is almost over. The setup resembles one of the typical chess puzzles such as white or black checkmates in a fixed number of moves."

I studied it, agreeing with him. "Can you solve it?"

"Probably, with a little time. But it will be tricky not knowing whose move it is or what the puzzle-solving outcome is."

"It's white's move," I said. "The chess timer is pressed down on black's side. That means white's on the clock."

My father-in-law looked up at me in surprise, or maybe grudging admiration. "That's a pretty clever way of letting us know," he said.

"It is. I think it's time to solve these puzzles. Winston, see how many ways you can come to checkmate. Alessa, Mia, and Clarissa, I'd like the three of you to work on the jigsaw puzzle, since I have a hunch the chess game and the puzzle are related. Gio, you check out the scale, and I'm going to take another look at the shooting gallery. Let's leave the Scrabble-style game alone for now. I suspect those remaining tiles are going to mean something to us at some point."

"What about the balloons?" Mia asked, pointing to the ceiling.

"They're too high to worry about right now," I said. "We'll have to deal with them later."

I glanced at the clock, noting thirty minutes had already passed and we hadn't solved a single puzzle.

Still, it wasn't time wasted. I'd already begun to get a feel for the style and patterns Mr. Zachetti enjoyed using. Understanding what we were working with before we started was an essential piece of solving the overall puzzle.

I went straight to the garish panel with the small doors, the carnival music already grating on my nerves. I tuned the music out and focused on the panel. The mini doors were closed tight and surrounded by small lightbulbs. No matter how hard I slid, pushed, or pulled on the doors, they wouldn't budge. On closer inspection, I noticed a rectangular display bar beneath the panel that could light up or display a digital message. Next to that was a small slot about the size of a credit card.

Interesting.

I turned to focus on the six chairs. They appeared identical, with a metal attachment on the right side that holstered the gun. On closer inspection, I saw the tiny, thin slot next to the holster that Gio had mentioned. The slot was in a location where one would typically insert a coin to start the game. I ran my finger gently across the slot. Gio was right—a coin would never fit. If we needed to start the game by putting something in that slot, we'd have to find something extremely thin.

I now focused on the plastic gun. It was held to the chair by a cable that was about four feet long and attached to the butt of the pistol and the base of the chair.

I sat down in a chair and felt it sink slightly. Curious, I pulled out the pistol attached to the chair and pointed it at one of the doors. I pulled the trigger, but nothing happened. I tried sitting in each of the chairs and doing the same thing with zero results.

But I felt as if I was on the verge of something.

"Hey, I'm number one," Gio called from the scale.

"And by the way, I examined every inch of this scale. It seems to be in working order and correctly measured my weight. But like the others, I got a number instead of my weight on this paper." He held up the same-size slip of paper Clarissa and Mia had received between his fingers.

I had a sudden inspiration. I stood up and dug into my pocket, pulling out the slip of paper I'd received from the scale. I tried to slide the paper into the slot on the first chair. It was precisely the right size, but it wouldn't go in. I tried all the other chairs with the same results.

No go.

Frustrated by my lack of progress, I plopped into one of the chairs. I felt the chair sink slightly. On a whim, I leaned over and tried to slip the paper into the slot again. This time there was a slight whirring sound before the chair sucked the paper from my fingers. There was a pause, but instead of the game starting, the paper was rejected.

"I think I'm on to something," I said.

I moved to the chair on my right and tried again. This time, when the paper got sucked in, a small blue light on the side of the gun and the shooting gallery panel lit up.

"Look at that," Gio shouted. "It worked!"

A digital message appeared on the rectangular bar beneath the panel—*Shoot Here to Start Game.* An arrow pointed to a small button at the end of the light bar. Elated, I pointed the gun and pulled the trigger. A second later, a message appeared stating the game would start in three, two, one.

"Game on," I murmured. "Bring it."

TWENTY-FIVE

Slash

I READIED MYSELF for a target. When the first door popped open, I shot and was rewarded with flashing lights around the door, indicating a hit.

Easy. Too easy.

I quickly got into a rhythm of shooting at the targets. However, as the game went on, the doors opened for less time and were widely separated. It became much harder for me to hit all the targets.

Suddenly two doors opened at once, and I could only hit one target at a time no matter how fast I pivoted. The pace continued to pick up until three and four doors were opening simultaneously, making it impossible to hit everything.

The game abruptly ended, with the light bar displaying a simple message.

NO WINNER.

I looked around, realizing everyone had gathered behind me, watching. Winston looked especially stunned. "That was incredibly accurate shooting. Aren't you a computer guy?"

"I am," I confirmed. "But, as you know, I've had some training in other areas as well." It was a huge understatement, but now wasn't the time or place to go into that. Still, if I wasn't mistaken, he looked slightly impressed. It wasn't much, but I'd take it.

"That was incredibly intense, Slash," Alessa said. "What do you have to do to win?"

"Hit all the targets, I guess," I said. "Which is technically impossible for me to do alone."

"I'll help," Gio said. "Remember, marksman is my profession."

He sat down in the chair next to me and inserted his ticket. It was sucked in by the chair but rapidly ejected. "Hey, why can't I play?"

"I had to try a different chair before I found one that worked," I said.

Gio tried another chair with the same results. "It's still not working."

"What if the number we got from the scale corresponds to the seat you have to use in order to play?" Clarissa suggested.

I looked down at my seat and realized she was right. The chair sank when you sat in it, which meant it could be recording our weight. The chair that had worked for me was the farthest away from the scale. I was number six, so Seat Six was mine.

"That's exactly it," I said, impressed with her observation skills. "The seat sinks down when you sit in it, so it must be activating a hidden scale that weighs the individual to make sure the right person is in the right chair. I suspect that means we're *all* going to have to play the game to win."

"I've never played a shooting game before," Mia said, throwing up her hands. "What if I can't hit anything?"

"Just aim, fire, and do your best," Gio said. "You'll get the hang of it after a few shots."

"Gio is right," I added. "We have to try. Everyone, please get your number out. If you don't have a number yet, go to the scale and get one. I'm sitting in Seat Six, so Seat One must be at the far end of me. Gio, you are number one, so go see if the first chair works for you."

Gio sat in the chair and slid the paper in. After a moment, his gun lit up. "It worked."

"Good. Everyone else, seat yourself according to your number."

"I told you we should have bought the body armor before we got to the castle," Winston said to Clarissa in an exaggerated whisper as he headed to the scale.

I pretended not to hear.

When everyone had sat down and inserted their papers, I began a countdown. "On the count of three, I'm going to shoot the start button and the game will begin. One, two, three."

Everyone started blasting, with us easily hitting all the targets, some taking multiple hits. But as we progressed through the game and the pace intensified, we began missing too many targets while hitting many of the same ones.

I swore beneath my breath as the game came to a crescendo and ended with a displayed message on the panel bar.

NO WINNER.

"We didn't win?" Clarissa said, sounding surprised. "Why? We shot so much stuff."

"We didn't hit all the targets," I pointed out. "Or at least, not enough of them."

"That's because we need to coordinate our efforts better," Gio said. "Like everything else, we need a strategy."

I nodded, so Gio continued. "How about if Slash and I take two targets apiece, and everyone else be responsible for just one target? Ignore all the other targets, no matter how tempting they are. But when your target shows itself, shoot everything you've got at it."

Gio and I took the top and bottom targets on the sides, as they were the most difficult. We assigned everyone else the remaining targets.

"Is everyone clear which target is yours?" I asked.

The team nodded, so we retrieved our papers that had been ejected from the chair slots and inserted them again.

"Just remember, focus on your target of responsibility and don't look at anything else," Gio cautioned us. "Also, the doors seem to open and close to the beat of the music. See if you can anticipate when your door will open by syncing your shots with the music. It might help you with your aim."

I started the game again, and we began firing. All seemed to be going well until the game, and by extension the music, began playing frantically. The targets came fast and furious, keeping me focused exclusively on my targets. Things were moving so fast I had no idea how everyone else was doing.

Finally, the game ended, and we lowered our guns. I glanced down the row of chairs, noticing everyone looked completely wiped out.

Suddenly Mia leaped from her chair, pointing at the message bar beneath the panel. "Look! We won!"

WINNER—TOTAL SCORE 6370. TAKE YOUR CARD.

A credit card-size piece of plastic popped out of the slot to the right of the display bar.

Mia danced around, high-fiving everyone in the room, completely pumped by the win. "That was more fun than a barrel of orangutans. Who knew I would take so well to shooting?"

"I'm just glad we don't have to do it again," Winston said, reholstering his gun. "That was more stressful than a week of cross-examinations in criminal court. Plus, I couldn't help but notice my wife hit every target. Remind me not to piss you off any time soon, dear."

"Good plan, sweetheart," Clarissa said, batting her eyelashes at him.

I couldn't help but be amused—and maybe a little comforted—by the thought that the in-law who liked me the least was the worst shot.

I glanced at the clock to see how much time we had left. Thirty-seven minutes. I walked over to the panel and retrieved the card that had been spit out near the display panel. Alessa joined me there.

"What does it say?" she asked, looking curiously at the card.

I examined it carefully on both sides. "Nothing as far as I can see."

"Put it in the ATM. Let's see what happens."

I didn't have a better idea, so I walked over to the machine and inserted the card. The screen leaped to life and asked for a PIN. Everyone crowded around trying to see.

"A PIN. Really? Is nothing ever straightforward around here?" Clarissa said with a sigh.

"Maybe we have to solve another puzzle in order to get it," Alessa suggested.

"Possibly." I watched the blinking message asking for the PIN. "Unless someone recalls seeing a four-digit number somewhere."

"Four digits," Mia said. "The final score. Wasn't the final score a four-digit number?"

"*Si*, it was," I said. "Is it still displayed on the panel?"

Mia ran over to the panel. "Oh, no! It's gone. The number is gone."

"I remember the first two numbers were six and three," I said, "but I'm not sure about the rest."

"It ended in a zero," Clarissa said. "I'm pretty sure of that."

"Well, that gives me a place to start," I said. "I'll take this from here. But we're running out of time, so everyone else, please get back to your puzzles. We need them solved as soon as possible."

As everyone dispersed, I methodically went through the numbers for the PIN until I arrived at the right number—6370. The machine flashed, and to my relief, the cash slot opened. However, instead of cash, a tray popped out holding two metal darts about eight inches long with plastic feathers.

I picked the darts up carefully, examining them. I wasn't sure what to do with them at this point, so I headed over to see how things were going at the puzzle table.

"What are those?" Alessa asked, pointing at the darts.

"That's what came out of the ATM."

Mia held a palm-size puzzle piece in her hand for a moment before Clarissa reached over and snatched it from her, sliding it into place.

"Do you know what to do with them?" Alessa asked.

"Not yet," I admitted. "I'm hoping you'll give me a clue." I took a closer look at the puzzle, realizing they'd finished more than half of it. "Good work."

"It's mostly Clarissa," Alessa admitted. "She has mad puzzle skills."

"That's kind of you to say," Clarissa said, not lifting her eyes from the puzzle. "Although I'll admit this one is tougher than most. It doesn't have a lot of pieces, maybe thirty-five or forty, but there are no straight edges, and we don't know the shape of the assembled puzzle. It isn't square or rectangular, I can tell you that. That means we have no edge or corner pieces to provide reference points."

Interesting how Lexi and her mom weren't as different as she believed.

I studied the puzzle further, noting another difficulty. "There are only black pieces on a white background, so you can't even assemble the puzzle using the background. That has to be extra difficult."

"It is," Alessa agreed. "But we're making progress."

They were, but clearly because of Clarissa's wicked puzzle skills. I had a feeling there was a lot more to my mother-in-law than I, and possibly her daughter, knew. I put the darts aside and helped them work the puzzle. It was assembled quickly with five of us working on it. When it was finished, we stepped back and studied it.

The message was clear. An arrow pierced the outline of a balloon.

"We have to shoot the balloons with the darts," Alessa said, looking up at the ceiling. "I presume the gold disc is hidden in one of them. But there are only two darts and a lot of balloons."

I looked at the clock. "And only twenty-five minutes to go. I don't see how we could pierce all of them in that time frame with just two darts." I walked over to Winston. "How are you doing on the chess game?"

"I have the solution—checkmate in two moves. It was the only possible solution, and I checked everything I could think of. But I don't know what to do next."

We all gathered around the chess table. "Can you show me your solution?" I asked.

"Should I move the pieces?" Winston asked. When I nodded, he picked up the queen. "The first move is the queen to the F6 square, putting the black king in check

190

from the white bishop. There are only two moves black can make at this point, but if he makes either one, the knight to E7 produces a mate."

"Well done," I said and was rewarded with a smile from my father-in-law. Was I sensing a slight thaw in our relationship or was it wishful thinking?

Winston moved all the pieces until he was able to checkmate the king. He clicked the timer when it was each player's turn to move and brought the game to a close. We all looked around the room, waiting for something to happen, but nothing did.

I rechecked the chessboard, the table, the timer, and flipped through the pad of paper, but found nothing. What was I missing?

"Why is there a pad of paper here?" I murmured aloud.

"Maybe we need to write down the solution," Clarissa said. "Can you write down the solution, Winston?"

"Of course, if someone could hand me a pen," he said.

"There's one at the Scrabble table," Mia said, racing over to pick it up.

Winston took the pen and wrote down QF7+, KD8, BC7#.

"The box combination lock," Alessa said. "This could be the combination."

I took the paper from Winston and headed for the box. I examined the lock and determined that Winston's solution matched the lock options on the pedestal box. "The solution works, with one caveat. There are only eight digits on the lock, and there are eleven in Winston's solution."

"Try using just the white moves," Winston suggested. "That should equal eight."

"OK, I'll set the combination as you read me the white moves," I said.

Winston listed each character, and I entered them on the lock. As I entered the last digit, we were rewarded with a clicking sound. To my surprise, Winston grinned, slapping me on the back and giving me a high five. That might have been the most positive interaction we'd ever had.

I carefully lifted the lid. A small green metal crossbow lay nestled on a white velvet cloth, along with another dart. I gently lifted the crossbow from the box and handed it to Gio.

"You're the man for this job," I said. "So, from this point on, it's your show."

"Fair enough, but what's the plan? Which balloon do I shoot? All of them?"

"There wouldn't be time," I said. "We have seventeen minutes left. By my calculation, there's no guarantee we'll be able to pop them all in time, even as good a shot as you are."

"Well, we can't just give up," Mia said, putting her hands on her hips. "Not after going through all of this."

"Perhaps we should look and see if there's anything else in the room that might pop the balloons," Winston suggested.

We did a quick search but found nothing. Inspired, Gio grabbed a laser pistol and started the shooting game again, this time firing at a balloon. When he shot at the balloons, it caused them to glow slightly but didn't pop them.

"That's strange," Alessa commented.

"Maybe we can stack the tables, stand on them, and pull down the balloons?" Mia said.

A quick examination of the game tables proved all were too low and anchored solidly to the floor.

"What about the Scrabble game?" Clarissa asked. "It's the only puzzle we didn't solve. I bet the answer to this resides at the Scrabble game."

We gathered around the table and began to examine the game more closely. As I'd noted earlier, the game was nearly over. Only one player had letters left to play. All the other tiles had been played, leaving a crowded and nearly full board. The tray with tiles had seven letters: M, J, G, E, Z, I, H. A piece of paper with the handwritten words *48 points* sat at the lower right edge of the board.

"That's where I found the pen," Mia said. "Lying right next to this piece of paper with these words on it."

"Maybe it means we need to pop balloon number forty-eight," Clarissa suggested.

"We wouldn't know which way to start counting to find balloon number forty-eight," Winston said. "It would take hours to count and then pop random balloons. There has to be another solution."

I picked up the paper, making sure there was nothing on the back side. "The clue must be here somewhere. Read the board carefully and check the tiles in the last tray. Maybe something will pop out at us."

We crowded around the board, looking for a clue. Clarissa and Winston focused on moving the tiles in the tray around, trying to form a word, since they had both admitted they were Scrabble addicts.

Time ticked past, and the pressure began to affect everyone. I'd come up with absolutely nothing, and neither had anyone else. I noted their actions had become more abrupt, almost frenetic. I felt their frustration. It was difficult to know the answer we needed was buried in the details right in front of us.

"The only words we can make with the letters in the tray are JIG, HIM, and HEM," Winston finally said.

"Clarissa and I can find places to play them on the board to make four-letter words like HOME or TIME, but nothing fits that would relate to forty-eight points or the balloons. We're completely stumped."

I closed my eyes and took a deep breath. Logic had to be the key. "Okay, let's try working this backward. How can we get forty-eight points? We have a lot of high-value letters, but we would still need to use a double-word or double-letter score to reach forty-eight points, right? So, let's look for the places where we might do that."

Since the board was full, there were only a couple of spots where we would benefit from a double-word score. As it stood, only one of the triple-word squares was uncovered. In fact, the only place to take advantage of the triple word score was to connect it with four letters to the start of a word already played. TEEN.

Clarissa suddenly squealed. "Eighteen! That's it! Eighteen."

She picked up the letters and added the EIGH to make eighteen. "If you count the points, we get two points for the G, eight for the H, which is a double-letter score, and all the rest are one point each. That totals sixteen points, and if we triple that, it's forty-eight points."

"Good work, darling," Winston said, kissing her on the cheek.

"I agree wholeheartedly with that," I said. "Good work to both of you."

"Okay, so now we have two numbers, forty-eight and eighteen," Gio said. "How do we determine what balloons to shoot from that? Come on guys, just give me something to shoot at."

I considered for a long moment. This decision could make or break the game for us. "I think we're only working with the number eighteen. The words *48 points* were already written out for us and didn't require any problem solving."

"That still doesn't help," Mia said. "How do we know which balloon is number eighteen?"

I strode to the base of the slide and turned back to look up at the ceiling. The balloons were divided by color and numbers. Did the colors mean anything? Those closest to me on the right were red, blue, green, and orange, in that order. On the other side of the ceiling, they were purple, yellow, brown, and black. Eight different colors.

A single width of white balloons divided each of the colored sections. I could discern no pattern to the colors. I stole another glance at the clock, noting we had less than seven minutes to finish.

Since the balloon sections were numbered, that had to be a clue. Numbers were my thing, so I had only to figure the pattern. The sections ran from one to four down the left side of the room, starting at the shooting gallery, with the right-side sections numbering five to eight back toward the far wall.

Eight was the highest number. There was no eighteen.

Big picture. Big picture. It was as if my subconscious was trying to send me an important message. It's right there in front of you—just wake up and see it.

But there was no Section Eighteen, and none of the sections had eighteen balloons.

I let my vision and thoughts drift as I looked down the length of the ceiling balloons. After a moment, I took a deep breath and snapped back into the moment. My eyes immediately latched onto the one sign to the left, and then the eight sign to my right. One and eight. Eighteen.

The answer *was* right in front of me.

Stepping forward, I pointed at the signs. "While there isn't a Section Eighteen in here, the one and eight sections are adjacent. I bet the balloon we're looking for is in this line of white balloons between the two sections here."

Winston came to stand beside me. "That, son, was brilliant thinking. Well done."

I wasn't sure I'd kept the surprise from my face at his compliment, but thankfully he wasn't looking at me, but at the balloons.

Gio, too, was staring at the white row of balloons. "But which balloon? There are twelve of them."

"I don't know," I admitted, looking at the clock. It slipped just under five minutes. "Shoot them all."

Gio set the dart, cocked the crossbow, aimed, and fired at a random balloon in the row. There was a loud pop and a fluttering of a tattered balloon, but nothing else, and no gold disc.

"Uh, we have a problem," Gio said. "The dart stuck to the ceiling. That means we're down to two darts and ten balloons."

"That gives us less than a 20 percent chance of picking the right balloon," Winston said, blowing out a breath. "There has to be something we're missing."

"If we're trying to find a golden disc, shouldn't we be able to see the outline inside the balloon?" Alessa asked. "Or, at least, won't one of the balloons look heavier than the other?"

"How can we tell in this light?" Clarissa complained. "If only it were a little brighter on the ceiling."

"That's it!" Mia said, running to the shooting gallery.

I immediately knew what she was thinking. "Come on, everyone," I said, following her. "We need to shine our laser guns on the balloons. Hurry."

Everyone except Gio rushed to their chairs, inserted their number, and got their guns ready. I shot the start button to start the game. The doors with the targets began opening and closing, but we ignored that and instead aimed our guns at the balloons on the ceiling.

Two minutes left.

"Aim at the first balloon," I instructed.

Everyone aimed his or her gun at the first balloon until it glowed. I couldn't see anything that looked like a dark shape hidden inside the balloon. "Nothing. Let's try the second one."

We proceeded down the line of balloons, skipping past the popped one. When we got to the seventh balloon, it looked different, darker.

This is it.

I glanced at the clock. Fifty-two seconds.

"Everyone, keep your gun aimed on the seventh balloon. Gio, it's on you now. Don't miss."

Gio inhaled a deep breath. He cocked the crossbow, stretched up, and fired. The dart glanced off the side of the intended balloon, popping the one next it.

"Oh, no!" Mia wailed.

"It's okay," I said, trying to assure everyone. "We have one more dart and one more try." Gio seemed unusually nervous, not that I blamed him. It was likely why his aim had been slightly off. I needed to calm him, help him focus, and there was one way I *knew* would work. We'd always been fierce competitors, and although I was the older brother, I'd never, *ever* handed him a win. If he'd won it, he did it fair and square.

"Would you like me to take this one?" I asked casually. "I'd hate to tell Vittoria you lost her luxurious honeymoon because you missed a shot. Wouldn't you rather I take the blame?"

Gio gave me a steely glare as he set the dart and

cocked the bow. "A most gracious offer, big brother, but missing wouldn't be nearly as bad as giving up the win to you. You'd never let me live it down."

He turned smoothly, aimed, and fired.

A balloon popped, and a second later, a brass disc hit the floor. Shrieking with excitement, Alessa scooped it up and raced to the door. "It says forty-five," she shouted, punching the number into the keypad.

The door opened with three seconds to spare, and we piled out of the room, cheering, hugging each other, and talking excitedly.

"That was an incredible shot, Gio," Alessa said, handing him the brass disc. "Well done."

"It did take him three tries," Mia groused. "And only after Slash goaded him."

I laughed, slapping Gio on the back. "Three tries, brother? Could this be an indicator of the systemic decline of the Italian special forces?"

"Very funny, hotshot," Gio said, grinning. "If *you'd* come up with the solution just a little earlier, I could have had some breathing room."

"What would have been the fun in that?" I answered, slinging my arm around his shoulder as he chuckled.

As we walked down the hallway, it occurred to me I hadn't had this much fun with my brothers in a long, long time.

I had Lexi to thank for that.

TWENTY-SIX

Lexi

I WAS THE most nervous I'd been since we'd arrived at the castle.

First, I was in a bathing suit. Granted, I'd put one of our shower towels around me, but it didn't make me feel any more comfortable. I'd already shown more than enough skin to too many people as it was in the short time we'd been at the castle. I was not looking forward to doing more of it.

Second, knowing our challenge would involve water caused my anxiety to spike, which was why Slash had shot me a worried glance when my team determined the water challenge would be ours. He knew how much water scared me. Although I could dog-paddle if I didn't have any other choice, I worried panic would drown me before my swimming ever did.

Get a grip, Lexi.

I glanced at Oscar, who looked as uncomfortable in his swimsuit as I did. We shared a little smile, acknowledging our mutual discomfort and like-minded reactions. It was strange, but I'd discovered that Oscar and I had a lot more in common than I'd ever expected. He seemed to dislike crowds, social situations, and dressing up as much as I did. We both were a little (okay, a lot) quirky. Of course that made me feel more comfortable around him. I guess it's true that kindred souls seem to find each other and, apparently, marry socially adept partners.

On the other end of the spectrum, despite being seven months pregnant, Vittoria looked as glamorous as a movie star in a sleek white two-piece, her thick black hair falling in stylish ringlets around her back and shoulders, proudly showing off her pregnant belly. Stefan and Tito could have passed for Greek gods with their ridiculous arm muscles and abs of steel. Even my mother-in-law looked lovely in a sea-green bathing suit.

Nope, I wasn't feeling insecure whatsoever. Ugh.

I gulped air and tried to look confident as we followed the gamemaster toward the left wing of the castle and down a flight of stairs. We stopped at a long glass wall, through which we could see a large indoor pool.

"Welcome to the water challenge," Brando said. He pointed to his left, where two dozen red swim caps hung on the wall. "Please choose a cap that fits and put it on. Then take a dry towel from the opposite wall."

So, we *were* going to swim. My anxiety hiked up another notch as I found a cap that fit. I pulled it onto my head, feeling a strange lump embedded in the back. It felt awkward but not uncomfortable, though the cap came lower down on the nape of my neck than I expected.

"Hey, there's something in my cap," Tito said, running his fingers along the lump. Guess we all had the mystery lump.

"Please do not touch it," Brando said. "I will explain in a minute."

Shrugging, I tucked my ponytail inside the cap and helped Vittoria into hers after she asked for assistance. She had so much hair, it took me a few minutes.

When I finished, she looked down at her protruding belly and winced. "The baby is kicking hard. Hey, Lexi, want to feel it?"

I totally, absolutely did not want to put my hands on her stomach. I didn't like strangers touching me, and I didn't like touching strangers. But Vittoria wasn't a stranger—she was soon to be my sister-in-law. The spreadsheet guidelines reminded me I needed to go out of my comfort zone for family, so I nodded.

"Sure," I said somewhat hesitantly. "What do I do?"

She took my hand and pressed it against a part of her belly. "Hold it there and wait."

I held my hand there. Sure enough, a minute later I felt a strong kick. My mouth dropped open. "I felt it! The baby kicked my hand."

"*Si.* He or she is quite the active one. Gio and I are going to have our hands full."

"That was really cool. I didn't expect that to be so cool."

She smiled. "You're going to be an aunt. Aunt Lexi."

"Yes, I am." Weirdly, I felt proud. "Neither of my brothers has kids, so this little one will make me an aunt for the first time." I leaned over close to Vittoria's stomach and lowered my voice to a whisper. "Hey, you in there. If anyone ever tries to make you take ballet lessons or play on the football team and you don't like it, your uncle Slash and aunt Lexi will be on your side. And, by the way, math is cool."

I straightened and smiled at Vittoria. Now I was going to have to look for coding books for babies when Slash and I got back to the States.

When we were finally ready, Brando had us line up. He walked behind us and pushed the lump at the back of our caps. I heard a click and wondered what the heck was going on. Brando, however, did not explain.

Instead, he opened the door to the pool and ushered us in. The strong scent of chlorine assailed me, but the room was warm, certainly heated. Brando instructed us to drop our towels on a couple of lawn chairs just inside the door before leading us to the edge of the pool.

I swallowed, my blindingly white limbs now completely exposed in my boring, navy-blue one-piece suit. Thankfully, no one even glanced my way.

The pool had five swim lanes and appeared to be about thirty feet long. Sunken stairs led into the water at both ends. The bottom of the pool sloped quickly toward the center, and the marking on the side of the pool indicated the deepest part was three and a half meters, or just over eleven feet of water. Identical stylized drawings of a fish had been drawn on the long walls of the pool.

A hot tub that looked like it could seat eight or ten people sat to the left of the pool. The tub was sunken several feet below the pool deck with steps leading down to it. Apparently, it wasn't working, as it held no water and had a maintenance sign in the middle of it.

Along the deck, a long-handled aluminum pool skimmer with a mesh scoop hung on the wall. Next to it was a coiled pool hose that could be presumably attached to a vacuum, although I didn't see one. Along the far wall, two dozen metal cans had been placed side by side on the floor. They looked like the old-fashioned gas cans with removable lids I'd seen strapped to the back of jeeps in some World War II movies.

Odd.

"Now, if I may have your attention, I will present the challenge to you," the gamemaster said. "If you look at the bottom of the pool, right in the center, you'll see something floating."

We all leaned over, peering into the water. I saw a large light-blue square.

"That blue square is a float attached by a one-meter chain to a heavy weight that lies on the bottom of the pool," Brando explained. "Underneath that weight, beneath more than eleven feet of water, is the golden disc you seek. Before you try to dive in and grab it, let me warn you that the swim caps you are wearing cannot get wet. They've been alarmed and will sound if they touch water, other than a light spray, or if you try to remove your cap. If anyone's alarm goes off, the challenge will immediately end, and you'll have forfeited the game."

Okay, that was weird. "Our heads can't get wet?" I repeated to make sure I understood him correctly. "The challenge is to retrieve the disc without activating an alarm. That's it?"

"That's it. Retrieve the disc and have it on the pool deck before the clock runs out without activating the alarm on your caps."

"But how do we get the disc if it's underwater and we can't get our heads wet?" Vittoria asked.

Brando smiled. "That's for you to figure out, my dear. Now, if you have an emergency or if you decide to end the game early, just push the red button on the wall over there. The challenge will be terminated immediately."

He studied us for a long moment, his eyes stopping on me. "I will add that no one has ever completed this challenge. A few teams eventually figured out how to do it, but they lacked the time to complete the necessary tasks. So, I sincerely wish you good luck, because if you solve it, your team will be the first. According to the pool clock, it is now 1:25. I'll see you in precisely two hours."

He walked away, locking the pool door behind him.

"Great," Oscar said, eyeing the pool. "An impossible challenge."

"Nothing is impossible," I said absently, already calculating. "It's just a puzzle we have to figure out in a compressed timeline. We can do this."

For a moment, we all stared into the pool at the weight lying at the bottom of more than eleven feet of water. Although I'd told Oscar nothing was impossible, retrieving that disc in two hours without going underwater seemed almost inconceivable. Except there *had* to be a solution, so our job was to find it.

"I'm going to start with the obvious," Stefan said. "How about one of us swim out there, keeping our heads out of the water, to get a closer look at the float and weight? I'm happy to volunteer. I can tread water for several minutes."

I studied the lump and its location at the back of Stefan's cap. "It's risky," I finally said. "If we get any water on the cap, we're finished. Let's see what else we have to work with first."

Vittoria pointed to the skimming pole hanging on the wall. "Could we use that to snag the float and pull it up? The pole has a hook on the end of the handle, so maybe we can use it to our advantage.

"I don't think that the pole is long enough unless it telescopes a lot," Oscar commented.

"Guess there's one way to find out." Tito walked around the pool and removed the pole from the wall to see if it could be extended like a small folding umbrella. He pulled on it, but it didn't extend. "Well, there went that good idea."

"Maybe if we were able to get closer, we could reach down and hook the float," Juliette suggested.

Her comment got everyone running around to see

what might float. Vittoria tried putting one of the pool recliners in the water, but it sank quickly to the bottom. She doubled down and dropped another one, trying to stack them in the water. However, the recliner drifted as it sank and only partially landed on the first recliner.

"Those are heavy," Juliette scolded. "You shouldn't be lifting them in your condition."

"They weren't heavy," Vittoria protested. "I promise."

"She's right," I said. "The typical aluminum recliner is light enough to lift, even if you are seven months pregnant."

"I hope we didn't need one of those to solve this puzzle," Stefan said with a tinge of annoyance in his voice. "We ought to be thinking this through instead of just randomly trying things. What if our solution was to disassemble those recliners and use the parts to make a longer pole?"

"I'm sorry," Vittoria said, somewhat crestfallen. "I didn't think of that. It just looks so impossible."

"It was actually a good idea," I said. "If it had worked, it could have helped us. Besides, given the location of the lounge chairs, we can hook them and pull them back up if we need them. Good try, Vittoria."

I glanced around the room and saw Juliette exploring the cans along the far wall. "You know, Lexi, these cans are empty," she said. "Perhaps we could fill them with water and drain the pool."

⸱ I did a quick calculation of the amount of water in the pool. I paced off the sides, estimating the pool was ten meters by five meters or thirty-three by sixteen feet. Given the average depth of approximately seven feet and seven and a half gallons per cubic foot of water, that would equal more than twenty-five thousand gallons.

"It's a good idea, Juliette, but it won't work. Even if

we could somehow drain one hundred gallons a minute and keep it up, it would take us more than two hours to drain even half the pool. Given the size of those cans, and the fact that there are only six of us, we'd be lucky to drain thirty gallons a minute. Plus, we have no place to put the water."

"We could dump it into the hot tub," Vittoria offered.

"We could," I agreed, "but it's only a fraction of the size of the pool. We might get the top foot of the pool in the hot tub, but that's it. And that wouldn't be enough to get down to that float."

Tito paced back and forth along the pool deck. "What if we tied a bunch of the cans together and made a raft to float out into the middle of the pool, where we could try to snag the float with the hook on the pool skimmer?"

"Does anyone see a rope?" I asked. "Or any way the cans could be tied together?"

While we were talking, Stefan started to go down the steps into the water. "Brrr...the water is cold."

Juliette said something to him in Italian, and I presumed she was reminding him not to get his head wet.

"I'll be careful, Mama," he said. "But I wanted to see if things looked any different from a water-level perspective."

He walked gingerly down the steps and sat down, so the water came up to his chest. He stared at the water for a long moment.

"Do you see anything?" Vittoria asked.

"Not really," he said in frustration and stood.

The motion sent ripples of waves down the length of the otherwise motionless pool. The waves continued as Stefan sloshed out of the pool. My eyes tracked the ripples until they crossed the point over the float in the center of the pool.

"Wait. There's something there," I said. "There's something under the water right over the float."

By the time I said it and the others had turned to look, the ripples were smaller and nothing was visible. "Do that again," I instructed. "Stefan, make a few gentle waves in the water, please."

Stefan stepped back into the pool and began making waves, careful not to splash his head. Again, the ripples changed as they passed over the float, but now I knew for certain something was there, invisible, and just under the water.

"I didn't see anything," Vittoria said, frowning.

"There's something there," I said. "But we need more waves. Tito, Juliette, can you help him?"

"Of course," Juliette replied.

She and Tito stepped into the pool next to Stefan. Carefully they bounced up and down in the water to make even bigger waves. Suddenly, an obvious square pattern emerged. From my rough calculations, it was about thirty inches per side.

"I see it," Oscar shouted. "Lexi's right. There's something there." He leaned over the side. "I can't quite tell what it is, but it looks square."

"It's square," I confirmed. "Everyone, out of the water. Any ideas how we can check it out more closely?"

"We can try poking it with the pool skimmer," Tito suggested, dripping water onto the pool deck.

"Let's try," I said.

Tito took the skimmer and poked at the object. "Yah. It's square and clear. It slides down the side under the water when I poke it, but the skimmer isn't long enough to confirm if the sides go down more than a few feet."

Logically, I considered what that meant. "Since it is just under the surface of the water, if we could lower the pool level a little bit, we might be able to examine it better. So, that means we have two main problems to solve. First, we figure out how to lower the water level. Second, we need to somehow get closer to the middle of the pool."

"The cans," Juliette said. "You said we could use them to lower the water level a little."

Tito, Stefan, and Oscar raced for the cans and started dipping them in the pool and dragging them over to dump into the empty hot tub. The cans were heavy, and the men were straining. After watching them for a minute, I quickly realized that wasn't going to work as a solution.

"Does the side of the can say twenty liters?" I asked Stefan.

He checked the can and nodded. "That's what it says. No wonder it's so heavy."

Twenty liters equaled about five gallons. That meant that if they were filled to the top with water, they weighed almost forty pounds apiece. To lower the water level several inches, we'd have to remove about 480 gallons. We had neither the time nor the strength to do that.

"That's not going to work," I said. "There's too much water for us to move and not enough time. Let's find another solution to lower the water level. Oscar and Juliette, can you circle the pool to see if you can figure out another way to get to that box? The rest of us will work on figuring out how to lower the water level."

I looked around the pool, hoping inspiration would strike. My eyes stopped on the pool hose hanging on the wall. And, just like that, I had an idea.

"Someone, help me with this pool hose." I ran over and grabbed the three-inch-diameter hose off the wall and hauled it over to the pool, throwing it into the water by the steps. I carefully stepped into the water and pushed the hose under. "I could use a little muscle here."

Stefan and Tito joined me in the water. "We're going to create our own makeshift siphon, which means we have to get all the air out of the hose," I explained. "Also, Vittoria, could you bring one of those cans over here?"

The three of us quickly got the hose submerged. Starting at one end, I pushed it lower so the air would move up the hose. I continued walking on the hose until it was completely submerged and floating just under the surface.

"Vittoria, give me the can now." She handed it down to me, and I filled the can completely with water, pressing the end of the hose against the can so the water wouldn't escape and no air could get in.

I carefully brought the can to the surface. "Tito and Stefan, get out of the pool and take the can and this end of the hose and put them in the bottom of the hot tub. Set the can on its side, keeping the hose sealed tight against the can until they're both lying down. Everyone else, help them by moving the hose as they drag it to the hot tub."

I stayed in the pool, moving the hose forward and lifting it onto the pool deck as the rest of the team dragged it across the pool deck. Thankfully, we managed to get it right on the first try. When Tito pulled the can off in the bottom of the hot tub, water started gushing out of the hose into the hot tub.

"It worked!" I exclaimed. "Great job, guys."

I carefully climbed out of the pool and padded over to the hot tub, watching the speed and volume of the flow. It was a rough guesstimate, but I calculated it would take about thirty minutes to remove the desired amount of water. That would make it about 2:20. That gave us just over an hour to complete the rest of the challenge.

Hopefully that will be enough time.

"Lexi, come here, please," Juliette said. She and Oscar had returned to the deck at the middle point of the pool and were talking softly. Juliette held the dripping skimmer pole. "While you guys were working with the hose, Oscar and I took a closer look to see if we could disassemble the last remaining pool recliner for parts. We might have been able to make a useful pole retriever if we had all three recliners and were able to quickly disassemble them, which, without tools, would be highly unlikely. Added to which, two of them are currently residing at the bottom of the pool. Oscar and I tried to pull them up with the pool skimmer, but they kept slipping off the hook."

"So, we're out of luck?"

"Not entirely, as we've just discovered something that looks promising," Oscar interjected. "Well, Juliette did." He beamed at his wife. It was so sweet, my heart tripped slightly. I wondered if I had the same adoring expression when I looked at Slash.

"What did you discover?"

Juliette shook the pool skimmer slightly, sending water droplets over my feet. "It occurred to me that maybe that square wasn't the only invisible thing in the pool. So, Oscar and I tried walking carefully around the edge of the pool, periodically sticking our feet in, looking for anything that might indicate the presence of another object. But we found nothing. Then I tried to put myself in the mind of the puzzle maker. He'd expect us to look for a pathway of some kind to get to the middle of the water, right? Logically, that pathway would have to be anchored to the sides. I told Oscar to get the skimmer and stick it in the pool at about a forty-five-degree angle. Within the first two meters, Oscar hit something. I think we've found one of the walkway anchors."

There was a splash at the end of the pool by the cans, and I turned to see Vittoria get in the pool, with her head perilously close to the water. She was hanging on to one of the cans, using it as a float. It was rocking unsteadily as she tried to ride on the can to keep her head out of the water. As I watched in horror, she almost tipped over as she tried to find her way back to the steps, her head coming within inches of the water.

Before I could move, Tito raced over to the steps and into the water. He slowed as he got close to Vittoria so the waves from his motion wouldn't further disturb her precarious balance.

"Hold still," Tito instructed her. "Keep your head up and I'll pull you back until you can stand up."

TWENTY-SEVEN

Lexi

TITO SLOWLY PULLED Vittoria to the pool steps. When she was finally able to stand, I realized I'd been holding my breath for the last minute.

"Thanks, Tito," Vittoria said. "That was closer than I'd like to admit. I've used floats in the water for many years, so I was confident I could ride one of the cans to the middle, but the shallow depth of the cans, the stiff sides, and my pregnant belly made them much harder to ride than I expected. Clearly, it didn't work. We'll need another approach."

"No problem, Vittoria," I said. "It's just one more option we can eliminate, which is useful in determining the best course of action." I pointed at the hot tub. "In the meantime, can you keep an eye on the water level and let us know when it's getting close to full?"

"Of course," she said, shaking the water from her hands and legs.

"Come on, Lexi." Juliette tugged on my arm. "I'll show you what we found."

My in-laws and I walked along the side of the pool, away from the end with the siphon hose. Approximately eight feet from the center, Oscar stopped and put the skimmer into the water. It hit something solid.

I bent down at the edge of the pool, peering into the water. Now that I knew it was there, I could see it. "It's a glass platform about a foot under the water. It looks like it's about a half meter wide and curves upward toward the edges. I bet that makes it harder to slip off if someone was to walk on it. I'm not sure how far it goes out, but my guess is all the way to the center of the pool, directly above the float."

To test my theory, Oscar pushed the skimmer as far out as it would go, and from that I was able to confirm the invisible shelf pointed on a diagonal toward the square in the center of the pool. Running the skimmer back toward the edge, the platform stopped about a foot from the edge of the pool.

"This glass or plastic walkway is our access to the float and eventually the disc," Juliette said. "We just have to be careful with the first step."

No kidding, I thought. We had a means to the middle, but what was the best way to test it out? If the walkway was a red herring solution—much like trying to float on the cans—and wouldn't hold our weight, then we'd be sunk, literally. I was also troubled about the slippery walkway and not being able to see it while walking on it.

Still, it was a way forward.

"This is amazing deductive work by both of you," I said to Oscar and Juliette. I felt ridiculously proud of my in-laws and couldn't wait to tell Slash about their contributions. "Well done."

Tito knelt beside me and reached out to touch the walkway. "*Das ist clever.* I'm confident the curved effect on the path will help keep us from slipping off."

"The key will be to make sure we don't accidentally step off the edge," Stefan said.

The mere thought of standing on a glass walkway in the middle of a swimming pool caused me to shudder. I hoped no one noticed.

"Maybe we could first lay out the skimmer pole out along the walkway to help identify where it is," Vittoria called out from near the hot tub.

"Great idea, Vittoria," Juliette said. "Especially since it seems the path goes straight toward the middle. We could use that to orient our steps."

"I'll do it," Tito said, giving me a grin. "Walk the glass pathway. I may be the heaviest, but I have wicked good balance and I'm pretty athletic."

His confidence was infectious, and I decided that there wasn't a better choice, especially since I really, *really* didn't want to do it.

We all looked at each other, and when no one objected, Tito slid the skimmer into the pool and along the walkway as far as it would go.

Oscar and Stefan stood on either side of him, holding his hands as he gingerly stepped off the edge of the pool. He carefully placed one bare foot near the handle of the skimmer and paused. Convinced it would support his weight, he added the other foot and stilled again, standing on the walkway.

The pool area fell completely silent. I think we were afraid if someone spoke, Tito would fall off.

"*Das ist* the moment of truth," Tito said. "Let go of my hands."

Oscar released his hand first, followed by Stefan. Tito was now alone, balancing on the walkway. He waited a moment until he felt he was comfortably balanced. He took a tiny step forward, almost a shuffle, and then another. After he'd gone a few feet, he bent down and slid the skimmer the rest of the way until it hit something in the vicinity of the square. Confident the path went all the way to the middle, he started to walk more confidently out to the middle. When he reached the glass box, he knelt and felt around the area.

"It's a box with an open top. As far as I can tell, it goes down pretty far, possibly to the bottom of the pool. It's definitely centered over the float." He stood, putting a partial amount of weight on the edges of the box, pushing down to see if it gave. "It doesn't move, which means it probably goes all the way to the floor."

"Use the hook on the skimmer to snag the float and see if you can pull it and the weight up," I instructed.

Tito took the skimmer and slid it into the box toward the float. He jabbed at the float several times before giving up. "We've got a problem. The float is too tight against the sides of the box, so the hook can't catch on anything. I can't push the skimmer past it."

"Any ideas how to proceed?" Stefan asked me.

Right now, I had nothing. I needed time to think, but we were running out of time. My brain was busy calculating a million things, and nothing made sense.

"Vittoria, how are we in terms of water in the hot tub?" I called out.

"More than halfway full," she said. "And the water is still coming out."

I estimated that at this point our makeshift siphon had drained at least an inch off the top of the pool. The result was that the top of the square box was now clearly visible, the sides protruding slightly above the water.

"I'm going to check the other side of the box," Tito suddenly said. "Maybe there's a latch or something that will set the float free." He set the skimmer down and carefully lay across the square on his stomach, reaching his hands down the other side of the box, searching.

"I've got something," he said excitedly. "I think it's another walkway. This one connects to the other side of the box. Would someone go check the other side of the pool to see where it starts?"

Stefan and Oscar went to check it out, and within a minute, they confirmed the presence of a second diagonal walkway. At this point my brain had started to come up with a potential plan.

Unfortunately, that plan meant I needed to see the box at the center for myself. I had to force the words out of my mouth.

"I need to get a look at the box and the float for myself," I said.

"Are you sure?" Tito asked, giving me a smile from the center of the pool. "Walking on a glass walkway requires confidence, balance, and coordination."

"Very funny. Don't worry, if I fall in, I'll just tell Slash you pushed me."

He laughed, and his teasing made me feel a little better, which maybe was the point, so I faced the walkway with determination. I took Oscar's and Stefan's hands to stabilize me on either side as I stepped onto the walkway, the water sloshing over my feet. My legs were shaking, which wasn't a good sign, but I forced myself to be calm and let go of both of their hands.

This was a bad idea. A terrible, horrible idea.

I stood there for a good minute, letting my body and mind get used to the idea I was on the walkway and summoning my courage to move farther. Eventually, I began taking tiny steps forward toward Tito and the middle square. Before I knew it, I was almost there.

"You've got this," he said encouragingly, stretching out a hand.

I made the mistake of looking at Tito's hand instead of my feet, and my foot slipped.

"Noooooooo!" I shrieked, reaching toward him.

TWENTY-EIGHT

Lexi

I HEARD NUMEROUS gasps as I teetered back and forth on the walkway, trying to regain my balance.

Please, please don't screw this up. Don't fall in.

Too late I realized I wasn't close enough to reach Tito's outstretched hand. Windmilling my arms and contorting my body to stay upright, I'd pivoted almost 180 degrees. For a moment, I thought I'd recovered, but I knew I was near the edge of the walkway, because I could feel the slope. I put my foot down to catch myself and felt…nothing.

I was going down.

A cry escaped my lips as I fell. Except, by some miracle, I didn't fall. Something snagged my right arm, and I straightened.

Stunned, I turned and saw Tito had caught me. He'd placed one foot on the corner of the box and, by leaning over, had just managed to reach me.

"Easy there," he said. "You gave us quite a scare."

"Holy crap." My heart pounded. "Not half as much as I gave myself. *Danke*, Tito." My foot finally found purchase on the walkway, so I steadied myself. Still clutching Tito's hand, I knelt next to the box and closed my eyes for a moment to get a hold of my emotions.

Once I'd settled the rapid beat of my heart, I got back to the matter at hand. The first thing I noted about the clear box was although the water level in the pool had sunk below the level of the box, the water level in the box itself had not dropped. The water inside the box was now higher than the pool level by almost an inch.

Interesting.

"Tito, look at this," I said as he knelt on the other side. "The water level in the box isn't dropping. That must mean that the box is self-contained and the water in the box is separate from that in the pool. Otherwise, it would push the water out the bottom and the levels would equalize."

"Okay. And that means exactly what?" Tito asked, his expression blank.

"It means we don't have to drain the entire pool," Vittoria called out. "We just have to drain the water in the box to get down to the float and the weight."

We all turned to look at Vittoria in surprise. She held up her hands. "What? I had physics in school, and I'm a schoolteacher. Just because I'm pregnant doesn't mean I lack brain cells. Not yet, anyway. I presume this means we can stop draining the water from the pool and start doing it from the box."

Grinning, I gave her a thumbs-up. "You're exactly right, Vittoria. Guys, help Vittoria raise the siphon in the hot tub as high as it will go *without* taking the end of the hose out of the water. That should slow or stop the flow, so we don't fill the hot tub with any more pool water. Then, someone needs to grab the end of the hose that's in the pool and move it here to the box so we can siphon the water."

"On it," Stefan said, wading into the water and

grabbing the hose with his feet, pulling it up. Holding on to the side of the pool and keeping one end underwater, he dragged it toward us.

Juliette and Vittoria lifted the hose in the hot tub to slow the drain. While they did that, I quickly began calculating how much water we could siphon out of the box and put into the hot tub. When I came up with a number, it meant we didn't have enough room in the hot tub.

"Guys, we're going to have to remove some water from the hot tub with those cans and dump it," I said.

"Why?" Tito asked.

"Because the volume of water in the clear box equals roughly half of what we've already removed from the pool. But since the hot tub is more than halfway full, we're going have to first remove several feet of water from the hot tub before we can make this work."

Oscar looked at me in surprise. "You just did all of that calculating in your head? Right now?"

"Yes, right now. Do you want me to explain my calculations?"

"God, no. I'm just…incredibly impressed. Well done."

Wait, my father-in-law was impressed by my mental calculation skills? Really? I was totally going to sit next to him at all our family functions.

"Lexi, where do you want us to dump the water from the hot tub?" Vittoria asked, still holding the hose.

"Well, we can't put the water back in the pool," I said. "And we can't afford to raise the water level here. Anyone see a floor drain?"

"There should be one here somewhere," Stefan said. "Almost all pool decks have a drain of some kind for deck washing or in case the pool has an overflow. It might be hidden. We need to look for it."

Everyone started looking around, except for Tito and I, who stayed at our post in the middle of the pool and Vittoria at the hot tub.

"It's here by the hot tub," Oscar finally cried out. "It had a cover on it, so it didn't look like a drain."

"Excellent," I said as Stefan arrived, pulling himself along the wall toward Tito and dragging the end of the pool hose with him.

"Tito, can you get that hose out of the water and into the box without letting any air into it?" I asked. "You'll have to press your hand tight against the hose end while moving it into the box water."

"*Jah*, I believe so. I have big hands and I don't have to lift it very far." He stood up and walked along the walkway to retrieve the hose.

"Stefan, hand the hose end off to Tito now. Everyone else needs to get that water out of the hot tub as fast as you can. Juliette, Oscar, and Stefan, please climb into the hot tub. We need to form a bucket brigade to get that water evacuated as quickly as possible. Juliette, you fill the cans with water and pass them off to Oscar and Stefan. You two take the cans to the edge of the hot tub where Vittoria and Tito, once he finishes here, will tip the cans over the side and allow the water to run toward the drain. I'll stay here and keep the hose in the water on this end."

"Good idea. We definitely don't want *you* walking on water again." He chuckled, and I rolled my eyes at him.

"But I don't understand, Lexi," Oscar said. "Why can't we just siphon the water into the drain directly?"

"Because the end of the siphon *has* to be lower than the level of water in this box in the pool," I explained. "If they're at the same level, nothing will happen since the pressure is equalized. Since the bottom of the hot tub is lower than the current level of water in the box, it will siphon until the water levels equalize. Every inch of water we remove from the hot tub is another inch we can siphon out of the box."

"But that means that we won't be able to drain all of the water out of the box, right?" Juliette asked. "Because the box in the pool is much lower than the bottom of the hot tub."

"Unfortunately, that's true," I admitted.

"So, how are we going to get the rest of the water out of the box?" Stefan asked, pulling himself out of the pool on the side and heading toward the hot tub.

"Well... I'm still working on that part."

Tito knelt on the walkway, pushing his hand against the hose opening and lifting it out of the water. He walked carefully toward the square and pushed it underwater in the box. I took over from there, making sure it stayed put under the water.

"Good job," I said.

"I have the easy job." He flexed a bicep, causing me to smile. "You're the brains and I'm the brawn."

"Oh, you have plenty brains, too. Not every muscular Swiss guy can make it to the Vatican's Swiss guard."

"Hey, Lexi!" Oscar yelled from the hot tub. "It's working! I can feel the water swirling around my feet. It's siphoning the water from the box."

"Excellent," I said. "Now get that water out of the hot tub and fast."

"We're already on it," Vittoria said, tipping the first can and spilling the water onto the floor.

"Tito, go help them," I instructed.

"*Jawohl*, General," he said, saluting.

I watched as he carefully navigated the walkway back to the pool deck and headed toward the hot tub. He might have thought I was a general and knew what I was doing, but I didn't feel nearly as confident as I should.

Everyone was counting on me to solve the puzzle, but I was running out of ideas and time.

Speaking of time, when was the last time I'd checked? Worried, I looked over at the clock and saw it read two thirty. That meant we had fifty-five minutes, or less than an hour, left. By my calculations, the siphon would remove less than half of the water. We needed to remove the rest once the siphoning stopped, and quickly.

What could we do to get rid of the rest? I considered and discarded the idea of lowering the cans into the box, filling them, hauling them up, and then dumping them over the side. My instincts told me that there wouldn't be enough time and the work would be very difficult perched on the walkway. Still, without getting rid of the water, there was no way to reach the float without getting my head wet.

What am I missing?

"Lexi, how are you doing?" Juliette called out. It warmed my heart that even in the middle of the pressure of the puzzle, she was worried about me. Or maybe she was worried I *wouldn't* figure things out.

I decided honesty was the best policy at this point. "I'm okay, Juliette, but I'm running out of ideas here."

"Don't try to overthink things. I find that our brains, like our muscles, work better when they are calm and relaxed."

Of course she'd say that. Juliette was a nurse, used to being a calming presence in the midst of a storm. She faced life-and-death pressure on a daily basis. Remembering that gave me perspective, and I began to relax a little.

Still, Juliette and the rest of the team had no idea how much Slash and I had riding on these challenges. There was much more at stake than a nice honeymoon for Gio and Vittoria. There were a lot of people, many of them young and vulnerable, counting on us to solve these challenges. Then, of course, there was the pope, who believed Slash and I could do anything. Which wasn't true, but when the pope is counting on you, what's a girl to do?

I had to up my game.

"What do you think our options are at this point, Lexi?" Juliette asked, interrupting my thoughts.

I took a deep breath and tried taking her advice to relax. "Well, after we siphon as much water as we can out of the box, we have to lift the float and the weight and somehow get the golden disc off the bottom of the pool without getting our heads wet. That's it in a nutshell."

"Why can't we use the cans to remove the water in the box like we're doing at the hot tub?" Stefan interjected.

"I thought of that, but there's too much water to move and not enough time. I need to come up with a faster solution. There are many other related problems to solve, but that's the big one."

"In my experience, we tend to make our problems more complicated than they really are," Juliette said. "The best first step is to define the biggest problem standing in the way of your goal. Often, if you solve that, the rest will fall into place."

Defining the problem was the easy part, in my opinion. But I humored her just the same. "Our biggest problem is getting all the water out of the box as quickly as possible. We have no other options until we can do that."

"Why can't we continue to use the siphon?" she said. "It's working wonderfully."

"For now, yes. But the siphon will stop working once the level of the water in the box reaches the same level as the water in the hot tub."

"Oh." She stopped to consider that for a moment. "So, if I understand this correctly, at a certain point, the problem is you can't lower the siphon any more to continue to drain the water."

"Correct."

"Then to use the siphon past that point, we have two choices. Lower the drain end of the siphon or raise the water in the box."

"Both are impossible, I'm afraid," I said. "We can only lower the siphon end in the hot tub as low as the bottom of the tub if it's empty. And raising the water is opposite of what we're trying to do, which is to lower the level of the water in the box so we can get the disc without getting our heads wet. Therein is the conundrum."

"Hmm…" she said, falling silent for a moment. "You know, this problem kind of reminds me of an old Aesop's fable I used to read to Romeo, Stefan, and Gio."

"An Aesop's fable?"

"Yes. All this talk of raising and lowering the water reminds me of a story called 'The Crow and the Pitcher.' You may have heard of it before. The crow badly wanted a drink, but the water in the pitcher was too low for him to reach. The crow couldn't tip over the pitcher, so instead, he figured out a solution. He dropped rocks into the water until the water rose to where he could drink it. I often remember that fable because afterward, the editor annotated the story with the quote 'Necessity is the mother of invention.' I've used that motto during many challenging times in my life. Now, I don't know where you'll find your rocks, but I have faith an intelligent woman like yourself can figure out a solution from that."

I stilled, finally understanding where she was going with the story. Why hadn't it occurred to me before? "Juliette, you're brilliant. You just solved this puzzle."

"I did?" she asked. "Because I don't know what comes next."

I smiled at her. "Don't worry. I do."

Rocks. I needed rocks, but what could I use in their stead? I turned and stared at the crew dumping water from the hot tub. They were slowing down a bit, but I could see the results of their efforts. They'd gotten into a good rhythm on the brigade, and the water in the box was already down well over a foot in just a few minutes.

Cans. We'd use the cans. We had twenty-four of them, and each can could hold five gallons. That would displace 120 gallons of water. I estimated the siphon would leave about 220 gallons in the box before I started using the cans as my so-called rocks. I wouldn't be able to get *all* the water out of the box using the siphon and the rocks, but there would be less than three feet left when we were finished. That should be enough. It *had* to be enough to retrieve the disc.

I didn't want to slow the brigade's progress, as it was critical to our success, but I needed some help. I asked Juliette to take a quick break from the hot tub.

"Would you please bring me the remaining empty cans from the end of the pool?" I asked her. "I think I've found my rocks."

TWENTY-NINE

Lexi

THE WATER BRIGADE was currently using only five of the cans, which left nineteen cans for me to use.

"Vittoria, would you please help Juliette bring me all the remaining empty cans?" I asked. "Stack them up right at the edge of the pool. Then go back to help at the hot tub. Tito, when Vittoria and Juliette are back on duty at the hot tub, can you come out here and help me? I have an idea."

The two women started bringing the empty cans to the edge of the pool deck, standing them side by side until all the cans were there. Juliette and Vittoria switched places with Tito, who came over to the edge of the pool, awaiting my orders.

"Bring me the empty cans," I instructed. "Two at a time."

He brought the first two cans, carefully walking along the glass walkway. I took one of the cans and filled it with pool water. I screwed on the cap, hefted it onto the edge and pushed it in the box, handle up. The water line rose slightly. Encouraged, I filled the second can to the brim.

Before I could push the second can into the box, Tito leaned over my shoulder. "I assume you've figured out how to get the cans back out of the box. Someone is going to have to go down there to get the disc, right?"

I paused, realizing I hadn't thought that far ahead. I needed to slow down and think things through or we'd never win this challenge.

Before I could come up with a solution, Tito reached around me and picked the skimmer up off the walkway. He waggled it in the air. "How about the hook?"

I took the skimmer from him and slid the hook onto the loop handle of the can at my feet. It fit perfectly. "You're the man. Thanks, Tito."

I pushed the second can into the box as Tito watched. "I have to be careful not to dislodge the end of the siphon hose when I drop the can in, handle up, so we can better remove them later."

The second can sank to the bottom, and we could see the water rise again and then fall as the siphon drained it away.

"Bring me the rest of the cans," I said.

He brought the rest of the cans, and together we filled them, screwed on the caps, and carefully pushed them into the box. By the fourth can, the water level in the box had stabilized, with the siphon draining off the water about as fast as we could add new cans.

"It's working!" I said, pumping a fist. "Stefan, how's the level of water in the hot tub?"

"It's about a knee-high from the bottom and about one and a half meters below the pool deck," he replied.

I glanced at the clock—twenty-seven minutes left. "Good. Keep going and do *not* stop. We've got to get as much water out as we can working in tandem."

This would work. It had to work.

"After ten more minutes, you guys can stop dumping

water out of the hot tub," I said. "Then as you empty each of the remaining cans, bring it to Tito for me to fill and drop into the box. We're going to need every single one of those cans to make this work."

"Understood," Stefan said, not breaking his stride. Everyone was working so hard, even Vittoria, who hadn't complained once. I was in awe of my family and friends. To say they were incredibly strong and intelligent would be an understatement.

In the meantime, I continued to monitor the water level. I never thought watching water drain could be so mesmerizing. I kept one eye on the clock, relieved the water level in the box had already dropped several feet below the surface of the pool. The siphon was continuing to drain, though it was slowing down. When the ten minutes were up, I eventually added the remaining five cans, pushing the siphon hose lower and lower into the water.

"I think the siphon has stopped," Stefan said, wiping his brow and leaning against the side of the hot tub. "I'm not feeling any water coming out the hose anymore."

"Me neither," said Juliette, perching herself on the rim of the tub next to Oscar as Vittoria sank to the steps leading up to the hot tub.

I glanced up at the clock—fifteen minutes left. "Okay, it's showtime. Let's get those cans out of the box." I pointed to Tito. "Bicep Man, you're up."

Tito flexed and then met me on the other side of the box. I pulled the hose out of the box and tossed it into the pool.

Tito knew what to do. He squatted and leaned over the box. Lowering the skimmer down into the box, he slid the hook beneath the handle of the can nearest the top and pulled. The can came up, and he set it on the walkway in front of me. I simply pushed the can into the pool and out of our way. The water level in the pool no longer mattered.

One by one, Tito effortlessly pulled the cans up and out of the water. Each easily weighed thirty-five pounds. I couldn't help but admire the muscles in his back. He was working like a machine. I was sincerely grateful he was on our team.

Finally, Tito pulled the last can out of the water, revealing less than a foot of water above the float. Tito sat up, stretching his back. "That was fun," he said. "Now what?"

"Well, one of us has to slide down into the box, grab the float, and pull it and the weight up and retrieve the disc. Then we have to figure out how to haul the person back up and hand the disc over to the gamemaster."

Tito peered down into the box. "Sorry, Lexi, it won't be me. I'm too big. Plus, you're going to need me here to help lower down and haul up whoever goes in. I think there is only one person suitable for this job."

I looked at the rest of the team. Stefan and Oscar were also too large, and Vittoria was seven months pregnant. That left me and my mother-in-law. No matter how scared I was, I was *not* going to ask her to take my place. Plus, Tito was right. Physically, I was a good four inches taller than Juliette and, according to my calculations, height would be an important part of this challenge.

Unfortunately, I was also the absolute *worst* person for this part of the challenge because...can anyone say *underwater glass coffin*?

I swallowed the panic that rose in my throat. The team wanted me to drop down into a glass box surrounded by water and not hyperventilate and pass out? Just the thought of it terrified me.

But there was no time to wimp out. Inhaling a deep

breath, I maneuvered myself into a sitting position on the side of the box, my feet dangling into the box. "Guess I win this lottery."

Tito leaned forward and gave me a peck on the cheek. "I'll lower you down as far as I can. Don't worry, you can do it. We'll be here to make sure you stay safe."

I narrowed my eyes. "You'd better, or I'm going to tell Slash about that kiss."

He laughed. "If he hadn't already married you, I would have challenged him to a duel for you. And you can tell him that, because he already knows. Now, come on and let's do this. We have only ten minutes left."

"Okay, but how are you going to get me out?"

"You let me worry about that part. You focus on getting that disc."

He stood over me, and I held up my hands. Bracing his feet against the side of the box, he grabbed each of my hands in a wrist lock. "Summon that courage, yah?" he said. "You can do this."

"Yes, I can," I said, my voice cracking as he began lowering me down, the water pressing in on every side of my mind. I closed my eyes and stretched out my legs until the motion stopped.

"That's as far as I can reach," Tito said. "I have to let go now. You ready?"

I wasn't, but what could I do? "You can let go of me, Tito. Just don't leave me."

"Never."

He let go, and I fell. I pressed my hands alongside the glass box to slow my descent. A couple of seconds later, my feet hit the float and my downward motion stopped. I froze, my heart pounding. Water began slowly oozing up the sides around the edges of the float.

"I made it," I shouted up to Tito.

I swallowed my panic, reminding myself to trust science and my careful calculations. As the water rose to my ankles, up to my knees, and finally to my thighs, I recited the Pythagorean theorem until I realized it had stopped.

I exhaled a breath. My calculations were sound, and I was safe for the moment. Turning diagonally in the box, I carefully squatted, the water rising to my waist. I stretched out my fingers, feeling along the edge of the float to get a grip on it. To my dismay, the top was curved and nearly flush to the sides of the box.

"I can't get underneath the float," I called up. "It's set flush against the side of the box, and I can't get a grip."

"Stand on one side of the float," Vittoria yelled. "See if you can get it to rise on the other side."

I tried, but the float still fit too tightly against the box. "It won't tip more than an inch or so, and I can't get my fingers under it."

I continued feeling along all four sides, but the float didn't give anywhere. Uncomfortable, I tried to adjust my position by pressing my elbow into the side of the box. I slipped and almost lost my balance when my right elbow slipped off the surface into an imperceptible indentation in the wall.

"Wait! I found something," I shouted. "Stand by."

I explored the indentation farther with my hands, discovering that there was a shallow opening on the opposite wall of the box about eighteen inches above the bottom. If I could maneuver the float at the same level as the opening, I should be able to get my hand under the float and then lift it.

Gritting my teeth, I put my back against the wall of the box above the indentation and tucked up my knees. The float rose until it was stopped by my butt. Carefully, I put my hands into the indentation and flipped the float, putting one of my feet on the bottom of the pool. The water reached to my upper chest.

No freaking pressure.

Standing on one leg, I reached under the float and grabbed the chain that held the weight. I pulled it closer and saw a metal object in the shape of a fish. Pretty, but it wasn't the prize I sought.

"Lexi, we're running out of time," Tito called down. "What's happening?"

"I've got the float and a fish weight in my hand. But I can't see the disc yet. How are you going to get me out of here?"

"We already have taken care of that," he said. "Just get that disc, and hurry."

I examined the fish weight further but found no hidden compartment and no way to open it. Where the heck was that disc?

I gingerly lowered my other foot to the bottom of the pool. Standing on my tiptoes, I began feeling around with my feet. Suddenly I hit something with the side of my foot. I maneuvered my foot over the object, clenched my toes, and somehow managed to lift it high enough to grab it without putting my head underwater.

The golden disc.

"I've got it!" I shouted, relief flooding me. "I've got the freaking disc. Get me out of here."

I slid the disc into the top of my bathing suit so I wouldn't drop it.

There was silence, and then Tito appeared at the top of the box, tossing something down to me. It hit me on the shoulder, and I grabbed it. A towel rope. The team had knotted several of the towels together and formed a loop at the bottom.

"Step into the loop and we'll pull you up," Tito called down.

I didn't know exactly who "we" was, but I stepped into the loop and pulled it tight, wrapping the upper part of the rope around my wrist. When I was ready, I gave the rope a hard tug. "Pull," I shouted.

As they began to pull me up, I realized at some point, they'd have to reposition themselves to avoid falling off the walkways.

"When you need to reposition, I'll wedge myself against the sides of the box," I shouted out. "Just be careful."

A minute later, they changed positions, so I wedged myself in. I'd lost all track of time since I'd descended into the box. I had no idea how much time we had left.

When I was about halfway to the top, Tito instructed me to wedge myself into the side of the box one more time. "I think that is far enough. If you can hold yourself there, I can reach you."

"Okay, but you'd better not drop me."

His face appeared above me in the box opening. "Oh, sure. Drop you and have Gio forever on my case for ruining his honeymoon or drowning his sister-in-law. *Nein, meine liebe frau,* I will not drop you."

He thrust his hands down, and I grasped his forearms. In seconds he lifted me out of the box and onto the walkway next to Stefan.

"You did it," he said, giving me a hug.

"*We* did it," I corrected him. "And careful, don't push me in the pool by accident."

I glanced at the clock, surprised to see we still had four minutes to go. It felt like I'd been down there for hours. "Let's get out of here."

"Yes, and everyone be extra careful. You do *not* want to fall off after all we've been through," Juliette warned. I held on to Stefan's shoulder as we shuffled toward the side. I was pretty sure I heard a collective sigh when I stepped onto the deck.

I dropped to my knees, beyond relieved to be on solid ground again. I pulled the disc out of my swimsuit, holding it above my head. Everyone swarmed me, cheering and laughing.

"We did it!" Everyone shouted and congratulated each other.

I had to admit it was a great feeling. I also knew there was a certain fable and aphorism I would never, *ever* forget.

After a moment, I walked over to Juliette and handed her the disc. "This win belongs to you. Slash was right. You really *are* an amazing woman. I know we've just met, but I'm already glad that of all the mothers-in-law in the world, I get you."

Juliette threw her arms around me. "And I know exactly why my Romeo fell in love with you. You, my dearest Lexi, are truly a rare gem. Nonna was right about you. You're absolutely perfect for him."

A loud buzz sounded, causing me to jump. I glanced up at the clock, noting our time had run out. The gamemaster walked through the door at that precise moment. For a moment, we stared at each other, and then Juliette held out the disc.

"We did it," she said simply. "Here's the golden disc."

I noted he wasn't surprised, so I figured he'd been watching us from a hidden camera or two, monitoring our progress. Still, his eyes swept over the wreckage in the pool room—the cans, chairs, skimmer and hose, and the long towel rope. Then his gaze landed and stayed on me.

"I'm beyond impressed," he said. "Are you sure you're just a family gathered together for a wedding? I feel like there is a lot more to you people than meets the eye."

"Oh, there's definitely a lot more," Juliette said, putting an arm around my shoulders and pulling me to her side. She snagged her husband with her other arm until the three of us were joined together. Oscar put his arm around Stefan, and Stefan pulled Vittoria to his side. I motioned to Tito, and he stood beside me, sliding an arm around my waist. We stood linked like that, facing Brando.

"We're a tight-knit family," Juliette said quietly. "Together we're strong, stubborn, loving, and…" she glanced sideways at me, smiling "…awfully smart."

A lump formed in my throat. I'd had no real idea what it would be like to have in-laws, but from most of the literature I'd read, I'd expected it to be more of an ordeal rather than a blessing. How wrong I'd been.

Brando clapped, the sound echoing through the pool room. "I do believe Mr. Zachetti will be most surprised. He might even have to make this challenge harder now."

"Oh, no!" we said, practically in unison. "It was plenty hard."

We laughed, and even Brando chuckled as he led us out of the pool room and into the hallway. As instructed, we hung our caps on the hooks and took fresh towels from the other side. We wiped ourselves down and wound them around our waists, still laughing and chatting.

I'm pretty sure I was the only one who noticed the gamemaster had fallen quiet on the way back to our rooms. If Slash's team had also succeeded, we'd be four for four.

That meant if we continued our winning streak, Brando would have to tell Mr. Zachetti he was on the hook for a substantial payout to the pope. It made me happy we were inching toward securing the money for the orphanage, but I had a feeling that things would only get harder after this.

Slash and I would have to up our game even more.

THIRTY

Lexi

WHEN I GOT back to the room, Slash was already there. "We did it!" I said, jumping into his arms and nearly knocking him over onto the bed. "I survived the pool, although barely. What about you?"

He dropped me onto the bed and sat down next to me. "We successfully completed our challenge as well. Your parents were incredible. They played an integral role in solving our puzzles, and most were complex. I couldn't have done it without them. I'm beyond impressed. After the challenge, your dad pulled me aside. He said I'd done a great job leading the team through the puzzle. He also apologized for insinuating I would hurt you. It all seemed quite genuine and not like your mother had forced him to say it. I was actually at a loss for words."

"Even my mother couldn't force my dad to say something if he didn't want to. That's great, Slash. Wonderful progress. And while we're speaking about our parents, yours are totally the bomb. I mean it. Oscar found the first walkway, and your mom solved the one critical obstacle I couldn't by telling me an old Aesop's fable. Tito saved me from falling into the pool, and Stefan and Vittoria came through with solutions and answers when I needed them. They were *all* invaluable partners."

He smiled, twirling a piece of my hair around his finger. "I can't wait to hear all the details."

"Likewise, but first I really need a shower to get the scent of chlorine off me."

After the shower, I put on a simple dark-green dress that I'd bought online a couple of weeks ago. It was the first time I'd tried it on, so I hoped it fit okay. The length was right, just a little past my knees, which wasn't always a given, since I'm tall. It had a modest slit along the right leg to give my legs some more mobility. The belt around the middle fit perfectly and highlighted my high waist. I put on a pair of low-heeled black pumps and the diamond studs Slash had given me. My brown hair hung loose around my shoulders, although I preferred it in a ponytail. Makeup was not my thing, but I swiped on some mascara, lipstick, and a little cream blush. That was as good as it was going to get.

After Slash got out of the shower, he dressed in navy slacks with a light-blue shirt and no tie. He looked and smelled amazing, as usual.

"We still have fifty minutes until dinner," I said as he enfolded me in a hug. "What do you want to do?"

"Sit by the fire and drink wine," he said. "And get caught up on all the details of your challenge."

He placed his suit jacket over the back of one of the chairs in front of the fireplace. He added a few pieces of wood to the fire and lit it. "Let me go see what wine I can find for us. I'll be right back."

I sank into the chair, relaxing and watching the sparks dance on the wood. After a few minutes I heard a soft knock at the door. I opened it, expecting to see Slash with a bottle of wine, but instead, Mia and Alessa stood there, giggling and looking guilty.

"Lexi, have you thought about our offer?" Mia said.

I looked at them, wide-eyed. "Ah... I haven't."

At that moment, Slash appeared in the hallway holding a bottle of wine. "Hello, ladies. What's up?"

Alessa smiled sweetly at him. "Hi, Slash. We'd like to borrow Lexi for a little girl time before dinner, but I can see we're interrupting something."

Slash shrugged. "The wine can wait. If Lexi wants to go with you, I'm fine with that."

He probably thought he was encouraging family interaction. I wanted to correct him, but I couldn't see a way to gracefully extract myself from the situation. So, girl time it was.

"Okay, but just for a few minutes," I finally said. "I don't want to be late for dinner."

Slash smiled, stepping past me, giving me a pat on the shoulder. "Have fun," he said before disappearing into the room. I *really* wished I could follow him.

"Come on, Lexi, we want to show you something," Mia said, tugging on my arm.

I followed them down the hallway. They both wore long-sleeved mini dresses, Alessa in a red one and Mia in electric blue, both with ridiculously high heels. It looked like a dangerous combination to me, but they seemed unaware of the potential risk and walked on them like they were pros.

I followed them down the marble steps, holding onto the banister, and we exited the front of the castle. I had no idea what was happening. It was cool and I wished I had a sweater. The girls led me to the left of the castle, where a small oval courtyard had been tucked away. Several marble benches, flowers, and bushes surrounded a pretty fountain with flowing water and a three-foot statue of a woman.

"Do you know who that is?" Alessa said when we all arrived at the statue.

Dusk was falling, so the lights from the front barely reached the area, but I took a closer look. "It looks like the Virgin Mary."

Mia pumped her fist and turned to Alessa. "See, I told you she'd recognize her. It's all up the hill from here."

"It's downhill," I corrected. "Mia, I know you're trying to sound like an American teenager, but trust me, most teenagers don't speak exclusively in slang phrases." I looked to Alessa for some backup, but she'd averted her gaze and was, wisely, staying out of this.

Mia's expression immediately fell, and I felt terrible for even mentioning it. "Are you being a wet bedspread about my attempts to improve my language skills, Lexi?"

"No. I'm *not* being a wet bedspread... I mean, a wet blanket." I tried to backtrack, realizing I'd hurt her feelings. "I think it's great that you're trying, Mia. Soon, you'll be a pro."

"Can I practice on you until then?" she asked hopefully, her eyes lighting up again. "Please?"

Oh, jeez. No, no, no. Why me?

I sighed inwardly and forced a smile. "Sure. Of course, Mia. You can practice on me until then."

"Great!" A smile crossed her face, and her arms dropped from her chest. "Thank you so much. Now, where were we?"

Resigned, I pointed to the Virgin Mary. "The prank. The statue."

"Oh, yes. The Virgin Mary," Mia explained. "You recognized her and you're not even Catholic...at least, that's what Vittoria said Gio told her."

I tried to figure that out, but Mia had already moved

on. "What that means is that everything is as perfect as spaghetti on, well, any day. Just kidding, Lexi. You don't need to correct me. I just made that one up. Anyway, my family has been teasing Vittoria because she got pregnant before the wedding. I said she should have told our parents the baby was the result of an immaculate conception to preserve their perception of her as an innocent one. All has turned out for the best with Gio, of course, but it's the perfect way to prank her. It'll be so much fun."

I didn't think it would be fun at all, but I didn't want Mia to accuse me of being a wet blanket again, so I kept my mouth shut.

"It's going to be brilliant, Mia," Alessa said, confirming my suspicion I was clueless regarding fun pranks. "Let's carry on."

Mia and Alessa kicked off their shoes, climbed into the fountain, and began tugging on the statue.

"What are you doing?" I asked, flabbergasted.

"We're going to nick the statue," Alessa said. "To be more specific, we're going to temporarily relocate the statue to Gio and Vittoria's bedroom. Then we'll hang a sign around the neck that says in Italian, 'This is the church-approved way to get pregnant before marriage.'"

"Won't that be *so* funny?" Mia asked, giggling.

Alessa must have noticed the horrified expression on my face, because she sought to reassure me. "We'll put it back. We discovered the statue is hollow, so it's light enough for Mia and me to carry it. It will be just a bit unwieldy. We're going to take it up to Gio and Vittoria's room after everyone has gone down to dinner. We'll bring it upstairs through a side door away from the main entrance. Mia has already propped open the door there. We'll use the elevator to the second floor and haul it down the hallway to their room. Once the statue is on their bed, we'll put the sign around the Virgin's neck, and we're out of there. We'll all be a little late to dinner, but no one will suspect us because we'll come in through the kitchen toward the back of the room. If anyone asks what we were doing in the kitchen, we'll just say we were seeing how the cooks prepare the wonderful food."

I thought for a moment, trying to find a flaw in their thinking. "How are you going to get into their room?"

Mia grinned and reached into the pocket of her dress, holding up a key. "I stole it from Vittoria. We've already made the sign, so we're in execution phase right now."

"Right now?" I yelped.

"Right now," Alessa confirmed. "So, let's not cock this up, ladies."

I held up a hand, a small kernel of hope blossoming in my chest. "If you already have this all planned out, you don't need me, right?"

"Wrong," Mia said. "We need you to be our lookout and let us know when Gio and Vittoria have left their room to go to dinner, then make sure no one comes back upstairs while we're moving the statue into their room. It's super simple, just a little thing. Will you help us? Please, Lexi."

"You want me to tell you when Gio and Vittoria have gone down to dinner and make sure no one else comes back upstairs?" I asked. "That's it in terms of my participation?"

"That's it," Alessa confirmed. "Go back to your room, and when you and your handsome husband head down to dinner, I'll intercept you again. Tell him to go on ahead and you'll meet up with him shortly. Then wait for Vittoria and Gio to go down to dinner. When they've left their room, take the elevator down and we'll be waiting there to load up the statue. You keep watch while we get the statue from the elevator, down the hallway, and into their room. Then we go down the elevator one more time and come into the dining room through the kitchen. Simple, awesome, and funny."

I had to admit they weren't asking too much from me, and maybe it was a *little* funny. Plus, if I cooperated, it might be the start of a closer friendship with Mia and Alessa. Slash might even have a laugh and commend me for going out of my comfort zone to interact with the other women in the family and participate in a silly girls' prank.

A lookout. How bad could that be?

"Okay, I guess I can be a lookout," I finally said. "That doesn't seem too difficult."

"Great!" Mia said. "That makes me happier than—"

"Stop, Mia," I interrupted. "I seriously can't handle any more stress right now."

Alessa must have sensed I was on the edge, because she linked arms with me. "It's time for Lexi to head back to her room. Remember, don't say a word to Slash."

I was having serious doubts about the whole thing as I returned to my room. Slash was just finishing up his glass of wine in front of the fireplace. I envied him.

"How did girl time go?" he asked, an amused look on his face.

"Honestly, I'm not sure."

He pulled on his suit jacket and buttoned it in the front. "Well, it's nice that you're trying. I'm proud of you."

"I had a talk with Mia, you know, about the slang thing."

He raised an eyebrow. "And?"

"And I tried to explain that American teenagers don't really speak in slang phrases." I threw up my hands. "Sure, they use a few words here and there, but it's not an entire language separate from English."

"There might be some parents who'd disagree with you," he said, amusement flashing in his eyes.

I pursed my lips at him. "Not helping. Anyway, she got upset until I told her I'd let her continue to practice on me."

"You caved?"

"Of course I caved. I couldn't figure out a way to say no without hurting her feelings even more."

Slash grimaced. "So, we're subjected to this for the rest of the week?"

"Apparently. But you can't fault me. I tried."

"I don't fault you at all. You did your best." He offered me his arm. "Ready for dinner?"

I wasn't and wished I had stayed in the room with him drinking wine. But now, instead of a quiet dinner, I had to take part in a crazy prank on my sister-in-law. I'd promised Mia and Alessa I'd help them, so no matter how much I didn't want to, how could I change my mind at this point?

I took his arm, and with my anxiety increasing, we headed toward the dining room. We were almost there when Alessa stepped out of the shadows of the corridor, nearly scaring the crap out of me.

"There you are, Lexi. Hey, Slash, can I borrow her again for just a few minutes more? We'll be in shortly."

Slash looked at me, raising an eyebrow. I wanted to confess everything right then, but apparently, he thought more girl time was okay, because he nodded and strolled on into the dining room without me.

"Go on," Alessa whispered to me, pushing me toward the staircase. "Head back upstairs and watch for Gio and Vittoria. Take the elevator down and we'll see you shortly."

She disappeared, so I dutifully climbed the stairs and waited for Gio and Vittoria. My mom and dad came out of their room, both laughing. It occurred to me I hadn't seen them this relaxed in a long time. They were really enjoying themselves.

"Lexi," Mom said when she spotted me. She and Dad walked over, and she kissed me on each cheek. "You look lovely."

"You and Dad look great, too."

She smiled. "Thanks, sweetheart. What are you doing?"

"What am I doing?" I guess it was weird I was just loitering in the hallway by myself. I hoped I didn't look guilty. My dad could see guilt with his eyes closed.

"Yes, why are you standing in the hallway?" Mom repeated.

"I...forgot something important. I'll be down in a minute."

"Lexi, what's going on?" Dad said studying me. "You look like you're ready to kidnap the pope or something."

"Ha-ha!" I said a little too loudly, worried that his guilt meter had gone off. But neither of my parents pressed it, and, to my great relief, they headed downstairs without further comment.

At that point I decided standing in the hallway was way too conspicuous. I returned to my room, left the door ajar, and waited. I stood just inside the room, listening for Gio and Vittoria. Finally, I heard them come out, laughing and chatting in Italian. I crept after them, ensuring they headed down the stairway and disappeared into the corridor leading toward the dining room.

As soon as they were out of sight, I hightailed it to the elevator and got in. When the doors opened on the first floor, Mia and Alessa were already standing there barefoot with the statue between them. Mia had the sign hanging around her neck.

"Good timing," Mia whispered as she and Alessa muscled themselves and the statue inside, smooshing me up against the elevator side.

"What happened to your shoes?" I asked.

"We left them down by the elevator. It's too hard to carry a statue in high heels."

At this point, I was sincerely wishing I hadn't agreed to any of this, but here we were, the three of us and the Virgin Mary crammed into the small elevator. It seemed like the start of a very bad joke.

Ugh.

When the doors opened on the second floor, I stepped out first, checking the hallway. "Clear," I hissed.

"Did you check to make sure everyone has gone downstairs?" Mia asked.

"No, was I supposed to?"

"Yes, go check," Alessa said impatiently. "We'll wait here, but hurry."

I walked up and down the hall tapping on doors, reminding everyone that it was dinnertime. When I heard no response, I headed back to the elevator, passing the top of the stairs.

"Cara?"

I almost had a heart attack on the spot. "Slash?"

He stood at the bottom of the stairs, looking up at me. "Is everything okay?"

THIRTY-ONE

Lexi

I FROZE, GUILT plastered all over my face. I was glad for the distance, because I was sure I would have been totally busted if he had a better look at my expression.

"Fine. I'm fine. Everything is fine, of course. I'll be down in a minute. I just have one more thing to take care of, okay?"

"Okay, just don't get carried away trying to make everything perfect." He headed back toward the dining room.

My heart pounding, I ran to the elevator, where they were trying to keep the doors from closing. I kicked off my own shoes, figuring I needed the mobility as well.

"The coast is clear," I said. "Hurry."

The two girls hefted the statue between them and started shuffling down the hallway. I stood near the staircase, but out of sight so no one would spot me. I watched as Mia opened the door of Gio and Vittoria's room with the key. Together they lifted the statue over the threshold of the door, setting it down in the room with a thump so loud it made me jump.

Why did I ever agree to this?

They disappeared into the room with the statue, but the door was still ajar. I checked the stairway, determined it was clear, then sidled down the hallway, peeking in to see how it was going.

From what I could see, the two of them had wrestled the statue onto the far side of the bed. Alessa was trying to prop it up while Mia tried to get the sign off her neck and onto the statue.

Just then I heard someone laugh from the vicinity of the stairway and crept back to see what was going on.

I almost passed out when I saw Vittoria and Gio headed toward the stairs.

Crap!

I ran back to the room, flipping off the light and nearly knocking over Alessa. Mia was fixing the sign on the statue, making sure it wasn't crooked.

"What are you doing?" she said in surprise.

"They're coming," I hissed. "Gio and Vittoria."

"*What?*" Alessa said, her face turning pale. "Why are they coming back up so quickly?"

"How am I supposed to know?" I whispered frantically. "I didn't ask them."

I peeked out the door again and saw Vittoria turning down the hallway. Gio wasn't with her. Either he was waiting for her at the bottom of the stairs or he'd been delayed by someone. I closed the door as quietly as I could and pressed back against the door, my heart pounding.

"Hide." I breathed.

Mia and Alessa dove into the bathroom, closing the door. Before I could move, I heard the doorknob rattle. I darted to the side of the bed, the farthest away from the door, scooted myself under the bed, and lay still.

Vittoria shouted Gio's name from the other side of the door, and it occurred to me that she must not have been able to find her key since Mia had stolen it. She yelled his name a few more times. Apparently, he couldn't hear her, because her footsteps faded, presumably as she went to find him and get his key.

That was my cue to leave. As I wiggled out from beneath the bed, I heard the bathroom door open, light footsteps, and then the room door open and close. Mia and Alessa must have made their escape.

I had just gotten to my knees and crawled around the bed when I heard voices approaching the door.

Oh, no! Too late.

I dived back under the bed just as the door opened and the light snapped on. Vittoria and Gio were talking in Italian until they stopped abruptly. There was a gasp, some possible swear words, and then a lot of laughter. Vittoria said something to Gio, and I heard his footsteps heading for the door and the door open and close.

Vittoria said something to herself, perching on the side of the bed and laughing some more. I figured she must have read the sign. Minutes later, the door opened with a cacophony of voices as the other guests presumably crowded into the room to get a look.

I just hoped no one looked under the bed.

There was a lot more laughing and shuffling around before I finally heard my dad ask, "What's that sign say?"

Gio translated, and the room erupted into laughter again. There was more talking and joking until finally it seemed as if things were winding down.

I started to think that I was going to survive this disaster, when I felt a sneeze from the dust under the bed coming on. I tried all sorts of techniques to suppress the sneeze, including reciting various math theorems. It seemed to be working, when suddenly I sneezed so hard, I hit my head on the underside of the bed.

The room fell deadly silent, until the bed skirt was

abruptly lifted. I saw Gio's face peering at me. "Lexi, what are you doing under the bed?"

Obviously, there was no good answer. I crawled out from under the bed, barefoot, my hair a mess, my green dress covered with dust. "This isn't what it looks like," I said, my cheeks burning. I tried to brush the dust off my dress, to no avail.

"Lexi?" my mother said in surprise. "*You're* a part of this?" I couldn't tell if she was appalled or impressed, and there wasn't really any way for me to ask.

Tito stepped forward, slapping me on the back and laughing. "Ha, ha, ha. So, *you* were the trickster behind this joke, *jah*? Good on you. Never knew you had such a wicked sense of humor. Excellent work on the sign, too. Your Italian is impeccable."

Gio stepped forward, narrowing his eyes. "You didn't write that sign, did you, Lexi? Who helped you?"

I glanced at the door, but Mia and Alessa were nowhere to be seen. As I wasn't sure of the proper protocol for throwing fellow pranksters under the bus, I said nothing. Slash leaned against the wall, his dark eyes assessing me. I had no idea what he was thinking or how upset he'd be that I'd embarrassed him and myself in front of his family.

Vittoria sidled up to Gio, slipping her arm through his. She seemed amused rather than mad, but I wasn't always the best judge of people, so how could I be sure?

"Confess now, Lexi," she said with a smile. "Who else helped you?"

"I… I—"

"I did."

I blinked in surprise as Slash stepped up next to me, putting an arm around my shoulders. "Lexi helped me. But you surprised us by returning to your room so quickly."

"I'm pregnant," Vittoria said, cupping her stomach. "I have to go to the bathroom...a lot."

There was more laughter, but I stood staring at Slash in shock. Had he just covered for me, Mia, and Alessa?

Gio said something in Italian and good-naturedly punched Slash on the arm while Stefan mussed up his younger brother's hair. Slash didn't seem to mind, and everyone seemed so cheerful, I thought maybe all was okay.

Maybe.

But just to be on the safe side, I kept my mouth shut.

Their merriment was cut short when Juliette stepped forward, tugging on Slash's ear. Her eyes narrowed, but I thought I saw a twinkle in them. "Romeo, is it kind to tease your little brother on his forthcoming nuptials?"

Slash looked duly chastised. "No, Mama. It just seemed like too good an opportunity to pass up."

"Your prank did not involve just your brother. You will apologize to Vittoria."

"Of course." Slash turned to Vittoria, who had a huge smile on her face. She seemed to be enjoying every minute of this. He bowed slightly to her. "*Ti prego perdonami,* Vittoria."

"*Sei perdonato,*" she said and then noisily kissed both of his cheeks. "You, too, Lexi." She hugged me and gave me kisses, too. "But both of you put the statue back before bedtime, *si*? There won't be room for Gio, me, my stomach, and the Virgin Mary in the bed."

There was more laughter, and everyone started filing out of the room.

"Stefan, please wait a moment," Juliette said. "I need to speak with you about something. Seeing the statue of the Virgin Mary reminded me of it, and I'd almost forgotten all about it. It involves Father Rainaldi and something he told me many years ago."

Stefan froze midstep, and to my surprise, so did Gio.

Puzzled, I glanced over at Slash, but he, too, had paused in motion.

It was like Juliette had dropped a bomb in the room.

"Gio?" Vittoria said, tugging on his arm impatiently when he didn't move. "Come on."

He murmured something to her in Italian, and she shrugged and left the room, leaving Juliette, Stefan, Gio, Slash, and me. Gio's expression had paled considerably.

Juliette looked at Slash and Gio in exasperation. "Are you two Stefan?"

Slash smiled easily. "Mama, we all remember Father Rainaldi, and seeing as how he passed decades ago, we're curious as to what he might have said about Stefan all these years later."

"*Si,*" Gio said with a forced smile, slapping a friendly arm around Stefan's shoulder. "What did the father have to say about Stefan?"

The room fell silent, and I realized something was going on that I had no idea about. But I was an extra wheel. My cheeks heated for not realizing it earlier. "Ah, I'm sorry. I'll leave now."

Juliette tore her gaze away from her boys and glanced my way. "Lexi, please stay. You're family now."

As uncomfortable as it was, a part of me was secretly glad I could stay, because I was *dying* to find out what was going on. I perched on a corner of the bed and tried not to look too interested in the situation.

"Many years ago, Father Rainaldi pulled me aside and told me when our family gathered for the first wedding of one of you boys, Stefan would have an important announcement to confess to me that involved the Virgin Mary. Seeing the statue just reminded me of that conversation."

"Oh...really?" Stefan said, looking increasingly uncomfortable and oddly...guilty.

"Father Rainaldi said the confession would be necessary for your soul, but he was quite insistent I wait until at least one of you was married. Romeo, you are the first to marry—although not yet in the church. Gio's wedding is in a few days, so I believe we are close enough for that confession."

Stefan visibly winced, while Gio shuffled his feet. My usually unflappable husband rubbed his stubbled chin, a pained expression on his face. Fascinated, I abandoned all pretense of not listening and leaned forward, not wanting to miss a single word.

"Juliette?"

We all turned to look at the open door. Oscar stood in the doorway trying and failing, to straighten his tie. "Dinner is served. Can whatever this is wait until after we eat?"

Juliette gave Stefan a pointed look. "We will resume this conversation after dinner. I look forward to it."

She swept out of the room like a queen, linking arms with Oscar.

As soon as she was gone, Gio sat on the edge of the bed next to me, rubbing the back of his neck.

"Damn," he said. "After all these years, it's coming back to haunt me."

"Haunt *us*," Stefan corrected and then pointed a finger at Slash. "And it's *all* your and Lexi's fault."

THIRTY-TWO

Lexi

SLASH HELD UP two hands in a stopping motion. "Whoa. How is it our fault?"

Now Gio pointed his finger at Slash. "*You* obviously told *her* everything, after we swore, *in blood*, we'd never speak of it again."

I leaped up from the bed. "Slash didn't tell me anything. I don't know what you're talking about."

Stefan started pacing the room. "We're just supposed to believe it was coincidence that Romeo picked the statue of the Virgin Mary to play this prank on Gio?"

"Slash didn't have anything to do with this prank." I put my hands on my hips, standing my ground. "He's covering for me. This prank was Mia's and Alessa's brainchild. I got roped into it and they snuck away while I got caught. I didn't want to tell on them in front of everyone, so Slash stepped in to take the heat on their behalf. They're the true pranksters."

"Alessa?" Stefan looked at me as if I'd lost my mind. "My girlfriend?"

"Yes, she was Mia's righthand prankster, and I was the designated lookout."

"Then how did you get under my bed?" Gio asked.

"I came to check on their progress, but Vittoria returned to the room before we'd finished arranging the statue. They hid in the bathroom, so I dived under the bed. When Vittoria went to get you, they slipped out, but I was stuck, and then I sneezed. I assure you, this was Mia's plan, Alessa's execution, and my screwup."

Stefan stopped his pacing and snapped his fingers. "Wait. How would Vittoria's sister know about the Virgin Mary thing unless…" He turned to Gio. "*You.* You told Vittoria, didn't you? And she must have told her little sister."

"I did *not* tell Vittoria," Gio said, spreading his hands. "Why would I tell her? I swore in blood I would say nothing of what happened, and I didn't. Besides, I have the most to lose here. I wouldn't do that."

"Enough!" Slash said, clearly exasperated. "Read the sign around the statue's neck. It's clearly Mia playing a prank on her older sister, teasing her for getting pregnant before the wedding. Immaculate conception and all that. It's just an unfortunate coincidence that sparked a memory with Mama. Now we have to deal with it."

"What's going on?" I asked, looking around uneasily. "Did you guys kill someone or something?"

Gio snorted. "If only it were that easy."

"Yes, if only," Stefan agreed. "Instead, I have to confess."

"Confess to *what*?" I asked.

"To something he didn't do," Slash said, taking me by the elbow. "Come on, we have to go to dinner, but at some point, after we eat and before dessert, when people are out of their seats and mingling, we need to step out onto the balcony and have a discussion regarding this *before* we speak with Mama. We all need to be on the same page. Stagger your exits, please."

The three brothers looked at each other and nodded. Without another word, we left the room and headed down to the dining room together.

"Are you going to tell me what's going on?" I whispered to Slash as we descended the marble stairs.

"You'll hear soon enough," he said, taking my hand, leaving me wondering what in the world was going on. "Don't worry."

Slash

I shouldn't have wasted my breath telling Lexi not to worry. That had never worked in the past. But Mama's revelation about Father Rainaldi had taken me off guard.

Sure enough, during dinner, Lexi repeatedly folded her napkin in her lap into a tiny square, a sure sign of anxiety.

I sighed inwardly. There was nothing to be done about it at this point. I ate my dinner and chatted in Italian with Father Armando, who sat next to me. I pretended all was well in my house when clearly it wasn't.

I'd have to fix that.

I kept my eyes on my brother, noting when Gio disappeared, followed by Stefan a few minutes later. When Father Armando got up from his chair, I took Lexi's hand and we slipped outside to the veranda. I found Gio and Stefan at the far end of the veranda, huddled together talking.

"You brought Lexi?" Stefan said in surprise when he saw us.

"I did. She's a part of it now that she knows something's amiss, and I'm not keeping it from her," I said.

Stefan rubbed his forehead. "Fine. Sorry we have to air the family dirty laundry in front of you, Lexi."

255

"I don't have to stay," Lexi started to protest, but Gio came over and put an arm around her shoulders.

"Stay," he said. "You're family now. Our laundry is your laundry."

Stefan nodded, too. "You're one of us now."

It was a small gesture, but their inclusion of Lexi meant a lot to me. At least that was settled. "So, where do we start?" I asked.

Stefan leaned against the railing, looking out at the moon hanging low over the water. "How about at the beginning? For Lexi."

"For Lexi," Gio murmured.

She looked up at me with a look that always seem able to melt my heart no matter what was happening. "Go ahead, Stefan," I said. "You're the oldest. You tell the story."

Stefan leaned back against the veranda. "Many years ago, long before Mama and Oscar decided to move to London, I came home to Sperlonga for a visit from the university. I believe I was nineteen at the time, which would have made Romeo seventeen and Gio ten, correct?"

Gio and I nodded, so Stefan continued. "Something you should know, Lexi, is that our family had been members of the local church in Sperlonga for many years. Nonno and Nonna were married there, as were their parents and grandparents. Mama and my father were also married there, and when he passed, he was buried in the church cemetery. Mama and Oscar, Gio's father, were married there several years later. So, in other words, our family has long been devoted parishioners of the church."

"Okay," Lexi said.

"By extension, Romeo and I were quite involved in the church as well," he said. "We were both altar boys in excellent standing for many years with the head priest, Father Mario Rainaldi."

"That's why Nonna sometimes calls you *chierichetto*," Lexi said to me. "Right?"

"Right." I remembered how shocked Lexi had been to hear I'd been an altar boy. "It's also a nickname she bestows on Gio and Stefan when she sees them."

"Anyway, Gio had somehow managed to avoid becoming an altar boy until his tenth birthday," Stefan said. "Unfortunately, unlike Romeo and I, Gio wasn't quite as diligent or conscientious regarding his duties."

"Gio was a bit of a wild child," I added.

"That's not fair," Gio protested. "I was diligent. I showed up every Sunday, didn't I?"

"Only because Mama made you," Stefan countered, cuffing our brother on the head with one hand. "Anyway, one day Gio had a brilliant idea. He decided to steal a small antique statue of the Virgin Mary that normally resided on the altar."

"I didn't just *decide* to steal the statue," Gio protested. "It was a dare from some of my school buddies. My manhood was being challenged, so, of course, I accepted the dare. I was just going to keep the statue for a few days and return it secretly. I doubted old, doddering Father Rainaldi would even miss it."

"Oh, great." Stefan threw up his hands. "Let's add speaking ill of the dead to your long list of transgressions."

"I'll take it from here," I said, stepping between the two of them. "Anyway, Gio used some tape to keep the latch from closing on a door at the side of the church after he finished up with his altar boy duties one Sunday. Later that night, he snuck back into the church and absconded with the Virgin Mary. I caught him as he was climbing back into our bedroom window. I insisted he return it immediately, but Gio refused."

"I didn't refuse," Gio broke in. "Not exactly. It was just that I'd already removed the tape from the door after I *borrowed* the statue, and I didn't have any way of returning it...yet. Then, you had to go and tell Stefan."

"He did," Stefan agreed. "As the older brother, I decided we would return it early in the morning and figure out how to get into the church before Father Rainaldi arrived and noticed it was missing. So, the next morning, we arrived very early at the church to find that all the doors were locked, including the one Gio had previously taped open. At that point, we decided to break in. Romeo, from his time as the family's *extraordinary* altar boy, was the most familiar with the building. He told us there was a window on the second floor in the choir loft that had become warped and needed repair for a long time. He suspected we could open it and get in that way."

"I was *not* an extraordinary altar boy," I murmured.

"Yes, you were," Stefan and Gio responded in unison. I rolled my eyes at them, then glanced at Lexi. She seemed amused by the revelation and my denial, but not surprised.

"Anyway, Romeo proposed that since Gio was the smallest and lightest of the three of us, he should climb the tree on the outside of the church, go in through the warped window, and come down to the back door and open it for us from the inside," Stefan said. "But Gio didn't want to do that. He was too scared to climb the tree."

"I was only ten," Gio protested. "A mere child. Don't forget that part."

"Good thing you were protecting your manhood," Stefan countered.

I stepped in, trying to keep them on track. "Anyway, I climbed the tree for Gio. We left Stefan with the statue by the church's side door. I made it up the tree safely, managed to open the window, and got inside." I paused, waiting for Stefan to pick it up.

"While they were doing that, I huddled by the back door waiting for them to open it," Stefan said. "I heard the rustling of Romeo climbing, but after a bit, I couldn't hear him anymore. I wasn't sure if it was due to the breeze carrying the sound away from me or whether he was no longer climbing and was already inside. After a few minutes, I suddenly heard a noise on the inside of the door, like the lock and latch was being turned. I held up the statue, ready to pass it off, and the door swung open. Except...*surprise*! It wasn't Romeo.

"It was none other than Father Rainaldi."

THIRTY-THREE

Slash

"OH, NO," LEXI said. "What did you do?"

"To say we were shocked to see each other would be an understatement," Stefan said. "I might have yelped in surprise."

"You screamed," I verified. "I heard it all the way up in the church loft."

Stefan narrowed his eyes at me but didn't deny it. "After the initial shock wore off, Father Rainaldi asked me what I was doing outside the church holding the church's precious Virgin Mary statue. I debated telling him the story, but I decided to cover for Gio, who still had many years of service to the church ahead of him. So, I told the father I'd lost a bet and had to perform a task assigned by the winner. The winner charged me with stealing the Virgin Mary from the altar. Naturally, he was shocked and dismayed by my behavior. He took the statue from me, looked it over carefully. When saw it hadn't been damaged by its adventure, he offered me a deal."

"A deal?" Lexi asked. "What kind of deal?"

Stefan leaned back against the veranda railing,

running his fingers through his hair. "He asked if Mama and Oscar knew what I'd done. When I said no, Father Rainaldi said that in recognition of my family's longtime service to the church, and because no harm was done to the statue, if I confessed my sinful ways and performed all the required penance, he'd keep my transgressions private and not tell my family...*for the time being*. I didn't exactly understand what that meant, but what option did I have? By this time, we'd all become a part of this unfortunate incident. So, of course, I agreed, and Father Rainaldi took my confession right there. I spent over two hours in the church with him that day, and just so you know, the penance lasted the entirety of my university holiday. I had to do many other duties around the church."

Gio put a hand on Stefan's shoulder. "I appreciate that you took the punishment in my place."

"And yet you failed to assist me with my penance," Stefan said wryly.

"I didn't want to tip off the father that more of us were involved."

"So, Stefan took the fall for Gio," Lexi said. "What happened after that?"

"Well, Romeo and Gio were waiting for me in the bushes outside the church when I finished my initial confession," Stefan replied. "Romeo had heard the whole thing, and after he'd climbed back down, he told Gio what had happened. Then they waited for me."

"I was furious at Gio and embarrassed for Stefan," I broke in. "But I understood why Stefan took the fall for Gio. I would have done the same thing. In the end, I couldn't believe Stefan got off so easy and Father Rainaldi had agreed not to tell Mama what happened."

"I did *not* get off easy," Stefan corrected me. "I lost my entire holiday, but it was worth it because Mama didn't suspect a thing, and she thought I was an angel for working so hard in the church during my time off."

"*Si*, bonus points with Mama," Gio agreed. "Worth its weight in gold."

"I guess I didn't get off as cleanly as I'd believed," Stefan said.

"What do you think Mama knows?" Gio asked. "You don't think she suspects me of anything, do you?"

"She doesn't know anything," I interjected. "But she'll want to know why Father Rainaldi told her that odd bit of information, Stefan. She's been waiting a long time, Stefan, and wants to hear what you have to say."

"I already confessed," Stefan groused. "And did my penance, too. Why do I have to do it again?"

"Because you promised Father Rainaldi," I pointed out. "He said he wouldn't tell Mama...at that time. Maybe this is just his way of getting you to come clean with her after you'd grown up. He probably assumed since you were the oldest, you'd get married first, and he wanted you to go into your union with a clean heart. I don't see any way around it, Stefan. You're going to have to tell her."

"Tell her what?" Stefan said in frustration. "That I lied to the priest to cover for Gio? Or do I repeat the lie I told Father Rainaldi and take the blame once again for Gio?"

"You should tell the truth," I said. "That's the point of this confession."

"No!" Gio exploded. "I don't agree with any of this. Why does Stefan have to tell her anything? Father Rainaldi is dead, Stefan already did his penance, and we swore in blood we'd never discuss it again. The matter is finished, as far as I'm concerned. Just tell her you have no idea what Father Rainaldi was talking about."

Gio had always been a bit of a wild child, so when

he'd ended up in the Italian special forces, where cooler heads typically prevailed, I'd been surprised. But Gio was fearless, smart, and the best marksman I'd ever met. The special forces had been a good fit for him. His reluctance to admit his culpability clearly stemmed from a fear of disappointing Mama. All three of us had that same vulnerability, which came from a place of absolute respect and love. But it was clouding his judgment here.

I considered for a moment and turned to Lexi. "Maybe what we need is an impartial opinion. Lexi, you're the only one without a stake in this issue. What do you think Stefan should do?"

"Me?" she said, clearly surprised by my question. "You want *my* opinion on this?"

"*Si*, Lexi," Gio said eagerly, perhaps hoping she'd come up with a way to get him out of confessing. "You're family now. What do you think we should do?"

She fell silent, clearly considering the situation. "Let me get this straight," she finally said. "All of this is about a childhood misdeed, and the biggest concern is disappointing your mother and/or dishonoring the memory of a priest who is now dead, but who covered for your transgressions at that time?"

"That succinctly covers it," I confirmed.

She looked between the three of us. "Well, if you'd asked me this question just one week ago, I likely would have had a different answer. But I've learned something important over these past few days. Honesty is the right foundation on which to build a family. I didn't know Father Rainaldi, but if he covered for you, Stefan, he essentially did what you did for Gio, and what Slash did for me tonight. In the end, it sounds like he just wanted you to tell the truth, to stop you from having potentially harmful secrets within your family...*our* family. Not necessarily this secret, but *any* secret. Slash and I have recently learned how harmful it is to keep secrets from each other. Since Father Rainaldi wanted to wait until one of you was getting married, it sounds like he desired to give you—or by extension, all of us—an important lesson on how to start our marriages. So, my advice to you, Gio, and to all of you, is to come clean with your mom, start fresh, and don't keep secrets from your spouse."

I couldn't have said it better, and the fact that my wife had been able to articulate it so beautifully made me love her even more.

After a moment, Gio kicked his foot against the railing and sighed. "Fine. You're right, Lexi. You're *all* right. I release you from your blood vow of silence. It's time I face my penance many years later."

"About damn time," Stefan said with a grin.

Smiling, I gathered my brothers, one on each side, before clapping them on the back. The incident with Father Rainaldi had been a childhood transgression, but it had also been symbolic of the times we'd had each other's backs while growing up. Despite the distance and different directions our lives had taken, one thing was clear to me. We'd successfully evolved from our childhood roles with one thing intact...we'd always be brothers who cared deeply about each other.

I glanced over at Lexi, who gave me a little smile. Meeting her had ignited a chain of events that had led me back to my family, and for that, I'd always be indebted to her.

THIRTY-FOUR

Lexi

I WAS EXCUSED from the after-dinner childhood prank confessional with Slash, his brothers, and their parents, thank goodness. I was glad, because I wasn't sure I could handle any more wedding drama. And it wasn't even *my* wedding.

After we returned to the dinner table, Mia and Alessa officially announced their participation in the prank, and everyone had a good laugh at it. The two girls made a big deal of praising me taking the heat for them, which embarrassed me. It was at that moment I realized the situation I'd found myself in was like one continuous family circle. Years ago, Stefan had taken the fall for Gio, Slash had covered for me today, and I hadn't given up Alessa and Mia. I wasn't sure what it meant in terms of us as a family other than we clearly took care of each other.

Somehow that was enormously comforting to me.

When Slash and his brothers left to speak to their parents, I stayed at the table with Father Armando.

"I'm so pleased by the progress you all have made in the challenges," the priest said, taking Slash's chair. "Of course, I had no doubt you'd succeed, but I must say, Mr. Zachetti is quite taken aback by your intelligence and resourcefulness. You're moving through his puzzles logically, rapidly, and efficiently. I don't believe he expected that. His pride is at stake, but I also think he's pleased and excited by your resourcefulness."

"Why do you think that?" I asked.

"If I put my father confessor hat on, I think it's because it reflects well upon him. Anyone can make a puzzle that's so hard that no one can solve it. There's no challenge in that. But the test of a true puzzle master is to create something so difficult that *almost* no one can solve it, but it's still possible. Today, you proved Zachetti to be the master that he obviously is. That has to be supremely satisfying."

"We can't get cocky," I cautioned. "We still have more escape rooms to go."

"Of course," he said. "But watching you attack each challenge and following along with your thinking is fascinating and, if I may say so, quite encouraging. I sincerely don't think there is anything you two can't handle."

"So, you're watching us while we complete the escape rooms?" I shifted in my chair, leaning toward him. "And the gamemaster, too? I thought he would, to make sure we don't cheat somehow, but it's interesting that you confirm this."

"Yes. I'm the pope's observer, after all."

"So, he has cameras hidden in the rooms?"

"He does. Honestly, I think he quite enjoys seeing you work through the process, although I sincerely think he did not expect you to get this far. As it stands now, you have solved the most escape rooms of any group that has ever been through. Although, I should tell you that Brando remains overly confident you will not solve the final challenges. I warned him not to be so smug. But we shall see."

I sighed inwardly, wondering how much harder Mr. Zachetti could make the final challenges and then decided I didn't want to know. Guess I'd find out soon enough.

I chatted a bit with my mother, who'd decided it was wonderful and clever how I'd begun to integrate myself so effortlessly into Slash's extended family. Vittoria gave her little sister a good-natured scolding, but she gave Alessa and me multiple hugs and kisses, which I interpreted to mean I was forgiven.

Since Slash hadn't returned from his family meeting, I went back to our room alone, got into my pajamas, and added more wood to the fire. I poured myself the glass of wine I hadn't had earlier and warmed my toes in front of the hearth. Slash arrived an hour later, carrying his suit jacket over his arm.

"Pour me a glass of that wine, would you?" he asked, tossing his jacket onto the bed and sitting down to remove his shoes and socks.

I poured him a glass and held it until he padded over and took it from me. "How did it go?"

He sank into the armchair next to mine and took a sip. "All is forgiven, of course. Mama insisted Gio will have some penance of his own at the church the next time he goes to Sperlonga. Yard work, a little carpentry, whatever is needed at the church. He'll also visit and clean Father Rainaldi's gravesite."

"Seems fair." I took a sip of my wine, adjusting my feet to warm the other side. "What about you and Stefan?"

"We were tasked with getting that bloody statue out of Gio and Vittoria's room and back to the fountain. How Mia and Alessa managed to carry that thing between them without breaking it is beyond me."

"They pulled, dragged, and dropped it a few times," I said. "But it was pretty impressive…and completely crazy." A little laugh escaped my lips.

He reached over and took my hand, squeezing it. "How are you doing?"

"I'm fine. Thank you for stepping up and taking some of the heat off me when I crawled out from underneath Gio and Vittoria's bed."

He chuckled. "*Mio Dio.* I noticed you were missing, and as soon as I heard the sneeze, I *knew* it was you. The expression on your face when you came out from under the bed was priceless. I'll never forget it, and likely no one else will, either. I'm afraid to inform you, it will become an important part of our family lore for centuries to come."

"Wonderful." I took another gulp of wine. "At least it's better than the Lego-up-my-nose story."

"I don't know. That one's pretty classic, too." His grin widened. "So, how did you end up under the bed?"

"Alessa and Mia were hiding in the bathroom, from which it was far easier to make a quick escape. I would have told you everything in advance, but they forbade me. It was a girl thing. But all seems forgiven. Vittoria apparently thought it was hilarious, Gio has a clean conscience, and Mia and Alessa think I'm a team player. So, cheers to me." I lifted my wineglass in a salute to myself and took a slug of my wine.

He leaned toward me, tracing my cheekbone with his fingertip. "You *are* a team player."

"If you say so. Other than Basia, and maybe Gray and Gwen, I really don't have any other close girlfriends. Now I have more than I know what to do with."

"Friends are a blessing," he said, taking another sip of his wine. "And so are families."

He was right, but it still made me nervous. "I suppose

this is a warm-up to what our church wedding will be like with all our family gathered again. Except then we'll be in the States and have your brothers, my brothers, Basia, Elvis, Xavier, Gwen, Angel, Gray, Tito, Hands, and the rest of our friends to add to the mix. I'm not sure I'm ready for that level of family."

"I don't think we'll *ever* be ready for that, but we'll get through it, like we do everything else."

I didn't disagree with that. "At least we won't have the pressure of the escape rooms to deal with. Do you think we can finish strong?"

"I think we can. But Zachetti won't have made it easy. I think we need to be prepared for anything."

"I really want to win for the orphanage, Slash. For the pope, for your dad, but mostly for those children, who were once like you." I took his hand and kissed it before holding it in my lap.

"Me, too, *cara*." He gave my hand a gentle squeeze then stared into the fire. "Me, too."

THIRTY-FIVE

Lexi

"GOOD MORNING, AND good luck today on your final day of challenges at Castrum Augustus," Brando announced as we gathered by the gigantic hearth in the dining room, where Dante Zachetti glared down at us from his huge portrait.

"Today, there will be two challenges for two teams in the morning. After lunch, you will take on the final escape room of your stay here together as one big team. Are you ready?"

Tito, Stefan, Mia, and Gio all shouted in the affirmative. Not surprisingly, everyone was lighthearted and confident. My dad seemed particularly happy and had stopped to chat with Slash and me twice just this morning. He'd personally thanked Slash for stepping up and taking the fall for the prank with me, even though he'd had nothing to do with it. I could hardly believe it, even though I'd witnessed it with my own two eyes. The time spent with Slash during the challenges had seemed to bring them closer. I could also see Slash relaxing more around him. Of all the benefits of competing in complex escape room challenges, having my dad and

Slash get closer, especially after their rocky start, had not been one I'd anticipated.

But I greatly appreciated it.

"For the first challenges, Mr. Zachetti allowed you to select your teams and which team would go with which challenge," Brando said. "For the next set of challenges, he permitted you to divide into teams of your choice with the challenge being assigned randomly. Today, both the team construction and the challenge will be left up to fate, except for one person, who will be assigned to Team B. Since the challenge for Team B will require someone with gaming experience, Mr. Zachetti has graciously decided to permit someone to volunteer for that duty and be placed on that team. Is there anyone who'd like to come forward?"

Not surprisingly, everyone turned toward Slash and me. I looked at Slash, and he stepped back, deferring to me. "You take it, *cara*. You're the better gamer."

That was a matter of debate, for sure, but regardless, I walked over to the gamemaster to volunteer. "I'll be the designated gamer."

"Excellent. Please stand to my right as the first member of Team B." Brando then held up a black velvet bag. "For the rest of you, inside this bag are small rocks. Half are painted red, and half are painted white. You will each draw a rock. Those with a white rock will be Team A, and those with a red rock will be Team B. However, we'll have one extra player today." He swept out his hand to include Father Armando, who stood discreetly to the side, clad in his modest black cassock. "Mr. Zachetti would like to invite you to participate in this challenge, Father, if you so desire."

I exchanged a surprised glance with Slash. Wasn't that an interesting development? Did that mean Mr. Zachetti was so convinced we wouldn't win that he was permitting us extra help? Or was there another reason?

Father Armando looked toward Slash for guidance. Slash shrugged, so the priest bowed slightly to the gamemaster. "How kind of Mr. Zachetti to invite me to participate. Of course, I'd be happy to assist either team as needed."

"Excellent. As a result, there will be one rock not selected to ensure the team Father Armando ends up on is completely random. Now, let us start choosing teams. I suggest starting with the engaged couple."

Gio and Vittoria stepped forward, and Brando held out the bag. "Ladies first," Brando said, motioning to Vittoria. She dipped her hand in the bag, rummaged around, and pulled out a white rock. Gio went next and pulled out a white rock as well.

"How fitting. The first two members of Team A are the engaged couple," Brando said, beaming. "Please stand to my right. Now, who would like to go next?"

"I'll go," Tito said. He reached into the bag and pulled out a red rock. Mia bounded up, also grabbing a red rock. Stefan and Alessa followed her, both picking white rocks. Slash's mother picked a red rock, and my mother got a white one. Mom was followed by Oscar, who chose a red rock, my dad, who selected white, and Father Armando, who also picked white.

That left Slash. He reached into the bag and pulled out a red rock. That meant Slash and I would be on the same team for the first time. While happy about that, I worried that some others might be concerned and undervalue their own capabilities. If there was one thing I'd learned since arriving at the castle, it was that Slash and I had seriously talented families. They could solve the escape room without us, I was sure of that. The only problem was that they might not be as motivated as Slash and me to win. Unfortunately, there was little I could do about it at this point.

I could see some members of Team A shuffling around nervously, glancing at Slash and me. Apparently, I wasn't the only one thinking this, which meant I needed to nip that anxiety in the bud.

"We've got two great teams," I said with two thumbs up. "No worries." My mom gave me a grin and blew me a kiss. At least she was on board.

"The teams are formed, so if Team B would please wait here in the dining room while I set up Team A, it would be greatly appreciated," Brando said. "As always, please empty your pockets and leave any extra items in the basket on the side table."

He swept his arms out wide, a smile crossing his face. "Now, let the final games begin."

THIRTY-SIX

Gio

GOOD. I WAS done with all the talking and ready to get to the action.

We could do this. An important part of the rigorous and difficult training for the Italian special operations unit involved the mental game. Each soldier had to be confident, *truly* confident, in his or her own capabilities and the abilities of all team members to perform in order to succeed.

The tougher the challenge, the better.

Although my team didn't have Romeo or his brilliant wife, there was no way I was going to be the weak link and give him the pleasure of needling me for the rest of my life if I lost my luxury honeymoon. He'd do it, too— I *knew* it. Plus, my buddies back at the unit would invariably find out, probably from my brothers, if I didn't relieve a billionaire of some of his money when I had the chance.

Nope. No way was I going to fail.

Vittoria must have known what I was thinking, because she sidled up to me, slipping her hand in mine. "You don't want to be 'little Gio' for the rest of your life, right?" she murmured softly. "You're just as capable as them, so prove it."

I set my jaw and squeezed her hand. "I will."

We followed the gamemaster down a corridor to a large room with huge double doors inset with stained glass windows. Peering through the glass, I could see the room was a large library. The gamemaster unlocked the room with an old-fashioned key and ushered us in.

"Wow," Alessa uttered as we looked around. "What a gorgeous library."

The room was two stories high, but windowless. Dark wooden bookshelves stretched to the ceiling along the wall to the left of the door, on the left and back walls, and along the right wall, running about a third of the way from the back. Several tall, wheeled ladders mounted on rails provided access to the upper-level books on each wall.

A book lover's dream.

An interesting glass-front display case containing two dozen World War II-era model airplanes stood along the right wall where the bookcases ended. Next to that was a small library card catalog cabinet. A gigantic map of the Mediterranean region set into a thick wooden frame hung to the right of the cabinet. A smattering of sofas, armchairs, end tables, and lamps filled out the room.

A waist-high bookcase, holding a magnificent antique scale and flanked by two taller bookshelves, took up much of the center of the room. The scale was clearly meant to be the focal point of the room, so I walked closer to get a better look. Upon closer inspection, I discovered it was made of bronze and had a balance point in the center. A metal arm extended approximately two feet to each side, and, as of this moment, the right arm was raised and ended in a single metal post pointing upward. The left side had an identical post, but four round weights of different sizes and colors were sitting on the post.

The scale was clearly unbalanced, so the left bar touched the top of the bookcase.

The gamemaster gathered the rest of our group around the scale. "I want you to know that it's quite impressive you've successfully completed the first four challenges," he said. "I warn you, this one will be more difficult than the previous ones, as will the escape room your companions will attempt concurrently. I've been authorized to tell you that no group has *ever* been as successful as you have been to date. Given your success, I doubt you need further motivation. Nevertheless, it will be interesting to see how you adapt to the increased difficulty and random team assignments. If you can continue your success, it might force us to reconsider our approach. Good luck. I am eagerly awaiting your performance."

"Now, a few words of advice," Brando continued. "This challenge appears simple on the surface. All you must do is use round weights to balance the scale. Once you do so, you must push the red button by the door, and I'll come verify you've completed the challenge. There are few rules. You may not leave the library once the challenge has begun, and you will have only two hours to complete the task."

He started to leave and then stopped. "Oh, and one more thing. When you balance the weights, you must have at least four weights on the left post. No fewer. Are there any questions?"

Oh sure, I had a million questions. I just didn't know what they were yet.

"Well, good luck," Brando said when no one spoke up. "The clock will start as soon as I close the door."

As soon as he left, we gave each other an uneasy glance and continued to study the scale. The weights on the post were colored—from bottom to top—red, orange, yellow, and green.

Stefan took the top one off the post and held it. "It's

metal." He tapped the other weights, confirming that they, too, were metal.

I ran my finger over the green weight. Embossed in it was the number two. The yellow weight had a five on it, the orange one a seven, and the red one a nine.

"Could the number equal the weight?" I asked.

Alessa took the weight from Stefan and held it in her palm. Then she removed the green weight. "Well, it feels like the five weight is at least twice the weight of the green one, so I think that's a good assessment, Gio."

"Well, if that's correct, it should make it much easier to calculate the weights we need on each post to balance them," I said.

"True, but if we must have four weights on the left post, there must be some additional weights somewhere in the library," Winston pointed out. "There are no weights on the right side."

Good point. I tried to remember what Romeo had told me Lexi's father did for a living. Doctor? Lawyer? Something impressive like that.

"I think that's a good assumption," I said. "We have to assume there are additional weights hidden somewhere in this room." I looked around at the thousands of books on the shelves and sighed. "Unfortunately, they could be hidden anywhere."

"Well, we obviously don't have time to check every book, so there must be clues that will direct us to weights," Lexi's mother, Clarissa, said. "I think we should start going over the room, looking for any clues that might help get us started."

That sounded like as good a plan as any to me, so we split up the room into sections and started to investigate. Winston and I ended up exploring adjacent areas in the back of the room. I hadn't been looking long when he called out to me.

"Gio, come look at this," he said, waving a hand.

I obliged and saw a beautifully finished wooden cone about two feet high with a wide base and a narrow top sitting on an end table between two stuffed chairs. The cone had a small hole in the center.

"What is it?" I asked, touching the cone. The sides contained a spiraling ridge that ran from the top of the cone to the bottom, looping around multiple times. To me it looked like a small road without guardrails spiraling down a steep mountain.

A single marble sat next to the cone in a small indentation in the table. I picked up the marble and studied it. "Do you think this goes down the ridge?"

Winston had been trying to open the end table's drawer, but it was locked. He looked at the marble and shrugged. "It's worth a try."

I carefully placed the marble on the spiral ridge at the top, but it quickly fell off the track as it spiraled down, picking up speed. I leaned over and picked up the marble off the floor. "We need a guardrail or another way to make the marble stay on the road."

Winston studied the cone. "What would be the point? Even if the marble rode the ridges, once it gets to the bottom, it would just roll off across the table and onto the floor again."

He had a point. "Would the marble fit in the hole at the top?"

"I think it would. But do we risk inserting it without knowing it is the right time? It is the obvious move. If we are wrong, we would lose the marble and perhaps the challenge."

He was right again. We couldn't risk it just yet.

I walked around to the back side of the table to get a better look at the other side of the cone. "Hey, there's something written on this side."

Winston joined me, peering at the inscription. "It looks like two words. The word near the bottom reads *libidine*. Over here is the word *haeresis*. Is that Italian?"

"It is not," I confirmed.

"Latin?" Winston mused. "I can't be certain, as my Latin language skills are limited to legal terms."

Lawyer. That was it. Lexi's father was a lawyer.

I straightened and looked across the room at Father Armando. "Emilio, can you come here for a moment? We have need of your expertise."

The priest walked across the room, joining Winston and me. "Can you tell me what these two words say? We think they are in Latin."

Father Armando studied the inscriptions. "The bottom word is Latin for *lust* and the top one is Latin for *heresy*."

"Now we're talking my language," I joked, and I heard Vittoria laugh from across the room.

"Save the exciting commentary for the honeymoon, love," Vittoria teased.

Winston grinned and studied the words again. "These are two strange words to write in Latin on the back of a cone. What do you think it means?"

"It sounds like a religious reference," I offered. "Like the seven deadly sins."

"Heresy wasn't a deadly sin, Gio," Stefan called out.

"I bet Father Armando thinks it should be," I replied. "Right, Father?"

"Right," Father Armando confirmed. "But Stefan is right. Heresy is not a deadly sin. However, looking at the cone from the side, I've noted there are nine spirals on it, which, combined with the words *heresy* and *lust* in Latin, bring to mind a particular book."

When we all looked at the priest blankly, he sighed. "The Italian master Dante Alighieri's *The Divine Comedy*. Anyone heard of it?"

THIRTY-SEVEN

Gio

IT RANG A vague bell, but Italian literature had never been my strong suit.

"I've heard of it," Vittoria volunteered.

I grinned. Of course she'd know—she'd been a literature major at the university and now, as a teacher, she always had her head in a book.

"Dante's *Inferno* and his nine levels of hell," she explained. "Heresy and lust are two of the levels, right?"

"Yes, Vittoria, you're right," Father Armando said. "There are nine levels of hell in his inferno. But, if I recall the levels correctly, lust is the second circle and heresy is the sixth out of the nine. So, it seems as if the word order is reversed on the cone, if we're presuming the reference to Dante's *Inferno* is correct."

I may not have known Dante, but I was familiar with hell. "Why not just turn the cone upside down so that hell is down and not up?" I suggested. "Isn't that the way it should be anyway? Hell at our feet." I lifted the cone off the desk and turned it over. "Look, there's a frame under here and a marble-size hole that enters into the desk." The frame was clearly designed to hold the cone mounted upside down. I carefully slid the cone in the frame that was anchored to the desk. Once inserted, the cone rested several inches above the desk, with the hole in the cone aligned directly over the one in the desk.

As I inserted the cone, Winston pointed out that the spiral ridges were reflected on the inside of the cone as well. Our excitement attracted the rest of the team. They abandoned their searches and gathered around to watch us.

"Put the marble in the ridge and see if it works," Father Armando suggested.

I picked up the marble, placing it at the top of the ridge. This time the marble spun faster and faster as centrifugal force pushed it out against the walls and kept the marble on the track.

Finally, at the bottom, the marble dropped out of the cone and into the hole in the desk. A faint click sounded. I grabbed the handle on the desk drawer and pulled it open.

"Success," I said, holding up a round, light-blue weight marked with the number four.

Clarissa frowned. "That seemed counterproductive. Why did we have to go through the whole spiral thing? Couldn't we have just dropped the marble in the hole and been done with it?"

"Maybe," Winston said, shrugging. "However, it's also possible the marble tripped something during its spiral. And what if we were wrong? We might have lost the marble and not been able to try again. So, Gio, what's next?"

I suddenly realized everyone was looking at me. Somehow, I'd been put in command. I suspected that was less because of any perceived skill at escape rooms and more because of my military training. I didn't mind so long as it kept us on track.

"Let's get back to looking around," I said, taking a page from Romeo's playbook. Looking for clues seemed the best way to go about this. "There are certainly more clues to find."

Everyone dispersed again. Alessa pulled up all the sofa and chair cushions looking for a clue, while Winston studied the large map on the wall near the card catalog.

Father Armando, Clarissa, and my love, Vittoria, diligently searched the bookshelves, pulling out occasional tomes, looking for hidden compartments or clues. I was beyond impressed by how enthusiastically she partici- pated in every challenge, giving it her all, even though I knew she must be exhausted. I was seeing a new side of her, and I loved it.

"Gio, I found something," she cried, holding up a torn strip of colored paper. "It was just lying here on the shelf. It has numbers written on it: 4075/1450 H15."

I walked over to check it out. "Does anyone have any idea what these numbers might mean?"

No one answered, but I didn't want to discard it just yet. "Even if we don't know what it means, let's assume everything is a clue." I handed the scrap of paper back to Vittoria. "Put it in front of the scale so we don't lose it. That'll be our spot for any additional clues or weights that we need to evaluate at a later point."

I'd just started examining a picture on the wall when Stefan called out. "Hey, guys, check out this old- fashioned card catalog. I haven't seen one of these in a long time. I presume it has information on all the books in this library." He pulled out a card and held it between his fingers. "Interesting. The information is printed in English on one side and Italian on the other. I wonder if this might allow Mr. Zachetti to reconfigure the room from Italian- to English-speaking groups by simply pulling out the drawers and turning them around. Clever."

I agreed. "Keep looking through the card catalog for anything out of place or any other clues. If the cards are in two languages, that must mean something."

I started to turn away and then had another thought. "Hey, Stefan, see if you can find any books that have titles relating to clues or weights. It's just a hunch, but we might get lucky."

"Great idea, bro," Stefan said. "I'll see what I can find."

For the first time, I noticed a sign above the card catalog that read *Please Return All Books*. Curious, I walked over and lifted the sign. Sure enough, on the other side it read, *Si Prega Di Restituire Tutti i Libri.*

Perhaps another clue.

"Guys, look for books that are out of place or not shelved," I called out.

Clarissa walked past me and plopped down onto a couch. "Like these books?" She picked up a stack of three books sitting on the end table. She put them on her lap, opening the first one and flipping through it.

I started looking through the drawer of the other end table.

"These books are written in Latin, too," Clarissa said. "Might that be important?"

I shut the empty drawer and sat next to her on the couch. I checked out the top book, confirming it wasn't in Italian. "Father Armando, can you check these books to see if there is any significance to them?"

Father Armando joined us, sitting on the other side of Clarissa. He examined the books and then started looking through them. "They are indeed in Latin. The top one is *The Aeneid* by Virgil, the second book is *The Divine Comedy* by Dante, and the third is *Il Principe* by Machiavelli."

"Well, we already figured out the significance of *The Divine Comedy* with the marble and the cone," Clarissa said. "These two other books are also written in Latin and penned by famous Italians or Romans." She took one of the books from Father Armando's lap. "But there's no library reference number on the spine of this book. There are on all the other books on the shelves."

I walked over to the shelves to confirm. Sure enough, all the books had reference numbers on the spines. Impressive. "I think you may be on to something, Mrs. Carmichael."

"Please, call me Clarissa," she said.

Lexi's mom was not only beautiful, but she was observant and clever. My brother would certainly have his hands full with two accomplished women in his life. Now that I thought about it, so would I.

"Maybe those are the lost books you're looking for," Stefan offered from across the room.

"Maybe," I said. "But how do they reshelve the books if they don't have reference numbers?"

"Let me see if I can find the books listed in the card catalog by title," Stefan said. "Maybe we can determine where they go."

"There are signs above some of the sections," Alessa called out. "That might help. Here's one that says, 'World War II History.'"

"There are some signs over here, too," Winston said from over by the scale. "These two bookcases that flank the scale have signs that say, 'Roman History and Culture' and 'Greek History and Culture.'"

"See if you can find a section called 'Italian Greats or Masters,'" Stefan called out to us, still rummaging through the card catalog. "I bet that's where they belong."

"Found it," Alessa called out a few seconds later. She

pointed to a sign on the second level on the back left wall that said "Italian Masters."

"Gio, can you check if there are empty spaces for the books to go there?" Stefan asked.

"I can." I strode over to Alessa and looked up at the sign. "Let me push the ladder over here, and I'll climb up and see what's there."

Father Armando put a hand on my shoulder. "I'll go. If there are more Latin books, it might be easier for me to figure out where they belong."

Made sense to me. "Sure." I pushed the ladder next to the section, made sure it was locked in place, and swept out my hand. "All yours, Father. I'll spot you at the bottom."

"Thanks, Gio. I appreciate that."

"Just don't break your neck, Father," Vittoria called out. "Or we'll never get married before the baby comes."

Everyone laughed as Father Armando began climbing the ladder. While he began his search, I glanced around the room to see what everyone else was doing.

Winston had wandered over to the display of WWII airplanes. I'd glanced at it earlier, noting there were aircraft from all the major countries that took part in the war. Most of the aircraft were fighters, and the craftsmanship was extraordinary. Clarissa was flipping through the books on the shelves near the scale, presumably looking for hidden compartments in the book covers or spines.

I glanced up the ladder and saw Father Armando surveying the array of books in the section. "Gio, can you move the ladder a little to the left, please?"

"Okay, Father. Hold on." I released the lock and slowly pushed it to the left until Father Armando told me to stop. "Do you see anything?"

"I do," the priest said, sounding excited. "I can see

gaps where it looks like the three books have been removed. It appears the books have been organized alphabetically by author's last name."

I watched as he stretched and slid a book into place. I hoped something would happen, but nothing did.

"On to the next one," Father Armando said. He found the gap and slid another book into place. Again, nothing happened. "That's odd. I'm sure these are the right places for the books."

"That's okay," I said. "Maybe all three have to go on the shelf before anything happens."

The priest replaced the last book, and we waited. Nothing occurred—no sign. Father Armando started climbing down the ladder when he spotted something on the bookshelf adjacent to the book he had just replaced.

"Gio, you told me to let you know if I saw something odd. I don't think *The Godfather* by Mario Puzo belongs in the 'Italian Masters' section."

"Au contraire," Stefan called out. "I consider that book a masterpiece of fiction."

"But does it really belong here?"

The priest reached over and pulled the book off the shelf, and a loud chime filled the room.

THIRTY-EIGHT

Gio

"WHOA." I SAID, startled. "What did you do, Father?"

Father Armando held the book in his hand. "I pulled *The Godfather* off the shelf and that chime sounded."

"Put it back and do it again," I instructed.

Father Armando carefully replaced the book and waited a minute. He then pulled the book off the shelf. The chime sounded again.

"Why is it doing that?" Alessa asked.

"I don't know," I said mystified. "Anyone got any theories?"

"I do," Clarissa said. "Father Armando is right. That book doesn't belong there. Mario Puzo isn't Italian. He's American."

"Italian American—maybe that's it," Alessa mused. "Perhaps we have to find the non-Italian authors in that section and take them off the shelf."

"Why worry about looking for non-Italian authors?" Vittoria said. "Let's just take *all* the books off that shelf in that section."

"That would take too much time," Alessa said. "Especially since they are on the second level and we don't know how many other puzzles we'll have to solve."

"Alessa's right," I said. "We don't have time. Father Armando, can you look over the entire section up there, and instead of pulling out every book, pull only those you think aren't true Italian masters?"

"I could, but I'm afraid I'm not the best person for that job. My knowledge of contemporary literature and poetry is quite limited."

"I can do it," Vittoria said confidently. "Come down, Father. I was a literature major at the university."

I narrowed my eyes. "You will *not* stand on a ladder in your condition, Vittoria."

"Gio, darling, I'm perfectly capable," she said, smiling sweetly at me.

Sometimes that smile worked on me, but this time it wouldn't. "Oh, I have no doubt you're capable." I blocked her way to the ladder. "However, you're still not going to climb that ladder."

"Perhaps I can assist?" Winston offered. "I'm fairly well-read in contemporary fiction, and Vittoria can assist me on the ones I'm uncertain about while safely planted on the ground. Fair enough compromise?"

I lifted an eyebrow and Vittoria finally acquiesced, understanding I was not going to budge. "Fine," she said. "I can do that."

Father Armando descended, after which Winston climbed up. Vittoria stood below ready to help. They began discussing titles and which authors were true masters and which ones weren't.

While Father Armando spotted the ladder, I drifted over to the display of famous World War II aircraft models Winston had been looking at earlier. As a military man, I appreciated the attention to the smallest details on the planes. The aircraft were arrayed on shelves starting at knee level and extending well above our heads. Each aircraft had a little card identifying it. I saw a P-51 Mustang, a Russian Airacobra, a US Navy Hellcat, a British Spitfire, a Japanese Zero, a Corsair, a German Stuka, a Japanese Kite, and Italian aircraft with numerical designations. All had been artfully presented on the shelves. I saw no obvious pattern among the aircraft or countries. I wasn't sure as to their point in the library other than as a cool display.

I heard a chime from the bookshelf and looked up as Winston called out, "I just removed a book by Plato."

"Good job," I called out. "Keep it going."

Winston pulled some more books from the shelves, dropping them down. There were chimes for each one, but nothing else happened. "I just got rid of Francis Ford Coppola, Homer, and Tomie dePaola," he called out. "I don't see any more suspect books. Everything else seems legit."

"You must have missed something," Vittoria insisted. "Start over."

Winston shook out his arms and started back at the far side of the shelf. After a moment, he stopped. "Was Archimedes Italian? I thought he lived in Sicily. Doesn't that count as Italy?"

"You're mistaken," Father Armando yelled from across the room. "Archimedes is Greek."

Shrugging, Winston pulled out the book, and another chime sounded. Suddenly, the sign that identified the "Italian Masters" section swung up, revealing a secret niche underneath.

"Look! We did it," Vittoria shouted, pointing to the niche. "Winston, can you see what's in there?"

"Gio, can you move the ladder over?" Winston asked.

I unlocked the ladder, pushing it until Winston could

reach the hole beneath the sign. He stuck his hand in the niche and pulled out a light-blue weight and a rolled-up piece of paper. "Another weight," he called out. "We're making progress."

"Great. Come back down carefully." I spotted him until he climbed off and handed me the weight.

"Another number-four weight." I walked it over to the scale table and set it next to the scale.

Winston unrolled the paper and read aloud, "What's greater than God? / More evil than Satan. / The poor have it, the rich need it, / And if you eat it you will die."

I sighed. "Riddles. I hate riddles. I can never figure them out. And now they want me to figure out a riddle in English?"

"I'm good with riddles," Clarissa offered, standing next to her husband while reading the riddle. "Let me have a go."

"Could it be a play on the letters?" Alessa asked. "Sometimes if you take the first letter of every sentence, it forms a word." She stared at the words, trying to make sense of the letters.

"Maybe, but I think the key to solving riddles is to focus on one part and use that to find something in common with the rest," Stefan said.

"What do the poor have that the rich need?" Father Armando mused aloud.

"I personally think the not-eating part must be the important clue in the riddle," Winston declared. "What things should you not eat? Chemicals, metal, poisonous plants? What do you think, Clarissa?" When she didn't respond, he repeated himself. "Are you listening, honey?"

She glanced up from the riddle. "I heard you. Nothing is all I can think of."

Winston looked at her in surprise. "Well, that shocks me. You never give up that easily. Riddles are your thing."

She patted him on the cheek. "My dearest husband, I've already given my answer. The answer to the riddle is *nothing*. Nothing is greater than God, if you eat nothing you will die, etc."

For a moment, everyone stared at her before it started to sink in. "She's right," I finally said. "Clarissa figured out the riddle. Nothing is the answer."

THIRTY-NINE

Gio

STEFAN GLANCED AT me, puzzled. "The clue is nothing? How does that help us, Gio?"

I tried to think what that might signify but came up with...nothing. "Stefan, go check in the card catalog and see if there's a book in the library that starts with the word *nothing* or has the word *nothing* in it."

"Or a synonym for nothing," Clarissa suggested. "Wordplays are big in riddles. So, check for words like *nil*, *zilch*, *zero*, *zip*, or *naught.*"

"That's too many words," Vittoria complained. "Stefan will be looking in the card catalog forever."

Something Clarissa said tugged at my memory. Zilch? No, zero. Where had I just seen something mention a zero?

"Wait a minute," I said, snapping my fingers. "There's a Japanese airplane in the World War II collection called the Mitsubishi Zero. It's a long shot, but worth a closer look. I'll need a ladder to reach it."

I hurried over to the ladder Winston had just used and pushed it toward the airplane display. Once I got it where I wanted it, I climbed up and carefully lifted the

Mitsubishi Zero from the display, handing it down to Winston. "Be careful," I warned him. "It's heavy."

Winston cradled the plane and carefully carried it to the scale table. I climbed down from the ladder and angled it under the lamp so I could get a better look.

"I think I see something." I carefully reached my hand into the cockpit, twisted my hand, and slowly pulled out a small round weight. This weight was dark blue and had the number six on it. Taped to the top was a small, folded note.

"Yes!" Alessa exclaimed. "Another weight. Way to go, Gio."

"Don't give me the credit. This is a total team effort." I carefully extracted the note and handed the weight to Stefan. He and Winston began trying to balance the scale with the weights we'd already collected.

"Read the note," Vittoria urged me, so I gingerly unfolded it. Like the others, the clue was in both English and Italian, but since there were non-Italian speakers in our group, I read aloud in English.

"My seas are dry, / My mountains rise no more. / My forests are green, but treeless. / My cities are many, / But of people, I have none."

"Sounds like an apocalypse," Alessa mused. "Dry seas, no people. The end of the world, an endless stretch of desert, or a nuclear winter, maybe."

"Perhaps it refers to the end of time," Father Armando offered. "In a biblical sense."

"But the forest in the riddle is green, not burned," Winston said, looking up from the scale. "That doesn't sound like an apocalypse to me."

"Perhaps it refers to the moon," Stefan mused. "It has a sea with no water."

"But the moon doesn't have cities or green forests," Vittoria countered. "So that doesn't make sense, either."

"Clarissa?" I asked. "Have any thoughts?"

Everyone moved aside so Clarissa could look at it. She maneuvered the paper beneath the lamp to see it better. After a moment, she looked up. "I think the riddle is referring to a map."

"A map?" I said, stunned.

Stefan threw his hands up in astonishment. "How. Do. You. Do. That? It's crazy amazing."

Clarissa bestowed Stefan with a dazzling smile, one that practically lit up the entire room. Romeo had told me that Lexi's mother had been a beauty queen or something when she was younger and, no kidding, that woman could still turn heads. Apparently, she also had intellect by the bucket load. Impressive.

"I told you I like crossword puzzles, riddles, logic, and word games," she said lightly, as if she hadn't just solved a complicated riddle in less than a minute. "I do one in the newspaper every morning, even when my favorite paper moved online. It's my thing, as is said these days."

"Well, I'm highly appreciative of your thing, Clarissa," Stefan declared, bowing and causing us all to laugh.

Since Clarissa had mentioned a map, I quickly moved to inspect the only map I saw in the room—the gigantic world map hanging on the right-side wall. If the riddle was pointing us to a map, there was no bigger one in the room than this one. It was mounted in a thick wooden frame and was marked as being from the 1600s. Its depiction of the Americas, Oceania, and eastern Asia was wildly out of proportion. Greenland and Antarctica were completely missing, and there were only a few representations of cities and an occasional name in roughly the right geographic location. Rivers were prominently displayed, but mountain ranges were not.

Unlike modern maps, this one lacked a compass that

oriented the map to the cardinal directions. Instead, whoever had mounted the map had placed a compass on the frame adjacent to the map to avoid damaging what was clearly a valuable historical item.

"What are we looking for?" Alessa asked, joining me at the map.

"I have no idea, but hopefully we'll know when we see it. Got any ideas?"

"Not a single one," she murmured.

"Father Armando, how much time do we have left?" I asked.

The priest checked the old-fashioned clock on the wall. "About an hour. I think we're making good progress. We've already collected three weights and several clues."

"Although, unfortunately, the weights we've found are not enough to balance the scale," Winston replied. He'd been trying to balance the weights we'd already found, with no success.

Stefan joined Alessa and me at the map, and the three of us stared at it for a while longer. Without knowing what we were looking for, it was impossible to find anything. We decided to regroup to see what options we had.

"In terms of clues, we have one pointing us to the map, but we're not sure what we're looking for," I said. "Just the same, Clarissa, Alessa, and I will keep looking at the map and see if anything jumps out at us. Stefan, head back to the card catalog and look for books that have to do with maps. Vittoria, Winston, and Father Armando, check the bookshelves and tables for any maps lying around or books that might have maps *in* them. We have to figure out why the map is our clue."

"Wait," Stefan suddenly said. "There was a dedicated section in the card catalog labeled 'Maps.'" He rushed back to the catalog and began thumbing through it. "Yes, it's here. But that's weird. From what I can tell, there are several hundred cards for maps. But where are all of these maps?"

I looked around but only saw the giant map on the wall. "Several *hundred* maps?"

"Yes," Stefan replied. "Maybe they're elsewhere in the castle?"

"We can't leave this room," Alessa reminded us. "They have to be here somewhere."

"I agree, but where?" He looked around the room again. "Gio, can you see if there's a library reference code noted somewhere on the map?"

I peered at the map in the lower right-hand corner near the ornate, raised compass rose.

"Well, is there a code or not?" Stefan called out impatiently.

"There is, but there's something wrong with this map," I replied.

"What's wrong with it?" Alessa asked.

"The compass rose on this map has north pointing east toward China, instead of toward the top of the map, where it should go."

"The compass is not attached to the map," Alessa pointed out. "Maybe it was installed incorrectly."

"Anything that's odd is most likely a clue," Clarissa reminded us.

I stared at the compass and then the map. "I might be able to adjust it. What if I try turning the compass to the correct position if I can?"

"Give it a shot," my brother called out.

I reached down and turned the compass rose ninety degrees counterclockwise. To my astonishment, the map, and the wood frame on which it was mounted, suddenly moved backward a few inches and slid sideways into the wall.

We'd found a hidden room.

FORTY

Gio

"WHOA," I BREATHED. "I didn't see that coming."

I stepped across the threshold, and the lights turned on automatically, abruptly illuminating the space. Dominating the center of the room was a life-size bronze statue of a wolf with two human figures crouched beneath it. The statue was perched on a large marble pedestal.

The rest of the room was filled with bookshelves and cartography tables. Mounted maps covered most of the right and back walls. The left wall contained a deep rack that supported hundreds of tubes, which presumably contained maps. A tall, wide metal file cabinet with dozens of shallow drawers stood in the back left corner of the room. To the right of that cabinet, a large flat table with swivel lights and magnifiers for map viewing had been positioned. The tubes and drawer fronts were clearly marked with library notations.

We'd clearly found the stash of maps noted in the card catalog.

"A map room," Clarissa said softly from behind me.

I turned and saw the rest of the group had crowded

inside with me and were looking around in awe. Vittoria slid up next to me, so I put an arm around her, pulling her against my side.

"This is incredible," she breathed. "Gio, look at that statue. It's an exact replica of the famous statue in Rome. You know, the one about the founding of the city."

I studied it for a moment. "You mean the Lupa Capitolina?"

"*Si*, that's the one."

"I've seen that statue in a museum before," Alessa said. "In Rome, I think. The wolf is suckling Romulus and Remus, the mythical founders of Rome. The twins were purportedly thrown into the Tiber River by their father—the god Mars—because he feared them to be a potential threat to his rule. The children were saved by Tiberinus, father of the river, who gave them to a she-wolf to care for and raise as her own. Eventually, Faustulus, a shepherd, adopted them and the twins grew up tending sheep, not knowing their true identities until much later."

"It's beautiful," Clarissa said, running her fingers along the marble pedestal.

"There are Roman numerals on the pedestal," Winston pointed out. "DCCLIII. Any idea as to the significance of that number?"

"Since the statue features Romulus and Remus, my best guess is that it stands for 753, the year Rome was founded," Alessa said.

Two maps hanging side by side caught my eye, so I moved closer to inspect them. The map on the left showed ancient Rome, while the map on the right showed modern Rome. It was an incredibly interesting comparison.

"It's truly fascinating that so many of the major

highways and streets today follow the same routes and paths from two thousand years ago," I said.

"Come look at this map, Gio," Father Armando called while examining a huge floor-to-ceiling map along the back wall of the room. "This map shows the Roman Empire throughout its various periods of history. It covers all the Mediterranean, the Mideast, North Africa, and much of southern and central Europe. It's extraordinary."

I walked over to get a better look while Alessa pulled out a couple of random tubes and unrolled the maps onto one of the cartography tables. "These maps are a mixture of ancient, old, and modern," she said. "The maps in the pull-out drawers, however, appear to be much older and probably far more valuable."

"There are valuable historical documents here," Vittoria said, coming to stand beside me. "I find it quite strange that Mr. Zachetti would find it acceptable to use them for a game. Please, handle everything with care."

I'd been thinking the exact same thing. I ran my hand over her hair, and she smiled up at me.

"So, what exactly are we looking for?" Alessa asked. "And yes, I seem to be asking that question a lot."

"I don't know," I said, blowing out a breath. "And I'm giving that answer a lot. There are too many things to see and not enough time to figure out what we need. We need another clue that gives us more guidance as to what we're searching for with the map."

"Not to be the bearer of bad news, but we only have forty-five minutes left," Father Armando said.

"Okay, team, what clues haven't we used yet?" I asked.

"We have the numbers and colors on the weights, and that's all I can think of," Alessa said. "We determined the numbers equal weight, but what about the colors?"

"And what about the scrap of paper I found on the floor?" Vittoria said. "It had some numbers on it, but they didn't make any sense."

"Let's take a look at that again," I said. "Bring me the paper, Vittoria, would you?"

She left the room and brought it back a minute later. "The numbers say 4075/1450 H15. Those don't seem like map coordinates to me."

"Let's try it anyway," I suggested. "We've got nothing to lose…except time."

"Let's assume the first number is the latitude." Stefan came over to stand beside me and peered over my shoulder. "I guess it could be 04 north or 04 south or 40N or 40S, depending on whether it's above or below the equator, and, of course, where the decimal place is."

Alessa flanked me on the other side, her voice sounding excited. "That's a great idea, Stefan. We could then assume the second number is the longitude. We try east and west and see if it could be 01 or 014 or 145."

"What about the H15?" I asked, tapping my finger on the paper. "What does that mean?"

"I don't know," Stefan said. "But let's see what the first numbers yield and go from there."

"All of that is a good plan," Clarissa noted. "But which map should we use?"

She'd asked a very good question. We were in a room surrounded by thousands of maps. Which one should we use?

"Let's use the giant world map that opened the door to this chamber," I decided.

"But it's hidden in the wall since we used it to open the door," Vittoria pointed out.

"I know, but the door was closed when we came in, so there must be some way to close it again, right?"

We all exited the map room and started searching

along the wall. "I think I've got something," Winston said, pointing just inside the right edge of the door. It was an inconspicuous metal symbol shaped like a compass rose.

"Rotate it," I suggested.

Winston rotated the symbol, and the door closed. We quickly began trying to map the locations on the wall using the different longitude and latitude combinations. Most of them landed in the middle of the ocean. A couple were in the middle of the Congo, one was off the east coast of Spain...but the last one landed on the west coast of Italy, near Naples.

"Italy, at last," I exclaimed. "That has to be it. Stefan, can you tell exactly where those coordinates are in Italy?"

"Not on this map. We need a bigger map of Italy."

"What about the map of the Roman Empire on the back wall of the map room?" Clarissa suggested. "That was much bigger and centered on Italy. I don't recall if it has latitude and longitude on it, but we can look."

We reopened the door to the map room and checked it out. Stefan and Alessa read me the coordinates, and I plotted them carefully on the map. My finger fell directly on the Roman city of Pompeii.

"What does it mean?" Vittoria asked me.

"I have no idea."

"Look," Vittoria said, pointing at the map edges. "There's another grid on the map."

I bent down to look where she'd pointed. Sure enough, letters ran across the top of a small grid with numbers along the side.

Vittoria measured from my finger on the map to the grid. "Pompeii is at H15. I think that confirms our deduction. Now, we need to figure how Pompeii figures into this."

"Who can find me a map of Pompeii?" I called out.

"Already ahead of you," Stefan said running out of the room and presumably back to the card catalog. After a moment, he shouted, "See if you can find map 930M88-1."

Winston, Clarissa, and Alessa began searching the tubes, while Vittoria and I searched through the pull-out map drawers.

"Got it," Alessa shouted a few minutes later, sneezing as she pulled out a tube. "Wow, it's dusty and heavy."

Clarissa pointed to one end of the tube. "That's because there is a weight attached to the end of the tube. Team, I think we've found our next clue."

FORTY-ONE

Gio

"YES!" ALESSA EXCLAIMED, pulling the deep-purple weight with the number eight off the tube and handing it to me. "We did it!"

There were a few whoops as I handed it off to Winston, urging him and Father Armando to take it to the scale and see if they could get the scales to even out. Then I gave the tube back to Alessa to return it from where she'd got it.

"Shouldn't we at least look at the map in case there's another clue there?" she asked.

"Good point," I said. I carefully slid the map out of the tube. In addition to the map of Pompeii, which I noted was based upon the archaeological record of 2015, there was an unsealed white envelope.

"I just hope it isn't another riddle," Stefan said sighing. "I'm pretty much done with that."

I opened the envelope and pulled out a card written in English on one side and Italian on the other. "No such luck, Stefan," I said before reading it aloud. "Not in the shade, but under the light / Balance the scale to come out right."

"I think this means we're getting close," Alessa said. "It seems to be telling us to use the weights now." She dashed out of the room with the riddle still in her hand.

"Let's go check how Father Armando and Winston are doing," Stefan said, walking to the threshold of the map room, then stopping, switching to Italian. "Aren't you coming, Gio?"

"I guess so. But something's telling me this has been too easy."

"Too easy?" Stefan said in disbelief. "Are you out of your mind?"

"I don't know," I said, shrugging. "It's just a feeling."

"Well, we still have twenty-five minutes if we run into any problems. Come on."

"I suppose you're right."

I followed him into the room where everyone was working on the scales. I peeked over Father Armando's shoulder. He and Winston had put the nine, seven, five, and two weights on the left and four, four, six, and eight weights on the right. The scale lifted slightly. Winston put the last weights on, but after a moment, the left end sank back down again.

"It's close, but we need to swap a weight to make it balance," Winston said.

"Try swapping a four-pound weight for a five-pound one," Clarissa suggested.

Winston switched it around, but now the scale tipped to the right. More suggestions came as they worked it, but no matter how many combinations they did, they couldn't get it to balance evenly.

"We're missing a weight," Winston said, sitting down on the couch and running his hand through his hair in frustration. "That must be it, because we're so close."

"We're out of clues," Vittoria said, joining Winston

on the couch and cradling her stomach. "What are we going to do?"

Clarissa stood alone at the table with the scale, not touching anything, but staring at the setup. "Why are the weights color-coded?" she finally asked.

Winston shook his head. "I don't know. I hadn't really thought about it." He glanced over at me. "Gio, have any thoughts on that?"

"Not a one."

"Well, perhaps we can use the colors to predict what color of weight we should be looking for," Clarissa said.

"That's an interesting idea," Alessa said, standing next to Clarissa. "And what if we stack the weights the way they were originally? Heaviest to lightest on the left. Then we can stack the ones on the right similarly."

"That's not going to even the scale," Stefan warned.

"Not yet," Alessa corrected him. "We won't know until we try."

"Alessa is right. It's worth a try," Clarissa said, stacking them by weight. "The one thing I noticed is that when we stack the weights by color, it follows the pattern of the color wheel, going from red to green to blue to dark purple. Perhaps that's significant."

"We haven't adequately addressed this riddle, either," Father Armando said, holding up the paper with the short riddle we'd found in the Pompeii map tube.

Not in the shade, but under the light

Balance the scale to come out right.

"That's right," Alessa said, rubbing her temples. "'Not in the shade, but under the light.' Which light?"

"Maybe there's a light switch we need to turn on to allow the scale to make a small adjustment," Father Armando said, looking around the room.

"Everyone look for a light switch," I ordered. "And fast."

Vittoria found the switch on the wall just inside the door where we'd come into the room. It was currently on. "Turn it off," I said. "Let's see what happens."

Vittoria flipped the switch, and the room darkened except for the lights in the map room, the table lamp on the small end table in the back of the room, and a pole lamp near the couch.

"I need someone on each light. Vittoria, stay on the room light. Stefan, take charge of the lights in the map room. Father Armando, stand next to the pole lamp. Winston, Alessa, and Clarissa, you watch the scale. Let's try different combinations of turning the lights on and off to see what happens."

We tried a variety of light combinations, but nothing changed in terms of the scale. "Nothing is happening and we're running out of time." Alessa's voice was heavy with disappointment, echoing what we were all feeling.

After several minutes of trying various light switches, I called it quits. "Turn all the lights on for now. Perhaps there's a hidden light or lamp we're missing. Let's see if we can find anything."

Clarissa returned to the paper with the riddle and studied it. Then with a laugh, she set the paper down. "No need to do that. I've solved the riddle."

I glanced up in surprise. "You did?"

"I did. It's not in the *shade*." She wagged the paper with the riddle on it at me. "Remember I told you about the wordplay? The riddle isn't talking about the shade as in darkness, but the *lampshade*. The clue says it's not in the lampshade. That's because it's *under* the light. Check beneath all the lamps."

"Do it!" I ordered as everyone scattered, heading for a light. I sincerely wanted to plant a huge kiss on Clarissa's lips, but instead, I ran to help Father Armando with the heavy pole light. The priest was already tipping it up to look underneath. Alessa had lifted the lamp on the end table, peering below it, while Winston ran toward the map room to check beneath the lamps in there.

"It's here," I shouted as soon as I saw the bottom of the pole lamp. "The base of the lamp is the final weight. It says 'thirty' on it. Someone, help me unscrew this thing from the pole while Father Armando holds it."

Stefan knelt beside me, and we quickly unscrewed the bolt attaching the base to the pole. I hefted the weight and carried it to the scale. "Take off all the weights on the right side," I said. Alessa and Clarissa quickly removed them, and I put the base on the right side of the scale by itself.

The scale leaned heavily in that direction.

"We need at least four weights on the left side to balance it," Stefan said. "If we presume that all the weights are proportional to their numbers, then we need at least four weights equaling thirty on the left side to balance it."

"Already ahead of you," Alessa said, efficiently loading the weights onto the scale. "If we use the nine- and seven-pound weights from the original set, and the eight- and six-pound weights from the new batch, that equals thirty." She put the last weight on, and the scale wavered back and forth…before it balanced perfectly.

"We did it!" Vittoria whooped, hugging Alessa, Clarissa, and then me. Everyone shouted and congratulated each other while I walked over to the red button on the wall and punched it. A glance at the clock indicated we'd finished the puzzle with less than four minutes to spare.

I returned to face Clarissa and Winston, who were standing arm in arm. I took Clarissa's hand, lifting it to my lips. "Clarissa, I'll always be in your debt. Your brilliance, and that of your husband and daughter, is much appreciated."

I hugged Vittoria and gave her a kiss before facing the rest of the team. "Everyone performed beyond expectation. I don't even know what to say, and those of you who know me well, understand that is most surprising. It's truly an honor to have completed this challenge with you. I'm proud to call you friends and family."

At that moment, the gamemaster walked into the room. His gaze flicked toward the open door of the map room as he headed for the scale. He carefully checked the scale balance and the weights before turning to face us.

"Congratulations," he said. "Once again, I'm astounded by your excellent performance." He handed me a golden disc with the number forty-five engraved on it. "You should know that over the years, others have solved this escape room, but you are the first to have done it by solving *all* the puzzles. How is it that you, a family without a single Nobel prize or scientific award among you, has managed to do something many of the brightest minds in the world have failed to do? Bravo." He then turned to Father Armando and dipped his head. "I see you were a valuable addition to the team, Father. Most impressive."

"It was my pleasure," the priest responded, smiling. "Sincerely."

"Well, thank you for those generous accolades, Brando," Clarissa said, fanning herself. "However, if we're done here, I'm hot and tired and greatly looking forward to relaxing and enjoying a wonderful lunch prepared by that genius chef of yours along with a glass of exquisite Italian wine to go with it. I'm quite famished."

"Of course, my lady. Your lunch already awaits you in the dining room." Brando swept out an arm toward the door. "Please, after you."

Everyone filed out of the room, but I hung back a bit and fell into step with Brando. "So, did the other team solve their escape room?" I asked.

The gamemaster glanced at his watch before giving me a smile. "We'll find that out in about six minutes."

FORTY-TWO

Lexi

WE WAITED IN the dining room while the gamemaster took the other team away. Ten minutes later, he returned and led us toward the front of the castle, down some stone stairs.

We stopped in front of a metal door with a keypad next to it. He punched in some numbers, and the door swung open. "Please, everyone, enter carefully. It's dark."

I stepped into the room, which was lit only by red lights coming from hidden fixtures. It took a minute or so for my eyes to fully adjust. The walls of the room were a checkerboard mix of black and mirrored tiles that gave the room an eerie atmosphere. One wall had a scorpion made entirely of red mirrored tiles.

Weird.

The room had only one piece of furniture: a small metal keyboard mounted on a pole and attached to a raised chair in the center of the room. There were two metal rings around the base of the chair that appeared to serve as steps. The chair faced a large video screen that was currently dark. Brando turned on the screen with a switch on its side before walking to a closed door on the left side of the room and pulling on it, apparently confirming it was locked.

The video screen jumped to life. A small, elevated track with three shoebox-size, radio-controlled cars came into view. The elevated track was hilly and curvy as it wound back and forth through a room about the size of a one-car garage. The narrow track was not much wider than the cars, and there was a drop of a couple of feet from the track to the ground, meaning the slightest mistake would cause the car to fall off the track. A raised platform with a ramp from the track was at the end of the track.

"Lexi, as the designated gamer, I ask you to take a seat in the chair," Brando said, sweeping his arm out toward the chair.

I climbed up the metal steps and sat down. A control console swung up from the side of the chair and in front of me. Hooked on one side was a pair of high-tech headphones.

"Okay, that's pretty cool," I said.

"Indeed," the gamemaster agreed. "Now, Lexi, you may not leave this chair until it's time to exit the room. I'll explain further in a minute."

I ran my fingers over the console buttons, getting familiar with them while the gamemaster continued.

"This challenge has two parts. The first part is a combination of skill and problem solving. The second part will test your teamwork, powers of observation, ability to communicate, and willingness to learn from your mistakes. To complete the first part of the challenge, Lexi must navigate at least one of the radio-controlled cars onto the platform at the end of the track. Doing so will unlock the closed door to my left so you may begin the second part of the challenge. To succeed at the second task, Lexi must navigate you to the platform at the far end of the room, where you'll find the code to exit this room. Be warned, you'll be able to hear Lexi, but she'll not be able to hear you. The room efficiently absorbs sound."

It sounded odd, but at least it appeared *relatively* straightforward...so far. However, since the challenges had become ridiculously harder, I doubted it would be easy.

Brando picked up a cloth bag off a thin counter that ran just under the front of the screen. He asked everyone except me to hold out their right arms while he affixed a small plastic bracelet around each wrist. When he finished, a dim red glow outlined the edges of the bracelet.

"Only I can remove the bracelet with a special tool after you exit the room," he said. "The purpose of the bracelet is to notify you when you're eliminated from the challenge. This will happen if you get to the second half of the challenge and step off the path in the far room. At that time, your bracelet will flash red, and a door will be illuminated on the side of the far room. You are to proceed to that door and exit the challenge. The bracelet will provide just enough light for you to safely exit the room. Until you do, the control room lights, cameras, and microphones will be inoperative. So, any delays will cost your team valuable time. You will then proceed and wait outside the entry door until the challenge is over."

"So, team members can actually be eliminated, and we can still win the challenge?" I asked.

"That's correct. I will explain further in a moment."

He put the bag that held the bracelets on the counter under the screen and picked up two more items that looked like flashlights. "These are strobe lights. You'll need them to complete the challenge. I warn you, however, they have an extremely limited battery life. So, if you attempt to use them for any other purpose, like to navigate the walkway, they'll not have sufficient battery life to accomplish their intended purpose."

"But there are only two strobe lights and six of us," Juliette said. "Who gets to use them?"

"That's entirely up to you," Brando responded. "Now, let me review the challenge once more. First, Lexi must drive at least one of the radio-controlled cars onto the platform. If she fails, the challenge is over. If she succeeds, the door to your left will open, and one or more of you will proceed in the dark along an obstacle-ridden path to another platform guided only by her instructions. If you step off the path for any reason, you're eliminated and must exit the game immediately. The game will be frozen until you are out, so I suggest you move quickly. If one or more of you manages to make it to the platform, there'll be additional obstacles. If you conquer those, you must solve the remaining puzzle to acquire a code. Once you have the code, at least one of you with a nonalarmed bracelet *must* return to the control room with the code and use it on the keypad for you and Lexi to exit the room." He looked around the room. "Any questions?"

I stared at the screen and back at Brando. "Just to be clear, I have to have at least one person with an alarm bracelet that hasn't been activated and the code obtained from the platform in order to exit the room and win the challenge."

"Correct. You'll have two hours to complete the challenge. After that, the screen, the cameras, the infrared lights, and the screen will turn off and the house lights will come up. I warn you, this room has *never* been solved before. In fact, only one team has even made it past the cars, so best of luck."

We all looked at each other as Brando exited the room and the clock over the door began its countdown.

"Okay, I guess the first part is up to me." I faced the screen, sliding the headset onto my ears and adjusting the mic in front of my mouth. I'd already briefly checked out the console. On one side was a high-end gaming controller with dual thumb sticks, four triggers, and four face buttons.

Slash climbed up one of the steps and examined the setup over my shoulder. "Must be Bluetooth-connected," he commented as I lifted the console and saw it didn't have any wires.

Several sets of multicolored buttons were on the left side of the console, and in the center of it was a square button labeled "microphone." Only three buttons on the left-hand side were illuminated.

I picked up the controller and tentatively moved the thumb stick but saw no response on the screen.

"Try that," Slash said, pointing to a green-lit button.

I pushed it, and one of the three cars came to life with a green light pulsing on its roof. I tried using the thumb stick again, and the car moved forward a foot or so. I pulled back, and the car returned to its position.

"While I would have preferred a racing controller, I think I can handle this," I said. "But it seems too easy. There has to be something I don't know yet, especially since only one team has conquered this section of the challenge."

Slash murmured his agreement as I briefly turned on each of the cars. I also pulled and pushed a couple of levers on the side of the console, discovering they moved my stool up and down and even rotated it.

"That's pretty sweet," I said, moving the stool into a position that gave me a full view of the track.

I started driving the green car slowly around the pad

to get the feel for it before driving it onto the track. In the process, I discovered one of the thumb sticks acted as a brake. That could be useful. I tried a few more moves before I uncovered a significant issue.

"The controls are backward," I said. "Slash, check this out." When I steered the car right, it went left. When I steered the car left, it went right. The forward and back movements were accurate, but the right and left were reversed.

"That's going to affect your accuracy, timing, and reflexes," Slash said. "Be careful with it."

"Easy for you to say. Okay, let me check that it's true for all three of the cars." I experimented a bit and confirmed the same setup on all the cars. "Well, this is going to make it a lot harder, but not impossible. I'll just have to go slow and steady, but we have to get moving."

"You've got this, Lexi," Mia called, and I smiled as I carefully maneuvered the first car onto the track. I moved it up the ramp and onto the track. I negotiated the first simple turn with a few small adjustments. Feeling slightly more confident, I picked up the pace slightly and made a couple more turns.

"It's not easy fighting my instincts honed from years of play," I said. "Right is left, and left is right. It's crazy."

Still, I was making progress, so that was good. In fact, I started to think I was getting the hang of it when I approached a steep hill on the track. I slowed as I reached the top, but once I started down, I was going too fast to make the hard right turn at the bottom. I tried to correct in the moment, but my instincts moved the car in the opposite direction, and the car tumbled off the track.

The room fell deadly silent.

Slash, who still stood watching over my shoulder, patted my arm. "Consider it a necessary learning curve, *cara*. You've got this."

Inhaling a deep breath, I fired up the second car with determination. I carefully retraced my steps, but the fact that I was eating up the clock was adding to my anxiety. I had to strike that delicate balance of accuracy and time, and it wasn't going to be easy.

I started driving again, and it felt like I was starting to get a handle on the backward steering. My confidence on the turns and braking increased even though I almost lost it a couple of times. I finally reached a set of four climbing switchback turns about three-quarters of the way into the track. I was close to finishing. I took the first two turns slowly, and then the third one with a little more confidence, but on the fourth, I made the same mistake. Needing to go left, I steered left, and the car slid off the right side of the track before I could react.

Gasps sounded in the room, and I closed my eyes. But I wasn't upset—I was mad. The track wasn't that hard. I'd played on dozens of tracks a lot harder than this and won them handily.

"It's part of the mental challenge," Slash said. "The more skilled you are at these kinds of games, the harder it's going to be for you."

"That's the problem. It really isn't that hard. But if I lose concentration for even a second, it's fatal. It's like trying to drive fast while going in reverse. I've always struggled looking in the rearview mirror. It would be fairly simple if I could reverse the course back to normal."

"What if you looked at the screen in a mirror?" Oscar asked. "Wouldn't that reverse it the right way?"

"Of course, but where would we get a mirror?"

"What about the mirror tiles on the wall?" Oscar suggested. "Looking at them made me think maybe one of them could act like a rearview mirror for you."

Slash jumped down from the chair. "Brilliant idea, Oscar. Let's see if we can pry one of them off the wall."

Everyone began pulling at the tiles.

"They're not coming off," Mia complained.

Suddenly Tito gave a whoop as one of the tiles popped off. "I've got one. How are you going to use it, Lexi?"

Slash held it up behind me, and after fiddling around and trying to sit sideways in the chair and work over my shoulder, I remembered I could pivot the chair. I rotated the chair, facing away from the screen. After Slash repositioned the mirror a few times, I fired up the final car and drove it onto the track.

"It's working," I said, making rapid progress.

"Don't get cocky," Tito warned.

I easily made it past the section with the four switchbacks and approached the final, sweeping turn right before the ramp to the platform. I drove confidently and was almost over the rise before the last turn.

"Stop!" Oscar suddenly shouted.

FORTY-THREE

Lexi

I USED THE brake trigger and quickly brought the car to a halt, although it almost skidded over the edge. My heart pounded at the close call.

"I'm sorry about scaring you," Oscar said. "But there's a problem with the final turn. I can't tell for sure in the lighting, but I think the track in the curve is banked away from the turn instead of into it. If you aren't creeping along that corner, you're going to slide off."

"I didn't know you were so well versed in car games," Juliette said to her husband in surprise.

"I may have played a time or two with the boys, just for fun," he said, his cheeks reddening.

"You're actually pretty good, Oscar," Slash said. "You surprised all of us with your need for speed."

While the others laughed, I peered at the spot where Oscar had pointed. I wasn't sure, but since it was the last turn, I wasn't going to take any chances. I slowed to a crawl. Sure enough, the track banked away, just as Oscar had suspected.

I blew out a breath. "Great save, Oscar. I'd have gone right over the edge if you hadn't warned me."

Easing around the turn, I hit the final stretch and gunned the car up the ramp and onto the platform. Amid the cheers from the others, a red light came on over the platform, and the side door in the control room slid open. The big video screen went dark and, simultaneously, a new set of buttons illuminated on the console.

We'd made it through the first part of the challenge. Unfortunately, I'd eaten up a lot of time.

Slash set the mirror aside and carefully stepped into the darkened room. "It's a complete blackout situation with only the first few feet of the floor revealed by the red light of the control room," he said. "The edges of the door are highlighted with the same thin ribbon of light as the edge of our bracelets. What's next?"

Not sure, I pushed one of the buttons on the console and the screen illuminated, although this time in black and white and much dimmer. The view gave me an overhead shot of the room. Most of the screen was dark, with the circle of a single spotlight showing me a small section of the floor. A meandering path cut across the pool of light and into the dark shadows beyond. The lighted areas and borders of the path shone on my screen in an eerie white—infrared—just like the gamemaster had said.

"The edges along the path must be heated slightly or have a mild current running through them to make them stand out under the infrared," Slash commented. "That could also be part of the alarm system if someone leaves the track."

I pushed the next buttons in succession, and as I did so, the prior light turned off and a new one lit up. I was able to walk the lights down the length of the room and around a corner, where I could see a raised platform. While the first two-thirds of the path was contiguous, the latter third had two large gaps. The second of those gaps was just in front of the platform at the end of the room. To cross those gaps, the team would have to take large, accurate steps, or even jump in the dark and solely on my instructions.

Jeez.

"Guys, come look at this," I said, tapping on the screen. "I want you to see these large gaps. They're going to be a real challenge. You should study these spots the best you can, so you'll know the length and general angle you'll need to step, or jump, over to get to the other side."

Everyone studied the map, but I knew it would be hard for them to figure how that would play out when they were standing in the dark on the actual path. I shone the last light, nearest the platform, but unfortunately, it did not light up much of that area. I could vaguely make out something round hanging on the far wall, but that was it.

"It looks like I won't be able to help whoever makes it up the platform. And remember, I won't be able to hear you. But I'll get you there." I glanced at the clock. "We have just over an hour left. Let's get our plan together. Slash, what do you think we should do?"

"I don't think you'll have time to direct everyone individually, so I think we should split into two groups," Slash said.

"How will that be faster?" Juliette asked. "She'll still have to give separate directions to everyone."

"I know, but I still think it's safer to have two teams. A scouting team will go first to check out the path. I'll go with Oscar, and we'll take one of the strobe lights. Tito will lead a second group with you, Mama. He'll take the other strobe light. Mia, you stay with Lexi and be available to assist her if problems arise."

"How are you going to give us instructions, Lexi?" Juliette asked.

I considered. "To make sure we're oriented in the same direction, before you move, I want you to stick one arm straight out in front of you. I'll tell you how big a step to take by using a clock formation using the position of your arm. Lift your arm straight up. That's the twelve o'clock position. Ninety degrees to your right would be three o'clock. The opposite side would be nine o'clock. Everybody got it?"

"While the idea of this plan is sound, I think there are some additional items to consider," Juliette said, crossing her arms against her chest. "First, Brando said there would be obstacles on our path. Other than the gaps, I didn't see any when Lexi scanned the room with the lights. So, I suspect they're invisible from her vantage point. But I'm sure they're out there somewhere. Brando also said Lexi won't be able to hear us in the other room. That means if the first team runs into obstacles, she may not understand what is going on. And worse, the team that follows might not as well unless we're all out there together."

I was struck by the logic and thoughtful analysis just presented. "You're right, Juliette," I said. "We have to account for the fact that I'm going to be blind to some, maybe all, of the obstacles. I'll be able to keep you on the path, but that's all we can reasonably count on."

Oscar nodded vigorously. "Yes. Romeo, I think the teams you have selected, and the order in which you wish us to proceed, does not reflect our best chance of success. It would require both you and Tito to be saddled with Juliette and myself, even though you, Tito, and Lexi represent our best chance for success. Logically speaking, Juliette and I should go first as a team. We'd serve a useful purpose in identifying possible obstacles or traps that might await us and put us out of the game. That would reduce the risk for you and Tito. One of you two is the player who needs to solve the final puzzle."

"Make that him," Tito said, pointing a finger at Slash. "I'm not even a third as good as he is at puzzles and codes."

Slash pushed his fingers through his hair, mulling over his parent's words. "The gamemaster thinks we're doing so well in the challenges because we're a family. I think that's true, but it's also because we listen to each other, communicate well, and respect all points of view, no matter the source. Communication for this challenge will be critical. Before we start the challenge, we need to figure out how to get information back to Lexi on what challenges we are facing."

"How do you propose we do that?" Juliette asked.

"I think that given the time constraints and your and Oscar's thoughtful analysis of our situation, instead of going as two teams of two, as I proposed earlier, we go in a long single line. Mama, you'll go first, followed by Oscar, just as you suggested. Tito and I will hang back and serve as voice relays of what is happening ahead. Mia will stand just inside the room by the door to hear us and pass the information to Lexi."

"Won't that take longer?" Mia asked.

"It does mean that we'll be slower to get started, since Lexi will have to walk us individually into position before we move farther on down the path. But it'll also give us the opportunity to get used to the environment and, more importantly, communicate efficiently with one another."

Mia clapped her hands excitedly. "I'm as ready as Meemaw's corn bread."

Slash opened his mouth to say something and then shook his head, deciding to let it pass. "You'll also have another critical role to play, Mia."

"I will? What is it?"

"To succeed, we must have both the code and someone with an unalarmed bracelet. We don't want to waste time or risk getting whoever is on the platform back to the control room in the dark. So, if you're still here with a working bracelet, then all we have to do is to get the code to Lexi and you walk out the door with her."

"How are you going to get me the code if I can't hear you?" I asked. "The platform is too far away for Mia to be able to hear what someone is yelling even if she's standing in the doorway."

"We'll use a visual code," Slash explained. "Whoever gets to the platform and gets the code should do jumping jacks to mark a number, one through nine. Does everyone know what a jumping jack is?"

He demonstrated it just in case. "Lexi will say, 'first number,' and then whoever has the code will start jumping for the corresponding number. Stop jumping when you've reached the desired number. Lexi will ask you to confirm the first digit. If it's correct, bow. If not, don't do anything. Once the number is confirmed, she'll say, 'second number,' and we repeat the process until we've given her the complete code. Lexi will enter the code on the keypad, depart the room with Mia and her unalarmed bracelet, and we win. Simple."

"That didn't sound simple to me, but I trust you," Juliette said. "If you say it's plausible, then it is."

"I can handle that," Lexi said.

"Do you know how to use the microphone?" Mia asked.

"I presume by using the mic button here on the console." I pushed it. "Testing, one, two, three."

"I hear it," Mia exclaimed. "It works."

"Be specific about whom you're giving instructions to, Lexi, and the rest of us need to be vigilant about listening and responding only to our names," Slash instructed.

I stared at the screen, hopping from section to section. "Unless I say otherwise, when I tell you to take a step, it should be about two lengths of your foot. If we get to a curve where I want you to take shorter steps, I'll tell you. Just put one foot in front of the other carefully. If you find something, if the path is uneven, or something surprises you, please stop and wave your arms over your head so I can see. That'll tell me there's a potential problem. Relay the problem to me through our so-called echo brigade. Once you're clear, swing your arms at your side until I say you're ready to proceed."

"All right, we need to get going." Slash started lining everyone one up. "Mama, you're going first. Lexi will position you a little way down the path and then advance Oscar. Then she'll move you farther down the path until we're all in place. We'll do this slowly but surely." He handed Tito a strobe light. "Tito and I will each carry one of these to use as needed."

Tito nodded, and I positioned my chair for a better look at the open door. I could just see the edge of the path on the floor on the other side of the door. It looked like there were two clear cables embedded in the floor. They probably produced the signature I could see with my infrared cameras. Atop of the cables was a thin white line demarking the edges of the path. They would be invisible in the dark room. Heck, they became invisible two feet from the door.

I returned my focus to the screen. "Okay, Juliette, let's start slow. Take two steps straight ahead and stop." She did as I requested. "Turn ninety degrees to your left. Back up a little to your right. Great. Now take two more steps forward."

It was slow going at first, but eventually everyone got the hang of it. I was able to maneuver all four into the other room, separated by about six feet. I'd just started moving Juliette forward again when she abruptly stopped and started swinging her arms. Apparently, there was a problem.

"Mia, what's going on?" I yelled.

She stuck her head back in the room, and I could hear shouting, although from my location, I couldn't hear what was being said.

"You're not going to believe this," Mia said, popping back into the control room. "It's bat-poop crazy."

Nope. I just couldn't deal with that right now. "What is it, Mia? What's there?"

"Security laser beams. Just like in the movies."

FORTY-FOUR

Slash

THIS CHALLENGE CERTAINLY created an unusual experience for me. It was a blackout situation, which I'd been in before, but not in circumstances like this. I was completely dependent upon Lexi's instructions for my every move. There was no one I trusted more than her, but not being in full control of my own actions wasn't my preferred mode of operation.

I knew there were three other people in front of me, but the darkness was so oppressive, I couldn't sense them at all. I could hear Lexi's periodic broadcasts of instructions to each one of us, but otherwise it was eerily quiet.

I'd just moved into place and verified my ability to still talk to and hear Mia at the door. Lexi had started moving my mother forward again when there was a call from Mama at the front.

"I think I've found the first obstacle," she shouted.

"What's the obstacle?" Oscar yelled.

"It's a red beam of light that shoots across the room at about knee height. The light is wavering like it is passing through some smoke or clouds."

"That's probably so you can see the beam," Tito

shouted. "Lasers are normally invisible to the eye unless they are reflected off something."

"I heard that," I shouted and then told Mia what my mother had found. I checked my watch and saw we were down to thirty-five minutes. This was going too slowly. We were running out of time.

We relayed information back and forth for a few minutes. Then Lexi told my mother there was a potential problem. The path made a left turn right at the spot the beam cut across, so the beam ran down the middle of the path. Fortunately, the path made a hairpin turn right there, so it would be possible for my mother to step over the beam and end up on the far side of the path where it looped back. Lexi told her where to step, and we waited.

After a minute, my mother shouted, "I made it."

It took another ten minutes before we were all past the first obstacle safely. We were getting farther away from the door, so it was getting harder to communicate with Mia. I estimated my mother was over halfway to the platform. Lexi was moving Mama again when she encountered a waist-high laser beam. We relayed the information back to Mia and Lexi.

"Got it," Mia yelled after I had to shout three times.

"Mia, wait," I added. "Tell Lexi we're almost out of time. We're going to have to change strategy and take some chances or we'll never make it." My comment met silence, so I had no idea if she'd heard me.

After a minute, I heard Lexi talking. "Here's the situation. Just beyond this beam is the first of the two gaps. To pass, you'll have to bend under the beam and stand up on the far side as close to the beam as you dare to risk. Then you'll need to take a large step or jump to bridge the gap. Unfortunately, the beam will prevent you from getting any sort of running start. Do you think you can do it, Juliette?"

"I'll try." There was a long pause, and then finally I heard my mother speak again. "Okay, I'm standing on the other side of the beam, but I lost my orientation as to where to take my giant step."

We passed the message along, and then Lexi replied. "Juliette, turn right to about your one thirty position. Okay, that's perfect. You can jump when ready."

Suddenly, a red light illuminated off to my side, and I saw a blinking light start flashing from ahead of me.

"Oh, no!" my mother shouted. "I'm so sorry. I guess I didn't take a big enough step and I fell off the path. Oscar, you might have to try and jump. It's a bigger gap than I anticipated."

"I will," he replied. "Be careful on the way out, and don't trip over anything."

"I won't. The bracelet gives me a little extra light to see things."

I could see the blinking red light of my mother's bracelet as she passed through the first laser beam on her way back to the exit door. There were no additional alarms or penalties when she did that.

Interesting.

Her movements gave me an idea. I was trying to flesh it out as Mama opened the exit door and the area was briefly illuminated. I squinted and managed to get a quick glimpse of my orientation in the room, the relative positions of Oscar and Tito, and the immediate path ahead.

Lexi's screen must have been reactivated, because she started directing Oscar forward again, giving him a small correction.

"Okay, I'm past the beam and ready to jump," Oscar declared. There was silence. "I'm across. I made it!" he shouted.

Suddenly the red light over the door came on and

another flashing bracelet appeared. "Oh, no," Oscar moaned. "I'm bloody sorry, blokes. I made the jump, but as I turned around to talk to you, I lost my balance and stepped off the path for a second. I can tell you, it isn't too big of a jump, and I can see by the light of my flashing bracelet the path goes straight for a couple more steps after you cross, if that's of any help."

"That helps," I called. "You did well, Oscar. We'll take it from here."

"Of that I have no doubt. Good luck, boys."

I carefully watched his bracelet flashing as he broached the second beam and then the first, much as Mama had and headed out the side exit door.

I had a plan, and it was time to execute it.

As soon the door closed behind Oscar, I called out to Tito. "We need to move, and I have an idea. I don't have time to explain it to you now, but here's what I need you to do. When Lexi gets you close to the beam, stop and wave your arms. I'm going to ask Mia to tell Lexi to move me up close to you. I'll explain the rest once I'm in position."

"*Verstanden,*" he replied even as Lexi started giving him instructions.

As soon as there was a pause in Lexi's instructions, I yelled as loud as I could, telling Mia to instruct Lexi to move me up next to Tito. Mia called something back to me, but it was too faint to comprehend. I just hoped she'd heard me correctly.

"Tito, take one more step and stop," Lexi said over the loudspeakers. "You're a half step short of the beam. Slash, I got your message. Mia said you want to be moved up next to Tito. If that's correct, raise your right arm."

I raised my right arm, so she continued. "Perfect. Then I need you to turn to the eleven thirty position and take one step. Good. Now turn to two o'clock. Stop. Go a bit more to the right, then take two steps. Turn left to the eight o'clock position. Perfect. Take one step, turn to the two o'clock position, and then a half step and you'll be next to him."

I followed her instructions until I sensed Tito's presence. I was able to judge his location by how his shape blocked out the occasional flicker of the security beam that wavered in whatever mist the gamemaster was using to make it visible.

"Slash, you're in position," Lexi said. "Please note that we have less than twenty-five minutes."

I loved how calm and logical she remained in a pressure situation—if it didn't involve bugs, animals, water, or flying. It was one of the things I admired about her most.

But now it was time for drastic measures because I fully expected additional obstacles ahead, and we didn't have time to locate and defeat all of them. It was an all-or-nothing gamble, but it was better than being bled to death by the clock. I'd committed the path to memory while viewing it in the control room, so I knew what I had to do and felt confident I could make it. The real challenge would be what lay ahead on that platform. I needed to save time to deal with that.

I reached out and touched Tito, my hand bumping against his shoulder. "This is going to sound crazy, but here's what I need you to do. We don't have time to continue as we are, so I'm going to take a long shot. It will require precise timing and your assistance. When I say, 'go,' I want you to step directly into the laser beam. Then step to the side so I can pass you while you're blocking the beam. While you're doing that, lean down and use your bracelet to help illuminate the gap for me to jump while keeping some part of your body in the beam. Can you do that?"

"I can, but we don't have to sacrifice one of us to get through the beam. We can both go under it. It'll give us another chance if it doesn't work out."

"I've considered that, but I also believe the path and the beam alarms are disabled while someone is exiting. That's why I need you to step into the beam on purpose."

"And if the path alarms are not disabled?" he asked.

"Then I'd better not make any mistakes," I said grimly. I looked at the red laser beam wavering across the path. "From here, I'm going to try and get to the platform in just a few jumps. I intend to use the strobe light to help guide my way. I've pretty much memorized the path after this gap, so I know where I need to land." I patted him on the shoulder. "Ready?"

"On your word."

"Make sure that you take at least thirty seconds to get out the door. Go."

Tito stepped into the beam, and his bracelet immediately started flashing red. He bent down close to the ground, so I stepped forward, vaguely seeing the dual ribbons of the path below my feet. Like Oscar had said, it wasn't a big leap, and I easily bounded over. I turned briefly to Tito. "See you outside in a few minutes."

"Viel Glück."

Remembering the path, I lined myself up and took two steps as he headed for the exit door. There was a switchback at this location I needed to bypass. I turned on the strobe light to be sure of my direction. It flashed twice, and I leaped.

I heard Tito curse and worriedly froze in place. "What's wrong?" I called out in German.

"The other strobe light," Tito said. "I forgot to give it to you. I'll leave it on the path in case you need it."

"I don't have the time to come back for it," I called.

"I'll leave it just the same. You've got this."   .

I did, but I had to jump before he exited. If I landed this leap, I could jump straight to the platform and be safe.

I oriented myself and took a deep breath, flashed the strobe, and leaped into the darkness. Behind me, I saw the flare of Tito opening the exit door.

FORTY-FIVE

Slash

I LANDED ON the platform, hit my knees hard, and rolled once before coming to a stand.

I'd made it.

I glanced over my shoulder, noticing the light over the door was out. Tito must have exited, and no additional alarms had gone off, thank God. I couldn't be sure if it was because the alarms were disabled or I'd gotten lucky. At this point, I didn't really care.

"Slash, is that you on the platform?" Lexi's shocked voice came through over the speakers. "How did you get to the platform already? I thought you and Tito had been eliminated."

I'd have to explain it all later, but for now, I had bigger problems. I didn't have my bearings. I wasn't sure where I was on the platform or where the walls were. I needed help.

I waved my arms, hoping Lexi would get the message that I needed direction. Sure enough, she came through.

"Okay, I don't know what you did or how you got there, but well done," she said. "Let's finish this. Turn

110 degrees to your right. You're now facing the back wall. You're about one quarter of the way along the platform toward the wall. Walk straight forward."

I stepped gingerly in the dark toward the back wall while Lexi informed me that we had less than twenty minutes left. I figured that would be just enough time if I could get the code and relay it back to Mia. I was tempted to use the strobe light to hasten things, but I wasn't sure how many flashes it had left. It had noticeably dimmed the last time I'd used it.

As I moved forward, I heard a deep humming sound and a swish, like a giant fan. But I felt only a slight breeze blowing on me.

I took another step forward, and the humming noise increased slightly in pitch, but the airflow didn't increase. Strange, it sounded like the fan, or whatever it was, had started to move faster the closer I got to it.

"Slash, it looks like there's something moving on the wall in front of you," Lexi said. "It might be a giant disc or something. I can't get much of a reading on it because it's the same temperature as the walls. But the center is now showing as warm, which means there might be a motor there, and the edges are warming from the air friction. You're about ten feet from the disc. Be careful."

I walked closer to the spinning disc, and as I did, it whirred faster. Possibly a giant fan blowing away from me. To test my theory, I backed up a couple of steps, and it slowed. That meant I controlled the speed of the fan by my distance. That was important somehow.

But time was slipping away, and I needed to see what I was dealing with. I had to risk using the strobe. I aimed it at the disc and pulsed it several times. The image spun, but my brain retained enough to see that it wasn't a fan but a large disc about as tall as a man. On the disc were one or perhaps two long shapes wrapping around the face of the disc. Another flash of the strobe light and I spotted some Roman numerals. Unfortunately, in the flashing light, the image jumped each time, and I couldn't read it.

I suddenly knew the solution. I had to synchronize the speed of the spinning disc to the flashing of the strobe light. At that point, the image before my eyes would freeze and I would be able to read the numbers.

Now I just needed to estimate where that exact spot would be.

Recalling my last images, the successive flashes had made the image to appear to rotate to the right. That meant that it was moving too fast for the strobe light, and I needed to move backward. I took one step back and heard the disc slow slightly. I should be close to the right spot. I raised the strobe light and pressed the button.

Nothing happened.

The battery was dead.

FORTY-SIX

Lexi

I KNEW SLASH had a plan, but I was stunned when Tito deliberately stepped into the beam, eliminating him from the game.

Then my screen froze. It seemed to take forever until I could see what was going on again. When I did, both were gone. At first, I'd thought they'd both been eliminated. I'd seen no movement in my camera view. I quickly scrolled the cameras forward, hoping against hope that Slash was somehow still alive. At the edge of the screen, near the platform, I thought I saw a brief movement. I switched to the platform view and realized it was Slash.

How did he get to the platform by himself in the dark?

I didn't have time to figure it out now. Mia told me she'd heard Tito yell something about leaving a strobe light on the track. I didn't know what that meant, but she'd also reminded me we had only fifteen minutes to finish, which meant I had to help Slash get that code and worry about the rest later.

I helped him orient himself on the platform and

watched as he moved back and forth on the platform in an odd manner. I had no idea what he was doing. After a moment, he stopped and waved his arms.

I hit the mic button. "Slash, is there a problem?"

He bowed, so I interpreted that as a yes. "Do you need something?"

He bowed again.

"Directions?"

He didn't move, which I took as a no.

"Maybe he needs the other strobe light," Mia said from her position by the open door. "Tito was yelling that he left it on the track. Maybe his burned out."

I turned back to the screen and pressed my mic button. "Do you need the other strobe light?"

Slash bowed quickly, confirming Mia's hunch. Before I could even think of what options we had, Mia shouted at me, "I'll get it for him."

"Wait, Mia!" I called out, but she'd already disappeared.

Worried, I flicked the light on for the first section of the room and thought for a moment she wasn't there. Then I spotted her on her hands and knees, crawling along the path. She approached a sharp left turn and, before I could say anything, swerved following the path. How was she doing that in the dark?

I turned on my mic again. "Mia, you have a curvy stretch ahead of you, so be careful. Slash, Mia's going to get you the other strobe light. I don't know if there's enough time, or exactly how she's going to get it to you, but we're going to try."

I watched Mia flawlessly navigate the curvy stretch on her hands and knees and then another straight patch. "Stop, Mia. You're approaching the first laser beam. It's knee high, so you will have to crawl on your belly to go under it. Then the path turns ninety degrees left. You'll have to remain on your belly as the beam will be just above your head. I'll tell you when you are clear to resume crawling."

She waved, so I presumed she understood. I wasn't sure how she was following the path, but I didn't care. She was making remarkably good time, which meant she was giving us a fighting chance.

She finally cleared the first laser. "Mia, you're clear and can resume crawling," I said.

Mia accelerated, twisting her way down the path toward the second laser. Several paces short of the second beam, she stopped and stood up.

My anxiety spiked. "Mia, what are you doing?"

She held her arms above her head, and I saw she had the strobe light in her hand. Success! She'd found it. Now how would she get it to Slash?

She was facing in the direction of Slash, and a quick glance showed Slash was facing her, probably turning to the sound of her voice. I presumed, or hoped, they were talking to each other. I desperately wished I could hear what they were saying. I flipped back to Mia just in time to see her cock her arm and throw the strobe light toward Slash.

Holy hail Mary!

She'd thrown him the strobe light in complete darkness. It would be a stroke of luck if she threw it in the right direction, let alone if Slash was able to catch or corral it before it rolled off the platform.

I flipped my view over to Slash. To my surprise, he was already facing the disc again. Did he have the strobe light? He acted like he was working on a puzzle moving forward and back again. I had no idea what was going on.

I checked the clock—just under five minutes remained. "Mia, start crawling back here as carefully as you can. There won't be time for me to guide you and get the code, so you're on your own. Just stay low and use your hands on the track to guide you."

I debated whether to tell Slash the time when I saw him start doing jumping jacks on the platform.

He had the code!

My fingers shook as I hit the mic button. "Slash, I see you and I'm counting. The first number is…four. Is that correct?"

He bowed and started jumping again. I scrambled to keep up.

"The second number is eight." I paused, but he didn't confirm with a bow, nor did he continue, so I assumed I was wrong. "Seven?"

He bowed and started jumping again. In seconds I had the three-digit code—476. Slash sat down, so I knew that it was. Now, all we needed was Mia. I dreaded even looking to see where she was. My stomach dropped when the clock indicated we only had forty-five seconds left.

I tried to climb down from the chair, but it was awkward to squeeze around the controller console that I couldn't figure out how to raise. I didn't have time to figure it out. Somehow, I managed to squish past. I hopped off the steps and staggered toward the door to the blackout room, my back and legs stiff from sitting for so long.

"Mia!" I shouted into the darkness.

"What?" she said, crawling into view and coming to a stand.

"You did it!" I reached out and grabbed her hand, yanking her toward me. "Holy crap, you did it all on your own."

"Did you get the code?"

"I did. *We* did. Come on, we've got to get that code keyed in now."

"My knees are all scraped up from crawling," she

moaned, looking down at her legs. "Vittoria is going to kill me. I'll ruin all her wedding pictures with my ugly knees."

"Haven't you heard of Photoshop? Besides, she'll *love* you for saving her honeymoon." I punched in the code. After a moment, the red light above the door turned green, just as the clock ticked down to zero.

I pulled Mia out of the room, holding up her arm with the bracelet like she'd just won a prize fight.

I briefly saw the gamemaster's shocked face before we were completely mobbed by our teammates. There was so much shouting and screeching, I was pretty sure I wouldn't be able to hear properly for at least the next seven years.

Tito lifted me off my feet, squeezing me so hard I couldn't breathe. He finally set me down, and I looked around. "Where's Slash? How did you do it? What happened?"

"I'll tell you later," I said. "He's still inside. Someone has to go tell him we won."

"I'll do it," Tito said and disappeared into the control room.

Brando approached me, his expression one of complete disbelief. He held out the golden disc. "I'm truly at a loss for words, Ms. Carmichael. You and your team have exceeded my expectations in every way."

I grinned. "Thanks, but I had the easy job. These guys did all the hard work." I spread out my arm to encompass the team, including Slash and Tito, who walked into the room slapping each other on the back. "Especially the youngest member of our group, Mia. If it weren't for her quick thinking and courage, we wouldn't have made it in time. I think *she* deserves to be presented the golden disc. Great job, Mia. How did you manage to navigate in the dark?"

"I had some extra time standing there in the doorway, so I started playing around. I discovered I could feel the path cables in the floor. They were barely raised but made of a different material. I wondered if I could follow the path by crawling and feeling the cables and staying between them. I wasn't sure, but when we needed the other strobe light, I figured I would try it, and it worked."

"How did you know where to throw the strobe light once you'd found it?" I asked.

"Slash told me to throw it. He said to turn it on just before I threw it because it'd help him estimate its location so he could catch it. He was worried I wouldn't throw it hard enough, so he told me to throw it as absolutely hard as I could. So, I did, and I guess he caught it, or at least got it. Then he shouted at me to head back to you as fast as I could."

"You're amazing, Mia. We owe this win to you."

The teenager bounced up and down on her feet, beaming happily. "Thanks. You guys make me feel like a million bucks. Hey, did I get that one right?"

"You did." I grinned. "At last, Mia, you got one right."

We laughed, and Slash gave her a kiss on the cheek after Brando handed her the disc. We clapped and filed out, chatting happily while heading back to the dining room for lunch.

As we walked along, Brando asked Slash for his thoughts on the escape room. "Tell Mr. Zachetti to lose the lasers," Slash said. "It's plenty hard as it is."

"I respectfully disagree," Brando said. "It clearly wasn't hard enough. I'm truly astonished at your capability and resourcefulness. What *is* it about you people that makes you so special?"

"It was the teenager who came through in the clutch,"

I said, grinning. "Or Slash's parents, who refined our game plan."

"Or the big Swiss guy who took one for the team," Tito added over my shoulder.

"How did the other team do?" Slash asked. "Did they successfully complete the challenge?"

"Why don't you ask them for yourself?" Brando replied.

FORTY-SEVEN

Lexi

"YOU'RE BACK," MY dad exclaimed as soon as he saw me, jogging across the dining room at an alarming speed to wrap me and Slash in a combined bear hug. I was so shocked that he'd included Slash in the hug, I was speechless.

"Did you solve your challenge?" he asked, finally releasing us.

I managed to find my voice. "We did, Dad. What about you guys?"

"We did, too," Dad said. "Gio was great, and your mother was indispensable. We're unstoppable. Lexi, I can't remember the last time your mother and I have had so much fun. Thanks so much for arranging this, pumpkin. And, Slash, I sincerely appreciate you including Clarissa and me in this adventure. It's been wonderful getting to know your parents and family."

Slash lifted an eyebrow at me over my father's head, and I smiled back. Who knew it would take a castle full of escape room challenges to bring our families together?

I didn't have time to process it, because we were immediately surrounded by the rest of our group. Everyone started asking questions and sharing exciting tidbits of who did what for each puzzle.

While it was interesting to hear how the other team had solved their challenge, it was too many people in too-close proximity. I started to get a headache from all the noise.

Brando finally had to intervene and ask us to sit down and eat so we could progress to the final challenge. I sat with Slash on one side of me and Juliette on the other. Chiara and Ciro served us bruschetta with fresh tomatoes topped with garlic, basil, and olive oil and served on toasted slices of thick Italian bread. There was a lovely selection of meats, cheeses, and olives, as well as some fresh fruit.

Slash was chatting with Vittoria, so I carefully put a few slices of meat and cheese on his plate, avoiding the ones I knew he didn't care for. I filled up my plate and then passed the tray on to Juliette.

Eventually, Slash turned to me, noting his full plate. He leaned over to kiss me on the cheek. "Eat the protein first," he murmured. "It will help with the headache."

I stared at him in surprise. How had he been able to tell that I had a headache? Was I that transparent?

Regardless, I did as he said, and my headache began to subside just like he had predicted. I even managed to chat coherently with my mother-in-law while sipping a small glass of fruity wine.

When Slash excused himself to go to the men's room, Juliette surprised me by putting her hand over mine. "Lexi, I wanted to be sure to tell you Oscar and I are impressed at how well you and Slash have performed in the challenges, together and separately. You are remarkably well suited for each other, more than I could have ever dreamed. When Nonna told me how perfect you two were for each other, I didn't believe her. Romeo is a complicated man, guarded and reserved. He takes care of everyone, but he rarely lets his guard down so someone can take care of him. I feared he'd never meet the right person, someone who could bring him the kind of peace, contentment, and happiness he deserves." She paused a moment, collecting her thoughts. "You're his true match, Lexi, and I don't say that lightly. I see the way he looks at you, the fierce love in his eyes. As his mother, that means everything to me. I couldn't be happier for the both of you."

I set my wineglass down without drinking any more. Her words touched me more than I could say. "Thank you, Juliette. I was so nervous to meet you because Slash adores you. I was afraid I wouldn't measure up, that I'd be lacking somehow. But you and Oscar have been so kind to me that not only do I feel welcome, but I feel accepted, and that's really important to me."

"You're everything Slash said you were and more," she insisted. "How lucky we are to have you in our family."

"That's exactly what Slash said you'd say."

"And he was right," she replied, smiling. "As usual."

I didn't have a chance to respond, because Brando clinked a fork against his glass, getting our attention. "Honored guests, please finish your lunch in the next five minutes, as we will proceed with the final challenge of your stay here at Castrum Augustus."

A few minutes later, Slash returned to the dining room and was promptly intercepted by my dad. Whatever Slash said to him caused Dad to laugh and give him a friendly smack on the shoulder. Their relationship had definitely moved to the next level. I didn't think I could possibly be happier or more relieved about it.

When lunch concluded, the gamemaster led all thirteen of us to the large high-ceilinged foyer of the castle. "Every group that has come through Castrum Augustus has been brought to this point and given the opportunity to solve the final challenge," he said. "Prior to this, none of our guests have solved more than three of the escape rooms leading up to this point. In fact, the average of the groups coming through the castle has been just one puzzle. What you've accomplished as a group has been truly extraordinary and quite unexpected."

His compliment made most of us smile. But when I glanced at Slash, there was no humor in his eyes, only determination. He wasn't swayed by the gamemaster's words or praise. Nothing was going to distract him from finishing the final challenge. In fact, I wasn't even sure his motivation was any longer about Gio's honeymoon, the pope's reputation, or even the orphanage. Somehow, this castle challenge had become personal. A test of his insight, creativity, and leadership. He was determined not to fail, and I was just as determined to help him win for whatever reasons were important to him.

"Even though those earlier teams were not nearly as successful as you've been, they were still offered the chance to tackle this final challenge," Brando continued. "Oh, I see it surprises you. Yes, indeed, it's possible for anyone to solve the final challenge without having solved each, or even *any*, of the prior rooms. Therefore, everyone gets one last chance. It's certainly far more difficult to solve this last challenge without any prior successes, but it's not impossible. Although all of you seem quite capable of solving the impossible.

"I truly commend you on your ingenuity and how you have all worked together. I did not expect several of these challenges to be solved for many years, if not decades. I have pondered why you've been successful when so many of the other, seemingly far more qualified teams have failed. My theory is that a primary weakness of the other teams was they were too dependent upon only a few people. The random process, especially for the last two puzzles, magnified that weakness."

He studied us for a long moment. "However, your team seemingly has no weaknesses, and you work well together regardless of the configuration of the team. The only thing I can attribute to that is you're a family. At least most of you." He acknowledged Tito and Father Armando with a slight nod of his head.

Slash spoke up. "Tito and Father Armando are as much a part of our family as anyone here."

Brando nodded. "Of course. I retract my statement. You are, indeed, an amazing family unit. In fact, I'd wager that given your success, you're a particularly close family."

I looked around the room, but to my surprise not single person disabused the gamemaster of that notion or mentioned that most of us had just met for the first time on the castle grounds.

"And because of that, Mr. Zachetti will permit Father Armando to participate once again in the final challenge, if he so desires," Brando continued.

"I'd be delighted," Father Armando said.

Brando led us from the castle foyer through a door opening under and between the two marble staircases leading upstairs to our rooms. When we walked through the door, we found ourselves in a dim, circular room with a high, curved ceiling. A large, elaborate marble table spotlighted by several overhead lights dominated the center of the room. Classically styled, cream-colored statues of two nude men supported the table on each end, almost as if they were carrying it across the room. The table held a huge, raised, flat, circular stone device.

We crowded around the table to stare at the oddity. The stone device had seven large, concentric rings, each about four inches wide. The rings were grooved along the edges, which made me suspect they could be moved independently. Embedded in all but the center circle were dozens of the same round golden discs we'd won at our challenges.

These discs appeared to be equally distributed around each circle, and all of them had numbers engraved on them. Rising from the center circle was a metal device that reminded me of the gnomons on the sundials in the garden maze. This one's angled shape rose over the rings, pointing away from the door we'd just entered.

As my eyes began to adjust to the dimness of the room, I realized the walls and ceiling were covered with small lights, as if stars were glimmering in a night sky. It made me think of a planetarium.

"The final challenge starts here," Brando said. "In order to claim success, you'll need to provide me with two names prior to dinner cocktails, which will begin promptly in the lounge at six thirty this evening."

"Give you the two names of what?" Slash asked.

"That's for you to determine," Brando responded. "In addition, the attire for cocktails and dinner is formal, as we are expecting additional guests. Please be sure to give yourself time to solve the challenge and clothe yourself appropriately. From this point on, I'll not take any further questions. Be advised you're free to roam anywhere in the castle or on the island, except for the kitchen and the staff's quarters on the upper floor, in pursuit of the answer to the final escape room challenge. I wish you the greatest success."

We all stared at him in disbelief as he exited the room.

"Wait. What just happened?" Stefan asked. "What's the challenge? What does that mean, we have to provide him with two names? Whose two names?"

I was as stunned as everyone else. I had no idea. Slash and I looked at each other uneasily.

"Well, that was unsettling," Mom said. "Here, team, solve a puzzle, but we're not going to tell you what the puzzle is."

"That's bizarre," Gio burst out. "He didn't explain the challenge at all. How do we form a strategy if we don't know what we're supposed to be doing?"

"Excellent question, Gio," Dad said. "I don't know how the gamemaster expects us to solve an escape room if we don't know what the point of the challenge is. We don't even know where to start."

"Yes, we do," Slash said, putting his hands on the marble table. "We start here. The gamemaster brought us here for a reason."

FORTY-EIGHT

Lexi

WE ALL LOOKED at Slash expectantly, but he didn't explain further.

"But how do we get started?" Oscar asked. "How do we solve a puzzle if we don't know what the puzzle is?"

"We figure it out," I said. "That's part of the challenge. We need to determine what the puzzle is and how we solve it."

"So, we just work as if there are no rules?" Alessa asked.

"There *are* rules," Tito said. "Well, at least two. We must finish before cocktails at six thirty, and we can go anywhere in the castle or on the island, except for the kitchen and the staff quarters, to get the answers we need. And, apparently, the answer is two names."

"What does any of this mean?" Mia moaned. "Names of what?"

I held up a hand, stopping any further questions. "None of us know the answers to these questions, no matter how important they are. Let's just start with this table and work outward. Perhaps as we figure out a few things, the challenge will become clearer."

"I like that plan, Lexi," Father Armando said, smiling at me and putting a hand on my shoulder. "One thing that leaped to my mind as soon as we walked through the door is that this room looks and feels like a planetarium."

"Yes," I agreed. "I thought the same thing."

"The room is kind of dark and the walls and ceiling look like they have stars," Vittoria said.

"Those gold discs are the same style the gamemaster presented us with after every challenge," my mom said. "And they have numbers etched on them, just like the ones we received. That can't be a coincidence."

"The gamemaster did say we might need the discs we won," Gio said. "But I didn't bring mine. I left it our room."

"Let's go get them," Alessa suggested. "Mine's in my room as well."

"Alessa is right," I said. "Let's bring all the golden discs we won from the challenges here. Everyone who has one, go get it."

Since I had the disc from the maze, I quickly returned to my room and retrieved it. Within minutes, those of us who'd gone to get the discs had reassembled in the planetarium and carefully laid them out next to each other on one end of the marble table.

In the meantime, Slash, Father Armando, Vittoria, Oscar, and my dad stood at the center of the table on one side, pointing at something on the stone device and having a deep discussion. Stefan and Tito were on the other side, arguing and adding commentary.

"Lexi, come here, please," Slash said, waving me over.

My dad made room for me to stand next to Slash. I realized for the first time the table was longer than it was wide, although it was easily the width of the banquet table in the dining room. The statues of the naked men who supported the table left the giant ring device in the center easily accessible from both sides.

Gio, Alessa, Mia, Juliette, and my mother joined the group on the far side of the table while we all studied the unusual stone ring from our vantage point.

"A closer inspection of the table indicates our supposition that this is a planetarium is confirmed." Slash pointed at some markings on the table. "These carvings surrounding the device are the sky, stars, and the moon."

I leaned closer to the tabletop to get a better look at the carvings, my arm brushing against Slash's. "Is there a pattern to them?"

"Not that I can see," Slash said. "Yet."

"There are six rings and a small center area with that metal part sticking out from the middle," Oscar said. "Like we saw on the sundials in the maze."

"And each ring on the device has a different number of discs," Stefan said. "Naturally, there are more discs on the larger outer rings, and fewer on the smaller inner rings. As far as I can see, though, none of the etched numbers on a disc have more than three digits. However, several of the discs have single digits."

"And the numbers on the discs on the circle are not in sequential order," Mom offered.

"Maybe we just need to put the discs in numerical order," Mia suggested.

I absorbed all the information, considering the best course of action. "It's a possibility, Mia. Do any of the numbers match the discs we won?"

Slash walked over to the row of discs we'd left on the table. "What was the number on the disc from the maze, *cara*?"

"It's 509."

"Everyone, look at the stone circle," Slash said. "Is there any disc that has the number 509?" he asked.

Everyone began searching, and then Vittoria cried out. "Yes. I found it. It's right there on the second ring from the outside."

I followed Vittoria's pointing finger and saw where it sat. "But we can't lift it out."

"Alessa, which disc came from the bull room?" Slash asked.

"The one that says 395. And I've already found it on the outer ring, here." She pointed at the spot.

"My disc from the blackout room has the number 476 engraved on it," Mia offered.

"And there it is on the innermost ring," my dad said, his brow creased in concentration. "What does it mean, Slash, that we're able to match our winning discs to the discs that are already on this device?"

"I'm not sure yet," Slash said. "How about the game room, Gio? Which number was on your disc?"

Gio's cheeks reddened slightly. "I'm not sure."

"What do you mean, you're not sure?" Slash said. "You just brought it down from your room."

"I didn't pay attention to the number."

Slash gave his brother an exasperated look. It reminded me how sometimes my brothers drove me crazy with their lack of attention to detail. Different family, same dynamics.

"It's forty-five," Alessa said, saving the day. "I typed it into the keypad in the game room."

"Thanks, Alessa," Slash said. "How about the disc from the pool room? Mama, you had that one, right?"

"I did," Juliette confirmed. "It's the one with the number sixty-four on it."

"It's on the fourth ring from the outside," Father Armando said.

"That leaves the library," Stefan said. "Clarissa, do you know the number?"

"I do. It's the one with 121, and it's sitting on the fifth ring."

Slash placed that disc to the side and studied all the golden discs we'd won at once. My dad joined him, and together they looked for a pattern or something that might be significant.

Figuring they had that covered, I kept my focus on the giant stone circle. "What I've noticed is the discs appear to be ordered consecutively with the challenges that we performed. For example, the gamemaster took your team, Slash, to the room with the bull before he came to take us to the garden maze. So, the bull room was technically the first challenge, and the garden maze was the second one. The number for the bull room, 395, is located on the outer ring. The number for the garden maze, 509, is located on the second ring, and so on. It's a precise match of challenges and position of the discs on the stone circle. That has to match up for a reason."

I looked up and saw Slash smiling at me. Had he been thinking the exact same thing?

"You're right, Lexi," Tito said. "That has to mean something."

"But what does it mean in terms of the big picture?" Father Armando asked.

"I'm not sure yet," I admitted.

"What are those holes for?" Juliette asked, pointing at the one-inch-diameter holes found on each of the rings. "There's one on every ring."

Gio leaned over, sticking a couple of his fingers into the hole. "It's round, like a pole or something should go here."

"So, maybe we should look for a pole or a broom handle to stick in there?" my dad asked.

"Possibly," I said. "But I suspect there's something special about the length or weight of the object. Let's look around and see if we can find anything that would work."

Everyone split up and started searching for a suitably sized rod or a pole. Several people left the room to look in other areas of the castle, while Slash, Vittoria, and my mom stayed in the planetarium room, as I'd started calling it in my head. It didn't take us long to clear the room, as it had no additional furniture or decorations.

I headed out of the room to look elsewhere and nearly collided with Stefan and Gio, who were running back into the room, Stefan held a marble rod about twice as long as the width of his hand out in front of him like a spear. I was lucky I hadn't gotten skewered.

"Sorry, Lexi," Stefan said, catching me by the arm and straightening me. "I yelled at everyone to come back to the room as soon as I found this. It was sitting in the drawer in the butler's desk right in the entryway."

"What does a butler need a marble rod for?" Vittoria wondered aloud.

"Everyone needs at a stiff rod at some time, right, Gio?" Stefan said, snorting.

Gio burst into laughter and smacked his brother on the back of the head. "You're lucky Mama didn't hear you say that."

"Here, Romeo," Stefan said, handing over the rod. "You take it from here."

Slash rolled his eyes at his brothers but took the rod. Holding it in front of him, he walked over to the stone circle, sliding one end into the hole on the outermost ring. It fit perfectly, sinking in about halfway. By this time, our entire team had reassembled back in the room.

"It fits," my mom said. "Now what?"

We looked around to see if anything happened on the device or the ring, but we saw nothing.

"Try the next hole," Oscar said. Slash removed the rod and tried the hole in the outermost ring.

Again nothing.

Slash tried sticking the rod in each of the holes on the device, with no success.

"Perhaps the rod acts as a handle to turn the individual rings?" I suggested.

"Good idea," Slash said. He reached over and pulled the rod, which was now in the innermost ring, trying to pull it toward him. After a moment, he put some real muscle in it. As he increased his effort, the ring began to rotate.

"Look!" Mia shouted, pointing at the wall. "The stars…they're moving."

FORTY-NINE

Lexi

SLASH CONTINUED TO slowly rotate the ring, and the stars moved with him.

"Not all the stars are moving," Alessa said after a minute. "It's only those in a band near the ceiling."

Slash stopped pulling on the rod, and the stars ceased moving. "Try the hole in the next circle," I suggested. "Let's see what happens then."

Slash moved the rod and pulled. The stars moved, but this time it was a different band immediately below the previous one. He completed this exercise for all the rings. As he moved outward on the rings, the band of stars that rotated moved down the wall as well.

When he finished the outermost band, he studied the stone device and then the stars. "So, now we know we can align and realign the stars on the wall by moving the stone circles."

"What does that have to do with the gold discs and the numbers on them?" Oscar asked, clearly confused.

"We haven't connected those dots yet, Oscar," I said. "We're still collecting data, so to say." I walked over to the wall for a closer look at the layout of the stars.

Although there was no boundary between the layers of stars—and they were just pinpoints of light—it was possible, on closer inspection, to tell they were somehow out of alignment.

After a moment, I returned to the table. "I think we have to line up the numbers on the discs from the prior challenges in order to get the stars in the proper alignment."

"I was thinking the same thing," Slash said. "Let's try it." He stuck the rod in the hole of the outer circle and pulled. "What number is on the outer disc?"

"It's 395," I said. "And it should be adjacent to 509 on the ring next to it."

Slash moved the circle into position and removed the rod, putting it into the hole of the next circle. "The disc number on the third ring is forty-five, followed by sixty-four, and then 121," Gio called out as Slash methodically worked his way through the circle. "The last number is 476."

Slash removed and replaced the rod in each ring, rotating it until the designated discs were all in order. I returned to the wall, noting the stars appeared to be aligned, and familiar patterns emerged.

"Is that Orion?" my dad said, pointing at some stars on the wall.

"It is," Mom confirmed, coming up beside me. She traced the constellation with her finger. "See it, Lexi?"

"I do," I said. But I didn't recognize any other constellations, and to my disappointment, nothing else had happened.

Slash stared at the stone circle, one arm resting against his forehead, the other hand holding the rod. "I think the problem is while I have all the numbers lined up, I don't have them pointed in the right direction."

"The direction," I mused. "Good thinking. But what would we orient the numbers against? The gnomon in the center, perhaps?"

Slash looked up, his dark hair falling over his forehead. "The snowman?"

I stared at him and then laughed, shaking my head. "No, Slash. Not a snowman, the gnomon. Like on a sundial. It's the metal part that sticks up in the middle and tells you what time it is by where the shadow falls. Gnomon."

"*Gnomone su meridiana,*" Father Armando quickly translated.

"Ah," Slash said and then grinned. "*Gnomone.* I'm disappointed. I was looking forward to seeing how a snowman fit into all of this."

Still chuckling, I pointed to the gnomon and said, "See what happens if you align the numbers with that, Frosty."

"Ha. Now I know who *that* guy is." He arced an eyebrow at me. "Which way do you want to align the discs? Toward the way the base is pointing or the other way?"

It was a good question. I looked both ways, thinking. "If we use the direction toward which the base is pointing, it'd turn us back toward the door we came in through. Let's try the other direction first. If that doesn't do anything, we'll follow the base direction."

"Fair enough."

Slash once again started moving the rings, slowly realigning the numbered discs so they lined up with the gnomon. We watched as the stars on the wall followed his movements. As the inner and final ring swung into place, two unseen spotlights on the ceiling suddenly popped on, shining at a spot on the wall where the gnomon was pointing. The precisely aimed lights illuminated the vague outline of something previously hidden in the shadows.

"It's a door," my mom gasped, stepping forward and squeezing my shoulder.

FIFTY

Lexi

TITO REACHED THE door first. He fumbled with the doorknob before pulling it open. Bright light flooded into the room, temporarily blinding us.

"Come on," Tito said, waving his hand at us. "Let's see what's in here."

Squinting my eyes and blinking, I cautiously followed him into the room. As my eyes adjusted, I saw it was a much smaller room than the planetarium. The walls were flat and adorned with stylistic drawings that looked vaguely familiar, which was odd, because I wasn't much of an art aficionado.

Where had I seen drawings like that before?

One drawing had a lion, another a goat. I could make out a ram, a scorpion, and some people. I felt like I should know what this was.

"Signs of the zodiac," Alessa promptly said, solving the mystery. "Wonder what that means."

I scanned the room as I automatically counted the drawings. There were twelve, as expected. There was nothing else in the room except for one empty frame against the far wall with a small shelf beneath it.

As I got closer to the frame with the shelf, I could see it wasn't completely empty. It contained six niches arranged in a circle. Each niche was about three inches square. On the shelf below the frame were twelve metal blocks, each with a sign of the zodiac engraved on the back.

"It looks like these blocks go into the squares in the frame," Juliette mused from over my shoulder.

As I mentally compared the sizes of the niches and blocks, my dad picked up one of the blocks and stuck it into one of the niches. It slid in perfectly and clicked, as if it sealing itself magnetically.

"Okay," Dad said. "That was easy."

"Yes, but is it in the right place?" Mom countered. She reached in and tugged on the block. There was another click, and it popped out right into her hand.

By this time the entire group had gathered in the front of the empty frame. We seemed to know this was the puzzle to solve in this room.

"It seems a fairly straightforward challenge," Father Armando said. "We must put the right block in the right hole to solve it."

"I agree," I said. "But which block goes in which hole?"

"Well, since there are only twelve blocks and six holes, we can try all the combinations until we hit the right one," Mia suggested.

I'd already started my mental calculator to determine the odds of success with that approach. "That's not a viable option, Mia. It could take up to 665,280 attempts to find the right permutation of six blocks from twelve choices while putting them in the right order. Even at one combination per second, that would take us over a week to complete. We have to solve this puzzle logically."

My mom tugged on my arm. "Correct me if I'm wrong, sweetheart, but we have two problems at hand, right? We need to determine which six of the twelve blocks we use, and what order we put them in."

"Yes, but there are three problems, Mom. In addition to determining which six blocks and what order, we need to figure out *where* to start placing the blocks in the circle. We could have the right order, but with the blocks rotated one spot to the left or right, it might not work."

"Might I suggest something?" Juliette said. "Before we get too involved with this puzzle, are we sure there's nothing else we should do first? One thing I've noticed is these challenges have had a lot of subtlety to them, and the direct solution has not always proved to be the best."

She was right, and I'd totally forgotten to factor that in. "That's an excellent point, Juliette. Do you have any ideas?"

"Unfortunately, I don't. I just thought I'd mention it in case anyone else did."

"There's nothing else in this room except for the drawings," Alessa said, looking around. "And we've already determined they're the signs of the zodiac."

Nonetheless, I walked to the middle of the room and studied the zodiac drawings as a whole. Slash joined me.

"I know nothing about horoscopes," Tito said, standing next to Slash. "Are there any missing?"

"There are twelve signs and twelve months, so I'm pretty sure that's the right number," Alessa said. "I don't see any that are missing, but I'm not exactly an expert in this area."

"I have an idea," Vittoria suddenly said. "I'll be right back." She exited the room, and we all looked at each other, shrugging.

"Okay, for the moment, let's presume that all twelve zodiac signs are accounted for, and none are missing," I said. "Let's see if we can properly identify each one."

We started at the far left, with Alessa calling out the ones she recognized and others helping with the ones they knew.

"Capricorn, Gemini, Libra, Taurus, Virgo, Aquarius, Cancer, Scorpio, Leo, Pisces, Sagittarius…and I'm not sure of the last one," she said. "It's the ram."

"Aries," Mom said. When I looked at her in surprise, she shrugged. "It's a common answer in crossword puzzles."

"Wait." Oscar spoke up suddenly. "I think I see a pattern here. All the challenges I participated in had a zodiac connection. Let's think about it. In the black room, there was a scorpion made from red mirror tiles. And when I was in the garden maze, the statue in the hidden alcove had a woman pouring water onto twins. That could either represent Aquarius or Gemini, depending on whether you focus on the twins or the water. And the pool had two big fish drawn on the side. Remember that, Juliette? That would be Pisces, right?"

"Oh, my brilliant darling," Juliette said. "You're absolutely correct. There *were* drawings of fish on the sides of the pool. And I was in the room with the bull that had a ring in its nose. That could be *Toro*."

"Taurus in English," Stefan said. "Plus, the library had the scale. That's Libra."

"I think we're definitely going somewhere with this, but what about the game room?" Alessa said. "What's the zodiac sign for that room?"

"*Sagittario,*" Gio said, stepping forward. He mimicked shooting an arrow at the ceiling. "The archer."

"That's six," I said. "Six signs, six niches. Guys, I think we have this."

"But which one do we use for the maze?" Oscar asked. "Aquarius or Gemini?"

"We'll try them both to see which one works," I

replied. "The number of different combinations to substitute between Aquarius and Gemini is manageable."

I walked over the shelf and separated out the seven blocks with which we would work. "Now the question is, in what order do we put them in the niches?"

"There's a couple of possible orders," Slash said. "We could use the order in which they occur on the zodiac calendar or, alternatively, we could try the order in which we completed the challenges. There are others orders we should consider, but those would be my first two choices at this point. Anyone else have any thoughts?"

"I vote for trying the order of the zodiac calendar," Tito said. "That seems to make the most sense to me."

"I concur," my dad said. "Most obvious first."

I shrugged. "Doesn't make any difference to me. Does anyone know the order of the zodiac calendar? I don't think these pictures are hung are in the right calendar order."

Everyone looked at Alessa. "Aquarius is first, I think," Alessa said sheepishly. "Sorry, while I know the zodiac signs, I don't know the exact calendar order."

I glanced hopefully at Father Armando, but he lifted his hands with a small smile. "Don't look at me for answers to pagan puzzles."

"Good point," I said. "In that case, let's pivot. We're going to have to try the order of the challenges instead," I said. "So, the room with the bull was first, followed by the garden maze, correct?"

"That's correct," Slash confirmed.

I studied the blocks and picked up the one with the bull… Taurus. "Where do I start, guys? At the top of the circle? Should I go clockwise?"

Everyone agreed that the top was as good a place as anywhere to start and that clockwise made the most sense. I placed Taurus in the niche. It slid in and clicked into place.

"Okay, what should I put for the garden maze? Aquarius or Gemini?"

"Let's try Aquarius first," Slash suggested. "Fountains imply water, and you said the woman was pouring water on the twins at the other fountain."

"Not to mention the only other statue in the maze was a woman pouring water," Mom added.

"Aquarius it is." I picked up the block and put it in the niche. After further discussion I placed Sagittarius, Pisces, Libra, and Scorpio. As I stuck the last block into place, we all waited expectantly for something to happen.

Nothing.

"Swap out Aquarius for Gemini," Stefan suggested.

I did as he asked, but nothing happened. I tried various combinations of the order of each of the challenges with no success. I finally stopped in frustration. "This isn't working. We don't even know if we're starting in the right place."

Vittoria returned carrying a book. "Sorry it took me so long to find this. I saw it in the map room during our challenge. I hope it'll help. It's an astrology book from the library." She handed it to Slash.

"That was a great idea, Vittoria," Gio said giving her kiss. "Brilliant, actually."

She smacked him on the arm. "I keep telling you that. See, I do not have pregnant brain."

We laughed as Slash flipped open the book. "Does it have the proper calendar order of the zodiac signs?" I asked.

Slash shrugged. "It depends on what you consider proper calendar order. Capricorn begins in December and goes into January. But if you start with that, you get Capricorn, Aquarius, Pisces, Aries, Taurus, Gemini,

Cancer, Leo, Virgo, Libra, Scorpio, and Sagittarius. Since Capricorn isn't one of our blocks, Aquarius will still be first."

"Okay." I put the six symbols from our challenge in the proper zodiac calendar order as he read them off. When he was done, I slid them into the niches. As I snapped the last block into place, I held my breath, but nothing happened.

I replaced Aquarius with Gemini, but still to no avail. "No luck," I said in frustration. "We must be missing something."

"Maybe rotate the whole circle one spot to the left," Dad suggested.

I tried that, but still nothing. "I'm not sure what to do now," I said, blowing out a breath. "It would take hours to try all the different possible combinations. There *has* to be another clue somewhere."

"But there's nothing else in this room," Mia complained. "This is just too hard."

"Maybe there's another clue in the planetarium room," Juliette said. "We were so focused on solving the stone circle and star puzzles, we didn't really give anything else in there much thought."

"There wasn't anything else in that room, either, except for the table and the stone circle with the brass discs, Mama," Gio said.

"It won't hurt to take another look," I said.

"I'll stay here and keep trying different combinations while everyone else looks for another clue," Slash said. He handed the astrology book to Stefan and took my place in front of the blocks. As I rose from the chair, he ran a hand down my ponytail, then tugged me toward him, brushing his lips against mine. "Good work," he murmured.

"Back at you," I said, touching our fingers together once more before I headed out with the rest of the group to see what we might have missed in the planetarium room. We all looked around, but Mia had been right. Other than the stone circle, the rod, the brass discs, and the table, there was nothing else in the room.

"Are those statues of twins?" Mom asked, walking back and forth between the statues of the naked guys holding up the table. "Their features are identical. Could that be a clue?"

"If they're twins, it could mean they're Gemini," Alessa offered.

"What do we know about Gemini?" I asked. "Stefan, can you read from the book about the Gemini twins?"

"Sure." He moved to the doorway so he could get enough light to read. "'Gemini is the third sign of the zodiac, and it covers May 21 to June 21. The sign is represented by twins, or in Egyptian astrology, by a pair of goats. In Arabian astrology, Gemini is a pair of peacocks. The brightest stars in the constellation of Gemini are Castor and Pollux, which help form the heads of the twins. According to Greek mythology, the twins have also been related to other celebrated pairs, such as the younger and older Horus in Egyptian mythology or Romulus and Remus for the Romans.'"

"Did that you say that Gemini was the third sign?" Alessa interrupted. "If so, we're one sign off. We put Gemini in the first block in place of Aquarius. We need to go back and make sure it goes in the third."

We hurried back to the room where Slash was trying different combinations with the blocks. Alessa told him what they'd uncovered about the twins and Gemini, but Slash didn't react like we expected.

"I've already tried it," he said. "In fact, it was the first set of combinations I tried, but it didn't work."

"Damn, I really thought that would be it," Alessa said, leaning against the wall.

"There might be something else to the Gemini or Castor and Pollux story we're missing," Slash mused. "Maybe it's the constellations. What if the stars were designed not only to help us open the door, but to tell us when to start? Maybe whatever constellation is over the door to this room represents the time of the year to start."

"Orion!" Mom, Dad, and I said at the same time.

"That's the only constellation we saw," I said. "But maybe we missed something."

We hurried back to the planetarium, closed the door, and waited for our eyes to adapt to the dim light again.

"See, there's Orion," my dad said. "Right by the door."

"What's that constellation to the left of Orion?" Slash asked. "Lower on the door."

I stared at the door until I saw what appeared to be a pair of angled snake eyes.

"Gemini," Alessa shouted before I could say anything. "That means the eyes on the door must be Castor and Pollux. Start with that, Lexi."

We opened the door again and surged into the room. I ran over to the frame and started placing the blocks. This time, when the last block clicked into place, the shelf slowly slid out, revealing a secret crevice.

"That's my girl," Mom said proudly, causing me to smile.

Just inside the crevice, I could see a business card-size piece of paper. I carefully pulled it out and read aloud. "Twenty-six Via del Colosseo."

FIFTY-ONE

Lexi

"WHAT DOES THAT mean?" Alessa said, reading over my shoulder. "It sounds like an address."

"Arrrgh," Mia complained. "Why won't this game ever end? Why can't it just say, 'The End, Go Eat' already?"

"It looks like an address, or at least part of an address," Tito said.

"There's no city or country listed, but the address is in Italian," Slash said. "And translated into English, it means 'the street of the colosseum.'"

"As in the Roman coliseum?" Dad asked.

"I would assume so. If we had our phones or a laptop, we could confirm there's a street in Rome named the Via del Colosseo."

"What if we had a map?" my mom asked.

"That would work," said Slash. "Does anyone know where we can find a map of Rome?"

Gio grinned and slapped his brother on the back. "I sure do. The map room. Follow me."

We followed Gio to the library and got a quick demonstration of how his team had found the hidden room. When we entered the map room, I looked in awe at the giant statue of a wolf suckling two human babies, as well as lots of shelves, drawers, and tables with maps, tubes, and cartography equipment. Gio bypassed all that and led us straight to a wall where two giant side-by-side maps of Rome hung. The map on the left was of old Rome and on the right was modern Rome.

"This is super cool," I said, checking it out. "Where's the Colosseum?"

"Here," Father Armando said, tapping the map of new Rome. "It's located in the center and oldest part of Rome."

"Score," Stefan exclaimed, peering at the map of ancient Rome. "I've found Via del Colosseo. It's right next to Colle Palatino and il Forum."

"What's Colle Palatino?" Mom asked.

"Palatine Hill is the oldest of the seven hills of Rome," Slash explained. "Legend has it that Rome was founded on Palatine Hill, and it's where many of the subsequent Roman emperors lived and built some of their greatest buildings."

"Via del Colosseo is a street running along the base of the hill toward the Colosseum," Stefan said, running his finger along the street. He switched over to the modern map of Rome, locating the same street. "Lexi, what's the street number again?"

"Twenty-six," I confirmed.

Stefan ran his finger along the street, his nose practically touching the map. His finger stopped on a small building northwest of the Colosseum. "This is it," he said. "On the map the address is identified as La Fine, R&R 753.

"What does that mean?" Dad asked.

Father Armando smiled. "*La fine* means the end. I suspect, or at least hope, we are close to the end."

"Oh, thank God," Oscar said. "I don't think my brain can take much more."

"Or my feet," Vittoria groaned. "I'm going to go sit on the couch in the library and take a rest."

Mom looked at Vittoria's swollen ankles and lifted an eyebrow at me, almost as if she was asking if it was okay to take Vittoria out of the equation before the problem was solved. How had I never noticed the subtle and kind ways my mom took care of people?

I gave Mom an imperceptible nod, and she smiled.

"I'm with you," Mom said in a loud voice, linking arms with Vittoria. "I'll come keep you company. Let's permit the rest of them to take it from here. You and I can relax and talk about all the wonderful Italian wine and dessert we've earned."

"Perfetto."

Mom and Vittoria left, and the rest of us stood looking at each other, not sure how to proceed.

"So, team, what do we think the two names are?" Tito asked. "Wasn't that what the gamemaster said? We had to give him two names to win the challenge."

"It was a really cryptic statement," I said. "Honestly, I've got nothing on that front. How about you, Slash?"

Slash pushed off the wall against which he'd been leaning. "Not a thing."

"Well, how about we focus on interpreting what R&R 753 means?" Stefan suggested. "Maybe something will come to us. What do you think it means?"

"Maybe it's a reference to another address, or perhaps a location in Rome?" Juliette asked.

"R and R could mean rest and recreation, or rest and relaxation," Dad said. "Just throwing it out there."

"My guess is that it's a person or persons," Father Armando said. "Maybe R and R are the names we have to give the gamemaster. Or maybe it's the name of a business."

"What about the 753?" I asked. "Is there any significance to that number?"

Alessa smacked her head. "Yes, of course. Why didn't I think of it before? Seven fifty-three is the year Rome was founded. I saw it etched somewhere during one of the challenges."

"Yes, I remember it," Gio said. "We were here, in this room, looking at—"

"This statue," Juliette interjected. She pointed at the base of the statue with the wolf suckling the two babies. "The number is etched here in Roman numerals—DCCLIII, or 753."

"*Si*, when we first saw this statue, Vittoria reminded me this is a replica of the famous statue the Lupa Capitolina," Gio said.

"Who are those babies?" I asked.

"Romulus and Remus," Juliette replied. "The founders of Rome. Could that be the R and R we're looking for? The two names we need?"

For a moment we all stared at Juliette, openmouthed. Then Slash swept his mother off the floor and gave her two kisses on the cheek. "*Si*, that's it, Mama, the two names. It was in front of us the entire the time."

"Yes," I said, everything clicking into place. "Those *are* the names we need to give the gamemaster. After all, he said it was possible to solve this escape room without having solved any of the other challenges, and he was right. He gave us major clues with every challenge. The twins in the fountain in the garden maze, the identical pair of fishes painted on the side in the pool, and this statue of the twins in the map room."

"Don't forget the identical columns at the entrance to the garden maze," Dad added. "Your mom noticed that right at the beginning of the challenge."

"Yes, and the twin Atlas statues holding up the table

in the game room, as well as the twin men holding up the table in the planetarium," Alessa said. "Could it have been a red herring to get us to think the twins might have been Castor and Pollux?"

"I don't think so," Father Armando replied. "Castor and Pollux were Greek. I expect we were supposed to recognize that, although we didn't. The *twins* were the point the gamemaster was making. Everything else about the castle and the challenges focused exclusively on Italy and Rome."

"If we'd recognized the macro picture of the challenges and recognized the emphasis on Roman history, sculpture, and twins, I suspect we might have come to the conclusion it was Romulus and Remus without having to solve a single puzzle," Slash said. "The gamemaster was right in his assertion. Impressive."

"So, you mean, the answer has been hiding in plain sight?" Gio asked. "Right in front of us, and we just didn't put the pieces together?"

"If we'd solved it too early, Gio, we would have missed out on all the fun," my dad said, clapping him on the shoulder. "And what an adventure it's been."

"It certainly has." Slash grinned and put an arm around me, kissing the top of my head. "Come on, everyone. Let's go get dressed and give the gamemaster our final answer. I think our work is done here."

FIFTY-TWO

Lexi

"ARE YOU READY, *cara*?"

I really wished he wouldn't ask me that question before a party. Ever. It wouldn't matter how many years would pass, I'd *never* be ready to go to a party, at least not socially or emotionally. But at least tonight I was dressed, and that was half the battle. Besides, there was the Italian food to look forward to, so there was that.

Taking a deep breath, I tucked my long brown hair behind my ears and smoothed the waist of the form-fitting, floor-length, sequined gold gown. The best part of the dress was the science behind the way the sequins caught the light and sparkled, no matter which way I turned. I knew that the glint and flash were due to specular reflection, a mirrorlike reflection of light waves off a surface. No matter which way I moved, the relative angles of the sequins would change with my motion, resulting in flashes of light. That part was pretty cool.

"Are you sure I look okay?" I asked.

Slash slowly walked around me in a circle, finishing up by wrapping his arms around my waist from the back. "*Bellissimo.* That gown is gorgeous, those earrings are perfect, and the shoes are a nice touch. It all came together nicely."

"Because you made the perfect suggestions."

"Only because you asked for help."

It was more like I'd *begged* him for help. Thank God he didn't mind helping me pick out dresses and outfits that would look good on me, be comfortable, and yet were totally appropriate for the occasion. Fashion was so subjective with too many variables, and I often got overwhelmed. I used to buy whatever was on sale for work, but I found myself enjoying how Slash patiently explained each fashion option and why he thought it would suit me. In the end, he made suggestions and let me make the final decision. That sensible approach to fashion worked for me, and, to my surprise, I was learning to understand what suited me best in terms of style and comfort.

"Now, let's relax and enjoy our final evening in this extraordinary castle," he said.

I turned around in his arms, placing my hands on his chest so I could face him. His dark hair brushed the shoulders of his tuxedo and framed his strong jaw, hinting at danger and passion. I smiled up at him. "You did it, Slash. You got the money for the orphanage, for the pope. So many people were depending on you, and once again, you came through." I knew how important it had been for him to secure the money for the orphanage, not only because it was named after his biological father, but because he'd once been an orphan himself. Even more, it was his way to give back and make amends for his past. A step toward forgiving himself.

He lightly traced a fingertip along the curve of my cheek. "No, *cara*, we did it. All of us. My family, your family, *our* family. Our wonderful, beautiful family."

I reached up, linking our fingers together, and he

pressed a kiss against them. "We're pretty lucky, aren't we?"

"We are. And to think I started life with no family, really. Then to end up with Mama, Father Armando, Gio, Stefan, Oscar, and, most importantly, you… I am truly blessed. Now I have the most incredible set of in-laws, brothers- and sisters-in-law, and friends I never imagined myself having just a few years ago. *Mio Dio*, I am a lucky man."

I stood on tiptoe and kissed him on the nose. "Then let's do this, lucky man."

He grinned and took my hand, and together we headed for the dining room. When we arrived, Oscar and Juliette met us and happily hugged and kissed us. It was strange, but I felt no awkwardness, no discomfort, just genuine acceptance and warmth from my new mother- and father-in-law. I'd learned, as is true with any relationship, there were always going to be hiccups, mishaps, laughs, and genuine affection when dealing with family members, even with those who weren't originally mine. Now they'd become mine…all of them. Strangely, especially for me, I didn't mind. Instead, like Slash, I felt remarkably blessed to be a part of this wonderful, wacky, amazing family.

Oscar looked dashing in his tuxedo and red bow tie, which was slightly askew, apparently because he kept tugging on it. Juliette caught him pulling on it once and whispered to him about it. He promised to stop, but I caught him doing it again a few minutes later, and I couldn't help but smile.

Juliette looked beautiful in a dark-blue gown with a belt, her dark hair piled on her head with lovely ringlets framing her face. She had such an approachable and soothing presence about her that I could easily imagine how Slash had fallen in love with her as a little boy. My mom had taken to her as well. She adjusted Juliette's necklace while the two of them keep chatting like they were best friends. Maybe they already were.

"Have you seen the gamemaster, Mama?" Slash asked his mother, putting an arm around her shoulders with obvious affection.

"I have not," Juliette answered. "In fact, I haven't seen any of the staff other than Chiara and Ciro, who are serving champagne." She held up a gorgeous crystal champagne flute as evidence. "I don't know where he is."

"How are we going to give him our answer to the challenge?" Mom asked.

Slash shrugged. "We'll have to assume he'll show up shortly for it."

We chatted for a few more minutes before Juliette happily linked her arm through mine and started telling me a story about when Slash was eight years old and dismantled her barely functioning blender, fixing it so it worked perfectly for another five years. I couldn't help but laugh.

Oscar and Slash brought us more champagne, and we spoke for a while with Father Armando before he left to speak with my parents. He wore a happy, satisfied smile I could only attribute to the fact we'd won the gentleman's agreement. Tito, Stefan, and Alessa joined us shortly thereafter, and we speculated on whom our mysterious guest would be.

Gio and Vittoria, the happy couple, made a dramatic entrance a few minutes after we did. Gio looked ready for a photo shoot for a men's magazine with his perfect hair, smile, and scruffy cheeks. Vittoria looked like a Roman goddess in a toga-style dress of ivory that draped gracefully over her shoulder, dipping into a deep open back. Golden jewelry sparkled at her ears, throat, and arms. They were an impossibly gorgeous couple.

My parents were the last to arrive, smiling happily and greeting everyone with hugs and air kisses. As I watched them—*really* watched them—together, it hit me how well suited they were to each other. Perhaps finding my own love had helped me see them in a different light.

Especially my mother. There was so much more to her than I'd ever realized. Smarts, kindness, a competitive spirit, and a logical mind. How had I not seen those qualities in her before? I wasn't the best at reading people, but my own mother? Had her efforts to shape me into a girly girl made me dismiss and ignore everything else about her? What kind of daughter did that make me?

Mom made a beeline straight for me and enfolded me in a hug. "My God, you look amazing, Lexi. I've never seen you dressed so beautifully. You're just glowing. I can't believe it, but my little girl has grown up and come into her own. Married—sort of—accomplished and taking care of business. I'm so proud of you."

I swallowed back the lump in my throat and hugged her back. "You look beautiful, too, Mom. You always do. I want to apologize that I never acknowledged how smart you are and how you've accomplished so many important things through your charity work and social networks. You're an incredible woman and a great role model. I'm sorry I've never let you know that."

She threw back her head and laughed, *really* laughed, her eyes sparkling. "And you thought the only thing I ever passed down to you was my long legs." She gave me a conspiratorial wink and lowered her voice. "So, now you know. But let's keep it our little secret, okay?"

A bell chimed, and we all turned toward the front of the table, from where the sound had come. Lorenzo stood there, looking sharp in a tuxedo and white gloves.

"Ladies and gentlemen, it's my sincere pleasure to

welcome you to the final official gathering of your visit to Castrum Augustus. I hope that your time spent here was engaging, interesting, and, above all, fun."

"It was the best," Gio called out. "*Grazie mille!*"

"Hear, hear," Dad said, raising his champagne flute. "The most fun I've had in years."

Everyone called out their agreement, and Lorenzo tipped his head at us. "I'm grateful to hear that, and I know my benefactor, the owner of the castle and the mastermind behind all of the challenges, puzzles, and escape rooms contained here within, would agree with me. However, I will let him tell you that himself, as Mr. Zachetti has decided to join you for dinner this evening and will be making an appearance shortly."

What?

My eyes widened as I turned toward Slash. The reclusive Dante Zachetti was making an appearance at our farewell dinner? How cool was that?

Slash raised an eyebrow back at me, seemingly calm, but I knew he *had* to be intrigued to meet the man with whom he'd just matched wits.

A moment later, Brando Porizio, our gamemaster, walked into the room. Gone were the hippie tie-dyed shirts and wrinkled pants. Instead, he was dressed in a fitted tuxedo, his long gray hair slicked back and tucked behind his ears.

"Congratulations to all of you. You've reached the final moment of the challenges presented to you at Castrum Augustus," he said. "You've done what no one before you ever has done before—solved every challenge so far. I eagerly await your answer to the final challenge. Who will provide me with the two names I require?"

For a moment, no one spoke, and then Slash stepped forward. "The two names you seek are Remus and

Romulus, R and R, twins and the mythical founders of Rome."

For a moment, Brando didn't say anything, and then he started clapping. "Bravo. You have done it. You've successfully completed *all* the escape room challenges this castle offered. I commend you on your creativity, ingenuity, and logical thinking. Well done, everyone. Well done, indeed."

He spread out his hands. "And now, for one final puzzle—and no worries, all will be revealed without any additional work on your part." He smiled and clapped his hands twice. "I now present to you the owner of Castrum Augustus and the designer of the escape rooms, Mr. Dante Zachetti himself."

FIFTY-THREE

Lexi

WE LOOKED TOWARD the dining room door, the kitchen, and then at Lorenzo, waiting for Zachetti's entrance, but no one entered. Puzzled, we shifted uneasily on our feet until Slash abruptly crossed the room and thrust out his hand.

"Mr. Zachetti, it's an honor to officially meet you."

Brando clasped Slash's hand, shaking it. "I assure you, young man, the pleasure is all mine. Please call me Dante."

Wait, what? Brando Porizio, the gamemaster, is Dante Zachetti himself?

There was a lot of murmuring in the room before Dante spoke again. "I apologize for the deception. I wanted a firsthand look at the family who decided to take on challenges that no one in the world, to date, had been able to solve. You, *all* of you, far exceeded my expectations in every way. The data you provided with your unique approaches and creative thinking to solving the puzzles has proven invaluable to me."

I looked up at the portrait of a younger Dante Zachetti, wondering how I'd missed it. I could now see

382

the resemblance, even though his hair was longer, thinner, and grayer, and he no longer had a beard. He'd completely fooled me, and the rest of us.

So, in a way, he'd won, too.

"You got me on that one," I admitted. "I had no idea."

"You disguised yourself as the gamemaster so you could personally watch us work our way through the rooms?" Dad asked, still in disbelief.

"*Si,*" Dante replied. "I'll be honest with you. I sincerely did not believe you'd solve even one puzzle. Watching your minds work and how well you played to your strengths and creativity has inspired me."

"Well, we do have a wide a range of complementary talents and skills," Dad said. "A lawyer, computer and math experts, a military marksman, a priest, puzzle lovers, a nurse, a teacher, businessmen, and even a teenager. There's more, but you get the idea."

Dante dipped his head. "I do, indeed." He nodded to Lorenzo, who disappeared out of the dining room without a word. "Now, I'm not the only the surprise guest at dinner tonight. Instead, we have a far more esteemed and distinguished guest with us. I've been informed that this guest considers himself a part of your family, as well. Please, welcome the Holy Father. Welcome to Castrum Augustus, Your Holiness."

The pope strolled into the dining room without escort, dressed in his traditional white cassock with an attached *pellegrina*, or cape, which was embroidered with the papal coat of arms. A pectoral cross suspended from a golden cord hung around his neck, and he wore red shoes and a white skullcap. His eyes searched the room, lighting up when he saw Father Armando, Slash, and then me. A huge smile crossed his face.

Zachetti immediately went to one knee, but the pope

urged him to rise, and the two men warmly shook hands. Slash knelt, too, kissing the pope's ring before rising. The pope engulfed Slash in a warm hug, patting him on the back several times.

I glanced over at my mom, who looked shocked. Vittoria, Alessa, and Mia wore matching awestruck expressions. Mia and Juliette both knelt, and I gave a small curtsy.

The pope held out his hands, as if ready to bestow a blessing on us. "Please, I ask you not to engage in formalities with me tonight, as this is not an official event. I humbly wish to take my place among family, as that is who you are to me. I hope that you will indulge me tonight and treat me as one of your own." He looked over at me. "Lexi, so good to see you again. How are you?"

I'd never seen my mom's eyes go so wide as when he called me by my first name. She threw me a glance that clearly indicated I had some explaining to do. A stunned expression had also settled on Dad's face as he looked between Slash, the pope, and me.

"I'm fine, thank you, Holy Father. It's great to see you again." Suddenly I wondered if he would make a comment mentioning how disappointed he was Slash and I got married in the rain forest, even though he knew we were having a church wedding in the spring. I paused, uncertain if I should say anything further or try to explain proactively.

He crooked his finger, urging me to come closer. When I stepped up next to him, he kissed me heartily on both cheeks and whispered conspiratorially in my ear. "I can't wait to hear all about your rain forest adventure. Make some time this evening for us to chat."

Relief swept through me, and I stepped back, nodding and giving him a thumbs-up.

"Well, now that His Holiness is here, I'd like to make an announcement," Zachetti said. "In honor of his visit, and your outstanding—if not astonishing—performance on the challenges, I intend to make a substantial donation to the Catholic Church toward the founding of a brand-new orphanage to be built in Salerno, Italy, and named in honor of one of the church's newest saints, Cristian Descantes."

Everyone cheered and clapped enthusiastically, no one more than the pope. I noticed there had been no mention of a wager, but I saw the twinkle in the pope's eyes as he glanced at me. I looked at Slash, and he smiled, taking my hand, and squeezing it gently. He hadn't told his family that he'd identified his biological father yet, but I knew he was going to take the opportunity to do so while we were all here together. I thought Zachetti's donation would be a perfect segue for that.

"As promised, the engaged couple will have free rein of my island, including my staff and my personal yacht for a period of ten days following their wedding."

"Does that include special nocturnal visits to the Virgin Mary fountain?" I called out, grinning. Vittoria laughed, and Gio threw a napkin at me and promptly got scolded by his mother for it.

"What about the beehives?" Oscar added, and it was my turn to laugh and cover my face with my hands.

"I strongly encourage caution unless you're with an experienced apiarist," I warned, wagging a finger.

"The entire island belongs to the couple for those days," Dante assured us. "Carlo, your chef, will prepare your favorite meals and exotic desserts. All expenses will be paid, and a generous stipend will be yours to keep. Let us lift our glasses to the happy couple. Congratulations!"

We leaped to our feet, lifted our glasses, and cheered our approval. After a moment, Dante indicated we should sit.

"Please, sit down and enjoy your meal," Dante said.

Even though the pope had told us not to engage in any formalities, no one else sat until he had. Dante took the place to the pope's right, while Slash sat to his left. I took the chair next to Slash, and my mom sat on the other side of me. We bowed our heads while the pope blessed our meal.

Even Ciro and Chiara looked awestruck to be in the presence of the pope. During the prayer, I peeked and caught them whispering by the kitchen door. Shortly thereafter, they served us the first course of the dinner, a rich tomato and bread soup. I was just glad it wasn't spicy so I wouldn't end up on the veranda with Oscar again.

"Lexi, you didn't tell me you knew the pope," my mom said between bites of soup. "How could such a detail slip your mind?"

"I told you I met him," I protested.

"Met him, not *knew* him," Mom said. "There's a big difference, you know."

"Well, I don't really *know* him," I said. "Although he did give me a necklace."

"The pope gave you a necklace and you never bothered to mention this to me?"

"It's a cross. Probably hopeful thinking on his part."

To my surprise, my mom laughed. "You must tell me all about it, young lady. What other secrets are you hiding from me?"

I thought for a moment, accepting her question at face value. "Slash and I are honorary citizens of Salerno. Although Slash complains he's yet to receive a hotel discount."

Mom set her spoon down and reached over to pat my hand. "We need to have a girls' night out before your wedding so you can catch me up on everything. And I mean everything."

I set my wineglass down carefully. "What exactly does a girls' night with you entail?"

"Whatever we want," Mom said, waving a hand. "As long as we have fun. And now you know we *can* have fun together, right?"

She had a legitimate point. The prospect of spending time with my mom didn't terrify me as much as it might have just a week ago. "Deal. As long as we set the parameters in advance."

"Great," Mom said, smiling and lifting her wineglass to me in a toast. "To a girls' night out."

"Okay, but before we make any more girl dates, I want to personally introduce you to someone. Come on."

Mom's eyes widened, but she stood up and followed me to where the pope sat chatting with Stefan and Juliette. When the pope saw me coming, he pushed back his chair and stood.

I immediately bent to one knee, so my mom tried to do the same—a bit awkwardly, since she was wearing a tight dress.

"What did I tell you about forgoing formalities for tonight?" he scolded me. When I rose, he kissed both of my cheeks and put his hands on my shoulders, studying my face. "It's such a joy to see you, my dear."

"Likewise. Thank you, Holy Father. I'd like to take a moment to introduce you to my mother, Clarissa Carmichael."

I would never forget this moment for as long as I lived. For the first time in my life, I witnessed my mother completely tongue-tied. She stammered something, so I smiled as I confidently and smoothly guided the conversation while she recovered. Gah! What had happened to me? Had I turned into my mother?

We chatted for a few more minutes, and my dad joined us, so I introduced him, too. We eventually returned to our seats, and my mom couldn't stop talking about how exciting it had been.

"I've learned a lot about you these past few days, Lexi," Mom said, placing her napkin on her lap. "You're no longer my little girl. You've found your path in life, and it's one in which you are exceedingly competent. You've changed from a shy, awkward girl into a confident, independent, and wildly successfully woman. Shame on me for not trusting your decisions."

I hadn't ever expected to hear those words from her, so it took me a moment before I could speak. "I don't know anything about being a mom, but I imagine it's pretty hard when you have an awkward little girl who would rather cite math theorems and tote around a laptop than dance ballet to the *Nutcracker*. You and Dad did good work. I guess I turned out okay."

Mom put her hand over mine and smiled. "Better than okay. The best."

For the rest of the evening, we feasted on beef braised in red wine, roasted artichokes, and thick, crusty bread, while the pope chatted easily with everyone. When the dishes were cleared and the limoncello, coffee, and dessert were served, Dante motioned to Lorenzo, who disappeared into the kitchen. He stood, clinking his glass to get our attention.

"Ladies and gentlemen, it is my sincere pleasure to have hosted you. As I've mentioned before, I had no expectation that you, a family gathered to celebrate the happy occasion of a wedding, would solve a single escape room, let alone every single one of the challenges. But you did, against all odds, and so, in addition to the all-expenses-paid honeymoon here on the island that I am offering Vittoria and Gio, I would like to present you each with a little memento to mark your time spent at Castrum Augustus."

Lorenzo returned, carrying a basket. He set it on the table next to Dante and stepped back. Dante reached into the basket and held up a small black velvet pouch. "Each of you shall receive an authentic, ancient, two-headed Roman coin for participating in the challenges. The two-headed figure is not Romulus and Remus, but the god Janus. Still, I hope it will remind you of the secrets of the castle. Ladies, for you, the coins have been fashioned as a pendant to be worn around the neck. Men, you will receive a coin mounted on a money clip. Father Armando, you will receive a coin as well, but as it's unlikely you'd wear jewelry with a pagan god on it or carry a money clip, I had your coin embedded into a block of Lucite that you can keep in your apartment or have on your desk. I hope that you all look back at your time spent here fondly."

There was a smattering of applause, and Mia wiggled in her chair as Lorenzo, Ciro, and Chiara handed out the gifts to each of us. Lorenzo handed me my bag, and I opened it, admiring the coin pendant. Totally cool. It would be a lifelong treasured item for me.

Once everyone received their gift, Dante spoke again. "Now that you've successfully solved all the puzzles in the castle, I would ask a favor. Please refrain from speaking of your experience here, other than in general terms, to protect the secrets of the castle, the puzzles, and their solutions. This will give me the opportunity to invite others to try to solve them, but also to refine my technique and approach. Since you've been singularly and astonishingly successful at solving even my toughest challenges, I extend an offer to you. As I develop new and restructured escape rooms, I would like to invite you to return in the future to test out any new challenges I've come up with—all expenses paid, of course. As compensation for your puzzle expertise, I will offer you all the amenities of the island during that time as a getaway vacation."

My dad immediately stood up. "Well, you can certainly count the Carmichael family in. What an absolute honor it's been to participate in these challenges, all while meeting my daughter's wonderful new family and..." he looked over at the pope "...friends."

Gio also leaped to his feet. "You can count on us, too. This was the most fun I've had in years, maybe ever. We'd love to come back to Castrum Augustus. And *grazie mille* in advance for the honeymoon. I know that Vittoria and I will enjoy every minute of it."

There was a lot of laughter and good-natured ribbing before Dante asked us if we had any questions about the puzzles.

"I have one," I said. "These challenges all seemed to feature numbers. For example, 753, which was the founding of Rome, of course, but there were numbers on the golden discs. Were the numbers random or was there any particular significance to them?"

Dante beamed. "Excellent question. The numbers on the discs were clues themselves, although it was not necessary to understand them to solve the final challenge. Still, they were there if the players were to recognize them. The number on the gold disc from the maze in the garden was 509. Rome first became a republic in 509 BC. The disc in the gaming room had the number forty-five, which was the year Julius Caesar crossed the Rubicon and defeated the Republic's army, establishing himself as the emperor. Rome, under Nero, burned in 64 AD, the number on the pool's disc.

Hadrian's Wall was finished in the year 121, which was the library's disc number, and that year also marked the height of the Roman Empire. The disc from the room with the bull was 395 AD, which was when the Roman Empire split into the western and eastern empires with capitals in both Rome and Constantinople. Finally, the fall of the Roman Empire and the official start of the Dark Ages is widely considered to be 476 AD, which was the number on the disc in the blackout room."

I shook my head. "Wow, so clever! We missed those clues."

"And yet you didn't need them," Dante said. "Just more opportunities to point you in the right direction, which was Rome, its founding, and its two founders— Romulus and Remus. But perhaps you didn't need those clues because the rest of the escape rooms were too easy."

The immediate chorus of "no" that filled the dining room was loud and clear.

"I assure you, Mr. Zachetti, the challenges were plenty hard enough," Stefan said. "As it was, we barely finished most of them, with luck playing somewhat of a role in at least one or two."

Others chimed in with their points of view. I wasn't sure they'd convinced him, but he didn't press us on it any further. We finished our heavenly dessert, coffee, and wine and then stood around chatting with the pope, Father Armando, Dante Zachetti, and each other. At some point, my dad approached Slash and me. He put a friendly hand on Slash's shoulder.

"Slash, I have to say, I truly appreciate the fact that since I've been in Italy, I haven't been shot at once or had my life put in danger. Which is a good thing, since this trip started off on the wrong foot. So, hopefully things are looking up on the danger front."

At that exact moment, a loud, sudden popping noise sounded from behind us. Without a shred of hesitation, my dad hit the floor, covering his head with his hands.

I looked over my shoulder and saw Gio holding a napkin over the top of a now-open champagne bottle. I bent down to tap my dad on the shoulder. "Relax, Dad. Gio was just opening the champagne."

My dad looked up, removing his hands from his head. "Oh, well. Old habits die hard."

We laughed as Slash stuck out a hand and helped him up. My mom joined us, and we talked for a bit more until Stefan and Gio came over.

"Excuse me, may we borrow our brother for a moment?" Gio asked. He wavered a bit on his feet and seemed tipsy.

"Sure," I said, although I wasn't sure why they had to ask my permission, or why I had to give it. Gio slung his arms around both his brothers as they staggered onto the veranda, talking rapidly in Italian.

"That's one good-looking group of brothers," Dad observed.

"No kidding," I said.

Mom gave me a sly smile. "So, I guess that means I'm going to have good-looking grandchildren."

"Mom!"

She laughed and leaned over to kiss me on the cheek. "It's just too easy with you. I'm kidding. Let's get through your wedding day first, okay?"

There was no way I going to argue with that.

FIFTY-FOUR

Slash

IT HAD BEEN years since I'd spent any significant time with my brothers. Life had become busy for all of us, and it was difficult for us to get together, seeing as how we were spread out internationally.

I hadn't realized until this weekend how much I'd missed them. Sharing a childhood with someone means there's no one else in the world who understands you like the people who've lived it with you. Although we hadn't talked much lately, I owed them a lot.

Growing up in the middle of two brothers, I'd discovered that sibling rivalry could be a powerful motivator. I'd worked hard for my achievements and success. I imagined Stefan and Gio had felt similarly motivated. Just thinking back on it made me smile.

"You guys know I love you, right?" Gio said, swaying on his feet. When he drank too much, it made him talkative and emotional. "I want to thank you for always being my wingmen, no matter what. Stefan, you took the heat for me with Father Rainaldi all these years ago, and Romeo, you came to my rescue when Vittoria and I were having trouble getting permission to get married in the church. I never really thanked you. You've always been there for me. Now, in two days, I'm going to be a married man. That's forever, you know." He gave us both a sloppy hug while I maneuvered myself between him and the veranda railing, just in case.

"Vittoria is gold, Gio," Stefan said. "She's the whole package *and* she's crazy about you, which is the part I don't understand."

"Very funny." Gio smacked Stefan on the arm. "She's going to have our baby. A little *bambino* to call our own. I'm going to be a father."

"You'll be a good husband and father, Gio," I said quietly. "And you'll have made Mama a *nonna*. You know how much that means to her."

Gio grinned. "Yeah, and I was the first of us to do it." He held up a fist. "I win."

We laughed as Gio turned to Stefan. "How is it that you're the oldest and yet the last to get married? What's taking you so long? Alessa's great, and she puts up with you, so there's that."

Stefan chuckled. "Well, about that…we're engaged. I asked her yesterday. I figured we'd been living together for four years, so it was about time. I had the ring with me, and I'd intended to ask her the night after your wedding. But last night we were sitting in front of the beautiful fireplace in the bedroom, drinking wine in this extraordinary castle, and the timing just seemed right. Lucky for me, she said yes. We weren't going to mention it to anyone until after the wedding, but since it's come up…" He swept out a hand, grinning. "…you're the first to know."

"And the last man falls," Gio said, laughing and clapping his hands. "No escape for you now, my brother. Many wishes for a happy life together."

"Stefan, congratulations." I gave him a hand slap,

then a hug. "I concur with all Gio said about Alessa. Although I just met her, she's smart, capable, and funny. She suits you and our family quite well. I like her very much."

"Thanks for saying that, guys. It means a lot. Alessa and I are thinking about a summer wedding in London or Ireland a few months after your and Lexi's wedding. After all this time, no need for a long engagement. I'd like to ask Father Armando to officiate, seeing as how he'll have blessed both of your weddings." He glanced over his shoulder into the dining room, where the pope and Father Armando were laughing and chatting with Dante Zachetti.

I followed his gaze, grateful there appeared no ill will that we'd won the money for the orphanage. "I'm sure he'd be honored to do it."

As we continued to talk and joke with each other, it occurred to me that in today's world, and particularly in mine, where meaningful things got pushed aside in the name of technology, my family—in-laws and all— would be, without a doubt, the greatest treasure I'd ever have.

How had it taken a visit to a remote castle with escape rooms for me to be reminded of that? Not only was my family growing with the blending of mine and Lexi's, but our extended family was getting bigger through my brothers and their families.

"Let's not wait so long to get together again," Gio was saying. "Although, I'll be honest. Any family activity we do after this will certainly be anticlimactic."

I clapped a friendly hand on Gio's shoulder. "Since the next family gatherings will be my wedding, presumably followed by Stefan's, I'm all for anticlimactic and serene."

My brothers laughed, and arm in arm we returned to

the dining room, where Lexi and our families were waiting. Lexi had a slightly bemused look on her face when I approached her.

"Everything okay?" she asked, leaning against me, lifting her face to mine.

"Everything's perfect," I replied, cupping her cheek with my hand as a shot of unfiltered love lanced my heart. She was my comfort, strength, and love.

My everything.

"I love you, *cara*," I murmured as I brushed her hair aside, my mouth grazing her ear. Words I'd never thought I'd say were so easy for me now. "Everything's exactly as it should be."

*Thank you for taking the time to read **No Escape**.*

If you enjoyed this story, the greatest way to say thank you to an author and encourage them to write more in the series is to tell your friends and consider writing a review at any one of the major retailers. It's greatly appreciated!

Check out the
Lexi Carmichael Mystery Series!

Get Your Geek On!

"The Lexi Carmichael mystery series runs a riveting gamut from hilarious to deadly, and the perfectly paced action in between will have you hanging onto Lexi's every word and breathless for her next geeked out adventure." ~ **USA TODAY**

The White Knights Series
by Julie Moffett

Geeks, Spies, and Teenagers! What an awesome combination. Check out the White Knights Mystery/Spy series for tweens, teens and the young at heart. Check Julie's website at www.juliemoffett.com for more information. You can find details and links on the website as to where to purchase the series.

JULIE MOFFETT is the best-selling author of the long-running Lexi Carmichael Mystery Series and the young adult, spy/mystery, spin-off series, White Knights, featuring really cool geek girls. She's been publishing books for 25 years but writing for a lot longer. She's published in the genres of mystery, young adult, historical romance, and paranormal romance.

She's won numerous awards, including the Mystery & Mayhem Award for Best YA/New Adult Mystery, the HOLT Award for Best Novel with Romantic Elements, a HOLT Merit Award for Best Novel by a Virginia Author (twice!), and many others.

Julie is a military brat (Air Force) and has traveled extensively. Her more exciting exploits include attending high school in Okinawa, Japan; backpacking around Europe and Scandinavia for several months; a year-long college graduate study in Warsaw, Poland; and a wonderful trip to Scotland and Ireland where she fell in love with castles, kilts and brogues. She almost joined the CIA but decided on a career in international journalism instead.

Julie has a B.A. in Political Science and Russian Language from Colorado College, a M.A. in International Affairs from The George Washington University in Washington, D.C. and an M.Ed from Liberty University. She has worked as a proposal writer, journalist, teacher, librarian and researcher. Julie has two amazing sons and two adorable guinea pigs.

Sign up at www.juliemoffett.com for Julie's occasional newsletter (if you haven't done it already) and automatically be entered to win prizes like kindles, free books, and geeky swag.

FIND JULIE ALL OVER SOCIAL MEDIA!

Facebook: JulieMoffettAuthor

Julie Moffett Facebook Fan Page:
https://www.facebook.com/groups/vanessa88/

Twitter: @JMoffettAuthor

Instagram: julie_moffett

Follow Julie on BookBub and be the first to know about her discounted and free books:
https://www.bookbub.com/authors/julie-moffett

Watch Julie's Lexi Carmichael Mystery Series book trailer on YouTube: http://bit.ly/2jFBsiq

Made in the USA
Las Vegas, NV
27 September 2021

31244016R00243